MAYAN STAR

Howard Allan

Mani, the Yucatán, 1562

The Franciscan monk responsible for bringing the Catholic faith to the Yucatán, by order of the King of Spain, sits in a rough and massive wooden chair, a primitive throne, in a crude adobe church. The afternoon buzzes with the sound of insects stirred by the heat. A jungle bird caws and is answered. A Mayan holy man - short, dark, dressed in an ornate feathered cape in spite of the heat - stands at a thick wooden table, reading one of the remarkable bark paper books of his people. Next to him, Garcia Fuentes translates into Spanish. Several other large bark paper books, each almost 2' x 3', rest on the table. The holy man has been reading, and Garcia translating, for over an hour. In spite of the heat, the monk listens, enthralled, like a child at bedtime. The Mayan glistens with sweat under his ornate cape, but like the monk, seems otherwise oblivious to the heat. Garcia wipes the sweat from his face and neck with a dirty handkerchief. He knows the monk understands the Mayan language, Garcia's translation is merely corroboration and he would prefer to be sleeping or fornicating. The monk does not make notes; instead he trusts his remarkable memory. He will write all this down tomorrow, in the cooler hours of the early morning after matins.

So far the narrative has been about succession and conquest. The translator shifts in his seat. The Mayan holy man reads.

There must be some mistake, the monk thinks. He looks at Garcia, waiting for his reaction.

Garcia hesitates. There is a pause in the rhythm of translation. The holy man looks at the translator and at the monk, waiting.

Garcia speaks to the holy man, asks him in Mayan – the monk understands this clearly – to repeat what he has just read. The priest rereads the previous sentence. Garcia pauses.

"Translate." The monk commands.

"I'm not certain this is correct," Garcia says and then he utters words that confirm the monk's own translation.

The holy man continues. Again there is a hesitation. But no one asks him to repeat himself. Garcia finally makes a halting translation, as if to distance himself from his own language.

The holy man reads and Garcia translates – but now his voice is almost gone, pared down to a mere whisper. He wonders if the monk can even hear him.

It doesn't matter. The monk is making his own translation.

The holy man reads. Garcia's translation is inaudible – his lips move, but no words come forth. The monk doesn't notice. He understands well enough. He stands. The holy man continues to read.

Garcia tells him to stop.

The monk looks at Garcia and says in Spanish, "Auto da fe." The monk approaches the table. He pushes aside his vestments and grabs the sword at his side. In a single fluid motion he draws the sword and stabs the holy man in his throat. Blood spurts over the bark paper books, and over the table and over Garcia. The holy man makes a gurgling sound and falls. The monk rushes to the dying man's side. He pushes the feathered cape back, and sees the priest's obsidian knife in his belt. He takes it and turns to Garcia, who is kneeling beside him.

"May you and God forgive me." He stabs Garcia in the chest. He administers the last rites to Garcia. He takes the obsidian knife, cuts his own arm and places the knife in the dead hand of the holy man. He calls out and soon two armed soldiers enter the church. He indicates the dead Mayan holy man: "Burn him."

And then he indicates the table piled high with Mayan bark paper books: "Burn them. Burn them all."

Later, the history books will note that Diego de Landa, the Franciscan monk, future bishop of the

Yucatan, and foremost expert on the Maya, destroyed virtually the entire record of the Maya as recorded in their books. No one knows why.

Chapter 1

Dr. Isabel Reyes

A jaguar.

Dr. Isabel Reyes was furious. She'd been pulled away from her clinic with a waiting room full of mothers and their children – all alive – to look at the mutilated carcass of the Norte Americano archeologist. Killed by a jaguar no less, which took a particularly potent combination of stupidity and bad luck. She drove her Jetta angrily – accelerating too quickly, braking too hard. The ride out to the site from Valladolid was 12 kilometers. Normally a ten to fifteen minute drive, but today was market day, and there was extra traffic, all of it slow, to contend with. Normally she liked market days. She hit the brakes as she came up too fast on a rusty white pickup loaded with cantaloupes, two barefoot ten year olds straddling the tailgate. There was no point in honking.

She knew a little about the archeologist, and hadn't, until today, thought of him as stupid. He showed some concern for his workers, the locals that cleared away the dense vegetation that obscured the site. He'd personally driven a heat-stricken worker – young, the older men knew better – to her clinic. The archeologist had found her attractive, but he'd made a clumsy attempt to hide it. It was the clumsy attempt to hide it that seemed unusual to her. The boys on the tailgate waved. They knew their truck was holding her up. She couldn't tell if the wave was meant to be taunting or apologetic. She didn't wave back. Did they recognize her, or her car, from the clinic? She spent most of her life ignoring men's waves: if you are a beautiful young woman in Valladolid, you learn quickly not to wave back. When she had first opened her clinic she was beset with men complaining of mysterious ailments in their cajones – would the doctora have a look? Now she saw only women and children. The boys in the truck waved again; her failure to respond was a challenge. She pulled out to see if she could pass.

A big blue bus of the ADO line was coming at her. She swerved back behind the white pickup. She resolved to be patient. She found herself wishing the jaguar had eaten Father McNeery – the archeologist's name came back to her – so that there would be no body for her to have to examine. The doctora was also the district coroner. This was a Norte Americano - they should have called someone from the cultural affairs office in Merida. Or the Bureau of Antiquities.

Anyone but her. She slowed the Jetta and dropped back, to better see around the pickup. The boys waved again. As she started to pull out she could see a large eighteen-wheeler pulling a cattle car in the opposite lane. She judged she did not have enough room to pass and pulled back in line. One of the boys brought his fists together in a mock collision. She noticed, chastened, that she had less patience than a ten year old boy. She would get to the site in another five minutes. Her patients at the clinic were used to waiting, didn't seem to mind it as much as she minded it on their behalf. At the turn-off for Mani, she waved good-bye to the boys in the pickup.

The access road to the site was bumpy, and after the first jarring hole she slowed down. She could see the pyramid shaped main temple ahead. A mound of red dirt and jumbled rock. A year ago it had been a green bump in the jungle. She wondered how they'd found it. In a couple of years it would have the haunting stature of Chichen Itza. Now it looked like a red mound, like something at the dump. There was a tent with open sides covering crude plank and trestle tables. She saw the late model Toyotas of the Valladolid Policia, and several men in beige uniforms smoking cigarettes and talking. She parked, grabbed her medical bag, and opened her car door. The wet heat hit her like a wall. The men turned to look at her. One man left their ranks and came toward her.

"I'm Captain Cepeda. Follow me."

The climb was made difficult by the imperfect state of the temple pyramid's restoration. The body was at the top. Once there had been steps, and there would be again, but now it was a steep climb over broken stone and dirt. By the time Dr. Reyes was half way up she was soaked. She could see dark stains under the captain's arms and on the back of his shirt. He seemed unconcerned that the stones his own ascent dislodged tumbled into her path. Finally he paused and turned, to see if she was keeping pace. A bird screeched. She nodded and continued up the temple slope. She was aware that the other Policia, the ones in the shade of the tent, were watching her. She slipped, fell and got up quickly. The fall made her furious.

The top was a flat area some 10 meters on a side. In the middle was a lumpy cloth. She smelled, or thought she did, a whiff of putrefaction. So soon? How long had he been dead, she wanted to ask, but of course that was for her to determine. Instead she asked "When did you find him?"

"A laborer says he found him this morning when he reported to work."

"What time was that?"

"When he told us?"

"What time did the laborer report to work?"

"About 6. Early, on account of the heat."

"And he called you – when?"

"We were called around 7."

And you called me about an hour ago, at noon, she thought. *Why the delay?* She said, "No one's here to watch the crime scene?"

"Why? He's not going anywhere. We watch from down there." He indicated the tent at the base of the temple.

Dr. Reyes stepped forward and lifted the tarp covering the body. A cloud of flies erupted from the corpse. She brushed them away from her face. The Captain had stood back, and now he registered his amusement.

There were long claw marks on the right side of McNeery's face, marks now black with congealed blood. His shirt was ripped open, and there were more claw marks on his torso, again on the right side. She waved off the flies. She looked around the corpse, but the only prints in the red dirt were human shoe prints. The worker's? The Policia?

She asked: "Has he been moved?"

"Not by us. We covered him. The flies."

Dr. Reyes noted the distance between the individual claw marks. She waved off the flies and examined his hands and arms. Both were free of marks. She said: "Bring the body to the Hospital General de Valladolid. I'll do the autopsy there."

"Doctor. We've had reports of a jaguar before. In this area."

She nodded. "A left-handed one?"

Chapter 2

Ex-Rabbi Simon Press

Rabbi Simon Press stepped up to the lectern, adjusted the microphone, thrust both hands into his pockets and began to speak: "Good evening. A remarkable thing happened in the Fourth century, a thing so widespread, so profound and yet so subtle that we have never really seen its like. A thing that has been for too long insufficiently remarked upon. A thing taken for granted. I intend to remark upon it this evening."

He had come at the invitation of the Religious Studies Chairwoman, an iconoclast herself in the field of the Christian Gospels. He'd come for her, because she was a friend, and for the stipend. He had a reputation for being an entertaining speaker: witty, enthusiastic, droll. His lecture an amalgam of history, archeology, anthropology, psychology, with a sprinkling of demographic science. He made it an intoxicating and provocative mixture. Plus, he was reliable. He kept his commitments in a field where tardiness and no shows were as common as on the rock band circuit. He'd dined earlier with the chairwoman, some faculty and a couple of honored undergraduates. Americans found his brogue charming, regardless of the contents of his remarks. If his colleagues were Jewish, his Yiddishisms, delivered in his brogue were, in the words of a friend, "verbal hors d'oeuvres."

Press continued: "In the Fourth century, most of the Western World changed its mind. Changed it willingly, I might add. Over 100 million people, most of the people of Europe, North Africa, the Middle East – became Christians. What had been a small sect of Judaism, itself a small religion; a sect so small that there is virtually no reference to it in the chronicles of the times; a sect so small that even its persecution went unremarked upon, became the dominant religion of Western Civilization. In about 100 years. Between 300 and 400 AD, the world changed its mind. In 313 the Roman Emperor Constantine issued the Edict of Milan, which removed the penalties for professing Christianity. He professed his Christianity and is regarded as the first Christian Emperor. But there's data to suggest that in this he was more follower than leader.

"Why this sudden mass conversion to Christianity? If the virtues of Christianity are obvious, as I suspect they are to you, my mostly Christian audience, you have to ask yourself two questions: One, why not sooner? And two, why did they cease being obvious when part of the world changed its mind again, 400 years later, and embraced Islam?

"To put it in perspective: imagine this audience 100 years from now. Only imagine that almost everyone in it is a Wiccan. No way, I can hear you say. And that's my point. No one in 300 AD would have predicted that Christianity would be the dominant religion of Europe by 400 AD.

"My job today is to try to account for this extraordinary change of heart and mind. My explanation is this: Christianity presented a better story than anything that came before. Not a better philosophical system, mind you; a better story."

"Liar!"

Simon Press saw that a gangly young man, in a state of considerable agitation, had stood to yell at him.

"Christ is the messiah, as foretold in the Old Testament, and His triumph was inevitable."

Simon Press said: "If you believe that, you've got two problems: Today Islam is growing faster than Christianity, and the Notre Dame football team had a losing season. I intend to finish my lecture, which is what these people came to hear. You can have the podium when I'm done, and anyone who cares to hear what you have to say can stay and listen to you."

The heckler pushed into the aisle and began to walk towards the podium.

Press saw this and said: "That's my best and final offer. Let me remind you that my faith does not require me to turn the other cheek."

The heckler moved down the aisle.

"The pagans, " Press continued, "what did they find attractive in this new Jewish cult? For the first time here was a message that spoke to their feelings of being an underclass, unfavored under contemporary systems of worship." Press paused to look at the heckler, now standing at the foot of the podium. The man placed both hands on the edge of the stage and hoisted himself up.

Press turned to him and asked: "Do you feel unfavored under contemporary systems of worship?"

"Your lecture's over." He pushed Press away from the microphone.

As a Jewish boy growing up in Dublin, Press had some experience with being pushed around. But he learned then that it always felt better to push back, even if the outcome, a sound beating, was the same. So reflexively, he pushed back. The heckler was not expecting this, and stumbled. He righted himself and pushed Press hard. Press' glasses were knocked askew, and he removed them. The heckler began to square off, but as he did Press jabbed him, quick and hard, in the mouth. The heckler swung back. Press blocked the swing and countered with two more jabs – to the nose and mouth. The heckler's face was bloody now. He swung again, wildly, and Press jabbed him twice more. And then Press was on him with a flurry of punches until the heckler staggered and fell. Press, his rage alive in him like an animal, had all he could do not to kick him. He was breathing hard and trembling, and it was all he could do to say into the microphone "This is why I am no longer a rabbi."

Press had hoped for applause. But the auditorium was silent. Then he heard one person clap. And then another. And then as counterpoint to this percussion there was a bass rumbling of boos that grew louder and louder. Press was stunned by the boos – he hadn't started this fight. He caught a slight movement out of the corner of his eye. He turned to look at his assailant and prepared for another attack. And then he understood the boos. There would be no further assault – the student wore a crimson beard of blood, and Press, presumably older and wiser had caused it. The audience was mostly students, and their natural sympathies were with one of their own. How many of them had been bloodied, albeit only figuratively, by the likes of Press. There was no more clapping. One student yelled "What the fuck" and his call was taken up by others and soon melded into a chant: "What the fuck! What the fuck!"

"What the fuck" indeed. Could it be that no one supported his right to speak, or to defend himself? But he understood. Still, he vowed to himself never to speak at an American university again. A room full of cowards. He glared at them. There would be no joy in delivering his lecture to the crowd before him. He shook his head. He gathered his notes and left the podium. The Religious Studies Chairwoman, his friend, was kneeling beside his bloodied attacker. He offered a hand to help him up, but the boy slapped it away. The Chairwoman gave him a quizzical look – or maybe it was a look of disgust – but in any event her look too said "What the fuck?"

In the wings, the young woman from the Department of Religious Studies who had introduced him was crying. For him? For the bloodied young man on the stage? Were these tears of anger or frustration? He would never know – she made no effort to speak. He'd been allowed to park in a place of privilege, close to the lecture hall. He made his way quickly to his car. He could see people leaving the hall as he got in his rented car and locked the doors. He had been given a room in the University House, a pseudo hotel, where visiting alums and guests of the university were put up. He drove there to retrieve his overnight bag. He no longer planned to stay the night. He parked in front and went directly to his room.

Back in his room, Press poured himself a scotch from the minibar, to take the edge off his lingering anger and to soothe the demons of adrenaline still frolicking in his system. The phone rang. His reflex was to answer it, but on his way to the night table his reflexive instinct was replaced by a more thoughtful one: whom, at this moment did he expect to hear from? The lecture organizer, with some lame apology? Some further vitriol from the heckler? The phone rang again. The police? No, they would come in person. Another ring. *Let it ring,* he thought, but in the end he picked it up, prepared for the worst. A familiar voice on the other end asked, "Simon?"

"Yes, Jackie, it's me." Jackie was his assistant. "Let this be good news. I've had quite a time of it here."

"I'm sorry then. It isn't. Father Colvin McNeery is dead."

"What?" He meant several questions by that.

"He's dead, Simon. He was killed by a jaguar in Mexico. I saw it on CNN – I suppose because animal attacks are always newsworthy."

"When?"

"I just saw it a few minutes ago."

"No, I mean when did he die?"

"I don't know. Sometime today or yesterday, I suppose. They didn't say. I'm so sorry. I know he was a friend."

"Thank you."

"Is there something I should do?"

"No. Not now. No wait. Yes. Get me on a flight tomorrow to Merida."

"OK. I'm sorry."

"Me too, Jackie."

He hung up. Why had he decided to go to Mexico? What did he hope to accomplish in the Yucatan? Another reflex, he thought: when somebody dies, the rabbi comes. But he was a lapsed rabbi, and McNeery was a Catholic, also lapsed. Perhaps that was the reflex. They were colleagues in more than their academic pursuits. Their lives had taken similar trajectories. How could he not go?

He gathered his belongings and went down to the front desk to let them know he was leaving.

Chapter 3

Detective Benito Rufino

Detective Benito Rufino looked through field glasses at the excavation 1000 meters away. A dozen workers with axes, spades, and machetes were clearing jungle from a small mountain. Two men with the telltale silhouettes of AK-47s stood guard – not facing the workers, but looking outward, as if protecting them. And then he heard it – the woomp woomp of a helicopter. The workers stopped and looked up. The helicopter was a camouflage green and landed in a small clearing. A couple of the workers dropped the machetes and unloaded Jerry cans and boxes from the copter. A tall man in fatigues got out, shook hands with the guards, and walked around the cleared portion of the hill. More handshakes. Then he got back into the helicopter and it took off. Rufino looked at his watch: 10:18. Right on schedule.

He took out a special satellite phone and dialed. When he heard his commander answer, Rufino said, "Tomorrow" and hung up.

Nine months earlier it'd taken something akin to an act of God to get the satellite photographs: a small hill in the Quintara Roo jungle, 100 km from Lazaro Cárdenas. There was a red earthen gash in the jungle next to the hill where two camouflaged bulldozers were parked. At the time he had called his colleague Max over. He pointed, but said nothing.

"How did they get there?" Max asked.

"Helicopter. But that's not the point. Why are they there?" Rufino answered his own question. "They're not with any of the archaeological organizations. First, they don't use bulldozers. Second, no one has any activity in this location - I've checked."

That was nine months ago. For the last 14 days Rufino had been here, in the jungle, watching as they scraped the vegetation away and the hill became a 1000-year-old temple. He hated to see them cut the huge stone glyphs, but now that they had they were in undisputed violation of the Antiquities Act. Tomorrow at 10:15 reinforcements from the elite Mexican special forces team would arrive on helicopters of their own. He swatted a mosquito – too late, as he looked at the bloody smear on his hand.

His phone vibrated. At first he didn't recognize the sensation. And then it registered. He took the phone and whispered "Talk to me."

"Extract immediately and go to Valladolid."

Rufino couldn't believe it. He said so.

The voice on the phone said, "I repeat. This one's over. I need you in Valladolid. It's more important."

Rufino was incredulous: "More important than a Mayan temple being stolen? What could be more important?"

The voice on the phone said "A codex."

Chapter 4

Humberto Perez

Humberto had been wary of Father McNeery at first. As a rule he avoided church, except when his mother hassled him so relentlessly that he judged it less trouble to just go than to continue to be hassled. He could have left the house, but he didn't like to walk out just before dinner, because when he returned there would be nothing left to eat. Anyway, he hadn't met Father McNeery at church. He'd met him at the dig, a job his tio had gotten him clearing brush and jungle off the Mayan ruins at Mani. It was hot, hard work, but if you found some jade you could sell it to one of El Gato's men – a bonus you gave yourself. But so far he had found no jade.

And then he found the codex. And with it, an opportunity. He knew it was valuable, but he knew it was too valuable to move through the black market channels he had access to. So he'd given it to McNeery, hoping thereby to gain a blanket trust that would cover his illegal traffic in the jade pieces he hoped to find. McNeery was so overwhelmed he cried. And when he was done, he explained to Humberto how rare and desirable it was, and how remarkable Humberto's honesty was. McNeery knew there was a black market, he said. And Humberto thought, *but you don't know how it works*. McNeery's trust gave Humberto free reign to rob the site blind, so long as he stole only the small stuff. And now his patron and unwitting accomplice was dead. Fucked by a jaguar.

Humberto had always been a little afraid of the jungle, but he conquered the fear. First, when he went there to look at the night sky. Later, when he was older, he went there to drink beer. Still later he went there with Maria for sex. But now, adding to the fear that roiled beneath the surface, was a new fear, very much above ground: he was afraid he was being followed. He was weighed down and slowed by his twin burdens: a Questar telescope and a Mayan codex.

Cobwebs brushed his cheeks and added to his torment. He was hot, thirsty, tired. He heard the jungle sounds, once familiar but now different – the cries of the animals louder, more desperate. He sensed, as he had never sensed before, the unheard presence of a jaguar. He knew that the jungle was no different. His circumstances were different, and he carried with him so much fear that it spilled over and stained everything. His foot caught on something and he stumbled, but he did not fall.

One moment he was on top of the world, his world, and now he was fucked. On his way to the top of the world he'd asked why a priest was interested in a Mayan Codex. McNeery surprised him with his answer: "Celestial observations. The Maya were great astronomers, the best of their time."

"I'm an astronomer." Humberto hadn't meant to say it. He looked at McNeery's expression – surprise? disbelief? – he wasn't sure so he pushed on. "I have a Questar, and most nights I look for new stars." He watched McNeery's look intensify. Finally McNeery had asked as he hoped he would:

"Do you ever find any?"

"A few. It's hard to find a new star." Humberto watched McNeery chew that over.

"When you find a new star, whom do you tell?"

"No one. I just make a note in my notebook."

"You should tell someone, and get credit for it. I have a friend in the astronomy department at the University of New Mexico. He's helping me with my research."

"Why do you care about the stars? Aren't you a priest?"

"I don't care about the stars. I only care about one star. Can you guess which one?"

Humberto shook his head.

"I care about the Star of Bethlehem. That's why I'm here. I want to see if the Maya have any record of it."

That's when they'd became partners: McNeery would translate the codex – mostly astronomical observations – and Humberto would tell him what the observations meant. It was hard for Humberto not to like this man who took him seriously. And now he was dead. Fucked by a jaguar.

He pushed through more jungle. He thought something brushed his leg, and he jumped in spite of his load. Then he ran, unmindful of the branches that whipped his face. Soon he was in the clearing, out of breath, his heart beating so hard he thought he would explode.

He was so fucked. McNeery had given him the codex and a translation that morning. And McNeery had also lent him his computer, to e-mail McNeery's astronomy friend at the University of New Mexico. Now McNeery was dead. By a jaguar. No one Humberto knew believed that. Okay, some did, but they were idiots. The police were idiots, but mostly they were lazy. The jaguar meant less work, so fine, let it be a jaguar. But no one was murdered in Valladolid without permission from El Gato, and even – so the joke went – the jaguars knew that and abided by it. So Humberto knew he was fucked, because sooner or later it was going to look like he was the jaguar who had killed McNeery.

Chapter 5

Ex-Rabbi Simon Press

Rabbi Simon Press could not say, really, why he was on Aero Mexico flight 627 to Merida. He was not a relative of McNeery's. Presumably the next of kin were already there. The local priest would handle the funeral mass. But he had not hesitated in his decision to go. Beneath him was the green jungle of the Yucatan.

He felt a pressure in his head as the plane began its descent. He had known McNeery for years. They had first crossed paths at a colloquium on Early Christianity at Notre Dame in 1986. Both were speakers. McNeery's specialty was dating the Gospels. He'd been in the forefront of the movement that postulated their writing some 70 to 100 years after the death of Christ. The notion that they were not written by contemporaries of Jesus, but later, was heretical to all but the scholars who made it their business to study these things. There had been talk of excommunication. An ordained priest, McNeery was never allowed a congregation. This was the basis of their bond: both were defrocked, congregationless, gypsy scholars. It was a small club. They had liked each other on first meeting, and had kept in contact over the years. As the plane touched down, so did Rabbi Press' thoughts. He was coming, he was reminded with a jolt, to bury his friend.

The service was at the Catedral de San Gervasio in Valladolid. Press made his way there and spoke with Father Eduardo, the parish priest. Father Eduardo was a young man, earnest, and full of pieties if not picty.

Press asked: "Who made the arrangements?"

"His university,"

"To be buried here?"

"Yes."

"Are you aware that he is a priest like yourself?" This took Father Eduardo by surprise.

"But he was a professor, an archeologist."

"And an ordained priest, like you."

"But his parish –"

"No parish. He was a scholar. But still a priest."

"And you?"

"A friend. A colleague."

"Then I am sorry for the loss of your friend. Let us pray."

"Thank you, but I already have. When will the funeral service be?"

"Sunday. At the 11 o'clock mass."

"Thank you." Press shook the priest's hand and began to walk away. A thought stopped him and he turned: "Who will deliver the eulogy?"

"I will."

"But you don't know him."

The priest said: "Perhaps you would like to tell me about your friend."

"I'll tell you what I know."

The day of the funeral was hot and sticky, like the days before it. And bright. Press couldn't get used to how bright the days were, or the sharpness of shadows. He felt he was in the Hopper painting, "Sunday Morning." The inside of the Catedral de San Gervasio was mercifully cooler than the day outside. In the end Father Eduardo was persuaded to let Press give the eulogy. Press was surprised at the priest's change of heart, but didn't question it. Press spoke briefly, and well, and was surprised when his own emotion forced him to pause on several occasions. He thought wryly that it was the similarity of their circumstances that made this so emotional for him. The eulogy would serve for his own funeral when the time came. The heat finally penetrated the church, and

Press was sweating by the time he finished. He was momentarily disoriented by the strangeness of his surroundings and by the circumstances. That thought kept him company for the rest of the service. He realized how badly he wanted to be in a familiar place, among familiar things: to be, he realized, back in Dublin. He was roused from his thoughts by the sound of his name.

"Dr. Press." The woman before him was young and striking. So striking that he wondered he had not noticed her earlier. She offered him a hand at the end of a straightened arm. He shook it, confused.

"Yes?"

"I am Dr. Isabel Reyes." A pause. "I did the autopsy on your friend." Press watched her look around. "Come walk with me for a minute." She took his arm and he let himself be led outside. The sudden burst of light added to his confusion. She asked "Were you very close?"

"We worked in related fields of scholarship. We respected each other's work." Press did not know how to explain that their lives had run on parallel tracks, that they belonged to a small brotherhood of out of favor clergy. He said, simply "In a way we were close." He wanted to add that they were both gypsy scholars.

She repeated herself: "I did the autopsy. There was no regular coroner available at Valladolid. I'm the local doctor, so I was summoned to the body when they found it."

Press could sense she had gone reluctantly. He felt he was missing his cue here, that she meant him to ask her something that would keep her telling her story.

He said: "You did the autopsy and..."

"I don't think your friend was killed by a jaguar."

Again he was being cued. "And?"

"This jaguar was left handed."

"I don't understand."

"Jaguars - all animals - are ambidextrous. They aren't left handed or right handed. Only humans have lateral dominance. Your friend was murdered."

"But they said he was killed by a jaguar." Denial. One of the stages of grief. He recognized it in himself.

"This is hard for you to hear. It was meant to look like a jaguar attack. But there was a bump on his head that preceded the jaguar mauling. I'm pretty sure he was unconscious when he was mauled in a way that was meant to look like a jaguar. The cause of death was loss of blood. I don't know what to do about it. I don't know what you should do about it. I thought you should know."

"Don't you have to file a report? Won't there be an investigation?"

"I don't think there will be an investigation. I suggested that it wasn't a jaguar to the police chief.

He chose not to hear me. He wants it to be death by jaguar."

"Why?"

"Because it's simpler. Who knows? If it's a murder, he'll have to investigate. He'll have the Norte Americanos asking questions. Maybe your police will come down here. There are other possibilities. There's a black market in pre-Columbian antiquities. It expects a certain percent of what's found. Maybe your friend was too honest. Maybe he wasn't honest enough. What I know is this: he wasn't killed by a jaguar."

"I'm pretty certain of my friend's honesty. Perhaps too honest, as you suggest. I'm sorry, I've forgotten your name."

"Isabelle Reyes. What will you do?"

"I don't know. Can you give me an autopsy report that indicates he was murdered?" Press saw her hesitate. "But that would be dangerous for you."

"And for you," she reminded him. There was a moment of silence. Then she added "I've already filed my report. With the police. They are choosing to ignore it."

"So you are already at risk. From the Policia?"

"No. They just think I am a silly woman doctor who doesn't know how to do an autopsy properly. They will lose my report."

Press paused. He was thinking about the danger from whoever had killed McNeery. "So the danger is from…"

She said: "…whoever killed your friend."

"Is there somewhere you can go? To be safe? Do you have a husband?"

"I work here. As for a husband, you are not very observant." She held up a ringless hand.

Press saw that she was annoyed that he had asked about a husband. He expected any husband would be less brave than she was.

She went on: "I'm not asking you to solve this. I just want someone else to know the truth."

Press watched her turn and walk away. He was reminded of a feeling from long ago, when his lover, Mary, had been beaten by her father: impotent rage. He felt the heat keenly now, and he took off his jacket. He walked a short distance to the gravesite. There was another prayer, and he watched as McNeery's coffin was lowered into the ground. He had always associated funerals with cold gray weather. It seemed wrong that his friend was being buried on a bright, hot day, a day at odds with the somber event. He looked around for Dr. Reyes, but did not see her. He shook hands with father Eduardo. He walked back to the hotel, where he hoped to figure out what to do next.

Chapter 6

Ex-Rabbi Simon Press

In spite of the heat, Rabbi Simon Press decided to walk back to the hotel. At first he marveled at the deserted streets – it was early afternoon – and then he recalled where he was: Mexico, and this was siesta. Anyone with any sense was indoors, away from this, the worst heat of the day. He was still keeping Irish time and Irish habits. He regretted his decision to walk: he was sweating copiously. He began to alter his route in favor of shade. He ducked down an alley off the main plaza for respite from the sun's hammer. The sudden darkness disoriented him. He thought he saw a man approach from the other end. As his eyes adjusted he could make out the man: young, Mexican, dressed in levis and boots. So not all Mexicans took a siesta. The alley was narrow, but wide enough for the two men to pass each other. "Buenas tardes," Press said as they approached. The man smiled and returned the greeting. They had just passed when Press was spun around and thrown hard against the wall. The man hit him in the face, in the stomach, in the face again. Press heard footsteps. Help, he thought. But his assailant spoke and the man grabbed Press's arms in a lock. The first man continued to punch him. Press tasted salty blood in his mouth. He got one hand free and landed a punch on his assailant's face. The man hit him twice more, glancing blows, and then Press was hit from behind with something hard. Press went limp, and when the man let go of him he slumped to the ground. He was conscious, but the fight was gone from him. He was kicked a few times, and then mercifully he heard them run away. He lay awhile, until he felt he could stand. Using the wall for support he staggered out of the alley to the plaza. The sunlight was a shock, and he sat down. His head throbbed. Two boys, about ten years old, stopped to stare at him. "Help me to a doctor," he said. They led him to a small clinic.

He was relieved to see Dr. Reyes.

She said, "Do you still have your wallet?"

Reflexively he felt his pocket. Still there. He was relieved. "Yes."

"Too bad. You should go, Rabbi. You're not wanted here. Next time, they'll kill you."

"Are you going to treat me first?"

"For what? Can you walk?" She helped him stand.

"I can walk."

"Good. Then go. The poor people here take someone's wallet when they take the trouble to administer a beating. The men who beat you didn't do it for the money – not for your money. You understand?"

Press decided it was the fog of pain that was making it so difficult to understand what was happening. He let Dr. Reyes' nurse help him to the door.

When Press left the infirmary he was relieved to see people in the streets, going about their business. It was still hot, but there was more shade, the sun no longer overhead. He walked slowly to his hotel, sticking to the main street, oblivious to whether the way provided shade. He tried to decide about filing a police report. Dr. Reyes implied it would be worse than worthless: it might actually increase the danger he was in. He entered the hotel lobby and felt its coolness. He realized he was reluctant to go up to his room alone. But he wanted a shower, some clean clothes, a pain reliever. He waited until he saw a family gathered at the elevator and joined them for the ride up. He got off at the fourth floor, checked the corridor, and then walked as quickly as his aching body would permit to his room. He unlocked the door, but did not enter immediately. He surveyed it from the door, looking for signs of disturbance.

Satisfied, he placed the key in his pocket and felt a piece of paper. He took it out and was surprised to see a sheet from the prescription pad at the infirmary. He didn't remember being handed this. There was nothing written on it. But Dr. Isabel Reyes' name was on the top and a phone number. He put it on the night stand, then checked the bathroom and the closet. Satisfied that he was alone, he bolted the door. He undressed and took a long shower, first hot, then cold. He dressed in clean clothes and dialed Dr. Reyes' number.

Chapter 7

Press & Reyes

"Hola." He heard a familiar voice answer.

"Is this the doctor who doesn't treat injured patients?" He was still hurt by his lack of treatment.

"I don't treat grown men who get in fights."

"That's not what happened. It wasn't a fight, it was an ambush."

"I know. Just as you know why I sent you away. When I asked you what you were going to do about your friend's murder you said nothing."

Press considered that Dr. Reyes was looking for an ally – a worthy ally, one as brave as she was. He had yet to demonstrate that he was that man. He felt accused by the silence. "Do you have a plan?" He had begun to ask "What do you want me to do?" but that sounded weak and cowardly.

"What's the English expression – I'm the brains of this garment?"

"Outfit. You're the brains of this outfit. Close enough. This is your country. I'm expecting you to know how it works."

"It works by mordida – bribes. Have you a lot of money, Rabbi Press?"

"No. How much is a lot? How much would it take to get the Policia to do their job?"

"I don't know. More than you have. You should leave town for a while. Go to Merida. There's a nice hotel there called Caribe. Don't book it from here. Just go and book a room when you get there. I have business there tomorrow. We'll talk then."

******

What struck Press about Merida was all the old Volkswagons. It was as if Mexico had been colonized by Germany instead of Spain. He took a cab from the bus station to the Hotel Caribe. He took some comfort in his anonymity; none of the million or so residents knew him. He checked into his room and called Dr. Reyes on his cell phone. "I'm here. When will you arrive? I'll meet you at the bus station."

"Stay where you are. I'll drive there. I'll see you later." She hung up.

This brief and unsatisfying conversation made Press aware again of the pain from his beating. He took some Advil and tried to sort out his feelings towards the doctor.

This proved impossible. She was good looking – beautiful even – but abrupt and cold. He thought about the peculiar nature of their assignation. In a normal context meeting a woman in a hotel in Merida - at her insistence yet—would be a romantic enterprise. But they were meeting to do what? Solve a crime? Plan revenge? Still, the meeting seemed illicit and he could not shake the romantic overtones of the situation. He wondered if she thought he was safe – celibate like the priests of her own faith. He wondered how he would clear that misconception up. There was the ambiguity of the room. She had not asked him to reserve a separate room for her. But surely she would make her own reservation. Ashamed of this train of thoughts, he turned his mind to McNeery. McNeery had an office somewhere, back at the University of New Mexico probably. There would be affairs to put in order. He smiled inwardly at the phrase. He lay down on the bed, suddenly tired.

He woke to a ringing phone. The room was dark, it was dark outside. He managed to find his cell by groping. "Hello."

"I'm in room 416. Come over."

It sounded to Press more like a command than an invitation. "In a minute. I was asleep." But she had already hung up.

As he walked down the corridor to her room, Press could not shake the wicked feeling that he was going to an assignation. This, he imagined, is how adulterers feel in hotels. He found her room and knocked quietly on the door, then a bit louder.

Dr. Reyes opened the door, acknowledged him bruskly and said "Come in" as she unfastened the chain.

Dr. Reyes was dressed casually, like a tourist, he supposed, in beige pants and a white shirt. She wore a simple silver cross on a thin chain around her neck. "Would you like something to drink? There's water, orange juice, soda."

"Nothing alcoholic?"

"Yes, but this isn't a date."

"Water then. If I'm going to be abstemious, I'll go all the way."

She handed him a bottle of spring water. "I didn't treat you in Valladolid because I can't trust my help not to tell whomever it was that beat you in the first place. How are you feeling?"

"OK. Sore. I've been beaten up before. I'll live."

"But sometimes you're the one who does the beating, no?" She smiled for the first time.

"What do you mean?" He thought he knew what she was referring to, but how could she have known?

"At your lectures. Someone gives you a hard time, heckles you, you – how do you say it? – you punch them outside."

"Punch them out. But how –"

"I googled you. So how come you lost the fight in the alley?"

"Mexican thugs are tougher than American college students. And there were two of them."

Chapter 8

Press & Reyes

"You've read Borges?"

Reyes nodded.

"In the original Spanish. You're lucky. Anyway, Borges has a story that makes me think of Colvin – Father McNeery. It's called "The Theologians." Do you know it?"

Reyes shook her head.

"It's about a heretic and his accuser. The heretic is burned at the stake. The accuser dies years later in a fire started by a lightning bolt. The end of the story takes place in heaven, where Borges postulates a god in whose unfathomable deity the heretic and the accuser are a single person. Colvin was trained to the priesthood. But he was more Jesuitical than Franciscan, and he felt, aggressively so, that faith was more important than its accoutrements. That faith superseded, and in fact was undermined by, miracles.'

Reyes: "You like this story?'

"Yes. Quite a bit. Actually, it's the idea I like. The story is a bit tedious. But I like the idea of a god who doesn't have a human perspective."

"You are strange, Rabbi, even for a Jew."

Press let the remark stand.

She picked up the thread of conversation. "He was a priest? A scholar?"

"He was both. He lost his flock because of his scholarship. His specialty was dating the Gospels, especially Matthew. He pissed off the Church when he claimed the Star of Bethlehem was the Gospel author's interpolation of the appearance of Halley's Comet in 66 A.D. So, he argued, Matthew was written after 66 A.D., and by someone who was not a contemporary of Jesus."

"So what was he doing here, excavating Mayan ruins?'

"I don't know. Looking for another Star of Bethlehem, one that would get him out of the trouble Halley's Comet had gotten him into."

"Archeologists look at the ground; shouldn't he have been somewhere looking up?"

"The Maya were the best astronomers of their time. He was hoping they saw something the ancient Hebrews, the Romans didn't. He was hoping they made a record of it. He'd done archeological work in the Middle East for the same reason." He watched Reyes digest this.

"Maybe he gets burned at the stake in the fifteenth century. Not now. Nobody kills him because he thinks the Star of Bethlehem is Halley's Comet."

"His scientific inquiries got him in trouble with the conservative faction in the Church hierarchy."

Reyes: "But he was an archeologist." So far, I don't see what his problem with the Church was."

"Begging your pardon, but the church doesn't take well to systems of knowledge besides its own. Deep down, they don't like science – don't make a face, it's true. They especially don't like astronomy – remember how they treated Galileo – and the Maya were great astronomers."

Reyes: "That's ridiculous. That was long ago."

"Colvin believed the Church relied too much on ritual and miracle to win over the pagans, and that distorted Jesus' message about both this world and the next. Faith is the belief in the absence of proof; miracles are proofs of a sort. He preferred a Savior who could bleed to death on the cross to one who could walk on water."

Reyes: "And which do you prefer?"

"I prefer the law: Torah. At least for this world. And I don't believe in the next. And you? What do you believe? You're a doctor - do you believe strains of bacteria and viruses evolve?"

"It's possible, you know, that all the strains are always present, and that when we kill off one strain, others thrive."

Press thought about that.

Reyes said: "I believe in evolution. I just didn't care for your smugness. How do you know McNeery? I never asked."

"We led parallel lives, and then they crossed. He's an ex-priest, or rather a priest without a flock. I'm an ex-rabbi, a rabbi without a congregation. He took a scholarly interest in - well, just about everything; but especially the gnostic gospels, books that got left out of the Christian canon. I took an interest in them as well, but it was a peripheral interest. My real interest in early Christianity is in how it spread so quickly. My theory is that the early church fathers chose the right stories: virgin birth, resurrection, star of Bethlehem, water into wine. The deity is in the details: crucifixion by nailing, when the common practice was to hang people on the cross by rope. Nails were too expensive to waste on criminals, even high profile ones. Professor McNeery's scholarly quest, his holy grail, was to understand Jesus the man, and like a true scholar, to try to reconstruct what actually happened at Calvary. You look offended."

"I begin to understand why people want to kill you."

"Yes. We're martyrs to our own particular brand of heresy – the truth."

He watched Reyes roll her eyes. Press shrugged. "I find violent people don't usually need much in the way of a reason. So McNeery's death by jaguar is something of a miracle for you?"

"No one's death is a miracle. And it wasn't a jaguar that killed him. I'm a doctor. I prefer that people live; and I'm after the truth too. You don't have a monopoly on that."

"You know, I would like a drink. Is there a beer in there?" He indicated the tiny fridge.

"You're serious. You drink?"

"Why not? Nothing in my faith forbids it. Your look says you think I murder babies too. I might have two beers. Do you want me to leave?"

Reyes shook her head. Press wasn't sure if this was exasperated dismissal, or whether she didn't want him to leave. He asked "Did you know McNeery?"

Reyes: "Yes. No, not really. He brought a sick worker to my clinic once. I tuned him away. I only treat women and children. The locals know that. McNeery didn't. He was indignant. I had to finally tell him to fuck off. That seemed to register with him."

"What happened to the patient?"

"He recovered. They usually do. He just needed rest and rehydration. I told him that. What? A rabbi can drink, but a doctor can't say 'fuck off'?"

Press shook his head. "Are you sure you won't have something to drink? Tell me why it wasn't a jaguar. Or is that going to spoil dinner? "

"Not for me. Maybe for you." Reyes paused, then went on. "The claw marks were all on the professor's right side: the right side of his face, the right side of his torso. There were no claw marks on his arms. So McNeery didn't try to defend himself. That seems unlikely, unless he was already dead or unconscious when he was clawed."

Press took a long drink.

Reyes: "Let's go to dinner. If you get drunk, I'd rather it not be in my room."

They walked a couple of blocks to a restaurant. Reyes said: "They get their beef from Argentina. You should order steak, unless you observe the dietary laws."

"I don't."

When they were seated, Press asked "How did you come to be a doctor?"

"Is that so unusual?"

Press: "For a woman in Mexico – no. Not these days. For a beautiful woman – and let's not have any false humility – you know you're a beautiful woman – all those people staring are not staring at me – so it was unusual for you to have become a doctor when I'm sure you had easier paths laid before you."

"Can't a beautiful woman be a doctor – and lets dispense with the rearhanded compliments – you're flirting and doing it badly –"

"Backhanded. You mean 'backhanded compliments'."

"How are you with Spanish idioms? 'Backhanded compliments'. OK."

"My Spanish is inferior to your English. So let's stipulate that you are smart as well as beautiful – is that a better compliment, by the way? – so we'll continue to speak in English."

"What was the question? I wanted to help people. Isn't that why you became a Rabbi? – so you understand - and I didn't look in the mirror to see if that was okay."

"And you run a clinic for poor people. Are you rich too, to afford to do that? Beautiful, smart, rich." He ticked them off on his fingers.

"My family is wealthy. Me, not so wealthy. But I have enough. I can pay for my own dinner. But not for yours."

"Fair enough. I was going to pay for both dinners, but I accept your offer."

There was a pause. She cut a piece of steak.

Press asked: "Are you from here? From Valladolid?"

"Mexico City."

"Does that mean something different than if you were from Merida or Monterey?"

He watched her consider the question. Finally she said "That's an interesting question to be asked by a foreigner. It means I'm cosmopolitan, what you would call liberal, attuned to politics. What about you? What does it mean to be a Rabbi from Dublin?"

"It means I cause a fair amount of cognitive dissonance even before I start in on Early Christianity."

"Why not early Judaism?"

"Not nearly so interesting. Look around. Every town here has a beautiful church. Most have several. Why not synagogues, or temples to Zeus? The world changed its mind between 100 and 400 AD. I just want to understand why."

"The world woke up. Is that so hard to understand? Your own alarm didn't go off."

"OK. Say that's true. Then the world woke up again between 800 and 1200 AD when Islam was the fastest growing religion. So the world, or a large part of it, changed its mind again. That's an interesting question too, but I'm only smart enough for one big question at a time."

"Those weren't Christians who converted to Islam."

"As a matter of fact, some were."

"I thought you didn't study that."

"I know a little about it."

There was a silence. Press could see her thinking things over. She said "Why did they kill your friend?"

"I don't know. I don't know who 'they' are. The Policia are happy for it to be a jaguar. Maybe they killed him. Is that possible? I know they are corrupt, but murder?"

"Not likely. Not these Policia. Mordida – yes. Murder - no."

"One of his workers?"

"I don't think so. I would say no."

"Why not?"

"Almost all the murders in Mexico are drug related or crimes of passion – a man finds his wife with another man. Mexican workers put up with a lot, and from what I can tell your friend was a better boss than most. So, not one of his workers. Could your friend have been mixed up in drugs?"

"No."

"Could he have been sleeping with someone's wife?'

"No."

"Then why is he dead?"

Chapter 9

Professor Owen Sterling

Professor Owen Sterling looked at the email from *yucatan2012@gmail.me* and shook his head. Inside were the celestial coordinates of a new star in the northern hemisphere sky. The third new star this correspondent had found in two months. Sterling remembered the first email: so laconic and matter-of-fact as to be almost rude: "There is a new star near Vega at declination 39 degrees, 16 minutes, 12 seconds and right ascension 18 h 36 m 14 s." Nothing about the discoverer. No salutation. He didn't think it was a prank. Pranks were more elaborate. So he had overridden that night's observation schedule to point the main refracting telescope at the portion of the sky yucatan2012 had suggested. There, as promised, was a new class M star. He sent off a report to the Naval Observatory, and a warm thank you to Yucatan2012. And then, nothing. No response.

Five weeks later he received another terse email from *yucatan2012@gmail.me*. Another new star. He confirmed it that night. He sent an uncharacteristically brief acknowledgement – two can play this game, he thought. No response. Still, there was a star-finding prodigy in Mexico. An uncharacteristically modest one.

Now this. Owen called down to scheduling and the observation plan was modified again. That night he found another new star winking at him, exactly where yucatan2012 said he would.

This time he wrote an effusive email:

Dear yucutan2012,

To find a new star is rare, to find 3 in 2 months is unprecedented. Please send me a brief biographical sketch and your CV. We'd like to give you proper credit. And if you're ever in New Mexico, please stop by. I'd like to buy you a drink. You've earned it.

All the Best,
Owen Sterling
Hubbell Professor of Astronomy
The University of New Mexico

A week later, when he still had received no reply, he resent the email. Another week passed, and still he received no reply.

"Who is this guy?" he said to his computer screen.

"Or gal." Megan, his grad student amended.

"I meant 'guy' in the inclusive sense." Owen knew he was being teased, but he felt a bit defensive, because he imagined yucatan2012 was a sixty year old man, someone like himself. Apparently his grad student was imagining someone more like herself. Except that neither of them had ever found a new star.

"How do you propose we find this person."

"Why do we have to find her?" Teasing again.

"If a modern Mozart was emailing symphonies to Zubin Mehta, wouldn't he try to find her? To give the woman her due?"

Chapter 10

Rufino, Reyes & Press

When Reyes returned to her clinic her receptionist handed her a pink message slip: "You were right about the jaguar. See me when you get this." – Det. Rufino."

Reyes looked at her receptionist.

"He called while you were away."

Reyes called Press. "It's no longer a jaguar. There's a new detective on the case. You might want to join me when I go to see hm."

At the Police Station, Reyes and Press were ushered into a small room, bare except for a wooden table and three chairs. An interrogation room, Press thought, and looked for signs of dried blood on the floor. He looked up when Detective Rufino entered. He heard Rufino address Dr. Reyes in Spanish: "Why do you hang around with this troublemaker?"

Dr. Reyes said: "This troublemaker speaks Spanish. Not well, but understands well enough."

Press saw the detective look at him. The expression he saw on Rufino's face wasn't embarrassment; it was annoyance. Press said "Hola."

Rufino chose to ignore him and speak to Dr. Reyes. "This is what we know, and it's enough. The teenager, Humberto, worked for Señor McNeery at the site. The morning after the murder, the morning we found the body, Humberto did not report to work. When I checked his home, he was gone, but we found McNeery's computer. We know, from informants, that Humberto was mixed up with the antiquities black market. You yourself said it was no jaguar that killed the professor – you were right. It was this juvenile delinquent. We suspect that the professor caught him stealing antiquities, and was killed in the confrontation that followed. When we find him we'll get a confession.

Press looked at the floor again, saw imaginary blood.

Reyes said: "You've solved the case so quickly. But I'm curious, why was the Captain of the Policia so quick to blame a jaguar?" She held up a hand as she saw Rufino was about to speak. "You've been a detective how long?"

"Twelve years."

"And how many teenaged killers, teenaged Indian killers, have you had in 12 years?"

"We arrest them all the time."

"But not for murder. For stealing, for getting drunk. But never for murder."

Rufino: "This one's different."

"How do you know? Because he was stealing artifacts? He's Mayan. They're more his than yours or mine or the Norte Americano professor's."

Rufino paused, let a smirk grow on his face: "Are you done, señora? There's one other thing. Humberto is left handed. What was it you said to Captain Cepeda about the jaguar – 'look for a left handed one'?"

Press watched some color come out of Reyes' face. It was a moment before she spoke: "Ten percent of the population is left handed. Fifteen million people in Mexico are left handed."

Rufino shook his head: "But all those other lefties don't have Father's McNeery's computer."

Press asked: "How do you know Humberto is left handed?"

"I searched his home. 'If my horse is missing, I may search my neighbor's barn.' The legal tradition here is the Napoleonic Code." Detective Benito Rufino looked at Press as he explained. "When we searched Humberto's home we found Professor McNeery's computer and an instruction manual for a

Questar Lightweight Titanium 7. We also found a baseball glove – for a lefty. We didn't find Humberto, your friend's killer, but we will. He was one of McNeery's laborers and a sometime petty criminal. We didn't find him, but we will."

Press stole a quick glance at Dr. Reyes. This lecture was for him. He heard the detective's subtext: *This is Mexico. There is no pansy-ass law against unreasonable searches; warrants aren't required as a matter of course, an hombre could get on with his work unimpeded when it came to catching bad guys.*

Press said: "You think he killed him to steal his computer?"

Rufino: "I think he killed your friend to steal a codex, or because he'd already stolen a codex and your friend caught him. I think he stole the computer because he wanted it. Did your friend own a telescope? Was he an amateur astronomer?"

Press: "I don't think so. I think he spent most of his time here looking down, not up. The Maya were astronomers. Maybe he took up astronomy to better understand them."

Rufino: "The Maya didn't have telescopes. They were astronomers with their eyes. We'll find Humberto." He turned to Dr. Reyes: "You were right about the jaguar. Some people owe you an apology, but you won't get it. You'll excuse me. I've got a murderer to catch." He handed Press his card on the way out.

Press started to leave. He heard Reyes ask "Where are you going?"

"To his rooms. To look through his notes. To pack things up."

Reyes: "You think the boy did it. Rufino convinced you."

Press: "Convinced? No. But it's hard not to think of Humberto as a suspect. I wish he wasn't left handed, that's all. You say these kids never kill. Not even each other. Why not? They get a little older and beat their wives, don't they?"

Reyes: "It's a cultural thing. They don't kill. Even among adults it's rare. Unless they get mixed up in the drug wars."

Press: "Couldn't he have been mixed up in that? By all accounts he was no angel."

Reyes: "By all accounts? No, by police accounts. Remember, these same police were happy to pretend a jaguar did it. They stink to heaven with their corruption. You asked about my family once. You asked about my relationship with them. One of the things between us is corruption: my father pays bribes, lots of them, and his businesses are allowed to flourish. They look the other way when he cuts corners. The Mexican way. My father pretends not to like it, but he plays the game."

Press: "It's hard to fight it if it's built into the culture."

Reyes turned to face him: "What is it with you men. So it's hard. Be brave. The policia came to me when I opened my clinic, for their mordida. They knew of my father; they thought I'd be the same. I told them to get lost. Suddenly, I couldn't get permits. Everywhere, I was in violation of this or that. So I went to the policia captain. I told him 'Someday, someone you care about is going to need a doctor. A good doctor, and maybe there won't be time to go to Merida. I'm the best doctor around, and even if I wasn't, I might be the only doctor who can treat your mother in time to save her life. Or maybe you or one of your men gets shot. Don't get in my way.'"

"And the Captain backed off?"

"He called me a stinking cunt, but he left me alone after that."

"Rufino isn't with the regular Policia." Press handed the card to Reyes.

She looked at it and said: "He's with the Antiquities Police. A separate entity from the local police. Supposedly elite, and less corrupt. Probably not. Every wealthy family in Mexico owns antiquities: Aztec, Olmec, Mayan. On display in their parlors and living rooms. 'If my horse is missing, I can search your barn.' They never search those barns. And it wouldn't matter if they did. 'Officer, that's been in my family for years, before the Antiquities Control Act. You've come all this way for nothing. You must be hungry – here's 100 pesos, please buy yourself some lunch.' 'Gracias, Señor.' I've seen it in my own home."

"Will he catch Humberto?"

"Sure. Humberto has no money. And Rufino will beat a confession out of him too."

"You don't know Humberto, but you think he's innocent. Why?"

"I know a hundred Humbertos. He's an indigenous kid. A trouble-maker – sure. A thief – maybe. Would he steal a laptop from a dead man who had no further use for it – I'm sorry to speak of your friend that way – yes. Kill him? No. These kids aren't killers."

"But he's left handed."

"How many Irish teenagers are killers?"

"I don't know. Not many, I'd guess."

"And yet you're a quarrelsome lot, badly behaved, am I right?"

Press nodded.

"A man killed your friend, not a boy. Certainly not a Mayan boy."

"How do you know it wasn't a jaguar? They attack humans. Certainly they could kill one."

"They don't attack humans. Or only rarely, and then only if the jaguar is sick or wounded."

"They're capable of killing cattle, for crissake. That's why ranchers shoot them."

"Yes, they kill cattle. Do you know how? You have a lot of jaguars in Dublin? They kill cattle by biting through their skulls into their brains. They don't claw them like a spurned debutante. And then they drag the body off to a quiet place to eat it. The detective knows this if I do. Even the idiot Policia captain knows this. But he wants to blame it on a jaguar. Why? And the Antiquities detective is in a hurry to blame it on a teenager. Again, why?"

"Why are you so angry? I should be angry – it's my friend who was killed."

"Angry, I'm told, is my natural state. And you? You go to give a lecture and it turns into a brawl. What? I googled you. You're not angry? Why are you so angry? I'm a hot-blooded Hispanic woman – so it's in my genes. But you, you're a rabbi. What's your excuse?"

"Same as everyone else's. I had a lousy childhood."

"A Jew in Dublin. A fish out of the lake."

"You mean a fish out of water. No, my problem was that I was rich, good-looking and smart."

"Rich is okay by itself. Good-looking is okay by itself. Smart is okay by itself. Even all three together is not a problem if you're a man."

"So you're angry because you're a woman? You can change that nowadays."

"You choose to misunderstand. It's not that I'm a woman. It's that I'm treated like a woman. Aren't you ever treated like a Jew?"

"Not since childhood."

"Stick around. You will be."

"They really don't attack humans? Other big cats do. Why don't jaguars?"

"Maybe we don't taste that good."

Press was going to hold the door for her, but she was already through it. He said to her back, "If I find anything, I'll let you know."

Outside he hailed a taxi. The driver saw Reyes striding down the street. He said, "That one's a hot one."

Press nodded. Whatever the driver meant by it, it was true. He gave him the address to McNeery's rooms.

Chapter 11

Ex-Rabbi Simon Press

McNeery's rooms were in the Calle Real. Press paid the taxi driver and walked to the front door. He rang the buzzer and was greeted by a short older woman wearing too much red lipstick. He introduced himself and explained he'd come for his friend's belongings.

"Where's your truck?" she asked.

"I'm just taking his papers today. I'll make arrangements for the rest. Maybe you know of some charity that could use his clothes?"

She nodded. "This way."

She led Press through a small stone courtyard with purple bougainvillea and small orange trees. "He was a nice man. A gentleman, your friend. I'm so sorry." They stopped at a door which she unlocked. "Here."

Press expected – what exactly? Yellow crime scene tape or something to indicate a police presence. But the room seemed to be as his dead colleague had left it.

"I'll leave you. Come get me if you need anything. Boxes?"

"Thank you."

The apartment consisted of a small kitchenette, a living room/dining room, a bathroom, and stairs that led half a flight up to what he guessed was a bedroom. The kitchenette showed little evidence of use. The living room/dining room was dominated by a large wooden table in the colonial style, dark and heavy, with matching chairs. The table was covered with manila folders, spiral notebooks, and books. Off this room was a bathroom, Press could see a tiled sink through the partially opened door. A small pile of books and papers rested on the first step of the stairs. He gave the pile a quick look and walked up to the bedroom. A bed of the same heavy wood as the dining room table took up most of the room. There was a cross over it, with a crowned and bleeding Jesus on it. By the window, on the wall farthest from where he stood, was a simple desk. There was a computer printer on it, and next to the printer an empty space where Press assumed McNeery put his laptop – the one found in Humberto's possession. There were notebooks to the right of the empty space. The bed had been made; the wastebasket next to the bed had been emptied.

Press looked again at the ornate cross above the bed, but he thought of another cross he'd seen in a church in Connecticut. He'd forgotten which town. The Congregationalist Church was pure New England Protestant: white siding, white steeple – the church on the green of a thousand picture postcards. The inside was sparse, with simple wooden pews and large windows divided into small panes. The huge cross at the back of the altar bore no image of Jesus. It was just wood: two railroad ties. It had put Press in mind of the thing itself: not a symbol, but the actual instrument of torture - empty, waiting for a victim.

Press crossed the room to McNeery's desk. He opened a spiral notebook that lay next to where the laptop had been. He looked at McNeery's handwritten notes: the cursive was beautiful. He thought of a young boy eager to please a long line of demanding parochial school nuns.

He read: "The codex is 92 cm tall by 60.5 cm wide and is comprised of 64 leaves including the front and back cover. The leaves are somewhat thick, so that the entire codex is about 6 cm tall. Some of this thickness is due to the warped nature of the pages themselves – think of a book left out in the rain and then dried. Like the Dresden and Madrid codices, the pages are entirely covered in glyphs and, again like the D and M codices, multicolored."

McNeery's own writing covered only half the page, up to a thin pencil line drawn vertically. Press assumed that McNeery had left the other half blank for the scholars inevitable footnotes.

He read on: "7.17.6.15.4 King Jaguar Brother ascended upon the death of his father, Snake Twin." On the side of the page reserved for notes McNeery had written "Dates are given in Mayan long count, but the calculated Julian/Gregorian dates will appear in parentheses. I'm using December 22, 2012 as the end of the Mayan long count and working backwards."

A second note explained that he would follow convention and skip 10 days, going from Thursday, October 4, 1582 Julian to Friday, October 15, 1582 Gregorian, in accordance with the first introduction of the Gregorian calendar. Press thought wryly of the Chicago song – "Does Anybody Really Know What Time It Is?"The simple answer was – for a long time – "no." Different countries followed different calendars before they got around to accepting the Gregorian. So it was that Shakespeare and Cervantes are said to have died on the same day, April 23, 1616. But Shakespeare died in England which stayed on the Julian calendar until 1752 and Cervantes died in Spain, which adopted the Gregorian calendar immediately, and so in fact they died 10 days apart, Cervantes first.

He continued to read: "Second Jaguar ascended on 7.17.9.8.2. In 7.17.11.1.7 he fought with Snake Brother and was captured and killed." Press was reminded of the dull roll calls of the generations in Genesis. He'd invariably skipped them and he skipped these. He began to scan the right side of the page - the side for notes. If McNeery had written anything more interesting than translation it would show up here.

The notes were mostly dates. Occasionally there were words or phrases followed by question marks – alternative translations. And then he came upon this: "Star of Bethlehem?!" He glanced over to the translation on the left: "During the rule of Plumed Serpent Son there was a new star…"

Press stopped. The Mayan date, 7.17.15.5.2, meant nothing to him, but the date in parenthesis gave him a chill: 4 BCE.

And here it was. Ironically, counter-intuitively - take your pick - scholars were nearly unanimous in assigning the date of Jesus birth to the year 4 B.C.E.

It was clear that McNeery had been looking at the original codex when he made his notes. Where was that original now? Stolen, of course. By Humberto? By the Policia? By the housekeeper? McNeery must have made some provision for the artifacts that were not part of the archeological site itself. Where were these kept? Was the codex among them? Press thought it likely that McNeery was working on the codex on the day he was murdered, and that it had probably been in this room. Whoever stole his computer could have taken the codex as well. Would the teenager have recognized its value? Surely someone working at an archeological site would.

He felt foolish, but he searched the room. He looked under the bed, in the drawers – where he found McNeery's clothes - in the kitchen cabinets. His search was quick and half-hearted – he was sure the codex had been taken. He was sweating now and stopped and sat.

He borrowed some boxes from the landlady. When he was done packing he had a dozen cartons of McNeery's books and files. He didn't think they would fit in a taxi, so he had the landlady call for a small truck. Twenty minutes later a boy of fifteen in a LeBron James jersey knocked at the door. "I'm here for the boxes."

"Where's the truck?"

The boy pointed to the street.

Is my Spanish so bad, Press thought, that this kid is resorting to gestures? He looked out the window and saw a small Toyota pickup at the curb. "Can you help me?" He indicated the boxes.

The boy picked up three, Press picked up one and they walked to the truck. Press gave his street address to the driver.

When they arrived at his rooms, the boy helped again with the boxes. After he'd been paid and left, Press sat down to look again at McNeery's notes. He went at it more slowly and methodically, now that he was in the comfortable familiarity of his own rooms.

His cell phone rang and startled him. He seldom got calls. It took him a moment to find the phone among the notes. "Hello?" Press always answered with an interrogative hello. It came, he thought, from not quite believing in the technology. He was always surprised to find a voice at the other end.

"Hola. This is Dr. Reyes."

"Hi."

"Humberto has a girlfriend."

"Does she know where he is?"

"She's pregnant."

Press was about to ask how she knew but then it came to him – the clinic. The better question was: "How did Dr. Reyes know this young woman was Humberto's girlfriend?" Reyes filled in the pause: "She came into the clinic. I'd seen her before. Ironically, about birth control."

"How do you know she's Humberto's girlfriend?"

"She told me. She's frightened. Humberto's gone, in trouble. So how would you counsel her, Rabbi?"

Press recognized the taunt. "I'd ask if she wanted to keep it, and assuming she did I'd remind her that her Savior was born under inauspicious circumstances – not in those words exactly – and look how that turned out. I'd tell her to take good care of herself and her fetus. What did you say to her?"

"Have you counseled many pregnant teenagers, Rabbi?"

"None."

"I didn't think so."

"She doesn't know where Humberto is?"

"Doesn't know, or won't say. I'm guessing she's been to where ever he's hiding out."

"Do the Policia know?"

"Why should they? I won't tell them about Maria – that's her name, by the way."

"Does Humberto know she's pregnant?"

"No. She just found out when she came to me. Why is everything about Jesus with you?"

"What do you mean?"

"Your advice: 'Tell her her savior was born under inauspicious circumstances.' And by the way, they were the opposite of inauspicious: there was the Star of Bethlehem and the Magi."

"Only in Mathew. The other gospels don't mention the star or the Magi. Everything is about Jesus because he beat my religion to a bloody pulp. Maria – does she need money? A place to stay? Will her parents throw her out? How old is she?"

"She's sixteen. Her father will probably throw her out when he finds out. And then he'll go after Humberto."

"Will he be any better at finding Humberto than the Policia?"

Reyes: "I think the Policia are looking harder now."

"Even so. Will they find him? Except for Detective Rufino, they don't seem to be a very diligent bunch. By the way, I found something interesting in McNeery's notes."

Reyes: "You're changing the subject. What about Maria?"

"You should take her in when her family throws her out. Or I will. There will be less talk if you take her in. In either case she'll have a roof over head and food. You'll look after her medically."

Reyes: "What about after the baby's born?"

"She can stay with me. I've helped raise a daughter. I know my way around babies."

Reyes: "I'm trying to imagine you with a baby. I don't think you're that patient."

"Not with adults. But I'm patient with children. What about you? Do you have children?"

Reyes: "No."

"No? Nobody wants to sleep with you?" When he heard the phone hang up Press considered that he'd gone too far. And he'd never told her about McNeery's notes on the codex. Also, he'd volunteered to take in a pregnant Mexican teenager, and as the doctor had pointed out, he didn't have any experience with that. He'd offered, he realized, because he wanted to improve the doctor's estimation of him. He was attracted to her; he couldn't deny it. And he thought her hanging up on him was a bit over-dramatic. So the game had begun. Press was still holding the phone. He wanted to talk to someone about what he'd found, and Dr. Reyes was his only friend here. He called her again. There was no answer on her cell phone. He left a disingenuous message about their being accidentally disconnected. Then he tried the clinic. The receptionist there said Dr. Reyes was busy, and besides she only saw women and children.

Press asked "Can I leave a message?"

"Si."

He left the same message he'd left on her cell phone. Even as the receptionist wrote his message down, he sensed he would have to do something more to get her to call him back. He set out for the Mercado.

Press could never get used to the unrefrigerated carcasses of animals hanging everywhere in this tropical climate. Beyond the open air meat market were stalls of vegetables, beyond these, fruits; and beyond these, flowers. He bargained for a large bouquet. This was the cornerstone of his apology. He headed to the clinic, where he knew he would be turned away, but where his flowers might at least be allowed to stay. He was feeling pleased with himself.

Press opened the door, looked around at the hurt and patient faces, then walked briskly to the receptionist and handed her the bouquet before she could register an objection to his presence. "For Dr. Reyes," he said, and quickly left.

Still pleased with himself, Press wandered over to the plaza, where he bought a fresh fruit cup sticky with papaya and guava. He considered calling Dr. Reyes and went so far as to take the cell phone from his pocket. He decided she was probably with a patient; he decided to call later. Then he ambled back to his rooms.

At the door he found his bouquet, considerably worse for wear, strewn about the entry way. There was a dark spot on the bottom of the door and on the step, and he couldn't help but think some animal had relieved itself on the broken bouquet.

He gave up all thoughts of the codex. Dr. Reyes was a more interesting puzzle. He kicked the flowers aside and entered his apartment. He was beginning to doubt his own charm and its most recent object.

He called the clinic. He was surprised when, after being put on hold by the receptionist, Dr. Reyes took his call. "Do not ever make a joke about my attractiveness." She hung up before he could ask whether she herself had peed on his doorstep, or had a proxy do it. He decided he'd try again, but not tonight.

He sat at his dining room table and began to go through the rest of McNeery's notes, looking he realized, for a distraction.

Chapter 12

Cardinal Sabatini

Cardinal Sabatini looked at the e-mail one last time:

Your Eminence,

Thank you for your efforts on my behalf. You asked about my work. I made the most wonderful discovery: a Mayan codex almost 1500 years old. Like Dresden and Paris, it contains mostly astronomical observations, including the appearance and disappearance of any significant celestial objects. I can't be absolutely certain of the translation, but it appears that a very bright star appeared in 4 B.C., the time that would correspond to the birth of our Savior, at least according to my calculations and those of other biblical scholars. There's more, a great deal more, all of it rather startling, but I want to recheck my translation before I share it with you.

As I hardly need to remind you, this completely refutes my previous scholarship dating the Gospel of Matthew. I am humbled, as I deserve to be.

Yours in Christ,

Colvin McNeery

Sabatini reread the e-mail and then clicked "delete." He called to his secretary, a young man whose balding head reminded Sabatini of a medieval monk, and said "Please cancel my appointments for today and tomorrow."

"Your meeting with his Holiness tomorrow at 11?"

Sabatini paused. He watched the blood drain from his secretary's face. "We'll keep that one. Cancel the rest."

Sabatini closed the door to the outer chamber, satisfied that his secretary was going about the business of canceling appointments. Sabatini picked up his own phone and dialed the number of the Prefect of the Archives, Msgr. Constantino.

"Archivo Segredo. This is Raphael."

"This is Ernesto Sabatini. Is Msgr. Constantino available?" Even if Constantino was not available, he would be now.

"I'll get him for you."

A moment later he heard the businesslike voice of the Guilermo Constantino: "Good afternoon, your eminence. How may I help you?"

"A good afternoon, Monsignor. There are two files in the archives I will need to have a look at. One is the correspondence from Diego de Landa in 1562, and the other is the transcription of his interrogation the following year. There may be others relating to Landa – I'll know better after I've had a look at these."

"When do you need them?"

"Now."

There was a brief pause and then the Monsignor said, "I'll retrieve them myself. Landa was Spanish, his letter will probably be in that language. Do you need a translation?"

"No."

"I didn't think so. But it's the custom to ask."

A few moments later Sabatini was off the phone and on his way over to the archives.

L'Archivio Segreto Vaticano - the secret archives of the Vatican – are the largest and most valuable archives in the world. 25 miles of bookshelves contain the official account of the trial of Galileo, the English lords petition to annul Henry VIII's marriage to Catherine of Aragon (and Henry VIII's love letters to Anne Bolyn), the private correspondence of the infamous Borgia popes, Napoleon's Treaty of Tolentino, and the private notes on all candidates for canonization, including their unsaintly behaviors and peccadilloes.

Sabatini stood, sat, stood again. He opened the door to the outer office. "What time is it in Merida, Mexico?"

The secretary hit a few keystrokes and leaned in towards the screen, "About 8:20 AM."

"Thank you." Sabatini closed the door and dialed an international call: "Leon Cortes please... Yes, you may. This is Cardinal Ernesto Sabatini."

Chapter 13

Press and Reyes

Press was hungry now, and decided to go out for something to eat. He would have liked some company, in particular, he realized, the company of Isabel Reyes. As he left his apartment he noticed the remains of the bouquet. He wondered what his housekeeper, Luisa, would make of this when she came to clean in the morning. He decided he didn't care.

It was a clear night, but Press did not look up. He took his cell phone from his pocket and dialed Dr. Reyes. She answered.

"It's Simon."

There was a silence, He was relieved not to hear Reyes hanging up. He decided to push his luck: "Care to meet me for dinner? I would bring flowers but they seem to have peed all over themselves. The florist assured me they were house-broken."

A pause. "OK. I'll meet you for dinner. At Cantina Las Campanas. It's loud. A rude place really. You'll be right at home. In thirty minutes. Norte Americano minutes."

"Thank you."

The Cantina Las Campanas was, as promised, loud and rude. The tables were close together. There was a long bar against the far wall, where a mostly young crowd was drinking and flirting. Neon signs above the bar advertised Mexican beers and tequila. Press decided to wait outside for Reyes, in the hope that, her point having been made, he could persuade her to have dinner in a quieter place. He looked at his watch. He was five minutes early. In spite of her insistence on Norte Americano time, he expected she would be late. Part of his punishment. He considered going in and having a drink at the bar. He smiled inwardly - this was the first third of every bar joke in the world: "A rabbi, a priest and a minister go into a bar..."

He looked down the Calle 11 for Dr. Reyes. He looked at his watch again. It was now exactly thirty minutes. He was about to begin his penalty minutes. He saw a woman that could have been Dr. Reyes at the far end of the street. As she drew closer he realized it was someone else. He decided that the noise from the cantina made a better backdrop for this wait than silence. Another woman – not Reyes – appeared down the street. He would try to think about the Mayan Star of Bethlehem – if that's what it was. Certainly it's what he wanted it to be. A young couple walked past him and into the cantina. He was hungry, and this made him consult his watch again. He was sure now that Dr. Reyes had insisted on his punctuality as payback. She would arrive on Mexican time, sometime in the next hour or so. Again he considered having a drink. He had a fleeting thought that something had happened to her - prompted, he realized, by his irritation. She'd pissed off the Policia, as she'd told him, and he had no difficulty imagining her making other enemies. He checked his watch. She was now ten minutes late. No big deal, really. But late enough to ensure that he would be here to meet her. Late enough to warrant him stepping inside for a drink. He took one last look down the street. It came up empty and he went into the cantina. He found a spot – no seats were empty – and ordered a Corona. What he really wanted was food. He turned to face the door. He meant to nurse his beer, but he discovered he was thirsty as well as hungry. When he finished he looked again at his watch. Isabel Reyes was now twenty minutes late. He wondered if she would come at all. Would she indulge her anger to that extent? He paid for his beer and went back out into the street. He considered calling, but decided against it – it would only reinforce her notion of his rudeness. Maybe he had misunderstood her reference to Norte Americano time. Maybe among Mexicans that meant late: just as the English called syphilis the

French Pox, and the French called it the English Pox. Venereal disease was always from somewhere else. Perhaps the habit of tardiness was too. He considered, as he looked back over this train of thought, that his intentions toward Dr. Reyes were not entirely platonic.

He saw a cab slowing down. The headlights made it impossible to see inside, but he was hoping the fare was Dr. Reyes. There was a pause after the cab stopped. And then the rear door opened and Dr. Reyes stepped out. She was dressed casually in jeans and an oversized white shirt.

"Waiting long?" she asked by way of a greeting. Press could detect nothing apologetic in her tone.

Press chose his words carefully: "I'm glad you agreed to see me. We've got a lot to talk about."

"So talk."

"Maybe we could sit down first." They entered the cantina and the host took them to a table far from the bar. The host held out a chair for Dr. Reyes, so the Rabbi was saved from that bit of awkwardness.

The host asked "Would you like something to drink?"

"Ice water." Dr. Reyes.

"Water for me as well." He turned to Dr. Reyes. "I was hoping we were going to be friends. I tease my friends – sometimes cleverly, sometimes not so cleverly. I didn't mean to offend you. I'm sorry."

"You were hoping we were going to be lovers." She said it matter-of-factly, emphasizing the word "lovers" as one might correct a child who had given the wrong answer.

Press was caught off guard. But he recovered: "Yes, that too, but they're not mutually exclusive."

"In my experience they are."

So that's what this is about, Press thought. She wants a friend, not a lover. His teasing had been a suitor's gambit, not a friend's. He had introduced the topic of sex into their conversation. How strange that must have seemed to her, coming from a rabbi – a Jewish priest in her frame of reference. Perhaps it felt to her like being hit on by a priest. He wondered if she'd had that experience. Not unlikely, given the sorry state of the clergy and her own good looks.

The waiter brought their waters.

Press said: "You think of me as a priest, just a different flavor. I'm not a priest. I'm no longer even a rabbi. But I can be your friend. As your friend, I will tease you occasionally."

He watched her give him a hard look.

He went on: "Most people find being teased a sign of affection. Usually they like the attention."

"Do you think I lack for attention?"

Press backed off: "No."

"I agreed to see you because I'm worried about Humberto and Maria. I thought maybe you could help. I talked to Maria about Humberto. She says he's nice, he's kind, he's smart – very smart about stars – but how would she know? She says he would marry her and take care of her and the baby, but now he can't because of a murder he didn't commit, but which he's been blamed for. And I thought you would help, but no, you just want to get tangled up in my underthings."

Knickers, he corrected, to himself. To Dr. Reyes he said, "I offered to take her in. I meant it."

"And what about Humberto? What will you do for him?"

"Whatever I can. Prove he's innocent. Will that make a difference – if he's innocent? He's mixed up with some bad people. How does a poor boy get his hands on a thousand dollar telescope? And whatever he didn't do, he did steal McNeery's computer."

"More likely, the Policia planted it in his house. You don't know how things work here."

"Police are the same everywhere."

The waiter came and they ordered. Press decided another beer would help.

Dr. Reyes said: "I can't get over that you drink."

"So?"

"You drink. You fornicate – or would like to fornicate me. You fight. You're not much of a holy man."

"Are you teasing me? Is teasing permitted now?"

"Do you steal? Do you bear false witness? Do you murder?" Dr. Reyes was ticking them off on her fingers.

"I just ordered a beer. If I decide to become a murderer, watch out. In the meantime, are you sure you wouldn't like a drink?'

"No."

When the waiter returned with his beer, Press felt he had less appetite for it. He let it sit. He said "I think the codex mentions the Star of Bethlehem."

"You said. But what does it matter? People who trade in black market antiquities don't care what they say – only that they're old, and rare, and forbidden."

Press felt a little deflated. The content of the codex was important to him, and obviously to McNeery, but that wouldn't obligate whoever killed McNeery to care. Like the Doctora said, it was enough that it was old and rare. It could have been a Mayan grocery list for all the killer cared. "Why did Humberto have a telescope? Did Maria say?"

"To look at the stars."

"I mean, why? Isn't that a strange and expensive hobby for a poor teenager? You'd think he'd rather have a car or a motorcycle. You're sure he was looking at the stars? Not keeping a lookout?"

He watched Reyes wave him off. "Maria said he would look every night. He showed her sometimes. Mostly he went alone. He's Mayan. They have a long tradition of astronomy. An unusually large percentage are cross-eyed – it's a trait they value – they believe, or used to, that it helps when looking at the stars."

"Is that truc? The high percentage of cross-eyed Mayans?"

"Yes. It's true."

Their food came. The cantina was more crowded now and noisier. As he reviewed the conversation in his mind, Press was ashamed: while Reyes had shown concern for Humberto and Maria, he'd been concerned with what was, at best, an intellectual puzzle. Of all the unrabbinical behaviors she'd questioned, this was the worst and she'd let it go. But it was in this that he was most derelict.

Press said, "I know how to help Maria. How do we help Humberto? Is there any chance we can find him when the Policia can't?"

Reyes shook her head. "I don't think so. The Policia will look only so long as they get pressure from the Americanos. Then it will go back to being a jaguar. Case closed."

"And Humberto will come out of hiding then?"

"No, he'll go to the United States. He'll get work. He'll send money back to Maria. He'll try to get her to join him there."

"She'll leave her family here?"

"Probably not. She's like most Mexican women – she's very attached to her family. She can't imagine leaving them. Not even for another place in Mexico, never mind the United States. Not everyone can be a vagabond like you."

Press did not think he was being complimented. So Reyes objected to what she felt was his rootlessness. He wondered about her family, so he asked: "You've always lived here? In Valladolid?"

"My home is Cuernavaca. That's where my family is. That's where I grew up."

"But now this is your home."

"No. This is where I work. My home is where my family is."

"So if you leave here, you'll return to Cuernavaca?"

"Yes." He could see she thought this was a stupid question.

"What about a place that's more exciting than Valladolid, or Cuernavaca? More exciting, more interesting culturally, intellectually?"

"I'd go there on vacation. Why should I live there?"

"To meet more interesting people." He said it to bait her, he realized.

"I meet interesting people here. They come to me. I meet an Irish rabbi, who's really an ex-rabbi, who drinks and fights and chases women. That wouldn't be so interesting, except in a rabbi." She touched his beer with her water glass.

Press felt the mood had shifted.

She went on: "Traveling, living in different places, do you find that exciting?"

"Not exciting, except of course for getting beat up. But enlivening. I feel more alive when I'm in a new place. I have to be more alert – I want to be more alert – more observant. And you, you're not bored, always in the same place?"

"My work keeps me from being bored. I find it comforting to be among familiar things. When I want something different, I go on vacation."

"So where do you go on vacation?"

"Cabo. The Copper Canyon. New York. Spain."

"Alone?"

"With my family. But that's none of your business, is it?"

"By 'your family' you mean your parents?"

"And my sister."

"So you have a sister. Any other siblings?"

"Just my sister."

"That's a small family for Mexico, isn't it?"

"My parents aren't very good Catholics in that way. Do you have brothers and sisters?"

"No, just me."

She nodded. "An only child. I would have guessed."

"Because?"

"Because you don't stay in one place. Because… I can just tell. You were either an only child, or the oldest."

Press wondered what about him made him seem like an only child. He suspected he wouldn't like Isabel's answer, so he didn't push her for an explanation. "Your sister – she's younger, I bet."

Her pause told him he was right. How had he known? She was a doctor, and high achievement was a first born strategy. He'd read somewhere that the original astronauts were all first born. It was something that interested him personally and professionally: the Old Testament made a big deal of birth order and sibling rivalry.

"She's two years younger. For her – she wants to get married. That's her ambition."

Press smiled. "You should introduce us." Was this teasing? Could he get away with it?

"I don't think so. I like my sister very much." She smiled back at him.

He'd walked right into that. He smiled back. But he thought he'd heard something beneath her barb. Something genuinely protective; something jealous? He couldn't say – relations between siblings were a foreign country to him. He'd studied the map – the Pentateuch was a map of that and a good deal else – but a map is not the territory. He wanted to meet Reyes sister: she might be a clue to the perplexing woman before him. Or a less perplexing version. What he said was "Since I'm not going to meet her, tell me about your sister."

Reyes said: "She's smart, but doesn't use it. She's more outgoing than I am. She's better looking – more fashion –

Press interrupted: "I doubt that, but excuse me for interrupting."

"- more fashion conscious. She's sweet, she's friendly – friendlier and sweeter than I am."

"I don't doubt that."

Press noticed that Reyes' point of reference for her sister's qualities was herself. That would have made more sense for a younger sibling.

"Watch it." Reyes said. She was still smiling.

"You're disappointed she didn't become a doctor, like you?"

"She doesn't have to become a doctor. She could be anything. But she should be something other than somebody's wife-in-waiting."

"She lives at home?"

"Yes, of course. We're a very traditional family. At least my parents are, and she goes along with it for the most part."

"You think she should live on her own?"

"No, not necessarily. I don't care where she lives: I care that she become her own person. But she's spoiled, and she let's herself be."

"So your parents tried to spoil you, but you wouldn't let them?"

"I let them spoil me a little. Look, sooner or later you're going to hear this. My parents are very wealthy and very well known. It's one reason the Policia backed off when I stood up to them about the mordida. 'Reyes' is a common name, but we are 'The Reyes.' Do you understand?"

"It's a burden having wealthy parents."

"You mock me?"

"No. Not about this."

"How do you know? Are your parents wealthy?"

"My parents are dead now, but they were prominent Jews in Dublin. It's a burden I understand. My father was the conductor of the Dublin symphony. My mother was a barrister. She took controversial cases. Famous performers and death threats were regular guests at our home." He saw something change in Reyes' expression when he said this. Perhaps they'd finally found common ground.

"Were the threats ever carried out?"

"No. People who threaten are cowards for the most part. It's the ones who don't take the trouble to threaten you first that you have to worry about. Being wealthy in Mexico carries with it some risk of being kidnapped for ransom, doesn't it?"

"In some parts. Not here. This is really a peaceful part of the country. Usually. It doesn't seem that way to you of course – but this is our first murder in some time."

"But it's still a burden being from a rich family."

"Men are after you for your money, your connections. Usually it's just sex, which is easy to see through. The ones that are after your money are subtler."

"Some, I suppose, are after both."

"Not as many as you think. In my experience it's one or the other."

Press watched as Reyes seemed to review some memory or other, as if validating her assertion. Then she changed her expression and asked, "Is it difficult for you to date? Do you date? I can't help but think you shouldn't be allowed to. Are you?"

"A rabbi can date. At least a reformed rabbi can, and that's what I was. Congregations, when they hire a rabbi, usually they want one who's married."

"Congregations hire the rabbi?"

"Yes. It's different from Catholic parishes, which get priests assigned to them. It's like any job application process. Well, not exactly. There's a broker, a bit like a head hunter – excuse me, an executive recruiter – who decides on several candidates based on the size of the congregation. The bigger congregations get more experienced rabbis. Smaller congregations get the guys – or gals – right out of seminary school. But your question was about dating. Promiscuity is discouraged. No one night stands. We only date women of the same degree of observance. As you might imagine, there are a number of women who want to fix us up. These are called 'Yentas' in Yiddish. Everybody else calls them pimps. Do you know the word?'

"The word 'pimp' I know."

"'Yenta' means busybody, but you get the idea. But I'm no longer a rabbi. So I can date whomever I please. For example, if this were a date, it would be ok." He watched Reyes for a reaction.

"So this is not a date? I have to pay for my own dinner?"

"If this were a date, I would take you somewhere nicer. So yes, you have to pay for your own dinner." He watched Reyes open her purse and take out a 100 pesos note and place it on the table. He took out his wallet and did the same.

Chapter 14

Det. Benito Rufino

Detective Rufino considered his options. He could go looking for Humberto in the jungle – sweaty work that was not likely to be successful, but work nonetheless, and the appearance of such activity would please his superiors who were getting pressure from their superiors who were getting pressure from the Norte Americanos. Or he could play a waiting game, certain that eventually Humberto would come out of hiding. He would need food, or he would get sick and need a doctor – Rufino thought of Dr. Reyes with mixed and complicated emotions – or he would want to see his friends. Humberto would come out of the jungle eventually.

Or he would run to the United States. That would be fine with Rufino. He would be the Norte Americanos' problem then. Let them find him. In the meantime he would organize a half-hearted search of the jungle around the excavation.

He decided to pay Dr. Reyes a visit, to remind her that if Humberto showed up at her clinic she had a responsibility to notify him. He went to the banos and checked himself in the mirror. He decided he liked what he saw, and then he stepped out into the bright sunlight and walked to the clinic.

When he entered, the receptionist said, "Dr. Reyes only sees women and children."

Detective Rufino produced his badge and explained he was here on Policia business, not for medical attention. The receptionist left her desk and went to the examining room.

A minute later Dr. Reyes appeared.

"Hola." He offered his hand.

Reyes looked at it. She kept her own hands on her hips. "What do you want?"

"Has Humberto been here?"

"No. Why would he come here?"

"Because –"

Reyes waved him silent. "If Humberto comes here, don't worry, I'll be sure to send him over to the Policia station to be tortured."

"We don't torture."

"Some of the people you don't torture come here afterwards to have their wounds tended to, their broken bones set. So they must just get clumsy when they enter the Policia station."

"You know I'm not with the local Policia. I'm with the Antiquities Policia."

Detective Rufino thought about Dr. Reyes as he walked back to the Policia headquarters. Local police were an embarrassment everywhere in Mexico – maybe everywhere in the world, but Rufino worked in Mexico. They took bribes. They tortured prisoners, sometimes out of anger, sometimes to get information, sometimes just for the sick fun of it – because they could. And Reyes had laid all these crimes on him. It was no use insisting to her that he was a good cop – there was no such thing in her world. No doubt she'd been hassled by these very clowns – the ones he saw lolling around as he walked into the station. It was hot and sticky. In the short walk to the station he was already perspiring. It was a bit cooler inside, but there was that smell, imperfectly masked by industrial cleaner, of sweat and vomit, tobacco and fear. Captain Cepeda was waiting for him. "How did it go with the puta?"

Captain Cepeda outranked Rufino, but was not technically his boss. And as a Federales, Rufino had the more prestigious job. Rufino said "She sends you her love. I think that's what she meant. Her exact words were 'Tell Captain Cepeda I hope he gets the clap and that his dick falls off."

"Fuck you, Rufino."

This was more of a response than Rufino had hoped for. He thought he saw some of the other Policia smiling. "She said she's tired of patching up the kids you torture. She's lying, right? You really don't torture children here, do you?"

"Continue to fuck yourself, Rufino."

"Because if you torture prisoners there would have to be an investigation. You don't personally sodomize them, do you?"

The Captain charged Rufino. Rufino stepped aside at the last moment. The Captain managed to grab one arm, but with his free hand Rufino delivered a vicious uppercut. The Captain went down immediately. Rufino braced himself for a second charge, but none came. He looked around the room. No one else made a move towards him. He noticed, or thought he did, that the room smelled much better.

Chapter 15

Det. Benito Rufino

Detective Rufino left the station and walked to the plaza. He hoped to find shade, and a quiet place to sit. There were only a few people in the plaza. An arborist was pruning the trees into a dense boxlike state. A vendor was selling ears of corn from a cart. There was a newspaper seller with copies of *Diario de Yucatan, El Sol de Mexico, Por Esto!* under lead bars. Rufino sat on an empty bench and allowed himself to fit Humberto to the facts. What he needed to do was to imagine the crime and all its details. Humberto wants a computer, the professor's computer. Rather than just steal it – it was at the site all day – his computer was stolen from his room. The plan to kill McNeery is part of the crime – because making it look like a jaguar seems premeditated. So this kid, in order to steal a computer from a professor's room plans an elaborate murder at the archaeological site 10 km away. Humberto has been in trouble before, but not for any violent crime, and never for anything that showed even a moment's premeditation. This made no sense.

Rufino tried another scenario. McNeery finds the codex at the site. Or rather, Humberto finds it, and decides to keep it. McNeery catches him, threatens to tell the police. In a panic, Humberto hits him, or they struggle, and in the struggle McNeery hits his head and dies. A panicked Humberto then concocts the jaguar cover-up and goes back to town to steal McNeery's computer. He also has to find a jaguar paw to lend credibility to this charade. McNeery's wallet is missing. So Humberto steals that, but still tries to make it look like a jaguar attack. And Capt. Cepeda chooses to believe it's a left-handed jaguar, apparently one who steals wallets. This makes no sense either.

The sun found Rufino and he moved to another bench.

Of course McNeery's wallet might have been stolen by one of the others at work. More likely, it was taken by the Policia. And why were they so eager to believe it was a jaguar, even after Dr. Reyes had mocked them? Laziness – to be sure. A jaguar would close the case and require no further investigation. Rufino got up and bought an ear of corn from the vendor. Then he got his car from the Policia parking lot and drove to McNeery's rooms.

He stopped at the landlord's office. "I'm Detective Rufino." He showed the landlord his badge. "I need to look at Dr. McNeery's rooms. Where are they?"

She told him.

"Do I need a key to get in?"

"No. They're open. The man was just here going through his things."

"What man?" Rufino was irritated.

"His friend. How do you say it?" She made a gesture pulling at her chin.

Rufino looked uncomprehendingly.

"The Jewish priest with a beard." She stroked her chin again.

Chapter 16

Rufino and El Gato

Rufino put on his hat and went outside to his car. With no Humberto, with no help from the Policia, there was nowhere else to go but to El Gato – The Cat. Miguel Felicio Catalan, also known as The Cat, was Valladolid's crime boss. Mostly he oversaw the cocaine and meth trade, but nothing illegal happened that he didn't have a piece of. Because he had no competitors – no rival drug cartels – he carved out his business peacefully and the Policia looked the other way. There was no violence; certainly no grisly murders with torture and decapitation, like in Chihuahua. In exchange for this relative calm the police left him alone. He paid them off of course, that was part of the elaborate etiquette between police and drug lord. But now the decorum had been violated: McNeery had been murdered.

He let the watch captain know where he was going. "If I'm not back in two hours come out in force." He knew full well they would do nothing of the sort.

El Gato's hacienda lay on land that had been cut out of the jungle. The jungle threatened to reclaim it, and the road leading to it. A road made for ambushes, Rufino thought. He called El Gato and told him he was on his way. Unannounced visitors often met with accidents.

The hacienda emerged from the jungle like a Mayan temple: large, blocky, it produced the same startling effect – civilization where it seemed most unwelcome. The smooth lines and regular geometry of the hacienda in contrast to the riot of vegetation surrounding it. Rufino pulled into the circular drive and stopped under a shaded portico opposite the door. He knocked and an armed man let him in.

El Gato's greeting was cordial, neither chilly nor effusive. Rufino was led to an inner courtyard, and there, in the shade, a middle aged woman brought them coffee.

Rufino sipped his coffee and said, "You heard about the American professor?"

"I heard. Stupid and unlucky to be killed by a jaguar."

"It wasn't a jaguar."

"I didn't think so. They're not in the habit of killing people." El Gato was saying that this murder was so far removed from him that he didn't have to pretend to believe the jaguar story. Rufino thought that was interesting.

"Maybe you can help me?" Rufino made it a question.

"I'll do what I can."

"I'm trying to figure out why someone would kill him."

"Not who?"

"That too."

El Gato looked relaxed, but alert. Feline. This, and not his last name, was why he'd been nicknamed El Gato. Or perhaps it was an allusion to his nine lives. He'd survived a couple of shootings as a younger man.

"Benito – may I call you Benito? – murder is a bad business. I don't need to tell you that. It frightens the tourists. Sometimes it breeds retaliation, and things get out of hand. I did not know the professor, but people who did tell me he was an honorable man. He paid a fair wage. He was good at his work, and respectful of the indigenous heritage. Who would want to kill him?"

Rufino noticed he didn't say our heritage. El Gato traced his ancestry to Spain, not to the Maya. El Gato was talking – Rufino waited to see if he would answer his own question.

"Was there a woman?" El Gato asked.

This was not where Rufino thought El Gato would go with his speculation.

"He was a priest. I don't think so." Rufino said.

"A priest. Still..." El Gato let the sentence hang there.

"An American priest."

"Ah, you mean the celibate kind. The kind that likes boys. Maybe there was a boy. Didn't one of the workers, the young one, run away?"

Rufino didn't let his surprise show. Of course none of this was secret, and information regarding crime was more likely to find its way to El Gato than to the Policia. But how subtly El Gato had switched roles: now he was the investigator. Rufino had been outmaneuvered and resolved to get back control of the conversation. He ignored El Gato's question.

"May I have some more coffee?"

"Of course." El Gato pointed to Rufino's cup and his housekeeper left to fetch the coffee.

Rufino asked, "You are a collector?"

"Yes."

"Do you collect pre-Columbian artifacts?"

"No, not really. A few. Mostly I collect church relics, and military artifacts."

"But you are knowledgeable?"

"A little."

"What would the most valuable thing you could find at a Mayan site be?"

"A Spanish sword. But that's not what you mean. Something Mayan and valuable. Jade. Carved jade.

They had books too, but Landa burned them. They were quite beautiful. A shame."

"How do you know they were beautiful?"

"Four survived. One is in Madrid. One is in Germany. The other two-" El Gato shrugged.

Rufino shot him a quizzical look. The coffee arrived.

"Come, Benito, don't look so surprised. A businessman can know a little about antiquities."

"Fair enough." Rufino took a sip of coffee. "But I would expect a businessman to know how much they're worth."

"The codices? I don't think they've ever been sold. They're priceless."

"But if a new codex were found? What would it be worth?"

"Tens of millions of pesos of course. But it wouldn't be sold. It would go to the Museo Nacional de Antropologio in Mexico City. You think the professor found a codex and was murdered for it. Let me think about that." El Gato stood, a signal that he didn't plan to say anything more to detective Rufino.

Rufino paused. He took a sip of coffee. Then he too stood. "Thank you. Always a pleasure."

They shook hands. The armed servant showed him out.

As soon as Rufino returned to the office he Googled "Mayan codex." He learned there were only four extant. The Dresden, the Paris, the Madrid and the disputed Grolier, the last discovered in a cave in Chiapas in the 1960s. The first three - about which there is no question of authenticity - were named after the cities in which they resided, but what stopped Rufino in his tracks was this: "These tables were designed to track solar and lunar eclipses; the appearance and disappearance of Venus in the night sky summer: and positioning of Mars against the constellations. Astronomical instruments occur in both Paris and Grolier codices as well."

Rufino went to another website that showed pages from the codex. Beautiful, he thought, mysterious and rare. On a hunch he checked out the Magna Carta. The only copy in private hands sold for $ 21.3 million US in 2007. And there were more versions and more copies of the Magna Carta than of the Mayan codices.

Chapter 17

El Gato

Great minds think alike, El Gato thought, as he watched detective Rufino drive away. The priest's murder bothered him. El Gato hadn't authored it, and while he knew that Rufino suspected him of all non-domestic crime in Valladolid – with some justification – he felt he'd convinced the detective that his paws were clean in this case. Not that it would've mattered. The detective couldn't touch him – or wouldn't – it came to the same thing. But Rufino's speculation confirmed what El Gato himself had heard: McNeery had found a codex and had been murdered for it. Better to have Rufino looking for it than to look for it himself. Where others bribed the Policia to get out of the way, El Gato found ways to make them work for him for free. But even the best, most motivated employees need supervision, so El Gato had him followed. Meanwhile he made discreet inquiries: could he purchase a codex, or a portion of one? Who would he be bidding against? What price should he expect to pay?

The answer to the first question proved to be "no" – a word he'd heard too much as a child growing up and almost never since. He smiled inwardly. No. We'll see. He liked a challenge.

He had a moment of annoyance. He'd let Rufino wrestle the conversation away from him at one point. It was subtle, and he hoped his bodyguard hadn't noticed.

El Gato had come up in the streets of Valladolid. Only the tough survived and only the very toughest prevailed. Toughness was equal parts courage and cruelty; he'd figured that out early and mastered it. But he was friendly and charming, so other kids tended to orbit around him. He had his own gang by 15. He was also smart and soon realized that most of those in his criminal underworld were not. Finally, he was lucky. He'd been shot three times and not killed. That's how he got his nickname – according to one version of his legend. Another attributed it to his physical grace: he was an expert dancer who moved with a catlike fluidity. He'd entered, and won, a samba contest at 14. Finally, there was the story of an actual cat. He'd found an injured stray and nursed it back to health. The cat had paid him back by sensing danger before El Gato did, a feline early warning system. But one time the cat had scratched him, and left a barcode of blood on his arm. El Gato had grabbed the cat and shoved it into a plastic shopping

bag and swung him against the wall. Again and again
– at this point most of the witnesses left – until the
sound of small bones breaking gave way to the sound
of meat being tenderized.

He never got another pet. Now his early warning
system consisted of bodyguards and a network of
informants. They were inferior in every way to his
former cat, but they knew not to scratch him.

He had made his fortune in drugs, an old story. He
invested in legitimate businesses: he held the cable
and cell phone franchises in Valladolid and several
other Yucatán towns. He owned a tequila distillery.
He sat on the boards of the General Hospital de
Valladolid and the Mercado de Artesanias.

When Esmeralda came to clear the coffee things
he took the tray away from her and danced a quick
samba around the room to the sound of an imaginary
Latin band. Then he bowed to her and left for his
study. There was work to be done and he was happy.
Some quick research confirmed what he thought he
knew: that if McNeery had found a codex, it was
possibly the first authentic one in four centuries. The
codex was missing – stolen – and therefore abiding in
the part of the world that he felt master of. He was
about to go on a treasure hunt. The first order of
business was to find Humberto. Challenging – but he
liked a challenge. Even the thought of hacking
through jungle in search of the boy held a quixotic

charm. But he knew he wouldn't find Humberto that way; finding someone in the jungle who wanted to be found was hard enough. The resourceful teenager – or so he imagined – made him in fact an avatar of his younger self. Finding a boy like that would be impossible. As a teenager, El Gato had hidden in the jungle. He knew that Humberto would keep contact with his family, his friends - probably a young woman. It was time to pay Humberto's family a visit. He called for his driver.

******

One of the many pleasures of being El Gato was the pleasure of making a grand entrance. He was not pompous – pomposity was, after all, the overcompensation for feelings of inferiority, and El Gato had no such feelings - but he liked to see a little ripple when he drove up to a restaurant or a church, ever expanding circles of awareness with El Gato at the center.

One does not visit empty-handed. When he arrived at Humberto's family home El Gato bore flowers and candies and a bottle of excellent tequila. Something for everybody he expected to find there.

He apologized for the intrusion. He knew Humberto was missing and that he had been unjustly accused. If there was anything he could do, he was their servant. He knew lawyers. He knew the judge. Hell, he owned the judge. At least that's what people thought. But it wasn't that way at all. They were really good friends. And Humberto? He understood Humberto. He'd been a troubled teenager himself – and had run away. He could relate to Humberto and their predicament. He was often unjustly accused himself. El Gato said all this and more, but mostly he listened: to the unfairness of it all, to the fact that Humberto was basically a good boy, that he worked hard and brought his money home. He was smart – you wouldn't believe how much he knew about the stars.

El Gato said: "He's frightened. There's no shame in that. The Policia –" he spit "– they don't care. They're too lazy and too corrupt to solve this crime. So they blame it on Humberto. They're watching your house. So if Humberto contacts you – and I know he will because he knows you worry about him – tell him to come to my casa and I will protect him."

Chapter 18

Dr. Isabel Reyes

Isabel Reyes had forgotten how pleasant evenings in Cuernavaca could be. None of Valladolid's stifling heat and humidity. It was a pleasure to dress-up when you weren't constantly sweating. She showered and felt clean and knew that the clean feeling would last. The symptoms that had driven her home had abated. She was looking forward to seeing Pascal, with whom she would share a co-conspiratorial laugh at their families' attempts to fix them up. Pascal was witty, often at his own expense, and articulate. He was a good listener and she felt the need to confide in someone other than her parents. He would have news and sarcastic commentary on their mutual friends. He was a bit self-dramatizing, and while she sometimes found that annoying she was glad that he would divert attention to himself and away from her. He would lighten the mood that had grown heavy with her arrival.

Pascal arrived early, as Isabel had hoped. After he greeted her and her folks and made a few minutes of small talk, Mrs. Reyes excused herself and her husband: "We need to check out how Consuela is managing the dinner."

"Can I help?" Pascal asked.

"Please keep my daughter company."

When they were out of earshot Pascal said "Your mom's pimping you now?"

"Yes. You can fuck me for 1000 pesos. She gets half."

"You haven't changed. It's good to see you."

"You too, Pascalito."

"No, no. Nobody calls me that."

"I do."

"So you're in town to find a husband? Or just to get laid?"

"I can get laid in Valladolid."

"My dear Isabel, you can get laid anywhere."

"You too."

"Yes. Thank you. And yet here we are, and neither of us is going to get laid tonight. Why are you back?"

"Keep this a secret. I had some tests at the hospital. Nothing serious. But periodically I feel like shit."

"Remind me again what you do for a living? What kind of diagnosis is 'I feel like shit'?"

"The patient kind of diagnosis. If the doctor in me knew what was wrong I'd still be in Valladolid."

A serious look crossed Pascal's face. "If you don't know what it is, how can you say it's nothing serious?"

"So you're a doctor now?"

"No, seriously. What's wrong?"

Isabel put her hand on Pascal's. "I'll be okay. Okay?"

"You shouldn't go through this alone. I'll go with you next time you go to the doctor, okay?"

"Okay." Isabel gathered herself. "So, are we going to make our parents proud tonight?"

"I'll devour you with my eyes all evening and discreetly squeeze your ass – or would that be over-the-top?"

"For this audience, who knows? I'll hang on your every word. It'll be like that movie, *Moll Flanders*. I should've asked – are you with someone special?"

"I'm with someone. I'm not sure he's the one. And you?"

"No one."

"No one? No one's interested in you?"

"No one that I'm interested in." She paused. "That's not quite true. I met a man, an older man. A rabbi. An ex-rabbi – it's a long story – from Dublin."

"I didn't think they had rabbis in Dublin. It's a little like saying you met a rabbi from the Vatican. Is he for real or is this an imaginary friend? We've all had those."

"I don't think I admitted it, even to myself, until just now. But I think I am interested."

"Is he interested in you?"

"Who wouldn't be?"

"But you're not Jewish. Would that disqualify you?"

"Apparently he's not that Orthodox. But tonight I have eyes only for you."

"This will be fun. You'll see."

"Have you ever tried women? Is that a horrible thing to ask?"

"Have you ever tried women – is that a horrible thing to ask?"

"I'm sorry."

"Apology accepted. When do I meet the rabbi?"

"Come to Valladolid. Anytime you like."

She watched Pascal make a face. "No thank you. Not my kind of place. But bring him to Mexico City and we'll double date."

Chapter 19

Humberto and Maria

Humberto was grateful for nightfall. The heat was less oppressive. He knew that no one would look for him in the impenetrable double darkness of jungle and night. There was the sky to read, until sleep overtook him. He was hungry. There was no food at the rendezvous point. He assumed that Maria had been watched and followed and couldn't come. He'd check again tomorrow. He thought about jaguars, for that was the shape his mind gave to his cumulative fears. He'd seen one a couple of days ago. It had been dusk. He was sitting stone still at the base of a banyan tree, obscured by undergrowth. He saw the rustle – there was no sound. A man would have made a sound, and his head would have been visible above the bush. It was like someone moving behind a curtain. In the smallest of gaps he saw a patch of black coat. That was it. The animal came and went in silence. This was why they didn't come looking for him. They were all afraid of that silent patch of black, that wind-like movement in the bush.

Now, in the darkness there wouldn't even be a patch of black. Everything was black. But not silent. There was the noise of the night jungle to keep him company. A steady thrum. The presence of a jaguar would make itself known by a change in that thrum. He looked at the stars, named the great constellations and the lesser ones, traced in the Milky Way, felt a velvety relaxation overtake him, knew he would soon be asleep.

The next morning he quietly made his way to the rendezvous point.

******

Maria filled the small backpack with water, fruit, and tortillas and slipped quietly from her home. She went to the bakery on Cabrillo Street, and bought two rolls. She ate one and placed the other in her backpack. She walked to the plaza, through it, into the Church of San Gervasio. The church was empty, except for two crones kneeling in the back pew. She placed the peso in the slot and a small electric votive candle sprang to life. She knelt, crossed herself and said a silent prayer. The light in the church was dim compared to the harsh light outside. If anyone opened the door she would know, even with her back turned toward it. If she was followed, they would wait outside.

She crossed herself again and stood up. She left the church. The light was temporarily blinding and she shielded her eyes with her hands. As she grew accustomed to the light she scanned the plaza. The usual vendors: the newspaper salesman, the candy and soda seller, the short dark man with a tall stack of hats. Two men were sweeping the walk. Another was pruning the plaza trees into their characteristic box shapes. A man buying a newspaper made her pause. His transaction with Aureliano, newspaper vendor, was brief – all business. If he had been one of the regulars, there would have been a conversation. That was the man charged with following her. She noted his clothes in her mind: sneakers, jeans, a white shirt with some embroidery work on both sides of the front. She watched him sit down with this paper, facing the church.

Maria was tempted to go back inside the church. She considered going to the market, to try to lose him there, but it was still early and she could not count on a crowd. She decided to walk towards the market - if he followed, she would return to the church. She walked briskly down the steps and turned right on Cabrera Street. She was still in sight of the plaza. She did not hurry, but walked in a way that implied she had business elsewhere and couldn't afford to dawdle. At the next corner she turned again - left on Calle 39, and threw a quick glance back at where the man with the newspaper had been seated. He wasn't there. She stopped. She pretended to search her backpack for something and then retraced her steps to the church. She passed him on the way back. He touched his hat. She nodded slightly in acknowledgment. In the church she found the parish's assistant, a young priest, thin, eager to please. She explained her predicament – or rather constructed a predicament that would enlist the young priest's help. A man was stalking her. The police would be no help. All she needed was another way out of the church – the back way. The young priest obliged her. He took her down a short set of stairs off of the nave, down the corridor towards a sign marked exit. He opened the door, looked around, and satisfied that no one was waiting, ushered her out. She thanked him and was on her way. She boarded a bus at the corner and rode with domestics and gardeners toward the edge of town. Nothing on the bus looked out of place. No cars followed the bus. She got off at the last stop. It was a half hour's walk to the edge of the jungle. The jungle began abruptly – entering it was like parting a curtain and stepping into a darkened room. She was sweating. The jungle canopy offered relief from the sun but not the humidity. A barely discernible path led to a large tree about 200 yards in. Kids came here to drink beer and cheap tequila, or for furtive sex when no other places were available. Maria took food from the bag, and water, placed them in a bag hanging by a long rope from a branch. She looked around, then quickly left.

Even in daylight, the jungle was a creepy place. There were occasional startling cries – monkeys, birds – and the rustling of unseen animals. There were snakes, most benign, but a few that could kill you. Of course there were the jaguars, representing dark death on a mythic level, even if the experts claimed that they generally avoided humans. Maria all but ran the 200 yards out.

Now she was a sheet of sweat. She looked around as she left the jungle. No one. She walked briskly towards the bus stop. Those waiting at this hour – mid-morning - were mostly older women and a few men, bound for the city center and errands. She felt her sweat made her conspicuous, even on this hot humid morning. She exchanged a few quiet "Buenos Dias" with the others at the stop. She had the urge to cry – from fear, from anger, from loss. She missed Humberto.

Chapter 20

Ex-Rabbi Simon Press

As a child growing up in Dublin, Simon Press had been put on mock trial for the murder of Christ by his schoolmates. This was the culmination of a year of bullying, so he knew that regardless of how he pleaded he was going to be mocked, beaten and humiliated. So in response to Sean Fogarty's question, "How do you plead?" he was silent for a moment. Then he threw out his arms, looked skyward, and asked, "Why hast thou forsaken me?" This should have caught them up short. But in the world of adolescents, this merely added to his strangeness, and they responded in adolescent fashion by proceeding with his beating.

Rabbi Press never stopped being amazed at how little Christians knew about the origin of their religion. In the scheme of things, he counted them enlightened if they knew that Christ was Jewish. If they knew that three of the gospels were at odds with the fourth - that made them geniuses. If they knew that there were other gospels, discredited by the early church and consigned arbitrarily to obscurity, that made them scholars, his colleagues.

Of his defrocking, the result of an adulterous affair with a young Irish woman, he said simply, "She gave me the apple and I did eat of it." It was more complicated than that. Mary O'Faolin was his student. In a defiant repudiation of her Catholicism, she had approached him about conversion. He advised her against it; had in fact insisted she discuss her loss of faith with her priest. In this he was blameless. Except he knew the priest, knew his bromides would only serve to further alienate young Mary and further her resolve to convert. She persisted, he resisted; and in this way rehearsed a drama they would replay later for more serious stakes. In the end he agreed to mentor her conversion.

"Is your religion too good for me?" She had taunted him.

He was not so easily baited. "Comments like that that make me think what you need is a spanking, not a conversion." He regretted his words immediately.

"Then spank me."

There it was. He had, he realized, elicited the offer, and she had offered. He wondered how much of his blush showed beneath his beard. He should have thrown her out of his study right then, the automatic and righteous response to her ...her what? Her sauciness, an archaic word but it fit her. He was used to having the last word, one of the prerogatives of a rabbi. But this round belonged to her.

He put his face in his hands, melodramatically, as if to say, "What can I do with you?" and shook his head. She pulled his hands away and forced him to look at her. He realized that the conversion he had resisted had already begun, and that he was the convert. Nothing more happened at first. She came for the conversion lessons, as chaste as her namesake, and he taught her. She was an apt student, friendly, polite, quick to grasp what he had to say, ready with perceptive and penetrating questions. They met once a week in his study. She dressed less provocatively than when she had been provoking him to take her on as a student. She dressed, he thought, like an acolyte, a nun in training. Long skirt, white blouse, her hair pulled back in a tight black bun. No make up he could detect, or else too subtle. He found himself looking forward to these weekly meetings more than anything else, and his greatest agony was when they ended. He limited them to one hour. He left the door to his study open. He avoided all small talk and launched immediately into his lesson, which was uncharacteristic of him.

As she intended, her conversion became an issue. There was a knock at his front door. He opened it to an angry and obviously drunk man a head shorter than he.

"What have you done to my daughter?" Mary's father, at last.

"Who might your daughter be?" He knew. They both knew.

"You've turned her into a Jew." He could smell the liquor on the man's breath.

"Mr. O'Faolin! Come back when you're sober and we'll talk about it."

"I've beaten her and now it's your turn."

"That will win her back to your faith, I'm sure." Religious conversion among the gentiles of Ireland had never been a delicate business. The rabbi stepped toward O'Faolin and closed the door behind him. He was fairly certain that O'Faolin wouldn't lift a hand to him.

O'Faolin stood his ground, but changed his tack. "She won't be coming here any more."

The Rabbi took another step toward O'Faolin, and thought *Please, take that first swing.*

"Fuckin' Jew bastard." O'Faolin glared a moment, nodded at some inner verdict that had awarded him the victory in this confrontation, and left, apparently satisfied with himself.

Later, Mary came to him. She'd been beaten, her father true to his word. She showed Press the bruises. And in the intoxicating mixture of his pity, anger, frustration and her exposed, bruised body, they consummated their affair.

Chapter 21

Maria and Humberto

This time, Maria came late, using the last light to find the rendezvous. It was darker in the jungle, night below the canopy, while the sky was still blue with the last of the light. Warm and humid, but without the oppressive heat of the sun overhead. She was frightened, and had to fight through it. She brought food and a message. When she arrived at the spot she crouched and waited. Humberto will be watching, she thought, he will come out to me.

She did not know how long she waited. Her fear, the darkness, the sound of the jungle all conspired to obliterate her sense of time. She heard rustlings, but they were small. She had learned to distinguish between the sounds of the person and those of the animals familiar to the jungle. She heard something larger move. She froze, tried to contract herself into something small, invisible, hard.

"Maria."

She recognized Humberto's voice in the whisper. "Here." She felt, rather than saw him next to her.

"Why are you here now, so late?"

"I needed to see you. El Gato went to see your parents. Brought them gifts, offered to help you."

Humberto considered this news. El Gato's generosity was well-known, as much a part of his reputation as his charm and his cruelty. But there was usually a point to it. El Gato must've known about the codex. It was the only thing that would account for his interest in a teenage boy accused of murder and sought by the Policia.

"When?"

"Yesterday. You can come out now. He will protect you."

"No, no he won't. I have to leave here."

"No, you're safe now. He'll protect you from the Policia. He owns them."

"No, I have to leave."

"He gave your parents gifts. Money."

"That's his way when he wants something. He gives gifts. It works too."

"He'll protect you."

"No, Maria, he won't. I have to leave here. He'll find me. He'll torture you, or my family to bring me out of hiding. He wants the codex."

"He was so nice to your family."

"He was nice to his cat. You know the story."

"If you go…" she didn't finish the sentence.

"I'll leave him the codex. He won't bother you or our families after that."

"Where will you go?"

"North. To America."

"How will you live?"

"I'll pick strawberries. I'll wash dishes. Maybe I'll go to the University of New Mexico because I'm the greatest star finder in the world."

"I'll come with you."

"No. It's too dangerous for a woman."

"It's too dangerous for you."

"I'll be okay. I can take care of myself."

"Like this? Hiding out? People bringing you food?"

"Not like this. If I give El Gato the codex, he will give me money to cross over. He'll do it because he'll want me gone."

"You won't come back."

"Eventually."

"No, you won't. You'll meet someone else."

"No."

"I'm going with you. El Gato will have to pay for both of us."

"Your family?"

"I'll send back money. I'll be a nanny."

Humberto handed Maria a large plastic bag. "It's in here."

"It's heavy."

"Take it home and wrap it like a gift. Don't bring it to El Gato yourself. Have your father take it. Don't go with him. Do you understand? Don't go with him."

"But the money?"

"El Gato will give your father money when he sees the codex. But if he doesn't, he should ask for a favor: passage for me to the United States. El Gato runs people from El Salvador, Guatemala and Nicaragua to the United States. He'll arrange it."

Humberto kissed her. He meant it to be a goodbye kiss, but she lingered, as he hoped she would. She held onto him and kissed him harder.

Later, they dressed and Maria slipped out of the jungle as quietly as she had entered, carrying the heavy plastic bag with the codex, their ticket to America.

******

Maria's father was stopped, as he expected, at the gate to El Gato's hacienda. He handed his gift over to a muscular man in the tight T-shirt holding a submachine gun. He was frightened, but he said as calmly as he could "I'll wait. I have a favor to ask of Señor Catalan."

The guard made a call on his cell phone and another man came down from the house. He took the gift and went to a work shed some distance from the main house. Moments later, Maria's father saw him carry a plastic bag into the house. "May I smoke?" he asked the guard.

The guard nodded. Maria's father offered him a cigarette. The guard took it and a light. His cell rang. After a brief conversation in which the guard did not speak, he looked at Maria's father and said warmly, "Señor Catalan would like to thank you personally for your gift. This way."

He pointed toward the front door, where El Gato was standing.

******

Humberto looked at the note. "Tomorrow at 7 AM you meet a white van at the corner of Calle 16 and 47. The driver is Jorge. Bring one bag with two days' food and water. No questions." There was no signature. There was a cheap digital watch. Humberto assumed the Policia would be looking the other away.

He'd heard the stories and was afraid. People were killed by their transporters. People were killed by rival gangs. People died in the desert: lost, dehydrated, starved. People were shot by the border patrol. People were caught and sent back and ran this gauntlet of death again. He did not think El Gato would have him killed; in fact he felt he was under his protection. He did not think a rival gang would pick a fight with El Gato. Challenging him was unthinkable. Humberto was young, healthy, strong, smart - he would survive in the desert if it came to that. Once in the U.S. he would pretend to be a student – he knew enough astronomy to get away with it. Still, the terse note frightened him. No gratitude was expressed for the codex. No mention of Maria. No questions were permitted.

He thought about his telescope. It had cost 10,000 pesos. He would have to leave it. He would hide it here, in the jungle. He knew the jungle would destroy it, no matter how carefully he protected it. There was no possibility of bringing it. He wrapped it carefully in a plastic bag and then he placed it in a second plastic bag. He dug a shallow grave for it, lined it with leaves, then placed the bag inside. He cushioned the sides with more leaves and put leaves on the top. Then he pushed the dirt over it. *There will be bigger, better telescopes where I'm going*, he thought.

He was at the rendezvous early. He stood in the shadows watching the road in every direction. Seven cars came and went. No vans. He began to wonder if he'd been set up. There was little traffic. He saw a police car and pressed deeper into the morning shadows. The car slowed at the intersection, but did not stop. He looked at his watch: 7:12. Had he missed the van? He'd been early – 15 minutes early – but still. Had they forgotten him? He looked again down the street. A rusty van that might have been white once drove down Calle 16 towards the intersection. It slowed, and Humberto stepped out of the shadows.

But it didn't stop. It turned onto Calle 43 and drove away.

Should he be in plain sight? He thought of the police car, and didn't see how he could. He looked at his watch again: 7:16.

An old VW minibus drove by. It was white and gray. It didn't stop.

He saw a man walking down the street towards him, dressed in boots, jeans and white shirt. 30-ish with a full black mustache.

"Buenos Dias"

Humberto replied, "Buenos Dias."

The man slowed. Humberto felt the panic rise in him. The man asked "Do you have the time?"

"7:20."

The man looked at Humberto's watch. "Then I am 20 minutes late for my meeting." He smiled "Humberto?"

Humberto was silent for a moment.

"I'm Jorge."

"I'm Humberto. Where is your van?"

"One street over. Walk with me."

Close-up, Humberto could see the man was strong, a weightlifter, maybe a boxer.

Jorge said "You've got money?"

"Didn't El Gato pay you?"

Jorge smiled. "It's a long trip. Water, food – these things cost money."

"He didn't say…" Humberto didn't finish the sentence. He started again: "I have enough." He tried to sound tough.

Jorge smiled again. "It's taken care of, my friend. Like you said, El Gato paid me." He clapped a hard hand on Humberto's shoulder. He directed Humberto into a short alley. At the end Humberto could see a white van with "Jalesco" written on the side and a picture of a crate of cantaloupes.

"Get in back. Try to behave like a cantaloupe."

The interior was dark and warm and smelled of rotten fruit. "Humberto." It was a whisper. As his eyes adjusted he could see Maria, and the others: young men - Indians – from Central America he would've guessed. They greeted him with their eyes only. He sat next to Maria. Jorge closed the door and they were in darkness. He took her hand, and he wondered: what had he done?

Chapter 22

Det. Benito Rufino

For two days after his meeting with El Gato, Detective Rufino was followed. He wasn't surprised, but he was annoyed with himself for failing to anticipate it. His tails were clumsy, and obvious, and their surveillance had a Keystone Kops quality that would have been funny if it wasn't annoying. On the third day it stopped. The thought came to him: El Gato was no longer following him because he'd gotten what he wanted - the codex. After McNeery had been killed, Humberto had ended up with it – and now El Gato had it. He had a sickening feeling. If El Gato had it there was a good chance Humberto was dead, his body buried somewhere in the jungle. All because he, Rufino, had gone to El Gato. He knew what he had to do and he dreaded it. He would have to pay a visit to Humberto's family.

He dressed in his uniform. He changed his mind. He removed it and put on a sports jacket and tie. He wasn't sure Humberto was dead. Perhaps they would have news of him. As he drove to Calle 12, where

Humberto's family lived, he checked his mirror often, and he made one random detour, but no one followed. He arrived at a nearby street and parked there. He walked to Humberto's home and knocked on the door. The boy of 10 or 11 answered. He asked the boy: "What's your name?"

"Alexander."

"Are your folks home?"

"My mother."

"May I speak with her?"

"I'll get her." Alexander left the door open and went to the back of the house, shouting "Mother, mother."

When Humberto's mother came to the door, Rufino said, "I'm Detective Benito Rufino. Have you heard from Humberto?"

"No." The answer came too quickly.

"I don't want to arrest him. But I think he's in danger. Not from the Policia. They stopped looking for him as soon as he went into the jungle. Have you heard anything from him? Of him?"

"No." There was hesitation in her answer.

Rufino pressed: "Maybe he left you a message. Maybe he sent a note to one of his brothers or sisters?" He looked at the boy who'd answered the door; watched him look at his mother. He turned to the boy: "Have you heard from Humberto?"

There was hesitation. He looked at the mother. "What has he sent?"

The mother shrugged. "Show him."

The boy ran returned with a tattered piece of paper. "It's a treasure map."

"May I see it?"

"You will give it back?"

"Yes."

The boy handed the paper to Rufino. It had been drawn in the style of the treasure map, with the thick cross indicating the location of the treasure. Rufino recognized some streets at the bottom of the map, and an arrow indicating where to enter the jungle. The cross was a mile or so into the jungle. There were some landmarks drawn in.

"I will make a copy of this and get back to you."

"It's mine. I'm going to find it."

"Yes." Rufino made an appealing look to the mother. "But there are jaguars in the jungle, and snakes. Deadly snakes."

"I don't care."

Rufino looked at the mother and shook his head. To the boy he said: "The treasure's yours. I'll bring it back to you." And then he left.

******

Rufino feared the worst: that the cross now indicated the location of Humberto's body.

Rufino returned to Policia headquarters and gathered two reluctant officers and some shovels. They drove to the spot at the edge of the jungle nearest the entrance charted by Humberto's map. Carlos, the larger of the two officers, asked, "What are we looking for?"

"A body." Rufino could see the look of revulsion cross Carlos's face. "Follow me."

The jungle had a heat of its own: moist, noisy, smelling of rotten vegetation. They had only gone a few minutes when Rufino stopped to drink. Small insects buzzed around them. The officers looked surly, mutinous. Rufino could barely contain his anger at that. "You've had a week to find Humberto, the kid your captain thinks killed the archaeologist. Now we have a map to his hideout. His 10-year-old brother wanted to come. I should have taken him instead. Drink and let's go."

At times Rufino felt he was on a crude path, but other times he was hacking his way through the undergrowth. After 15 minutes he stopped again and drank. By way of encouragement he said, "We're close. In a couple of hundred yards there is a small clearing, a break in the tree canopy."

He pushed on. He thought he saw light ahead and aimed for it. Moments later they could see bright jungle. Another 10 yards and they were standing under an opening in the canopy. He formed a line with the two officers and slowly they worked their way over the space. Near a banyan tree he could see the signs of disturbed earth. "Here." He indicated the ground. "Dig. Carefully."

Slowly they pried away the dirt with their shovels.

"A bag." One of the officers pointed into the hole.

Rufino looked down into the shallow hole. He could see the gloss of a black plastic bag. With his hands, he pushed away dirt and leaves.

"Careful." He indicated they should widen the hole.

More of the bag came into view. Rufino took a pocket knife from his belt and carefully slit the bag. Leaves. He pushed them aside and felt something smooth like skin, something hard underneath it. He pushed away more leaves and could see his hand resting on another plastic garbage bag. He carefully slit this too and saw curved black metal. He pulled on the bag and after a second the earth released it. It was lighter than a body. He tore the bag off.

"What is it?" Carlos asked.

Rufino paused. Then he knew: "It's a telescope."

So this is where Humberto had been, Rufino thought. Had been, but was no more. He'd bring the telescope back for Humberto's brother. To the men he said: "Look around. See if anything else is buried here."

He watched their haphazard and halfhearted search and shook his head. Slowly, methodically he walked back and forth through the clearing as if he were plowing it with an invisible team of oxen. He saw no other signs that the earth had been broken.

Satisfied, he said to Carlos, "Take the bag with the telescope. Let's go." He indicated to the other officer, Hernando, that he should lead. He would follow them both. In spite of the heat, and their previous exertions, they left the jungle much faster than they entered it.

Rufino returned to Humberto's home and handed Alexander the telescope. The boy looked disappointed. "Where's the treasure?"

"This is what Humberto wanted you to find."

"This isn't treasure. It's his telescope."

"Humberto thought it was treasure. Maybe you should keep it for him. Maybe he'll ransom it from you with real treasure."

"Put it in your room, Alexander." His mother said. Reluctantly the boy took the black garbage bag away. She questioned Rufino with her eyes when he left.

"He's not there. He's left. I think he'll contact you. He seems to care about his family."

"That telescope was what he cared about most."

Rufino nodded and left. On the way back to the police station he considered those words. The telescope was what he cared about most, and yet he'd left it. Humberto was on the move, no longer hiding out, and he was traveling light. Where?

Chapter 23

Prof. Owen Sterling

Owen Sterling's own words ate away at him. If Zubin Mehta was getting symphonies from a new Mozart wouldn't he go searching for him? He called over to the computer science lab and asked for the director. Owen hoped his name had the necessary clout.

"Can you locate someone geographically from his e-mail address?"

Kryszten, the director said: "Hypothetically, yes. But usually spammers and other troublemakers make an effort to hide their whereabouts by using proxy servers."

"This isn't a spammer. Please give it a try." Sterling gave him Yucatán 2012's e-mail address.

Later, a smug looking Kryszten appeared at Owen's office. "Yucatán 2012 e-mails from Valladolid. It's in the Yucatán."

"Could this be a proxy server, like you suggested?"

"It could. But given his e-mail address and the fact that there's no reason for him to hide, I think it's the location of the actual server. Valladolid's not a small place, but it narrows things down a bit."

"Is there a college or university there? Something with a telescope?"

"Not that I know of. I thought this guy was an amateur."

"He would still need the telescope. No matter. I'm going to Mexico."

It was unconsciously axiomatic to Sterling that prodigies, even shy ones, would stick out in their native surroundings. Without really thinking it through, he assumed he would get off the plane in Valladolid, ask a few of the local notables, and be directed to the hacienda, or maybe the private school where Yucatán 2012 performed his miracles. If it took a little sleuthing, so much the better. A true recluse would have hidden his e-mail better. Or hers.

The flight took Sterling to Mexico City and then to Merida. There he rented a car for the drive to Valladolid. He had hoped, because he'd never heard of it, that Valladolid would be a charming picturesque place of flowers and crumbling stone. This proved to be the first of a series of disappointments.

Sterling was familiar with heat, but not the damp heat of the Yucatán. The dry heat of New Mexico provided a kind of clarity. It was one-dimensional heat. But the heat of the Yucatán was a complex skein of irritants. His skin erupted with sweat and as each layer dried he felt shellacked with his own perspiration. Then there was the weight of it. New Mexico heat was weightless, while this heat was a constant burden. The air – and he was reluctant to call it that – was something in between a gas and a liquid. It pushed back. And then there was Valladolid itself: he took to calling it Squalidolid in his mind. A humid mess of poverty. Carrion eating birds pecked at the remains of small dead animals in the road. Of course that could be anywhere, but here it seemed emblematic. He found the hotel where he'd booked a room and parked the car. He checked in and explained the reason for his visit. The degree of incomprehension that he met with made him reconsider the entire venture. The innkeeper, a polite woman in her 40's, assured him there was no astronomy observatory in Valladolid. There was no university either. He let his disappointment show and she offered him a phone book. He explained that he was a professor, hoping that the implied stature would prompt a more helpful response. The innkeeper let a concerned thought pass across her face. Sterling saw it and asked: "What?"

"There was another North American professor here, but he was killed. By a jaguar."

Sterling's heart sank. "An astronomy professor?"

"He was digging up the ruins. What are they called?"

"He was an archaeologist?"

"Si. An archaeologist."

"No other professors?"

"His friend. A Jewish priest, but a professor too, I think."

"Should I ask at the police station?"

She laughed. "No." She shook her head. "Ask at the church. Ask the priest."

Sterling picked up the key and his bags. "I'll just put these in my room. Where is the church?"

"On the plaza. You can walk from here."

Sterling walked back into the heat. The church, when he stepped inside, was dark and cool. He stood at the back, just inside the door and let his eyes adjust. There was an old woman kneeling in the front, and another lighting candles. Finally one of the women crossed herself and rose, and walked toward the back.

"Excuse me," Sterling said. "I'm looking for the priest."

She pointed to the confessional.

Sterling thanked her. He did not know, he realized, the protocol for interrupting a priest at confession. He himself was a lapsed Protestant who hadn't been in a church since his childhood. He walked to the outside of the confessional and just stood there, pondering his next move.

Eventually a young man emerged. "May I help you? Are you here for confession?" Sterling thought the young priest sounded hopeful at the prospect.

"No thank you. I'm Protestant. I was told at the hotel that you might be able to help me though. I'm looking for a local astronomer."

There was a blank look on the priest's face. Owen pushed on. "I should introduce myself. I'm Owen Sterling. I'm an astronomy professor at the University of New Mexico. I've come here to find someone and all I know about him – or her – is that this person is a genius at finding new stars. I don't know this person's name. All I know is that he sends me e-mails from somewhere here in Valladolid."

"There are no colleges here, no professors."

"A gifted amateur? Someone passionate about astronomy?" Sterling was feeling foolish.

"Oh. That would be Humberto."

Sterling saw his face darkened. "Humberto?" Sterling left a blank with his intonation. He was looking for a last name.

"Humberto ran away." The priest shook his head.

Sterling couldn't believe his ears. He found and lost his prodigy in the time it took to utter a sentence. "He ran away?"

"Yes. A priest, an archaeology professor was killed. They think Humberto did it. So he ran away."

"How old is he? Will they find them?"

"He's 16. A nice boy. Gets into trouble now and then. But not murder."

"How do you know he's an astronomer?"

"He has a telescope."

"But other people have telescopes."

"Not here. Not in Valladolid. You should talk to the police."

"I was told they would not be helpful."

"They have a computer they say Humberto stole from the dead professor."

Sterling understood. Perhaps he'd been e-mailed from this computer. "Thank you. Where is the police station?"

"Across the plaza."

Sterling left the relative cool of the church and was assaulted again by a wall of Yucatán heat. He walked through the plaza, trying to stay in the shade of the sculpted trees. He tried to imagine persuading them to let him look at the laptop – now evidence in a capital felony. He could not imagine it going well. When he got to the police station the officer at the desk was wearing an assault rifle. Sterling considered how to begin. "I'm Owen Sterling, from the United States. Do you speaking English? I'm sorry, I don't speak Spanish."

"I speak a little."

"Okay. Good. I received an e-mail from someone in Valladolid. I'm an astronomy professor." Sterling realized this was not coming out in any sort of order. He pressed on: "I think the e-mail might have been from Humberto."

"When?"

"A while ago. I think it might have been from him. I don't know. His e-mail address was Yucatán 2012@gmail.me. It came from somewhere here in Valladolid."

"Why did he send you an e-mail?"

"It was about astronomy. I'm an astronomy professor at the University of New Mexico."

"The e-mail was not from Humberto."

"Maybe. It was from an address called Yucatán 2012. But that's just an e-mail address. The priest said Humberto had a telescope, that he was interested in astronomy."

The officer looked at him blankly.

"Look, I'm sorry I don't speak Spanish. Is there someone else here I could talk to?"

The officer indicated a chair. Sterling sat. When it was clear that Sterling would wait, the officer left. He spoke to one of the other officers in Spanish and pointed to Sterling. Then he disappeared into another part of the police station.

A couple of minutes later he returned with an older police officer. The older officer stopped in front of Sterling and Sterling stood.

"I'm Captain Cepeda." He held out his hand. Sterling shook it.

"I'm Owen Sterling."

"Tell me, why are you here?"

Sterling repeated his story.

"Why do you think this Yucatán 2012 is Humberto?"

"I don't know. He was interested in astronomy. He owns a telescope. Humberto, I'm told, was also interested in astronomy and owns a telescope."

"Humberto is a troublemaker, a criminal, and a murderer. Not an astronomer."

"Couldn't he be both?" Sterling tried to be placating.

"He didn't go to school. He had no money for telescopes. For liquor, yes. For drugs, yes. For a telescope, no."

"But he had the laptop. Could I see it?" Sterling expected the officer to laugh at his request.

The captain smiled. "Why not?" He led Sterling back into another part of the police station to his office. He pointed to the laptop. "Go ahead, look."

Sterling hesitated. This was supposedly evidence in a murder. The captain noticed his hesitation. "Go ahead. We found it in Humberto's home. There's no issue with fingerprints."

Sterling turned the laptop on and waited for it to boot up. He was relieved that it booted up in English, and then surprised. Shouldn't it have booted up in Spanish? But then he remembered: the murder victim was American. He opened the e-mail application and sorted the inbox by "from." He was hoping to find his own e-mail and yet when he saw his name he was still startled. He checked on sent items. He sorted by "to" and found his name again. He found the familiar terse e-mails he'd received from Yucatán 2012. He checked the "from" line: Yucatán 2012@gmail.me. He checked other e-mails: all were from Yucatán 2012.

"When was Prof. McNeery killed?"

"A week ago. We found the body the next day."

The last e-mail Sterling had received from Yucatán 2012 had been before that. None since. So Humberto had killed not just an archaeologist fellow professor, but the world's greatest star finder. "Thank you, officer. I hope you catch him."

He followed the captain out of the police station. He thought about McNeery, a man he was now even more bitterly disappointed not to have met. A man, he told himself, who spent his days looking down, and his nights looking up – in both cases to great effect. He had to admit it: he felt a little jealousy.

The heat was there of course, but it did not intrude on his thought. He walked back to the hotel, deciding if he should stay over, or push to see if he could catch a flight back this evening.

Chapter 24

Det. Benito Rufino

Rufino drove out to El Gato's hacienda. He was greeted cordially by the armed man at the gate and led to the main house. He could see El Gato at the door.

"Welcome, my friend. How can I help you?"

Rufino couldn't help but notice El Gato's ebullience. *This will be fun*, he thought. "It's nice to see you again too, Señor Catalan." *Two can play this game.*

"Please come in."

Rufino followed El Gato to the patio. They sat, and soon coffee appeared. El Gato asked, "Did you find Humberto? I heard you found his jungle hiding place."

Of course the police Rufino had brought with him into the jungle had reported back to El Gato. El Gato was showing off – not usually his style.

"We found a telescope, but no Humberto. Maybe you heard?"

"A telescope. Not a body. That's a relief."

"Yes. Some of the police are squeamish about dead bodies. Can you imagine?" Rufino took a sip of coffee. "This is a strange case, don't you think?"

"In what way?"

"In every way. For example, what was the motive? Or take Humberto. The wild boy, the hooligan. But he owns a telescope. A good one. What sort of hooligan owns a telescope? You were young once. Did you have any interest in telescopes? Another thing: I was being followed for a while, and suddenly, that stopped. I have to ask myself: why? Now I know how involved you are in this community and I know many people confide in you. More than confide in that skinny priest at the church. So has anyone told you who killed the professor? No need to deny it – no one has told you. Don't you find that interesting? That no one's told the police – that's not a surprise. But that no one's told El Gato – that's hard to believe. And yet, I believe it. You and me: we don't know who killed Father McNeery. I'm used to it: I'm like a mushroom. People keep me in the dark and dump shit on me." Rufino stopped. He hoped he'd nicked El Gato's pride by making them partners in ignorance. He searched El Gato's face for some clue that he'd hit a nerve.

Rufino saw El Gato force a smile at the mushroom comparison. El Gato turned his coffee cup, but did not drink. Finally he spoke: "Why are you here?"

"To warn you. I think you're in danger. There's a killer out there. The priest found something and he was killed for it. I think whatever he found has made its way to you. So I think you are in danger now. I realize you are not as naïve or as defenseless as the American priest, but I think you're in danger." Rufino lifted his cup, then put it down. "I don't think the professor's killer was an amateur." He pushed the coffee away. "I have to go now." Rufino rose. He noticed that El Gato stayed seated. Pinned to the chair, Rufino hoped, by his message.

******

Rufino heard about it before he actually saw it. A black cat was found hanging in the plaza by one of the morning workers who came to prune the trees. No note. The police questioned some of the local teenagers who hung around the plaza. They vehemently denied any responsibility. Rufino considered another visit to El Gato, but he decided that El Gato had already heard. The worker who found the dead cat was called back and questioned at length: where exactly was it found? How far from the ground? Describe it. Had he seen this cat around? It was comical really except that Rufino knew that El Gato was behind the questions: he wanted to know exactly what message was being conveyed. The answers: across from and in view of the church. High in the tree so you had to look up to see it. The cat was all-black. The cat, as far as anyone knew, was not from around here.

******

The letter had been written by someone with excellent penmanship. The handwriting made El Gato think it had been written by a nun - his main association with excellent handwriting. The message, however, was assertive, masculine: "The codex in your possession will only bring you grief. It does not belong to you. Return it to the ruins, where McNeery's body was found. If you're afraid, have one of your men do it. On the day you plan to return it, go to the church and pray."

There was no signature. The envelope had been postmarked in Merida. He looked again at the handwriting. It was excellent, and beautiful. He considered again if anyone other than a woman could've written it. Or perhaps it was dictated, and a woman had written the dictation.

The threat did not bother him. He'd been threatened before, although not lately. But the information contained in the threat concerned him. He had a leak in his organization and that was intolerable. First Rufino, and now this. He considered whether Humberto could've told anyone. His girlfriend of course, but she was on the way to America with him. His family? Her family? Neither would be likely to tell Rufino. They distrusted the police, for good reason, and feared El Gato, also for good reason. He thought about his antiquities dealer.

El Gato had never cared for his antiquities dealer, Alessandro Sussero. Something about the hiss of all those sibilants. A fitting name: Alessandro had a snakelike quality. He moved noiselessly; he was, in fact, the quietest person El Gato had ever known. A man of few words, and soft-spoken when he did speak. El Gato had asked him discreetly to find a buyer for the Codex. Now that discretion seemed flawed. El Gato called Alessandro.

"Hello."

"Talk to me."

"My impatient friend. As I told you, this is not like other sales. This will take some time."

El Gato tested the words, trying to determine if he heard anything patronizing in them. He realized one consequence of Alessandro's soft voice was that it became hard to hear the nuance in his tone. He listened for, but could not hear, anything defensive either. Alessandro was making a simple statement of fact. It made sense. The pool of buyers was small – how many people had 200 million pesos to spend on a Mayan artifact? The most likely buyers, museums, had to be excluded because of the artifact's lack of provenance. El Gato considered whether or not to confront Alessandro. Instead, he broke the unspoken rules of their relationship: he asked him whom he'd approached.

Alessandro remained unruffled. "The only way this can work is with anonymity all around. I never say who the seller is. I never say who the buyer is. Everyone is protected. Most importantly, you get the best price. Would-be customers can't collude."

And yet El Gato knew the system wasn't perfect. He asked: "Did you indicate the location of origin?"

"No. Only that its authenticity was unimpeachable."

Still, when a Mayan codex turns up - Alessandro's assertions notwithstanding - a man about to spend 200 million pesos does a little research. What sites are currently being excavated? Who's doing the excavation? How far along is it? Anything unusual going on at this site? And of course they figure it out. While many sites are being excavated, only one has a murder associated with it. So now the buyer is suspicious of Valladolid. They do a little more research: who has weight in Valladolid. El Gato, of course. So now the buyer – a man like himself – knows El Gato has a Mayan codex. He could buy it for 200 million pesos or -.

"Señor, you should call me whenever you feel like it. It's always good to talk to you. And I will call you when I get a nibble. Right away."

"Thank you." El Gato would do some research of his own.

******

Leon Cortes crossed himself and rose from his knees. He rose quickly, in spite of his bulk. He walked down the church aisle like the father of the bride. He nodded and smiled benignly at the other worshipers. Some he knew, all knew him. He was Santa Maria's chief benefactor.

Just outside the door, a thin younger man with a leather binder leaned toward him and spoke. They walked together to the waiting Lincoln town car, and the aide held the door for Leon Cortes and then walked around the car and got in next to him.

"It's done." The aide said.

"Now we wait."

The aide nodded.

Chapter 25

Leon Cortes

Leon Cortes led a charmed life, and he got down on his knees and thanked his Savior every day for it. He was healthy, wealthy, and powerful. He was becoming wise. He'd been born into the oldest family in Mexico, and he had increased its wealth and influence. He was a guardian of the old order: Catholic, Spanish, political. He stood against pagans, the indigenous, leftists. He was grateful for his responsibilities to his faith, his heritage and his country. He was grateful to have the power to carry out those responsibilities. He fought the drug cartel in the Yucatán as long as he could, and when he saw he couldn't defeat it, he took it over. There would be no bloody drug wars in his territory. The drug business was an inevitability and he was a pragmatist. It was going to exist, and the only question was whether it was going to be run with a minimum of bloodletting by a benevolent competent man, or by a bunch of thugs. It was the hardest business decision – the hardest decision – Leon ever had to make. Elsewhere, in the border states, there were 25,000 drug-related deaths a year. There were less than a dozen in the Yucatán. He reminded the governor of this from time to time. Cortes' hacienda was not the most opulent in Mexico, but it was the oldest. His personal office was modest, almost spartan in its furnishings. The servants found him to be fair and generous, and they revered him. His family felt the same way.

Chapter 26

Alessandro Sussero

"Do you have any idea how old it is?" Alessandro asked.

El Gato shrugged. "I don't know. It's old. It was found in the ruins they're excavating near here. Why does it matter?"

"It's part of the authentication process. Also, the older it is, the more valuable. How old are the ruins?"

Now El Gato let his impatience show a little. Alessandro took the hint. "I'll find out. I'll let you know." He watched a half smile return to El Gato's face, followed by a nod.

Alessandro left El Gato's office, and privately chastised himself. He should never have asked El Gato how old it was, and he should not have explained the importance when El Gato said he didn't know. It was a rare lapse of professionalism on his part. He had hoped to take a shortcut, never a sound policy in his line of work.

The dig near Valladolid had not yet produced any scholarly papers, a fact Alessandro's quick research turned up. But of course: the chief archaeologist had been murdered. His replacement had been on the site less than a week. The city being unearthed near Valladolid would have spanned centuries, perhaps a millennium. Contextual aging of the codex would be a problem. Certainly McNeery's notes would indicate where it had been found, but that too presented problems. As a venerated object, it could've been created years before its surroundings, and handed down from priest to priest, ruler to ruler. Clues from the codex itself would prove definitive. For that Alessandro needed a Mayan expert – the last sort of person he would want to alert to the codex's existence. A Mayan expert would insist it be turned over to the national archives.

Alessandro needed a date for this codex, and he decided an approximate one would have to do. Radiocarbon assay would give him a date plus or minus 130 years. He reluctantly snipped an unpainted corner and delivered it to a discrete lab he worked with in Mexico City. Even as he did this, he knew the objections: the process would only establish the age of the paper, not the images painted on it. Still, they could reasonably be assumed to be close together.

Two days later, Alessandra visited the lab to pick up the results and his sample. The receptionist asked him to wait and indicated a chair in the foyer. Soon a small man with a goatee came out and approached him: "Señor Sussero?"

Alessandro rose and shook his hand.

"Please come with me."

Alessandro felt a wave of anxiety wash over him. Usually, he was just handed a report by the receptionist. The sample was small, discreetly so, he'd hoped, but there was always the danger that if it were old enough it would arouse suspicions. He followed the goateed man back to an office. The sign on the door said Hermes Soriano, Director. Another wave of anxiety washed over him. Alessandro calmed himself by considering the possibility that they had damaged the sample, or lost it or in some other way had failed to date it.

Director Soriano closed the door and offered him a seat opposite his desk. He shook his head before he spoke, the conclusion of some private argument he was having with himself. "The sample is very old. That's what the radiocarbon assay says. We couldn't believe the first results, so we tested it again. A little different results the second time, which is to be expected, but still very old."

"How old?"

"1500 years old, plus or minus 130 years."

Alessandro considered this news. Old was good. Old increased the value. But this was older than he could credit. Something was wrong. He didn't speak and Señor Soriano continued: "You understand the fundamentals of radiocarbon dating. We compare the ratio of carbon 12 to carbon 14. Carbon 14 decays at a constant, known rate. Counting is imperfect, hence the plus or minus range. We assumed this was Mayan. This dating would place this at the dawn of Mayan civilization. But this is paper, which we always thought came later. What I'm saying is that radiocarbon dating is only one measure of age. Occasionally we get anomalous results, results that are at odds with all the other data. It doesn't mean we made a mistake – it means – well one possibility is that the sample was contaminated."

Alessandro nodded.

"That, and the other caveats and disclaimers are all in the report. It's part of the usual boilerplate. But in this case there's a real possibility that the radiocarbon dating was wrong. I thought you should know that."

Alessandro could see that Director Soriano was uncomfortable. He rose and shook his hand. "Thank you. I understand." There was no point in asking Soriano to run the tests again – he'd done that. He let the director show him out and he could detect his relief as they got to the door. Alessandro thanked him again and left. When Alessandro got to his car he turned on the air conditioning, but he did not drive away. He sat and read the report and the disclaimers.

He thought about Director Soriano. Why was he so uncomfortable with these results? Why would he care one way or other? Of course, Alessandro was a customer, and a good one, and normative results would have been helpful. Were these results unhelpful? Too old. That's what had bothered Soriano. What Soriano was hoping for, because he assumed it was what he, Alesandro, was hoping for, was 700 years old plus or minus 130. That would make this piece of ancient Mayan paper contemporaneous with the other Mayan codices. Soriano was no fool. He figured out that the sample came from a codex, and he was uncomfortable with the magnitude of the antiquities crime he'd become an unwitting accomplice to. Of course Soriano had dated other black-market antiquities. But always behind the veil of ignorance. His lab dated samples. He was not obliged to ask what, or where they came from. But the magnitude of what the sample implied had spooked him. Was he lying about the sample's age in an effort to further distance himself?

The report, on Alessandro's careful rereading, made no mention of what the sample was. It was simply sample 53971. He tried to recall if the other reports he'd gotten from Soriano were so circumspect. In the past he'd never bothered to notice - he was only interested in the putative date. He put his car in gear and drove away

Suppose the codex was 1500 years old: what then?

Chapter 27

Ex-Rabbi Simon Press

His cell phone, when he found it, was still warm to the touch, but it worked. He called Reyes. "I have news and I have news. Somebody just threw a firebomb through my window. And McNeery's notes and translation shows that the gospel of Matthew is in the codex. But you might still be in danger too."

"Are you burned? Are you okay?"

"I've got some burns. Nothing serious. I stopped being okay when I came to Mexico."

"Are you safe now? Are the police, the firemen there?"

Press said, "The firemen are here. So I feel safer than if I were with the police."

"Stay there. I'm coming over. If your burns aren't treated properly they'll get infected."

"You make house calls? You treat men?"

"Just this once."

Minutes later Press saw Reyes walk through his door. Instead of a black bag she was carrying white metal first aid kit. She said, "Where are you burned?"

Press held out his hands, palms up. Reyes opened the white metal first aid box and put on latex gloves. She took his hands and Press winced. She asked, "It hurts?"

"Yes."

"That's good. Reyes saw the look on his face and added "It means they're first or second degree. No pain would be more serious." She retrieved a tube from the first aid box and squeezed a worm of antibiotic cream on his palms and then on the back of his hands, spreading it around. Press grimaced. "Don't touch anything. I can wrap them, but they will heal quicker if I don't. Where else are you burned?"

"I'm fine everywhere else. I want to show you something." Press looked around, confirmed that the firemen were outside, backing up their equipment. He walked to the fridge and opened the freezer compartment. Reyes warned him to watch his hands. Press ignored her and retrieved McNeery's notebook.

"Just when I thought you couldn't get any stranger."

Press said, "You're in for a treat. It's about to get stranger." He showed Reyes McNary's notes culminating in the "This is the gospel of Matthew!"

"So?"

Press said "It means someone got here before Hernando Cortes. Someone got to the New World before Columbus."

"Couldn't it just mean this codex was written afterwards?"

"Maybe. The events recorded are old, and only old – they stop. The recorded history stops almost 1500 years ago."

Reyes said, "Maybe that's all they chose to record in this codex. Not every one of our history books continues to present."

"That's not how the Maya record history." He watched the thought sink in.

"Then maybe there's more. You don't know if McNeery translated everything."

It was Press' turn to think. This was the last entry in McNeery's notebook. In this notebook. He supposed there could have been others.

Reyes was holding Occam's razor – the simplest explanation was that the codex was written after Hernan Cortes had arrived. There was nothing to solve. Again Press asked himself: why was he rooting for such an early date? The case was simple really. McNeery had discovered a codex, worth $10 million. He'd been killed for it. By El Gato, or someone working for him. The codex was post-Columbian, and that explained the inclusion of the Matthew gospel. Post Landa, probably. Perhaps the Mayan figured that if they included a Christian narrative in their codices Landa wouldn't be so quick to burn them. It was a kind of inoculation. He thought all this, but then he said to Reyes: "So why are they still trying to kill me here?"

Reyes patted him on the arm, above the burns. "They try to kill you everywhere you open your mouth. Not just Mexico."

Press watched Reyes smile at him. "True enough. But back to McNeery's notes: the Matthew gospel isn't just added on, it's interwoven with the Mayan dynastic history. And that history ends in about 500 A.D. Likewise, the celestial observations end in 500 A.D. The author was writing the history to his present, and his present was 500 A.D. We don't have the actual codex anymore or we could date it using the carbon isotope method."

"How would they know about Jesus in the Yucatán in 500 A.D.?"

Press said. "I don't know."

Reyes persisted: "Who would've told them?"

Press shrugged. "There are some unorthodox historians – and when I say unorthodox I'm being kind – who claimed there were pre-Columbian contacts with the New World. There is evidence that the Norse got to Newfoundland about 1000 A.D. There is evidence that a great Chinese fleet got to the New World in 1421. Suppose a Portuguese coaster sailed off course while exploring its way down Africa and ended up in our hemisphere. But 500 A.D. is too early, even for the unorthodox historians."

"So will you accept that it was written much later? After Hernando Cortes arrives. Maybe after Landa has his bonfire. Maybe this is volume 1 and another codex traces their history from 500 A.D. to 1600 A.D."

"Again, because someone is trying to kill me. I don't have the codex. I don't know who does. I came to this party late, and all I'm bringing is a question. What's so dangerous about a question?"

"The answer."

Press reviewed what he knew about early Christianity. In one hundred A.D. there were outposts in Rome, Pompei, Thessalonica, Smyrna, Antioch, Athens, Corinth, Damascus, and Bethlehem. By 300 A.D. there were enough Christians in the Roman Empire to make them worth persecuting. By 312 A.D. the Emperor Constantine had converted to Chritianity. By 512 A.D., the last date recorded in the Codex, Christianity had spread through what was left of the Roman Empire. But nobody in what was left of the Empire was able to sail across the Atlantic.

Reyes interrupted his thoughts: "What did McNeery think? "

Press shot her a questioning look.

Reyes continued: "About the gospel of Matthew, about how it found its way into this old codex. He made notes, yes? What do his notes say?"

"The Portuguese. With a question mark and an exclamation mark."

"But you don't think so."

"I don't know. If the codex were from the 1400s, like the others, sure, why not? They were the best seamen of their day. They made their way part way across the Atlantic and discovered the Azores. So sure, if we're handicapping the discovery of the Americas in the 1400s, I would have bet on the Pertuguese. Before that, the only seagoing people were pagan: the Norse, the Phonecians." Press sat down, as if the weight of his deliberations had suddenly become heavier. If he could get himself to believe in the 1400s dating, some things would be easier. It would be the Portuguese. They were capable and Christian. They failed to return, so their claims on this new world weren't on record. That was plausible. Lots of expeditions didn't return. Cape Verde was at the same latitude as the Yucatán and they could have stopped at any of the Caribbean islands and pushed on, driven by the belief that they were oh so close to the fabled East. They drank the same Kool-Aid as Columbus, but they would have drunk it sooner, and like Columbus, overestimated the size of Asia. The idea grew on him.

Reyes said, "You're thinking deep thoughts, Rabbi."

"Let's say you're right. The codex is from the 1400s. Let's say the Portuguese landed in Mexico - they're the only Europeans – the only Christians - remotely capable of it."

He stood up suddenly, startling Reyes. "I know why Landa burned the codices. Idolatry had nothing to do with it. Think about the year 1562. Go back in your mind. The Spanish just discovered the richest deposits of silver in the world in Guanuato. And Landa discovers evidence that the Portuguese had beaten the Spanish to Mexico. But nobody knows it – the New World has been divided – by the Treaty of Tordisillas. Spain gets everything Columbus discovered, everything west of the mid-Atlantic line of demarcation. Portugal gets everything east of it, including a chunk of Brazil. Everybody's happy.

"But now Landa discovers that somebody Christian beat Columbus to the New World, and that can only be somebody Portuguese. Goodbye, Mexico. Goodbye, silver. At the very least, there's a war. So Landa makes a brilliant political decision – destroy the evidence."

Reyes smiled. "That would explain someone trying to kill you in 1562. Why now?"

Press said down like a balloon that the air and let out of. He shrugged. "Maybe there's something else in the Codex."

Press thought about it. But his mind kept returning to 1562. "Of course Landa would burn the codices, destroy the evidence. This destruction was an outrage to the church – which didn't know the reason for it – and so they called him back to Spain for a spanking. But when he returns to Mexico he's been promoted to Bishop. Some spanking. When he tells the Spanish authorities – and the Pope – why he burned the codices, they love him."

"So why are they trying to burn you now? And who's they?"

Press thought about it. "They aren't trying to kill me. If they were, I'd be dead. They could have killed me in the alley. This firebombing was scary but not that dangerous. These were all warnings. What are they afraid I'm going to find out?"

Chapter 28

Ex-Rabbi Simon Press

Press would have missed it, except for the crowd it gathered. He was pleased when he heard his name called and turned to see Isabel Reyes walking towards him. He saw her look and then felt her pull him away. Press asked, "Why don't they take it down?"

Reyes said, "They're afraid of Leon Cortes."

Press asked, "So who is Leon Cortes?"

Reyes replied, "What's the expression – a piece of labor –"

"A piece of work."

"A piece of work. The current patriarch of the oldest family in Mexico. Descended from the Conquistador. Still acts like one. A man of contradictions. Goes to church every day. Every day. The family had money of course. He made it much wealthier with investments in agriculture and telecommunications. He couldn't stand it that the drug dealers were killing each other and innocent bystanders, so he quietly, ruthlessly took over the drug business in Yucatán."

"Ruthlessly?"

"How else do you take over the drug business? It was like the Godfather movie. One day all the major druglords were killed. He got help from the Federales."

"How does he square that with going to church every day?"

"Christianity is about sacrifice, he'd say."

"Why does he want to get rid of El Gato? I thought El Gato was doing a good job of keeping the peace around here."

"Until your friend was murdered."

"But not for drugs."

"How do I know? But it doesn't matter. A breach of the peace. So Cortes is stepping in."

"Will he solve the crime? I suspect he has ways of getting information that are more effective than those available to us or even the Policia."

"He thinks he has solved the crime. The dead cat means he thinks El Gato killed your friend."

"What do you think?"

"Maybe."

"Why did he kill McNeery? Wouldn't it suffice to just administer a beating?"

"That's what I don't understand. A beating would suffice. Unless the beating got out of hand."

"You saw McNeery's body. You did the autopsy. Was he badly beaten? You can tell me."

"No. He was killed by a single blunt trauma to the head."

"So you need another theory."

"What about you? Don't you need a theory? He was your friend."

"Knowing who killed him won't bring him back."

"What about justice?"

"You've lived here all your life. How much justice do you see? I don't mean to pick on Mexico, Ireland is only marginally better." He looked at Reyes, tried to gauge if his remark had offended her.

"That's why I'm not a lawyer. We should get something to eat. I think Humberto knows, but he's gone." Reyes stood. "Over there, okay?"

Press nodded. Reyes started to walk in the direction of the restaurant and the Press joined her.

Chapter 29

Dr. Isabel Reyes

Reyes felt a tinge of homecoming as she drove to the ABC Hospital in Mexico City. She had done her internship and residency here, and knew many of the physicians. Her appointment was with Dr. Salvador Torres. He was a short bald man whose hyperkinetic energy was at odds with the diseases he specialized in, most of which were marked by extreme torpor. She liked Dr. Torres, but found his seemingly boundless energy draining. But this morning she felt fine, and in fact had considered canceling. She knew better: whatever ailed her came and went. Today she was asymptomatic. But something was clearly wrong with her.

She checked in with the nurse at the reception desk. The waiting room was full, although it was still early. She was still choosing a magazine when she heard her name called. "Dr. Reyes." The nurse was standing at the door that led to the examining room. Dr. Reyes put down the magazine and followed her.

"Remove your top and pants." The nurse handed her the gown.

A moment later Dr. Torres entered. "How are you? Wait – I'm supposed to answer that." He shook her hand – two quick pumps.

His examination was quick, but precise. He felt the lymph nodes in her neck, and armpits with deliberate care. "Put your clothes on and we'll talk."

She dressed and walked to his office.

"So," she said. "What's wrong with me?"

"You're Jewish," he paused, "or Armenian. You have Familial Mediterranean Fever. Or rather, you have all the classic symptoms: abdominal pain not accounted for in any other way, pain in your leg joints, but usually only one, and I'd expect occasional fever without any other symptoms. Let's take your temperature right now, when you're feeling fine."

A moment later he looked at the thermometer reading "101.4 - You felt warm to me when I examined you. I want to do a gene test."

"You're serious?"

"Let's do the test. That was a strange expression that just crossed your face. What are you thinking?"

"A coincidence. I just became friends with a rabbi. From Dublin. In Valladolid. Now you're teasing me about being Jewish."

"I'm not teasing you. You could be Armenian, the other ethnic group that has the condition. But you don't look Armenian."

"I look Jewish?"

"You look more Jewish than Armenian. And yes, now I am teasing you."

"My family goes all the way back to Spain."

"I don't doubt it. So do Jews – at least until 1492 – when they were kicked out, or converted."

"What are the other possibilities?"

"You know most of them, and if they were the right diagnosis you wouldn't be here, would you? Would you rather have some other disease, or some other ethnicity?"

"I am a Catholic of Spanish descent – not a very good Catholic, to be sure; but a Catholic nonetheless."

"Let's do the gene test. I'm sure we'll find some Catholic genes too." He took out a swab. "Open up."

Reyes opened her mouth and let him swab her cheek.

He said, "You haven't asked about the cure."

"For being Jewish?"

"For Familial Mediterranean Fever. There is no cure for being Jewish."

"Is it fatal?"

"Life is fatal. You'll be fine. We'll start you on some colchicines."

She was surprised that her first thought was to tell the Rabbi. Not her folks, not Pascal. She needed to wait for the gene test, she reminded herself. "How long for the results?"

"Call me in two days." He stood up. She rose and shook his hand.

It was bright outside. Too bright. She pulled on her sunglasses and walked to her car. Her cell rang. "Hi. It's Pascal. How are you?"

"How am I? I'm Jewish. How are you?"

"Still gay. How did you become Jewish?"

"At the doctors. I have Familial Mediterranean Fever, a disease unique to Armenians and Sephardic Jews."

"Can they cure it? Will you be all right?"

"They can treat it. I'll be fine."

"Did you catch this from your rabbi friend?"

"It's not that kind of disease. Oh, you're kidding me. They took a DNA sample. I'll know for sure in a couple of days."

"And then?"

"And then what? I'll start drinking the blood of Christian children."

"No need to become Orthodox. And look on the bright side – you won't need to be circumcised."

"Well, yes, there's that of course."

******

"This is Salvador."

"Hi, this is Isabel Reyes."

"How are you feeling?"

"Better."

"I have the results of the DNA test. You have the gene, as we suspected."

"So I'm Jewish."

"Some of your ancestors were."

Isabel thought about her mother, who wore her Catholicism lightly. A woman who practiced birth control and went to church every Sunday. She thought about her grandmother, who hadn't practiced birth control, who went to church almost daily, and who was, according to DNA evidence that much closer to her Jewish roots. Her family had come to Mexico from Spain in 1632. Her father's family had come 100 years later. She thought of the rabbi, but she called Pascal. "Hi. It's me. It's official. My ancestors were Jewish."

"Maybe we could have a joint coming-out party. What do you think?"

******

Later, while she was waiting for her flight to Valladolid, she called Rabbi Press. "I have some strange news. Can you meet me for dinner tonight?"

"About Humberto?"

"No, not about Humberto. Can you meet me for dinner?"

"Of course. Our usual place?"

"No. Yes. That will be fine."

"Are you okay?"

"In a general sense, yes. I'll be okay. Look, this is not a conversation I want to have over the phone. Eight o'clock?"

"Okay. Are you in danger?"

"Only the existential kind. Eight o'clock?"

"Okay. I'll see you then."

******

Press tried to imagine what would constitute existential danger, but quickly realized he had no idea what she meant. Existential was one of those words – you never know what someone meant by it. He felt a vague annoyance, he'd been deliberately kept in the dark; it was a bit of a tease, and self dramatizing – a quality he despised. It tarnished her allure. He was sorry to think that, but Isabel Reyes had just diminished herself in his affection, with a ploy he felt was intended to do just the opposite. Existential danger. What the hell was that? Sophisticated babble. He was becoming increasingly familiar with the real kind of danger. He'd been assaulted; a friend had been murdered; an innocent boy was hiding in the jungle from a bogus police investigation; this was danger. He wondered how existential danger was different from a bad hair day. Still, he could not help it, he was looking forward to dinner.

He arrived at the restaurant a few minutes early. An unnecessary precaution - he was certain that Isabelle would be late. It was still warm outside. The sky was a deep blue black, freckled with stars. The plaza was crowded. Teenagers huddled quietly but conspiratorially: boys in one group, girls in another. Pigeons pecked at spilled food. The church façade was lit up in a contrast of light and dark recesses. This was its most solemn face. He thought of his former synagogue, a less imposing and less sinister building. He checked his watch: 8:09. He made a mental note to be 10 min. late for any future meetings. The plaza was pleasant enough, it was only his impatience that made the wait annoying.

He saw her enter the Plaza from the Calla 36. Her walk was purposeful, but not hurried: it gave no indication that she felt she was late. Her hair was pinned back. She wore a large white shirt and jeans. She waved and he rewarded her wave with a smile, her tardiness forgiven, as it had no doubt been forgiven a thousand times before.

She stopped to speak to a woman selling bracelets. His first thought was that she was making a purchase, and his sense of annoyance returned. But then he saw that she was not looking at the bracelets, but at the woman. He watched Reyes put a hand on the woman's shoulder. The woman nodded, and then Reyes was on her way again. A patient, he thought. It was possible that every woman and child in this plaza was a patient. Dr. Reyes was conspicuous not just for her looks but for all the looking after she'd done. He began to understand why their first meeting had to take place elsewhere, in Merida. She was a celebrity here in Valladolid, or as close to a celebrity as this town had.

He crossed the Plaza to meet her. "A patient?" He asked.

"They're all patients. Or will be."

Press thought he detected a mixture of pride and resignation in her voice. He knew the feeling, or had, but only a couple of times a year, on the high holy days at his former synagogue. He held the door and she led the way into the restaurant.

"How's the level of existential danger?"

He saw a quizzical look on her face and then one of acknowledgment. She smiled. "I called it that, didn't I? How dramatic of me."

"What's going on?"

"How much do you know about diseases unique to Jews?"

He paused. "A little. There's Tay-Sachs. And then there was what Grace Paley called an outbreak of Jewishness in Europe in the early 1940s that killed about 6 million people."

"I know. Some Jews came to Mexico when they couldn't get into England or the United States. Have you heard of Familial Mediterranean Fever? It affects Armenians and Sephardic Jews. I have it."

"Are you okay? That sounds like a more than existential danger. Are you okay?"

"It comes and goes. I'll be okay. I saw a specialist in Mexico City."

A waiter approached the table and asked them if they would like something drink.

"Dos Equis." Reyes said.

"Two." When the waiter left, the rabbi turned to her and asked "How serious is it?"

"I'll live."

"So obviously people other than Sephardic Jews and Armenians get it. Are you Armenian?"

"No. I had a DNA test done. I have the same mutation as the Sephardic Jews who have the disease."

"So one of your ancestors was Jewish."

"Probably more than one."

"Your family, your distant ancestors, were Conversos." Press considered the woman sitting across from him.

"We could be related."

"Probably not. My family is Ashkenazi - Eastern European. Do your parents know?"

"That I'm Jewish?"

"That you're sick."

"No. I don't want to worry them."

"They're parents. They worry whether you give them cause to or not. You should tell them."

"What's it like to be Jewish?"

"You are in existential danger. I don't know how to answer that. Actually, I know too many answers to that. Everywhere, except Israel and some neighborhoods, you're an outsider. You have what others call a chip on your shoulder" - he saw her look at him quizzically – "it means a grudge – you carry what others call a grudge and what you call the Holocaust. You feel special. You check out how many Nobel Prize winners are Jewish – lots – and you're smug about it. But when someone does something terrible your first impulse is to hope the person isn't Jewish. You should read Philip Roth. Have you read him?"

"No."

"Are you thinking of becoming Jewish."

"You're teasing me about this?"

"I guess I am."

"Why?"

"Because I don't think you change who you are because you found out something about your family's distant past. You certainly don't do it because you got sick. Your ancestors converted 500 years ago. That's about 25 generations."

"I know exactly how many generations ago it was. My family keeps track of these things."

The waiter returned with their beers and asked if they were ready to order.

"Shall we have chicken soup?"

"Why do you make a joke of this?"

"It's a Jewish thing. I'm teaching you." He turned to the waiter: "We really haven't decided yet. Give us a couple minutes."

"I never felt particularly religious, certainly not particularly Catholic. I don't go to church except with my parents. I use birth control. I don't go to confession. Mostly, I'm uncomfortable with my Catholicism."

"How you feel about Jesus?"

"Do I believe he's the savior? I don't see much that's saved. I see a lot that needs saving. I don't know."

"That's why you're a doctor."

"Yes."

Press leaned forward in his chair. "If you want to learn about Judaism, I can teach you. If you want to convert you should learn about it first. What's it going to be?"

"You mean Judaism or Catholicism?"

"I mean to eat."

Reyes shook her head. "So, will you teach me about Judaism?"

"Sure. Do you want the short course or the long course?"

"Let's start with a short course."

"Do not do unto others that which is hateful to you."

There was a pause. Reyes looked at him. Press smiled. "That was the short course."

"That's just the Golden Rule."

"No. The Golden Rule is: do unto others as you would have them do unto you. There's a difference, a significant difference. Do you see the difference?"

"Yes. But I don't see that it's a significant difference."

"A trivial example. Suppose I like being tickled –"

"Do you?"

"It depends. But suppose I do. The golden rule requires that I go around tickling everybody. Do you like being tickled? How would you like it if I tickled you?"

"I don't like being tickled."

"So, the golden rule doesn't work in all situations. Now suppose I like being baptized. I should go out and baptize everyone I meet. A nontrivial example. The golden rule does not prevent us from imposing our likes on others. That's what's wrong with it. Judaism's rule is better. Mostly it requires me to leave you alone, and specifically prohibits me from harming you. It respects the other."

"The subtext is that Christianity doesn't respect the other."

"Diego de Landa burned all the Mayan codices."

"The Maya practiced human sacrifice, a lot of it."

"I agree it would be better if everyone observed the Judaic principle, not just Christian bishops. You really don't like being tickled? Never?"

"Where is this negative golden rule written? In the Old Testament?"

"Hillel, the great rabbi, was asked to teach Judaism while standing on one foot. Apparently he couldn't stand on one foot very long. So that's what he said."

"Who asked him?"

"The Spanish physician. One of your relatives?"

"A Spanish doctor? Are you serious?"

"No. I'm teasing you."

"Is this how you teach?"

"I tell stories. I give examples. I pose hypotheticals. I try to involve my students. Sometimes I do that by teasing them."

"What if they don't like being teased?"

"Everyone likes being teased. It's a form of attention and everyone likes attention."

"Not shy people."

"Shy people most of all. But unless I'm mistaken, you're not shy."

"A little. I try to act otherwise."

"I didn't realize that, but I should have. Some of your boldness is overcompensation."

"You think I'm bold?"

"Yes. What's more you know this about yourself. I suspect shyness is a cultural norm for Spanish women in Mexico. Forwardness would be construed as either unfeminine or sluttish."

"Not for modern Mexican woman. But I was shy as a child. Ask my parents."

"I will. Am I going to have that opportunity sometime? Guess who's coming to dinner."

Press saw a puzzled look on Isabel's face. "'Guess Who's Coming to Dinner' was an American movie from the sixties. With Spencer Tracy and Sidney Portier. A white woman brings her black boyfriend home to dinner. A very shocking thing to do at the time the movie was made. You know the history of race relations in the United States. It beat out 'The Graduate' for Best Picture at the Academy Awards. By my allusion I was suggesting you bringing me to dinner might be uncomfortable for your folks."

"What you are suggesting, as I understand your explanation, is that you're my boyfriend."

"I guess that is what I am suggesting. Do you have a boyfriend? Is the position open? Can I apply for it?"

"Thank you for making being my boyfriend sound like a job. I've had many boyfriends – none of them ever thought of it as work."

"All real relationships are work. On this all the women's magazines agree. And they're right. But you haven't answered my question: do you have a boyfriend?"

"If I do you wouldn't be interested? You don't seem to want the job of being my boyfriend very much, to be put off by some competition." She moved her cup. "Why is it so hard for you to say you like me?"

"I'm shy. I like you."

"So your boldness is overcompensation too. That's how come you recognize it in others. By the way, my parents are well-educated, cosmopolitan people. They would have no problem with my bringing a Jewish scholar to dinner. I think they'd enjoy it. So, will you come to dinner?"

"As your boyfriend?"

"As my guest."

"I still like you, even if you're not ready to reciprocate. What can I bring?"

"You're charming self. And wine."

"Is Manischewitz Concorde grape okay? Or would you prefer their white?"

******

Isabel called her mother. "I'm going to be in town again this weekend. I'm bringing someone I'd like you to meet, and who would like to meet you and father."

"Of course. The new boyfriend? What happened to you and Pascalito?"

"Don't pry, mother. Just be your gracious self."

"Does your guest have a name?"

"Simon Press."

"The North American?"

"He's from Dublin. A rabbi, if you can believe it."

"Do we need to prepare anything special? Anything he can't eat?"

"He's not Orthodox. I'll double check, but I don't think he observes the dietary laws."

"I'll have Consuela prepare fish to be safe. So: a new boyfriend? Pascal will be heartbroken. Does he know?"

"Pascal and I are just friends. We flirt because it's fun. He won't be heartbroken."

"It's just as well. I always thought he was gay."

Dr. Reyes realized, a little guiltily, that she was having Press meet her parents to dazzle him – with her family's sophistication, cosmopolitanism, and prestige. Why? Why did she feel this need to impress him with more than her own person? It was childish, and she hoped, out of character. She considered calling him to cancel. There was something smug about the rabbi that called forth this response in her. Something too self-satisfied, and proud. It needed to be met with – with what? Her own pride, and the manifest reasons for it. Or was it his otherness that so confounded her usual repertoire of responses, that she needed to call in reinforcements? She would call and cancel. She could not imagine the dinner except in the most awkward terms. The presence of her parents would infantilize her. She called the rabbi. "Hi. Before you meet my parents we need to talk. Meet me at seven, after work."

"It's always a pleasure to see you, So you think I need to be briefed on meeting your parents."

"This evening at seven in the plaza."

"My pleasure."

The rabbi sat on a bench in the plaza, opposite the clinic. He brought a notebook of McNeery's, but reading through it was not a sufficient distraction. So he closed the notebook and just took in the plaza. Evening was its finest hour. Families with small children began to gather near the corn on the cob vendors; groups of teenagers began to gather in the darker regions, from which the occasional shout or commotion broke forth and then subsided. The setting sun lit up the church façade. Mexico at its gentlest and most familial. It was hard to reconcile the tableau before him with the fact that his presence here was due to the murder of his friend.

He was looking at the church, his back to the clinic when he heard the rapid telltale footsteps. He turned and saw Dr. Reyes. She offered him a stiff handshake.

"I'm sorry I'm late." She tossed her head back toward the clinic, by way of excuse.

"I understand. I was just thinking, looking out at the plaza, how strange that I'm here because of the murder. By the way, any more thoughts about that?"

"You remember the cat?"

"Yes. But other than it being a sick prank, I don't know why it's so portentous."

"It's a message. It's a message to El Gato."

"Of course. But who would send that kind of threat? I thought El Gato was the local boss."

"He is, so the message isn't from someone local. Someone more powerful is announcing a change."

"How do you know? I mean how do *you* know. Do you moonlight as doctor to the narco gangs?"

"Moonlight?"

"Moonlight means work a second job."

"No. Why would you think that? Why would you say that? Everyone understands the symbolism of the hanging cat. That's why it was done publicly. Most local people understand this."

"I apologize. So why is El Gato being replaced? Who's doing this?"

"El Gato is only the local crime lord. It's a medieval structure really. He owes his allegiance to the King. The King is Leon Cortes. So it's Leon Cortes that's sending the message. You know it was a long time before anyone took the cat down. The police were questioning everyone here to find out who took it down. It disappeared, just as quietly as it went up."

Chapter 30

El Gato

El Gato remembered the night of Leon Cortes's ascension to power. It was the Day of the Dead, the pagan holiday that had been reluctantly brought into the Christian fold. El Gato was working for Javier. He didn't much care for Javier - the man was dirty and lazy, crude and stupid. Too quick to pick a quarrel, and then have his men do the actual fighting. His trademark execution was the hood ornament: he put the dead man's head on the hood of the man's car and parked it in front of his home. On the night of the Day of the Dead Javier's head was found adorning the hood of his Range Rover. El Gato had received a picture, and the note: "I understand you're looking for a job. Come work for me. Leon Cortes."

El Gato remembered going to Merida to meet Leon Cortes. He'd gone armed, with bodyguards. He'd gone by way of the back roads. He'd gone feeling a mixture of curiosity, awe and fear – this last feeling one he had some difficulty identifying. He was told to meet Leon Cortes in the church of Santa

Maria, in the morning. Instructions for the meeting had given the time, and place and this reminder: "Dress for church." El Gato wondered if it was a warning not to bring weapons.

He was met in the church foyer by Leon's man, not a body guard, but a small older man who handed him a garment bag with a dark suit, a white shirt, and a tie. "Please change into these." The man pointed to a rest room.

El Gato thought briefly of the photograph of Javier. He took the garment bag – stopped – made a slight bow of his head and said "Thank you. It's been a long drive."

"You're welcome."

The suit fit. El Gato was pleased at first, then alarmed. How had Cortes known? He returned to the foyer and the servant indicated the broad back of a man seated in one of the front pews. The church was sparsely attended, but not empty. Some old women in black sat alone or in pairs in several pews. El Gato walked to the pew the servant had indicated.

"Buenos Dias, Señor Cortes."

"Buenos Dias. Thank you for coming. The suit fits you well. It's not for me. It's for the church."

Leon Cortes was a large man, thick of neck, shoulder, chest, middle. His nickname, if he had one, would have been "El Toro." But he was the descendent of the Conquistador, and he had no need of nicknames.

"I come here every day to pray. Do you go to mass? Of course not. But you should. I'm not a violent man, or an evil one, just an ordinary sinner. Sometimes we are required to mortify our flesh in His name, and sometimes our souls. Drugs are an abomination. The gang war was a worse abomination. I did what I had to. You will run Valladolid. No more killing. Javier was a pig. You have the makings of a gentleman. See that you become one."

Leon kneeled and prayed. El Gato kneeled, but no prayer would come. He just knelt in silence in strange clothes, in a strange church, next to this strange man.

When he was done, Leon rose quickly, with an agility El Gato would not have expected of the large man. Leon said "Come with me."

El Gato rose and walked out of the church with Leon Cortes. The limousine was parked in front, the liveried driver holding the door open. Cortes gave some money and words of encouragement to the old Indian women begging on the church steps. He indicated to El Gato that he should enter the limo. El Gato did and found himself praying that Leon would join him. Otherwise he knew he was destined to be a hood ornament too. Leon spoke a few words to the driver and got in.

"You will tithe your church in Valladolid. Go to mass every week. It would please me if you would go every day, but I'm patient and some things must be done of one's free will. Give money to the poor. You should get married, because you're going to fornicate, and fornication outside of marriage is a sin. But again, I'm patient and this too must be done of your own will. Run our business without killing. You must be a harsh disciplinarian, but you may not kill. The commandment says so."

El Gato thought of the hood ornament, and held his tongue.

"My share is the customary 50%. You will not be bothered by the Policia, either the locals or the federales. Your first allegiance is to Christ, your next allegiance is to me. We are going to my home, because I want to show you how nice family life can be. Do you need anything?"

"If I'm going to be your guest, I'd like to stop and get some flowers."

Leon smiled. "Of course."

El Gato felt Leon's huge hand grab his neck and bring his head forward until it almost touched Leon's. "You're going to be fine, relax."

Chapter 31

El Gato

Alessandro called: "The codex is old. Much older than previous ones."

"So that makes it more valuable."

Alessandro said, "Yes. Definitely. But there's a problem. We need more testing."

More testing meant more money. "Why?"

"It's too old. Its authenticity will be called into question. That's why we need a second set of tests."

"Old is good. Too old is not good?"

"Exactly."

"How old is too old?"

"About 1500 years, give or take 130. That's what the radiocarbon dating says. The lab director is making all kinds of excuses. The problem is that no one will credit a codex that old. It's at least 800 years older than the others."

"How old is the site?"

"This site is old. But we don't know for sure how old. Possibly it is old enough, but again, scholars don't think there were codices 1500 years ago."

"Will more tests change their mind?" El Gato knew, or suspected, that Alessandro got kickbacks from the testing labs. If he were in Alessandro's shoes he would. The tests were expensive. And there was the prestige of being entrusted to test an artifact of this caliber. "Okay, test it again. But it comes out of your commission." El Gato knew this was a breach of their unwritten agreement, but he was angry.

"As you wish. I'd like you to come to the lab this time. I want you to hear it directly. Or maybe if you talk to the director. Suggest a more reasonable date."

"Where's the lab?"

"Mexico City."

El Gato wondered if Alessandro had heard about the dead cat. He said "Mexico City then."

"The lab there is at the Instituto DeTechnologia. I will get them a sample tomorrow. We'll have results by Friday. So on Friday?"

"Yes, on Friday." El Gato hung up.

El Gato decided to go early. He would be safe on a plane, and safe in Mexico City. Later that afternoon he left in his SUV, with the driver and two bodyguards, for the ride to the Merida airport. He watched for cars following him and saw none. There was no traffic coming the other way either. And then ahead he saw a mottled, mostly brown mass.

"El toro." The driver spoke.

"Hit one, we'll have lunch."

El Gato looked at his watch. A five-minute delay would not cause him to miss his plane. If he had to, he could hire a private jet for the one-hour hop to Mexico City. Still, he was annoyed. He looked around for some sign of the rancher, or his cowhand. There was dust everywhere. Finally he saw a small thin man with leathery skin and a long switch. He spoke to Jamie, his bodyguard, "Tell him to move this fucking herd. Show him your gun."

Jamie opened the car door. The strong odor of manure seeped in. "Watch where you step," El Gato called after him. The driver and Luis, the other bodyguard, laughed. Jamie slammed the door.

El Gato watched Jamie walk carefully toward the rancher. He saw the rancher look up from his cattle and wave his hat at Jamie. It looked like an apology of sorts, so El Gato was surprised when Jamie turned and looked back at the SUV.

Or beyond it. El Gato turned in his seat to look behind them. A second herd of cattle had entered the road. He turned and was about to get out of the car himself when he saw Jamie stagger and fall. And that's when he knew.

What happened next happened quickly. El Gato shouted to his driver, "Get out of here!" But they were in the middle of the sea of cattle. He could no longer see the rancher. "The horn!"

The chauffeur hit the horn. There was a startled pause as the herd seemed to momentarily stop and then began to run. The SUV was rocked as the cattle brushed by. But no opening appeared. The driver kept his palm on the horn and inched forward. El Gato look for signs of the rancher and others he was sure were out there. He took a semi automatic pistol from the floor. Luis had an automatic rifle pointed out the window. The horn continued to blare. The herd picked up its pace and began to stampede, but they were running down the road now in front of the SUV. El Gato turned to look behind him. The road behind was clear. "Turn around!"

The driver slammed on the brakes and let the SUV fishtail. They were perpendicular to the road – halfway turned around. He swung the wheel hard as he backed up to finish the u turn. When El Gato heard the shot, the glass was already shattered and his driver was thrown back against the seat. El Gato felt the fine mist of blood on his face. The SUV's momentum slowed and it ran off the road into a ditch.

A voice shouted: "If you want to live, step out without your guns."

El Gato looked at Luis. "We're going to die. Let's die like men."

Luis slowly shook his head and opened the door. El Gato raised his pistol and fired. Luis fell in the ditch. "They would've tortured you, Luis. I'm sorry."

He crouched in the backseat looking for his assailants. He heard the lowing of panicked cattle and then hoofbeats. There was the explosion and the window behind him sprayed him with glass. He turned. He could see only cattle. He thought he saw a figure in front of him and he fired. Again. Nothing. He waited. The sound of the cattle was moving away. He felt a fly tickle the back of his head and instinctively swatted it. It didn't move. He didn't understand. The fly didn't move. It became a stick in his hand. Then there was a crack on his head in which his consciousness exploded and then darkness.

El Gato awoke in darkness. His head ached. He was confined, but he couldn't understand how. He thought he was in some sort of hammock - he felt rough canvas all around him. He had a moment of panic: he was in a shroud, they'd thought he was dead, and had buried him. He found it difficult to breathe, and his panic gave way to fear. They'd buried him alive. He didn't smell earth, and his first impression, that he was in some sort of hammock, returned. He was not resting on the ground, much less in it. As he forced himself to calm down, he found he could breathe just fine. He was not tied, at least his hands and feet were not tied. When he tried to move, he found his hammock swayed. He groped for an edge in the darkness, but his hands found only the pliant wall of canvas. He reached as high as he could:

more canvas. He ran his hands around: canvas. So he began to consider the possibility that he was not in a hammock, but in a giant canvas bag. He found he could arch his back and feel beneath himself: more canvas. He smelled sweat - not his own. The canvas smelled of sweat. He fought the urge to vomit. He was thirsty. He reached down his leg for the knife he'd strapped to his calf. It was gone. He felt the other calf. No knife. Of course they'd taken it. He listened: nothing. He felt his pockets. His cell phone was gone; his keys were gone. Nothing. His exertions made the bag he was in sway slightly, and he heard the creak of a chain being strained.

"You're awake. Good. We were going to wake you soon anyway."

El Gato recognized the voice of Leon Cortes.

"Whatever you want, you can have it. It didn't have to come to this."

"But it did. It did come to this. How did you get your nickname?"

"I was a samba champion. People said I moved like a cat."

"I heard it was because you seemed to have nine lives."

"That too. I was shot a couple of times. I lived."

"I heard it was because you once put a cat in a bag and beat it to death."

El Gato felt the bile rise in his throat.

El Gato heard Leon yell "Start." He heard the thrum of machinery. He felt a jerk, and then he felt that the bag he was in begin to rise, accompanied by the whine of winches. It stopped. Then he felt his cocoon pulled sideways as the machine sound started again. It stopped, but his cocoon continued to swing. It reached the end of its arc and swung back. His nausea overcame him and he vomited. The swing back stopped abruptly as he crashed into a hard surface. He felt a sharp pain and heard a crack as his hip shattered. He heard the machine start up and he felt, through his pain, the beginning of another swing. When he reached the apex of this swing he started to brace himself: there was the pause and then he felt his cocoon accelerate as it swung toward the unseen wall. He seemed to be going faster this time. He felt the shock of pain as he hit the wall and his arm and shoulder shattered. The inside of the bag was sticky now with blood where broken bones had pushed through his skin. He heard this machine and felt the start of another swing.

On the ground, Leon Cortes looked at the operator of the crane: "Seven more. Then deposit the bag at the clinic in Valladolid."

******

Dr. Reyes saw the canvas bag from across the plaza. It was early. Workers had just begun their work pruning the trees, the news vendor was putting the lead bars on his piles of newspapers. The sky was orange and purple, the sun barely out. She stopped and bought the local paper. She didn't expect to have much time to read it until lunch. She looked again at the canvas bag. It was leaking, and the ground around it was stained. She felt the familiar rage. A bag of manure, or pig shit. She looked instinctively at the police station. A policeman with a vest and carbine stood by the door, oblivious. She addressed the news vendor: "Did you see who left me the present?"

"No Señora. It was there when I got here."

She decided she believed him. She made a point of walking past the police station and wishing the man at the door "Buenos Dias." She was closer now and she knew: That wasn't shit leaking out; it was blood. She stopped and then she ran. The thought, which surprised and terrified her, was that she would find Simon Press inside. She dropped her newspaper. She yelled for the police she just passed. There was a note on the bag. She read: "El Gato requires medical attention."

She smelled shit and bile. The bag, which was like a canvas mail sack, was closed by a rope drawn tight through steel eyelets on top. The rope had become brown with dried blood. She went into the clinic and pulled on latex gloves. She grabbed a scalpel and cut away the top of the back just under the eyelets. It opened. She turned her head away from the stench.

The crowd was beginning to form some 20 feet away. The distance gave her pause: what if this were booby-trapped? Too late, she thought; she'd already opened it. She could not recognize the contents. She expected a body or even discrete body parts. She looked away and staggered to her feet. What she'd seen was an unrecognizable mush of meat and bone. She saw the police man standing in the door. She walked to him and said: "He's dead. He belongs to you now." She walked back to the clinic and locked the door behind her. She went to the bathroom and threw up. Her first fear, that it'd been the Rabbi, returned in a different form. Not the Rabbi – not this time. She dialed his number, knowing she would wake him, not caring.

His "hello" was surprisingly chipper.

"It's Dr. Reyes. Did I wake you?"

"No. I get up early. This can't be good news."

"The body of El Gato was deposited at the door to my clinic this morning."

"Dead?"

"Beyond that. I don't even know how to describe it. I threw up when I saw it."

"Are you okay?"

"Yes and no. There was a note."

"Addressed to you?"

"No. Just 'El Gato requires medical attention.' A joke. Maybe I was the nearest clinic."

"I'll come over. Are the police there?"

"They're no help. When I saw that what was left of him was dead I told them it was their problem. But nothing will be done. Whoever did this was more powerful than El Gato, and the Policia are already afraid of him, so now they'll shit themselves six different ways before they investigate this."

"I'll come over."

"Sure. Okay."

"I'm curious: why did you call me? Glad you did, just surprised."

"When I first saw that it was a body, I was afraid it was you."

Press heard her hang up.

******

Press saw Reyes at the door to her clinic and he walked around the barricades to where she was standing. "Do you have to do the autopsy?"

"No. I'll refuse. They'll send it to Merida. Look at them," she indicated the police. "Everyone in this plaza knows who did this: Leon Cortes. The Policia know it. But wait, they'll blame it on Humberto, or some low-level thug. They found his bodyguards and his SUV in the ditch not far from his home. They were shot and died instantly."

Press looked at her.

"Those bodies will go to Merida too. You see why I limit my practice to women and children?"

"Can I bring you some coffee?"

"I have coffee inside."

He heard a slow siren, and watched as an emergency vehicle pulled into the square. Two uniformed EMTs brought a gurney out of the back and placed the bag with El Gato on it. They carried it to the emergency vehicle and placed it in the back. Slowly, with lights flashing, they drove away.

"Why did this happen? I thought these things were self policing."

"Who knows? Maybe Leon thought El Gato was cheating him. Maybe he was. El Gato was ambitious; maybe Leon felt threatened. Maybe he was just bored. Can you imagine women doing this to each other?"

"I have difficulty imagining men doing it to each other. I have a faulty imagination. The priest should do a brisk business today."

Reyes shook her head. "Just the regulars."

"Why did you think it might have been me?"

"I don't know. You were attacked before. You should've left town after that, but you stayed. Usually you don't get more than one warning."

"Was this a warning?"

"I don't know."

Chapter 32

Leon Cortes

"Hello, it's my sad duty to tell you that El Gato is dead. I'm Leon Cortes."

The housekeeper looked at the large well-dressed man before her, flanked by two large well-dressed younger men. Leon saw her shock and terror.

"This is a terrible shock to you. We will help you. You have nothing to be afraid of. We will take care of you. You should stay here as long as you like. I'm sure Señor Catalan provided for you. Do you need a ride to church?"

The housekeeper nodded. "I must change."

"We'll wait here. Felipe will drive you when you're ready."

Later, as Felipe drove the housekeeper to the church of San Gervasio, Leon and his men searched the house that she had neglected to lock in her shock and grief.

"It's not here."

Leon said, "I didn't think it would be. But you never know, so we look. I would put it in the safe deposit box at the bank. But El Gato was from a poor family, one not inclined to trust banks. If he's trying to sell it, then perhaps his dealer has it. See who's on his cell phone. And please tell me you took his cell phone before he had his accident."

Chapter 33

Det. Benito Rufino

Rufino read the autopsy report. And then he read it again. And then, because he was stuck, he picked up the phone and dialed the number for Dr. Isabel Reyes.

When she answered he said, "It's Detective Rufino. And I'm sorry to do this, but I need to ask you about El Gato's body. It's all in the autopsy report, which I don't understand."

"What don't you understand? I'm sure it says something about blunt trauma. He was beaten badly."

"I want to show you the report. It's not as simple as a brutal beating. It was more."

"What difference does it make? Find the killer. But that's the easy part, because everyone knows who did this. Even you. The hard part is arresting him and proving it."

"That's why I need to understand the report. If I know how he was killed, I might be able to figure out where. I'm coming over."

"As you wish."

Rufino had hoped for a warmer reception. He walked across the plaza to the clinic. He held the autopsy report in a huge manila envelope, which also included x rays, the strangest x-rays he'd ever seen.

When he entered the clinic and showed his badge, the receptionist said "Please sit. The doctor is with a patient. She should be out in a minute."

Rufino sat, but soon he was standing up again, too agitated to remain seated. He walked from wall-to-wall, reading posters: about hand washing, about birth control, about vaccinations, about nutrition.

Dr. Reyes came into the waiting room and said, "Outside."

Rufino followed her out. He felt the eyes of the waiting patients on his back.

"Show me."

He handed Dr. Reyes the envelope. She took one x-ray and looked at it. She brought one hand to her forehead to shield her eyes from the sun. Then she walked into the plaza, to a shaded spot under a tree. Rufino followed her.

She looked at the x-ray, then read the report, then looked at the x-ray again.

"He wasn't beaten with a metal pipe or anything like that. This is the kind of damage we see if someone is hit by a car – no – by a truck. But not just once. Hit by a truck over and over again. It's not just that every bone was broken; it's that the bones were broken over and over again and the splinters driven throughout his body. He was a human piñata, except he wasn't hit by a stick, he was hit by a convoy of trucks." She pushed the x-rays and report back in the envelope and started to return to the clinic.

Rufino tried to imagine it: El Gato stuffed into a canvas punching bag, suspended from an overpass, and truck after truck driving into him. It was hard to believe he wouldn't have been killed instantly. "Was it painful, or did he die after the first blow?" Rufino shouted to her back.

"Unimaginably painful," she said. Then she stopped and turned. "Did you ever see him dance?" She saw a question form on Rufino's face. "He was really something." She turned and went into the clinic.

As crimes went, El Gato's murder wasn't particularly hard to solve. He was the local drug lord, so only someone with equal or greater power would have the courage to kill him in this way. A subordinate would have simply shot him: no warning and no elaborately grisly death. In territory controlled by Cortes, no rival would've made the move except under orders from Cortes. They'd remember the hood ornaments. And then there was the business of the cat in the bag. This was Cortes' handiwork, Rufino was sure of it. The problem was how to tie him to it.

He followed her to the clinic.

"What?" Her voice was weary.

"You said he was hit by trucks. Could he have been swung repeatedly against a wall?"

"Like the cat in the bag? Everyone knows the story."

"Yes."

"Yes, I suppose he could have been killed that way."

"Okay. Thank you."

Rufino tried to imagine it: El Gato stuffed in a bag and swung against the wall. How? Where? Like a human wrecking ball; except the human got wrecked. Wrecking balls were suspended from cranes – big ones. There were lots of these, but the number was finite. Probably one was owned by one of Leon Cortes's companies. And within a three hour drive of Valladolid, if the coroner's time of death was correct.

He called a friend in the construction business. "How do I find out where all the cranes are within 150 miles?"

His friend said: "Talk to a rigger. Cranes need to be rigged; you don't just drive up in one and start working. You have to be a professional rigger to set one up. There aren't very many of them."

Rufino thanked his friend and checked the Yellow Pages under riggers. No luck. He called the nearest heavy equipment dealer and spoke to the sales manager. When he got off the phone he had three names. One turned out to be retired. The other two told him to fuck off – they weren't going to give him the names of their customers even if he was a detective, which they didn't believe, and told him so.

Rufino got in his car and drove to Tinum, about 20 kilometers from Valladolid, where the rigger who made the anatomically impossible suggestion lived. A large pickup truck sat in the yard. He parked behind it, almost touching it and got out. Soon a middle-age man with the largest forearms Rufino had ever seen came out the door.

"Who the fuck are you?" By way of a greeting.

"Señor Rojas?" Rufino pulled out his badge. "I'm Detective Rufino. Did you think you would tell me to fuck myself and that would be the end of it? Is that usually what happens? You tell a guy to fuck himself and he takes his dick out and tries to shove it up his own ass? I'm investigating a murder. You're not a suspect, unless you don't cooperate. Then you become a suspect. You don't want that. I want your customer list. I won't steal your customers."

Rufino watched Rojas consider.

"Okay. It's in the house."

"Bring it out. I'll be right here." He knew there was some chance Rojas would come out with a gun, but Rufino didn't like the idea of going into the house, where Rojas might have reinforcements. "I'll sit in my car and make a copy. Then you can have it back." When Rojas returned with the book he took it and went to his car.

It didn't take Rufino long to copy what he needed. There were, after the crossed out names had been subtracted, about two dozen customers. He recognized some of the names - national companies like Bechtel and Mitsubishi. He copied the company name, phone number, the contact. For the defunct companies, he wrote down the name. He got out of his car and gave the book back to Rojas. "Thank you."

"You're welcome." Rojas spat.

Back at the office Rufino got on the website for Cortes' company, Toledo Industries, and searched the names. He supposed Cortes was eager to prove his legitimacy, or he was just showing off, but all the subsidiary companies were listed, many with their own websites. After an hour of searching the links he was down to two subsidiaries on Rojas's list and Cortes': both were close enough to fit the coroner's timeline.

The Trujillo wrecking company was an hour's drive, towards Merida. It was mid-afternoon now, and hot. Rufino glanced at the clinic, considered stopping in, thought better of it, and drove away.

The Trujillo wrecking company was in Piste, off a dirt road. There was a chain-link fence topped with razor wire, beyond which he could see rows of partitions made from massive concrete blocks, each filled with rusty scrap. The crane was hard to miss. The gate was open. There was a tiny hut beside it, empty. He drove into the compound.

The crane stood in front of a partition filled halfway with a tangle of metal rebar. Windshield wipers had erased a swath of dust from the crane's control cabin window. Recently used, Rufino thought. He looked at the concrete walls of the partition. He expected to see – what? Not the telltale outline of a man, surely. A blotch maybe. Dark brown. But the rust was everywhere. On the left the concrete was almost white in the sun; on the right, in the shade, it was gray, almost soft looking.

He saw it. Halfway up the white partition a reddish-brown smudge, like a big handprint, caught his eye. A closer look meant climbing on the rusty rebar. He took a picture with his cell phone, then moved closer and took another. The smudge was maybe six or seven feet above the rebar if he stood on it. He could scrape the sample off the concrete. He walked to the rebar and tested it. It shifted a little, but seemed stable. He wished he had work boots instead of sneakers. He took one more look around the yard and then began to climb. The rust got on everything. Soon he was sweating and orange rivulets ran down his arms. He slipped and his right foot got stuck. He pulled and there was a slight shift. His foot started to come free from the tangle of rebar and then he felt his ankle squeezed. He was off balance and sat down, trying to twist his ankle free. He was annoyed – as he would be with a knotted shoelace. He tried to pull hard – a mistake – his foot was now wedged tighter. It occurred to him that he might need help to get out. It was embarrassing, and he dismissed the thought. He'd gotten stuck so easily that his personal logic insisted that he should become unstuck with the same ease. He pointed his toe and slowly tried to pull his foot out. He felt the rebar sag. Nothing. Perhaps sitting down on it was a mistake. He pushed himself up. He was mindful of his free foot and he tried pointing his toe again. Nothing moved. He knelt and felt along his trapped ankle to where the crossing rebar had imprisoned his foot. He tried to pry his foot loose. Nothing moved. He heard the machine start up with a dull whine. He looked around, and saw nothing. He looked at the driver's cab of the crane. Only reflected sunlight bounced back at him. Still, he didn't see any other machinery. There was a change in the reflected light: the cabin was moving. He looked hard at the cabin but he could still see only the reflected light. Then the crane was moving - slowly, and he was relieved to see, away from him. He called out and waved. The crane arm continued to move away from him. The crane arm stopped and lowered a huge disk shaped plate towards the scrap heap in the partition beyond the wall. It was lowered out of sight and then he heard the crash of metal. He shouted again, louder. He heard a different, higher pitched whine and watched the disk emerged from behind the concrete partition with a tangle of rusty scrap attached to it. It's a magnet, he realized. When the magnet and the attached scrap had cleared the height of the partition it stopped. He heard the other whine, the deeper one, and saw the magnet and scrap move across the wall and head toward him. He pulled hard on his trapped foot. Nothing moved. Remembering his gun he pulled it out of his shoulder holster and fired a quick shot into the air. The crane stopped. He waved. The crane started up again. He fired another shot in the air, but the magnet and the scrap kept coming. He fired a shot at the glass window of the cab, but missed. He steadied himself. He fired again and watched the glass window explode. The magnet and the scrap kept coming. It was over him now. He fired again and again into the black hole of the cab. The magnet was overhead now. He covered his head instinctively, a futile gesture given the weight of what was about to crash down on him.

The magnet passed over him and kept going. His first thought was that the crane operator had misjudged. The magnet kept going. He turned to watch it and he felt his ankle slip free.

Rufino's impulse was to scramble off the pile of rusty, twisted rebar. But the magnet was no longer overhead, and he was afraid of getting his foot stuck again. He got down on all fours, distributing his weight, and crawled slowly to the edge of the junk pile. Holding his gun made it more difficult. He glanced upward and back at the magnet, which had come to the end of its arc and stopped. He stood up and slowly approached the cab. He climbed up to the cab and took a quick look in. There was blood and glass everywhere. Pieces of glass were stuck in the operator. The operator was sprawled back against the seat, his right eye gone and replaced by a gaping hole where Rufino's bullet had entered his face. There was blood and gray brain matter on the back of the cab.

Rufino's next thought was not his most compassionate: this was going to be hard to explain. The magnet with the scrap now hovered over the partition to the left of the one he'd been climbing on, no longer posing a threat. He had a nauseating moment of doubt: had the crane operator not seen him? Not heard him yell? Not heard his shots? Rufino could see clearly out of the opening where the windshield had been, but could the operator? He checked the position of the sun. It was high in the sky, but if the driver had been looking at the magnet and the top of the crane… he let the thought trail off and die.

Another thought came unbidden. Where was everyone else? Was the crane operator the only employee on site? That seemed unlikely. Still, he heard only the sound of the crane's motor.

He looked at the crane's control panel. He realized he was trying to figure out how to move the magnet back, back to where its cargo of scrap posed a threat to him as he investigated the blotch on the wall. He knew how it would look if he kept things as they were: "Cop where he shouldn't be shoots a working man doing his job; all because he's afraid of some machinery." Chance for the local chief to get rid of him and show that the Antiquities Police were corrupt after all. In all this Cepeda would be helped by Leon Cortes.

He wondered if he'd been set up. He thought about the rigger. The plan, if there had been one, was to bury him under a load of scrap and have it look like an accident. This was even better for them.

Still no one came. The only way he could hope to explain this was to find El Gato's blood on the wall. He turned the crane off and was startled by the crash of metal. The magnet had released its load. He took the keys to the crane and went back to the rebar. He crawled carefully over it to the spot beneath the mark on the wall. He stood up slowly and scraped a sample of the rusty blotch into a glycerin envelope. He hoped it wasn't just rust.

Rufino pulled on latex gloves and returned to the crane. He found the dead operator's cell phone and dialed 911. And he got into his car and left. The federal police lab in Mexico City was 20 hours away. He would have lots of time to figure this out on the way, but one thing he was sure of: he had to get the blood sample to the only police lab he trusted. Then he could turn himself over to the inevitable investigation and suspension.

It occurred to Rufino that an investigation and suspension wasn't the worst thing that could happen to him. He had a glimpse of the worst thing. Two glimpses: a couple of tons of metal falling on him, and the bloody smudge on the concrete wall. Still, he reasoned, if they needed him dead, someone else would have finished the job at the junk yard. He called Dr. Reyes with his cell phone.

"It's Detective Rufino."

Her response was cooler than he'd hoped for. He pressed on: "I think I found where El Gato was killed. A junk yard in Piste. I scraped some dried blood off the concrete partition and I'm on my way to Mexico City with it. By any chance did you take a blood sample from the body they dumped at the clinic?"

"No. The police took it away to Merida for the autopsy. I thought you knew that."

"I did. But I ask again: did you take a blood sample?"

"No. But there's blood on my coat and on the gloves I used to open the sack."

"Save them." He paused. "If it's not too late."

"Not too late. But the coroner's report will have everything."

"I expect that when the time comes that the report matters, it will disappear, or get changed. The junkyard where El Gato was killed belongs to Leon Cortes."

"So your plan is − after he's corrupted the police and the coroner's office − it'll be my evidence and testimony that brings him down? So how will that work out for me? A bloody bag with my broken and unrecognizable body will be delivered to my parents? Thanks. How about this: instead you just shoot the evil bastard. You're a man. You've got a gun. You're sure he did it. Kill him and leave me out of it."

Rufino was silent. She had a point.

Dr. Reyes hung up. She went to the closet where the soiled linen was kept and dumped the bag on the floor. The bloody lab coat had been on the bottom, now it was on the top. She found a plastic bag and placed the coat in it, then sealed it up and put it on a high shelf above the other medical supplies: boxes of latex gloves, sterile pads, big rolls of white paper that went on the examining table.

She washed her hands and return to the examining room, where a frightened 14-year-old girl complained of nausea. "Take this stick. Go to the bathroom and pee on it. Put it in the cup. A nurse will bring it to me." She squeezed her shoulder: "Whatever it is, it will be okay. Okay?"

The girl left. She took out her cell phone and returned the last call. Rufino answered. She said "I've got the sample on the lab coat. I'll put it in the trash behind the clinic. Stop by and you can take it to Mexico City too." She did not wait for reply.

When she sat down to look at the file on her next patient, she was overcome by nausea. She felt hot and clammy. First she thought it was fear – she remembered what El Gato looked like in that bag. But the feeling didn't pass. Her joints began to ache and she knew: this was another bout of the Mediterranean Familial Fever. The nurse knocked and let herself in. She was holding a cup with the stick. She said "Are you okay?"

"I'm having an episode. Show me the stick."

The nurse handed her the cup and frowned. Reyes looked and said "Send her back in."

The nurse started to protest. Reyes shook her head. "She's scared to death, she might as well know."

The nurse returned with a 14-year-old girl. Reyes indicated she should sit. "The good news is that you're not sick. You're pregnant. The nurse is going to explain to you how to take care of yourself and your baby. Do you know who the father is?"

The girl nodded.

"Call him. Tell him he's going to be a father."

******

Press answered the phone. He was pleased to hear Isabel's voice.

"Rufino, the detective, found where El Gato was murdered. A scrap yard owned by Leon Cortes."

"Why does that matter? We know Cortes had him killed. Everybody knows that. Wasn't that the point – for Cortes to let everyone know what a powerful sadistic bastard he is?"

"But now there's proof. There will be, when Rufino gets the blood samples matched."

"So now some lucky policeman is going to Leon's home and put him in handcuffs? Is Detective Rufino going to do that? He'll be the next bag of blood and bones at your doorstep."

"It won't be Rufino. He's going to be suspended. He killed the man at the junkyard."

Press considered that he'd been too harsh in his opinion of Rufino. The man was brave. And he had a dangerous job. Press thought he heard something in Isabel's voice – admiration? He hoped not. "What happened?"

Isabel told him.

"Are you going to be okay? Does this put you in danger?"

"I'm okay. Actually I feel terrible. I'm having another episode of Jewishness."

"The Mediterranean Fever?"

"I think so. I have to convalesce for a couple of days."

"Do you have someone to take care of you?"

"I'll take care of myself."

"Still, it's nice to be taken care of when you're sick."

"Are you offering?"

"Yes. I am. I won't change a bedpan or do any of the gross stuff, but I'll keep you company and bring you food if you'd like."

"Let me think about it."

******

The doctor was right. He should just shoot the bastard. His own life was already forfeit. His career was probably over once the killing at the junkyard was investigated. Cortes had sufficient pull that he would be stripped of his badge. He might or might not be prosecuted. He would certainly be killed in jail if it came to that. Otherwise outside, if it didn't. He had a delivery to make first. He decided to drive to Merida and take a plane to Mexico City.

He took a look at his rearview mirror and then drove off. The Merida airport was about 150 km away. Once there he would be safe. He'd once been afraid to fly. Now he was looking at it as a place of refuge.

In about 10 km he would pick up the main highway to Merida and the airport. It was well-traveled, probably safe from the kind of ambush that had been El Gato's undoing. But the next 10 km were exactly the sort of road El Gato had been ambushed on. He reasoned that it would have been much easier for them to kill him at the junkyard. He looked again in his rearview mirror. Clear.

Chapter 34

Det. Benito Rufino

On the drive to the highway Rufino looked in his rearview mirror almost as often as looked ahead. Occasionally a truck would appear, a farmer driving to market. He felt relieved when he got on the ramp to Hwy 180 west. The sign said 150 Km to Merida. There was traffic – not a lot – but enough so that any mishap would have plenty of witnesses. He pushed his Toyota up to 120 kph, and began passing trucks and buses. He calculated he would reach the Merida airport in an hour and a quarter. He saw the red tail lights of braking traffic ahead and reluctantly began to slow down. Traffic stopped. When it didn't start up again he pulled onto the shoulder and began to drive along it, passing a long line of stationary cars, trucks and buses - one of the perks of being a police officer. He would miss it when they suspended him and took away his badge. He could see flashing lights ahead so the police were already at the scene of the accident. He looked for signs of a fire truck or an ambulance. As he approached the flashing lights he slowed and took his wallet out of his pocket. He strained, but he couldn't see the accident. He saw a police car blocking one lane, lights flashing, and several others on the shoulder. There was no accident, at least none that he could see. He slowed to a crawl. Four officers with rifles stood on the shoulder, while a fifth bent over to speak to the driver in the first car. He watched the officer straighten and wave the driver through. He was fifty yards from the checkpoint when one of the officers with a rifle pointed it at Rufino. He slowed, but didn't stop. The checkpoint officer held up his hand, palm towards Rufino.

Rufino lowered the window. The police approached the car, rifles aimed at him.

"Rufino."

"I'm not Rufino."

"You're driving his car. You look like him." He showed Rufino an ugly likeness of himself on a fax.

"I'm driving my car."

There was a pause. The officer stood at the open window. "Show me some ID."

"It's in the glove compartment. Okay if I get it?"

"Get it. Slowly."

Rufino opened the glove compartment and retrieved a black wallet. Inside was a 500 pesos note with the face of Diego Rivera, nothing else. He handed the wallet to the officer. "You'll see my ID inside. I'm Diego Rivera."

"Like the famous painter."

"Yes, like the famous painter."

The officer looked in the wallet, then at Rufino. He removed the 500 pesos. He turned to the men with the rifles and waved at them, indicating that they should lower their guns. "It's not Rufino." He handed the empty wallet back to Rufino. "Have a nice trip, Señor Rivera."

Rufino nodded. He put the car in gear and slowly drove on, wondering if he'd overpaid.

Chapter 35

Det. Benito Rufino

The forensic science laboratory in Mexico City was a glass and steel building on the Ave. Constituyentes in the Belen de la Flores colonia. Rufino asked the receptionist to call up to Señor Xaviar de Sousa. Moments later Xaviar de Sousa appeared in the lobby. He gave Rufino a hug and said, "Don't talk. Just follow me. We'll talk in my office."

Xaviar's office was on the second floor. "We'll take the stairs." Rufino followed. The office was down a long corridor. Inside, he was surprised by the orderliness, the stark contrast to his own cubicle and that of almost every investigator he knew. The surface of Xaviar's desk was empty. No telephone. No mug of pencils.

Rufino asked "Did you just move in?"

"No. The desktop is a work surface, not a storage area. Now, why are you here my friend?"

Rufino took the evidence bag out of his pocket. "I think this is dried blood. It used to belong to El Gato, our local crime lord. This is the coat of a doctor in Valladolid who examined his remains."

"I heard about this. And a good deal else. You're in trouble, my friend. You know that."

"I know. I'm lucky to have made it this far. Can you get a DNA sample from this? I hope so, I risked my life to get it."

"Probably. But then what?"

Rufino saw something old and resigned in his friend's face. Xavier was in his 50s, but he looked older now: some slackness in his face, perhaps some lines. His hair was gray at the edges. Some weariness in his eyes. It was contagious. Rufino said "I don't know. We prosecute Leon Cortes for ordering the murder?" It came out as a question.

"Sure. Why not?" Then your successor and mine will be tracking a bag just like this one and it'll be our dried blood inside. Why don't you just shoot the bastard?"

"You're the second person to suggest that."

"Who was the first?"

"The doctor in Valladolid. She shares your concern." Rufino looked at the evidence bag.

Xavier said, "But suppose the blood matches. Then what?"

"It proves El Gato was killed in Leon Cortes's junkyard."

"So?"

"You think just anybody could waltz into Cortes's junkyard and kill somebody there in this elaborate fashion without Cortes's knowledge and consent?"

Xaviar answered: "I don't think El Gato could have been killed at all, anywhere, without Cortes's consent. The difficulty is proving it. It would be better if the jacket with El Gato's blood on it belonged to Cortes."

Rufino nodded. Yes that would be better. It never would happen, but it would be better if it had. "You'll run the tests? As a favor?"

Xavier nodded.

Rufino said, "You look tired, my friend."

"What I look is old. What I look is world-weary. But it's nice of you to say I only look tired."

Rufino said, "I can find my way out. Thank you."

Xavier waved him away. "Use the stairs."

Chapter 36

Det. Benito Rufino

"Rufino."

Rufino looked up, then ignored the officer shouting his name.

"Rufino."

Rufino considered whether there was any point in running. He saw officers approaching from two directions. Behind him was the crime lab, where, he realized, Xavier had just betrayed him. How else could they have found him so quickly? Ahead was the street, filled with traffic. He stopped.

"A word with you, Rufino." The speaker was a tall young man, with a smarmy officious look of an officer on his way up the ranks.

"*Detective* Rufino." Rufino corrected the slight, knew it didn't matter.

"Your weapon please."

There were other officers at the four cardinal points of the compass. He was surrounded. Rufino unholstered his service revolver and handed it handle first to the officer.

"Your badge."

No "please." Now that they had his gun all courtesy would stop.

Rufino handed the tall officer his badge. His first thought, as he handed over the badge, was that they would torture him. Or they would turn him over to Leon Cortes. This made other thoughts difficult. What Rufino saw, in his mind's eye as they pushed him into the back seat of the police car, was a room whose floor sloped gently to a grate in the center. The slope, and the grate were there to wash away the blood. This is what the room he would be interrogated in would look like.

He found when he stopped thinking about the room he feared he was being taken to, that he resented how young the arresting officer was. He was a puppy, wet behind the ears, a by-the-book brat, puffed up by his quick rise through the ranks, helped perhaps by a wealthy father, and some aggressive ass kissing. He thought he could register the contempt of the officer's older subordinates in the momentary delay between receiving a command from their upstart lieutenant, and their carrying that command out. He'd practiced the same temporal insolence himself with superiors he hated or disrespected. There was also something jaunty in their speech – a bit too gung ho – technically irreproachable, but mocking. He'd done that too.

The car was slowed to a crawl by traffic. The Lieutenant ordered the siren and flashers turned on. Cars parted awkwardly to let them through.

At the station Rufino was led to a room with a scratched wooden table and two chairs. A florescent light hummed overhead. The walls were pale green. The floor, Rufino was relieved to see, lacked both slope and grate. When they got around to torturing him, it would be somewhere else.

The Lieutenant entered the room with two subordinate officers. Crime everywhere, Rufino thought, and there were three of Mexico's finest in this room – four, he corrected, including himself. The Lieutenant placed a tape recorder on the table and said, "Tell us what happened at the junk yard, Rufino."

Rufino made a point of looking at the officers standing at each end table, and then looking at the Lieutenant. He told his story.

"Did you get a blood sample from the wall?"

"Yes."

"You didn't first check to see if the man you shot was alive?"

"I did. He was dead."

"How do you know?"

"I'm used to blood and bullets. The shot entered his face just below the left eye and blew away most of the back of his head. He had no pulse."

"You checked his pulse?"

"I checked his carotid artery for a pulse. There was no pulse."

"But you are not a doctor."

"His brains were falling out of the hole in the back of his head. He had no pulse. He was dead. You are correct, I am not a doctor."

"Did you call for an ambulance?"

"No."

"Why not?"

"He was dead."

"So you say."

"He was dead, and I thought he might have accomplices, and that I was still in danger."

"Did you see anyone else?"

"No."

"So why do you say you were in danger?"

Rufino knew that his only answer to this question was weak: *It's a sense I had. A man had just tried to kill me. He works for a known drug kingpin, and generally these men don't work alone.* Rufino looked for understanding from the officers standing at each end of the table. They were older than the Lieutenant, might have been in danger themselves. And then the answer came to him. He said: "Are you in danger now, Lieutenant?"

"Answer the question: why do you say you are in danger?"

"I am answering it. I'm handcuffed, and you have two armed officers here to protect you. So you have a sense that you're in danger, and have taken precautions. No one has tried to kill you in the last 5 minutes. And we are in a room in police headquarters. I was on the property of a drug kingpin, his men had just tried to drop two tons of metal on my head. I was alone. Was I not entitled to at least the same sense of danger that you clearly feel in this room, with two bodyguards to protect you from a man in handcuffs?"

The lieutenant switched off the tape recorder. "These officers aren't here for my protection. They're here for yours."

The federales routinely put out press releases about anticorruption task forces, to placate the human rights watch groups, or the North Americans, or to burnish some corrupt politician's image. It seemed the young lieutenant had read these press releases and believed them. Or he wanted Rufino to believe he had.

Rufino said, "You can put the tape recorder back on."

"You plan on answering my question?"

"Yes."

Lieutenant turned the recorder back on. "Why do you say you were in danger?"

"A man had just tried to kill me. I thought there might be accomplices."

"Were there?"

"I don't know."

"Did anyone else try to harm you at the junkyard?"

"No."

"Did you see anyone else?"

"No."

Rufino saw what was coming next, and a sickening wave of doubt swept over him. If Leon Cortes had meant to kill him at the junkyard, he would have succeeded. Why wasn't anyone else there? Was it possible that only meant to intimidate him? That the two tons of metal wasn't going to be dropped on his head? Again, why wasn't anyone else there?

The Lieutenant asked the question Rufino was fearing: "Is it possible the crane operator didn't see you? Did you tell him you were going out onto the junk pile? "

"He saw me."

"How do you know? Did you do anything to make yourself visible? Did you wave to him?"

"Yes."

"Did you call out to him?"

"Yes."

"How do you know he saw you?"

"I was standing where he was going to drop his load. I could see him. Well enough to shoot him." Rufino hoped the Lieutenant hadn't been to the junkyard, wouldn't have figured out the sun would've been in the crane operator's eyes, and bouncing off the windshield, making it impossible for Rufino to see into the crane's control cab.

"He didn't hear you?"

Back on safer ground. "It would have been hard not to."

"Did you fire a warning shot?"

"Yes."

The lieutenant turned off the recorder. "You see how this looks, Rufino? You go to a place of business secretly. You shoot a man who was just doing his job, because you became frightened."

The Lieutenant stood up. "We'll investigate this further. You're suspended. At least for now. Go back to Valladolid; stay there; stay out of trouble. In fact, it would be best if you just stayed indoors." To the guards he said: "You can release him." They removed his handcuffs and stepped back, their hands on their truncheons. Rufino wanted to rub his wrists, but didn't. He stood slowly, stared at the door. The Lieutenant said, "It's unlocked. You can go." Rufino gave each of them a hard look and left.

He considered a visit to Xavier; then thought better of it. The time would come to settle scores, not now. He was shocked by the light when he stepped outside. He'd lost his sunglasses somewhere during this ordeal. He stood a moment, shielding his eyes with his hands. Then he found his car. On the passenger seat he saw sunglasses on top of a brown folder. He put them on, then considered the envelope. It was bulky and he considered the possibility that it was a bomb. When he saw the insignia of the federales on it, his concern was not diminished. A fatigue came over him, and with it a fatalism. He lifted the package, and when it didn't explode he ripped it open. He emptied the contents onto the seat and was surprised to see his gun, his badge and a note that said simply, "Be careful."

Chapter 37

Ex-Rabbi Simon Press

Press called Reyes. "I'll bring you some food."

"Some of that famous Irish cooking?"

"I know we're a gastronomically challenged people. We ate potatoes when no one else in Europe would touch them. No one looks forward to a new Irish restaurant opening."

"Why is that?"

Press said, "The English always took everything worth eating. I'll bring some Mexican food by."

Later, Press arrived at Isabel's apartment. He shouted through the door "It's Simon. I brought you soup." He listened and heard footsteps. The door opened and Isabel Reyes stood there in a red bathrobe. Under different circumstances it might have been sexy. But Isabel looked terrible: the face of sickness.

She said, "Come in. I debated letting you see me looking like this. And then I thought, what the hell. I could use the company. And the food."

He followed her to the dining room, where she took his soup and poured some into a bowl. "Keep your distance. I smell about as good as I look."

Press said, "Can I get you anything else from the kitchen?"

She shook her head. He watched her eat a couple of spoonfuls of soup. Then she put the spoon down. She said "I don't have much appetite. Maybe later. Let's sit in the living room."

Press followed her to the living room, where she sprawled on the couch. He took the chair opposite. He said, "We can just sit. There's no need to make conversation."

"I wasn't going to. That's your job. Why don't you deliver that lecture that started the fight. It must be some lecture. And you'll be safe – I'm in no condition to try to beat you up."

Simon stood up. "I usually lecture standing up. I pace a little; it uses up the excess energy."

"Okay."

He started, "Twenty centuries ago in a restive backwater of the Roman Empire, there was a routine execution of a local troublemaker. Of the literally hundreds of documents that survived from that time, only one, written by the Jewish historian Josephus, mentions the incident and the troublemaker. And he only mentions it briefly, and in passing. Elsewhere in the Roman Empire, and most particularly in Rome here's what was going on: the Roman Emperor Tiberius had semi-retired to Capri, and Sejanus, the head of the Praetorian Guard, was the de facto ruler of the Roman Empire. Trouble was brewing, and Sejanus, sensing a threat to his power, began a series of show trials against Senators and other prominent Romans he felt were capable of challenging his power. So Rome, the most populous and powerful city in the world, was in the midst of a season of political intrigue, purges, and ultimately, retribution. Sejanus would be denounced and executed a year later. Events in Judaea would be about as important to the average Roman as events in Guam are to the average American.

Press continued, "Seventy years after the incident, as near as we can tell, the first sympathetic account of the incident occurs: the gospel of Mark. Fifty years after that, one hundred and twenty years after the incident, other Gospels appear: Matthew, Luke, and John, and the troublemaker who was executed was thought by a small minority, mostly poor women, to be the Jewish Messiah. Paul, formerly Saul, is spreading the word in Antioch, Rome and elsewhere. Gatherings of these believers, called Christians, are not large or troublesome enough to be persecuted until 66 CE, the year of Nero's fire. Mostly they argue among themselves: do we keep Jewish law or not?

"Why was Christianity – the belief that Jesus was a Jewish Messiah – catching on? Who was it catching on with? Disaffected Jews? People who previously believed in and sacrificed to local deities? Animists? How fervently were these other religious beliefs held?

"The problem is that our notion of what happened is colored by the New Testament cannon – a conflicting, inaccurate set of accounts with axes to grind. There are lots of other documents, better historically, that are known only to scholars, which is to say practically unknown.

"Today we would use the word viral to describe the spread of Christianity." Simon stopped and looked at Isabel. "Can I get you something else? I don't usually make that offer during my lectures."

"I'm okay. Keep lecturing. It's distracting. That's what I need now – distraction."

"Watch it, Señorita. This is my life's work you're calling a distraction."

"Does this attract women? Do women come up to you after your lecture and want to sleep with you? Or does everyone just want to beat you up?"

"Some of each. Some of the women actually want to do both."

"I can understand that."

Simon smiled inwardly, but decided not to point out the concession Isabel had just made. He decided to resume his lecture. "Should I continue? Have you had enough? On the one hand you're still awake; on the other, you haven't punched me."

Isabel said, "Go ahead"

"The first converts were the most disenfranchised – to use a modern word – members of their society. Or marginalized. Poor women. The first converts were Jewish, and an early church father, Paul, was struggling with how much of Judaism – the laws – they needed to observe. There was a question – really it was *the* question – whether non-Jews – Gentiles – could become Christians. The first Christian communities, the first small congregations really, sprung up in cities where there were existing Jewish communities. This was not, in these early days, a religion bent on conquering the world. It was a movement to reform Judaism.

"To whom did Christianity appeal, and why? It appealed to women. Why women? What was the message here that particularly appealed to women? Or to put it another way: what about Christ's message was particularly appealing to these poor, marginalized Jewish women?

"We need to look at what was happening historically to Jews at this time. Romans had crushed the Jewish rebellion, captured Jerusalem and torn down the Temple in 70 CE. Christ had been crucified 40 years earlier. The Gospels according to Mark and others hadn't been written yet. The last Jewish resistance was crushed at Masada. The remaining Jews were expelled from Israel. They went to Babylon. Most of the men had been killed, as well as many women and children. The Romans were not nice people - in the words of a professor of mine, a noted scholar, they were and I quote 'the worst mother fuckers in history.' That's saying something, when you consider the competition."

"That bad?"

"Think about it. Crucifixion is a pretty horrible way to die. It's slow, it's painful, it's humiliating.

"But back to my lecture. We have to look at the portrayal of women in the Old Testament. Eve is evil, the cause of man's downfall. Sarah is barren initially, a threat to the whole Jewish enterprise until a decidedly male Yahweh fixes her. Think about just how far we've come from the celebration of female fertility with that. This is an emphatic denial of the fertility principle at the heart of so many religions that were contemporaneous with early Judaism. With Mary and the virgin birth, fecundity is reasserted, and female birth is center stage. In the Old Testament, Adam is made from earth – an autochthonic myth – and Eve is made from Adam, so the primacy of the male in reproduction is at the core of the religion. When God destroys the world with a flood, repopulation is due to male ingenuity – Noah's ark – not female fecundity. Moses, to continue the theme, is adopted by the Egyptian Royal family – again the natural mother and son relationship is demoted."

"Stop."

"You've had enough?"

"I want to go back to the business of women who want to sleep with you and then kill you."

"No, actually I think most would prefer the order reversed. I want to go back to something else too: are you in danger? Would Leon Cortes have you killed? I'm unclear about the scope of Mexican chivalry."

Isabel considered, "He would not have me killed. Tortured, perhaps."

"And me?"

"Tortured and killed. Unfortunately, in that order. You're a man, a Jew, and an outsider. Had you been an American, that might have given him some pause – but you're Irish, and Ireland is far away."

"And Rufino?"

"Same as El Gato."

Press considered that by far the wisest course – the only sane course – was to go home to Ireland. There was nothing he could do for McNeery. Justice was a joke in Mexico as it was in so many other places, but here it was an open joke, a joke to tell out loud, before an approving audience. But he would stay because he did not want to show fear in front of a beautiful woman. It was pathetic, moronic, and perverse.

Isabel continued, "Why do you stay? Mexico is not safe for you. Because of McNeery?"

"Not McNeery. Not because of McNeery. You. I stay because of you."

"Because you think you love me? Because you want to sleep with me?"

"Yes, because I want to sleep with you."

"You'd risk torture and death to sleep with me? I'm good, but not that good."

"You're you. How good you are has nothing to do with it. I'm not that good myself."

"So if I sleep with you, you'll leave? Go back to Ireland? Save yourself?

"Yes, if that's what it takes. And then you can go to work for the Bureau of Deportation. But I think if you sleep with me I'll want to stay, and if you don't, I'll still want to stay, in the hope that you'll change your mind."

Isabel patted his hand. "Go back to Ireland, Rabbi."

Chapter 38

Alessandro Sussero

The news of El Gato's death found Alessandro at home in his library where he'd wandered with the newspaper. He sat at a desk made from a 1/2 inch glass sheet spanning two pre-Columbian stone glyphs, and faced a wall of books, most oversized folios of art and antiquities in a range of languages: Spanish of course, but English, German, Italian, French – all of which he spoke, some (English and Italian) fluently and the rest passably. He wore a bathrobe of Turkish cotton. He sipped an espresso. He had planned to only skim the paper, nibble pastry, and then return to Delia, the young woman who was currently sleeping in his bed. It had been a good night; it would be, shortly, a good morning. "The body, battered beyond recognition," he read, and wondered *how do they know it's El Gato?* – but subsequent paragraphs explain the ambush, the slain driver and bodyguards.

Alessandro had never been fond of El Gato, had in fact been afraid of him, and for good reason. He sipped his espresso, and let the thought that was beginning to bubble in his mind percolate to the surface. He was in possession of a 200 million pesos codex, whose rightful owner – whose rightful owner was the people of Mexico, a naïve thought – but whose de facto owner was, until yesterday, El Gato; whose current owner, by happy accident, was the individual into whose care it had been entrusted: Alessandro. As the magnitude of this windfall presented itself to Alessandro, he felt his heart pump, and his blood surge, especially to his loins and he put his espresso and pastry down and returned to the bedroom, where he silently shared his good fortune with the drowsy but receptive Delia.

He was rich, or would be shortly – not beyond his imaginings, because he moved in wealthy circles and his imagination was healthy – but he was rich enough, or would be, to take his place in the society he had until now only served. As an agent he was genteel and sought after, and his knowledge commanded the respect of those he served, but in the end he was not a member of the club. Now he would be. There was much to do and precautions to be taken. He had been afraid of El Gato – he could admit that now; he was terrified of Leon Cortes. There was the nagging matter of the codex's date – previously an annoyance, but growing into a full-fledged problem as he saw a fortune almost within his grasp. In his mind he began to explain the thousand year discrepancy to Leon

Cortes. He would make the anomaly a virtue, but he knew he could not push it too hard or Leon would suspect this was part of the negotiation. He pored over his books on Mayan antiquities, he surfed the Internet for the latest research on Mayan writing. He despaired – just this once – of his predicament: he couldn't contact the scholars who would be most helpful in justifying the excessive age of the codex. He thought, unhelpfully, of McNeery and El Gato. He made, and sipped, another espresso. Delia had showered and dressed and now wanted the attention she felt she'd earned last night and this morning, but his attention was elsewhere.

She wanted to go out to breakfast and, with exquisite irony, to go to the marketplace and haggle for some Indian handicrafts.

Alessandro equivocated. He found himself mumbling about something that had come up at work.

She challenged him: "On Sunday?"

"The artifacts are timeless and indifferent to time. Their owners, and those that would be their owners, are rich and also indifferent to time, especially other people's." He had discovered that this professional way of speaking sometimes had a quieting effect on the young women he brought home for sex. It was shameful, it was shameless, but it reminded them that he moved in important circles, and of course that was what attracted these women to him in the first place.

He agreed to meet her later – a meeting he would break when the time for it came.

Now that he was alone, he began to make a list of potential customers. There was the matter of price. He picked, as a placeholder because his fantasy of wealth was concrete, 200 million pesos. But the codex was unique, which meant there was no established range for its price. It was literally priceless. There were four other Mayan codices, and none had been sold in the last hundred years. The two hundred million peso figure came from some quick research he'd done on the Waldseemuller world map of 1507, which the Library of Congress bought for $10 million US. An original copy of the U.S. Declaration of Independence had sold for $8 million US. The Waldseemuller map was the map that gave America its name. And to be honest, the codex was much more beautiful. It was also, although there was no need to say so, more relevant to the heritage of most of his customers. Undermining its value was the unfortunate fact that it was contraband. The usual discount for artifacts that circumvented the antiquities laws was 50%. But again, that applied to lesser objects where there was ample precedent. And there would be the inevitable haggling. Perhaps, Alessandro thought, he should meet Delia later at the market as promised, for the practice.

Chapter 39

Alessandro Sussero

Alessandro did not recognize the number when his cell phone rang. "Hola."

"Hola, Señor Sussero. This is Leon Cortes's secretary. Señor Cortes would like to meet with you regarding some antiquities you have for sale. Would nine AM tomorrow at his home be convenient?"

Alessandro thought of El Gato.

"Señor Sussero? Would that be a convenient time?"

"Can I check my calendar and get back to you?"

"I'll hold while you check. Señor Cortes is a busy man, but this is important to him."

"One moment." Alessandro resisted the impulse to throw the cell phone away. It wouldn't matter. Cortes would find him. He considered leaving the country. But he suspected he was already being followed. "Tomorrow at 9 AM would be fine. What is the address?"

Alessandro tried to consider his options, but the picture from the news interposed itself. He'd dealt with powerful men before – in fact he only dealt with powerful men; some, like the late El Gato, were narco bosses. Selling pre-Columbian artifacts to killers came with the territory. Even the crudest of them wanted to burnish their reputations and elevate their status with some trinket from their heritage. But not so soon after a brutal murder which, if rumors and common sense could be trusted, Cortes had orchestrated. The doctor who had first seen the corpse had lost her breakfast, if reports could be believed. He would go to Cortes. He would leave the codex in the safe deposit box. He told everyone he could trust of the upcoming meeting. Though not a religious man, he went to church.

******

"Apparently you are a busy man too, Señor Sussero, so I'll come right to the point: you have a Mayan codex. How much is it worth?"

"It's difficult to say, Señor Cortes. There is a problem with its age. If it were 800 years old, it could be worth $20 million US. But radiocarbon tests suggest it's almost 1500 years old. That would make it worth considerably more. But these tests also call into question its authenticity. The Mayan codices were all thought to be around 600 to 800 years old. This upsets much of what we thought we knew about the development of Mayan writing."

"What's your commission on the sale? 10%?"

"It varies. 10% is the average and customary commission."

"The codex doesn't belong to you, does it?"

"No."

"The person who commissioned you to sell it is dead, isn't he?"

"Yes."

"Who will pay you your commission?"

"Whoever inherits it from Señor El Gato."

"But it doesn't really belong to El Gato, does it? It belongs to the people of Mexico. Don't answer. We both know the problem here."

Alessandro waited. *Where was this going?*

"It doesn't belong to you. El Gato is dead. What's to be done?" Cortes smiled. "I have a solution. We will backdate the sale from El Gato to me. I'll pay the 10% commission – clearly El Gato isn't going to pay you. Turn the codex over to me – I assume it's in a safe place somewhere. In fact, El Gato and I had agreed on the sale a while ago. Now it will be awkward for you to explain commission on contraband of this value, so we'll call it a consulting fee. You advise me on my antiquities collection. I'll show it to you some time – you'll be impressed. I'll give you $500,000 US now as a retainer. The rest when you've given me the key to the safe deposit box and I verify the contents."

Cortes passed him the check. Alessandro sat frozen, the check in front of him. He felt it was wrong to look at it, it would signal some level of distrust, or worse - disrespect - for Leon Cortes.

Cortes bailed him out: "Go ahead. Make sure I spelled your name correctly."

Alessandro looked, but not at his name. He looked at the amount: 5 million pesos. $500,000 US. He was used to checks for large amounts: $500,000 US was not unusual for an antiquity. What was unusual was to see the amount made over to him. He put it in his pocket, suddenly aware he'd been looking at it for some time.

"Have I spelled your name correctly?"

Alessandra managed to say "yes," although he had no idea.

"So you'll tell me the name of the bank and we'll make an appointment to visit it."

"Yes, yes of course. Excuse me. Banco Mexico."

"Shall we meet there tomorrow at 10 AM?"

"Yes, of course."

"I'm sure you're busy. I'll leave you to your affairs." Cortes rose and shook Alessandro's hand. "Tomorrow then."

Chapter 40

Det. Benito Rufino

If Maribel could be believed, McNeery and El Gato and his bodyguards had been killed for a Mayan codex. He'd known that Leon had ordered El Gato's murder, now he knew why. But where was the codex? Why was it so valuable? He drove. He found, when he stopped to think about it, that he was on his way to El Gato's hacienda, probably the last place on earth he should visit if he wanted to keep a low profile. Still: he needed to talk to the help, if they were still there, and whichever one of El Gato's girlfriends was in the residence. He wondered who would be manning the guardhouse. He pulled over half a mile before the entrance. He checked his gun. Then he got back into his car and did a k turn so that it was on the other side of the road and facing away from El Gato's. He pulled his hat lower on his face and walked toward the hacienda.

It was hot. It was late morning, and the heat was already full upon the day. There was no question of cutting through the jungle to the house – El Gato would have established a perimeter with wire, surveillance, possibly booby-traps.

The police were in the guardhouse. Two young officers he didn't recognize. When they saw him they stood up, rested their hands on their carbines. Rufino said, "Hola."

The taller guard said, "Hola."

"Where's Luis?" Rufino tried to sound confused.

"Who are you?"

Rufino gave him his prepared answer: "I owe Luis money." He pulled a carefully folded wad of small bills from his pocket. "Where's Luis?"

"Dead. Where have you been? El Gato too."

"Mother of God!" Rufino fell to his knees and began to pray. Then, when he finished, he stood and dusted his pants. Then he started walking towards the house.

"Can't you hear? He's dead."

"But I must pay my respects."

"His body is buried."

"Still, I must pay my respects even if only to his housekeeper."

The guards looked at each other. The wad of bills was still in Rufino's hand.

"You'll steal something."

Rufino said, "No. Never."

"Leave your money as collateral. We'll frisk you when you come back."

Rufino pressed the money into the taller guard's hand. "240 pesos." Then he walked up the stone drive to the house.

When he rang the bell, the housekeeper he remembered from his previous visit answered. He barely recognized her. Her face was puffy from crying. He took her hand. "I'm sorry for your loss."

She remembered herself. "Come in. Can I get you some coffee?"

"Yes, please."

She led Rufino to the same table in the courtyard where he'd had coffee with El Gato before. It was cooler here than outside in the sun, but still warm.

"Make a cup for yourself and sit with me awhile," he called out to the kitchen.

A moment later the housekeeper return with two cups of coffee. Rufino pulled out a chair for her and she sat down.

She said, "I know he did some bad things, but for it to come to this? He was always kind to me."

Rufino nodded. El Gato dealt drugs, sold women and guns, loansharked, and enforced criminal activities with brutal beatings. Yes, in a manner of speaking, he did some bad things. Apparently he'd been nothing but kind to his housekeeper. Rufino sipped his coffee "Thank you."

"You know who did this to him."

Rufino couldn't tell if this was a statement or question. He said: "Who do you think did it?" He made a question, with some difficulty.

"Cortes, that pig."

"Why Cortes?"

"No one else would dare. No one here, anyway. It had to be someone from outside. Someone powerful. Most people deferred to El Gato, but El Gato deferred to Cortes. He was here once, you know. I mean Cortes. Gordo. A fat man."

"When was he here?"

"A couple of weeks ago."

"Was it the last time?"

"No. He had the nerve to come to pay his respects after he killed Señor Catalan."

"Did El Gato go to see him?"

"I don't know. I keep this house so I know who comes here. I don't know where he goes when he goes out. I mind my own business."

Of course you do, Rufino thought. She was afraid now. He couldn't blame her. El Gato, his driver, two bodyguards – all dead. She knew these people. She'd served them hundreds of meals. Had cleaned up after them. Had experienced their charm.

"Why do you think Cortes killed him?"

"Who knows. Money. It's always about money. Or respect. Maybe he felt that Señor Catalan was disrespectful towards him. Who knows? He was a pig. Does a pig need a reason?"

"Even a pig needs a reason. Did El Gato ever mention a book? Something from the archaeological site?"

"I saw it. It's not like a book. It's much bigger. It smelled bad. I complained to him about the smell. He said, laughing, 'We should all smell so bad.'"

"What did he mean?"

"It was worth a lot of money."

"Do you know where it is?"

"No. His friend, the effeminate one, has it."

"The effeminate one?"

"The antiquities dealer."

"You know his name?"

"Of course. I didn't call him the effeminate one to Señor Catalan, or to his face. His name is Alessandro Sussero. You're interested in this book. Is that why you think Cortes killed him – that stinky book?"

"Maybe. Like El Gato said: we should all smell so bad. Thank you for the coffee."

On the way out Rufino remembered he still had to be frisked at the guardhouse. Then he remembered his gun. This will be interesting, he thought.

He walked slowly toward the guard station, his head down as if trying to look invisible. But the police saw him and came out. Only one held a rifle, the other, the one who was apparently going to frisk him, was unarmed. They told him to stop.

Rufino said to the guard with the rifle, "El Gato left something for me." He held a small ring before him. When the guard bent forward to look Rufino drew his gun and brought it hard to the man's temple. "Put down your gun. Give me my money back. Fucking incompetents."

Slowly the guard took a wad of pesos from this pocket and handed it to Rufino.

Rufino said: "Handcuff your partner, in front." He did as he was told. Rufino turned to the handcuffed man. "You handcuff him now."

The guard objected: "The handcuffs."

"You can still do it. If I were to shoot your hands off, then maybe not. You can manage."

The handcuffed policeman fumbled, but finally handcuffed his partner. Rufino said, "Now walk towards the house. Don't look back. I see your face, I'll shoot it off." They walked slowly towards the house. Rufino grabbed their rifles and walked backwards, watching them, as he went to his car.

Chapter 41

Det. Benito Rufino

Rufino considered his options, which were considerably fewer, now that he was officially on leave. He knew he couldn't go back to the junkyard, and any evidence he found would be "lost." He thought of paying Xavier at the forensic lab a visit, but that would turn ugly - he wanted it to turn ugly – and he knew it was a waste of time. The lab, his friend, were in Cortes' pocket. He decided to pay a visit to the family of El Gato's dead bodyguard.

Luis was survived by a young widow. He drove to her home in Valladolid.

"I'm Benito Rufino." He watched as Luis' widow, Maribel eyed him cautiously.

She asked "One of El Gato's?" She spit.

"No, Señora"

"Then who?"

"I used to be police. No more. I'm sorry for your loss. I want to find the man that did it."

"Leon Cortes did it. The stupidest child in school knows that. So I just saved you a search. Now what are you going to do?"

"May I come in?"

Maribel gestured toward the room with her head. He followed her into a living room of heavy furniture, bright orange and purple cushions.

She asked, "You want some coffee?"

"Yes."

She indicated a chair and Rufino sat. She went to the kitchen and returned with two mugs. "Con Leche?"

"No. Black is fine." He took the mug from her hand. He sipped, waiting to see if she would speak. She sipped her own coffee, seem to find it distasteful. She put it down. "What are you going to do? You could shoot him in a church – I hear he's a regular church goer."

"That's an idea. But won't that make it harder for him to go to hell?"

Maribel seemed to pause to consider the theological implications. Then she said: "Who cares. Shoot him in church."

Rufino wondered that she didn't do it herself. She was a small woman, but there was something sharp about her. She seemed all edges. He couldn't picture her with a gun. A knife, perhaps. He said, "It's an option I keep in my back pocket. Why did he ambush your husband and El Gato?"

"We weren't married. Luis and I weren't married."

"I thought… I didn't know."

"It's okay. Better this way. Why did he ambush them? Who knows? Some squabble over money. Luis didn't bring the work home – to protect me. He'd tell me stories – silly things, stupid things that went on – but nothing important. El Gato had a complicated romantic life – he'd tell me about that – women hiding in closets, like a farce on TV. Stuff like that."

"You think that's why he was killed – over a woman?"

"No. Are you kidding? Over a woman? We know our place. No, it was over money or something like that."

"What about the American that was killed? Did he ever talk about that?"

"The American who was killed by a jaguar? Prof. Jaguar – that's what Luis started calling him. I said 'hush.' It wasn't funny. But it was. He comes all the way to Mexico. A professor. A smart man. Gets killed by a jaguar."

"He wasn't killed by a jaguar."

"I know. Everybody knows. But it's helpful – it frightens the children, keeps them from playing in the jungle."

Rufino considered the woman before him. Despite her claims to the contrary, she knew things Luis had told her, or that she'd overheard. She was the sort of person who liked to be in the know. Also, she was trying to impress him. He said, "The police think it was a jaguar."

"The police would think it was Santa Claus if they were paid enough. 'Oh, look sleigh marks, and what's this – a red cap.'"

Rufino smiled, nodded slightly, to egg her on.

"Look, this scat must be reindeer shit. That proves Santa Claus did it. Case closed. We can't arrest him; he's from the North Pole. We don't have an extradition treaty with them. But wait, maybe we can blame an elf, or a local boy who was naughty."

"So who killed the professor?"

"You are not paying attention. I explained: Santa Claus killed him. Or maybe one of his reindeer, or Santa's helper."

"Are you okay?"

"No. Luis is dead. Santa Claus is dead." She stood up, searching for some dramatic gesture, when nothing came to her, sat down again.

Rufino asked, "El Gato is Santa Claus?"

"Around here, he knows who's been naughty and who's been nice."

Rufino nodded. "I always thought so. I just never knew why."

Maribel said "The book."

"The book?"

"A Mayan book."

"What kind of Mayan book?"

"Ask the archaeologist, Professor Jaguar."

Chapter 42

Prof. Owen Sterling

Professor Owen Sterling's secretary knocked as a warning and then stuck her head in the doorway. "We've got a problem. There's a Mexican kid here to see you and he won't go away."

Owen gave his secretary a look that he hoped said *this is the sort of problem you're supposed to solve without bothering me.*

"A student?'

"No. I don't think so. He doesn't speak much English."

"Is he looking for work?'

"I don't know. I don't think so."

"I have, conservatively, about fifty things I have to get done in the next hour. Send him to someone else. Send him to admissions. They can give him a tour."

Shelly's look said, *Don't you think I tried that.* But she vocalized it, just to be sure: "I tried that. He doesn't understand or he just won't go."

"So call security. When he sees the uniforms he'll leave."

"He's quiet, but kind of agitated. I don't know — he's kind of freaking me out." Shelly stepped into the inner office.

Now their roles were effectively reversed: she'd made it his job to protect her from this unwanted visitor. Sterling asked, "What am I going to say to him? I don't speak much Spanish." But he found himself getting up from his desk. "Where is he?"

"In the corridor. I told him he had to wait there."

Owen considered. He wasn't young, or particularly strong, but he was tall. Sometimes that, and an imperious manner were enough. He walked past Shelly's desk and opened the door to the hall. He saw a short stocky boy, dark, with straight black hair. He looked to be about sixteen. "I'm Dr. Owen Sterling. How can I help you?" He tried to sound as unhelpful as possible.

"I am Humberto Perez."

They looked at each other. The boy said "Yucatan dos mil doce"

"In English, por favor."

The boy pushed a piece of paper at Owen.

Owen looked at it. It took a moment for the coordinates on the paper to make sense. Then he asked, "Who sent you?"

The boy before him looked blank. He said again "Yucatan dos mil doce"

"I don't understand."

The boy grabbed a pen from the desk and wrote "Yucatan 2012".

Owen shouted over his shoulder to Shelly: "Get someone up here who speaks Spanish."

"Security?"

"Anyone but security. Do it now."

Humberto considered the lanky Norte Americano standing before him. He'd assumed the professor would speak Spanish. Professors in Mexico spoke English. His assistant had been sent – for the police, for a translator – Humberto couldn't tell. The professor seemed confused.

"Agua?" The professor was offering him a bottle of water.

"Gracias." He took it and twisted it open. He drank, and then offered it to the professor. Outside, Maria was waiting for him. He'd seen signs in English and Spanish everywhere and he'd assumed language would not be a problem. He wished now he'd learned a little English to go with his Quetchen and Spanish. Too late. He wished that Dr. Owen Sterling, who'd had more educational opportunities than he'd had, had learned a little Spanish. He heard footsteps and looked quickly down the hall. If she brought the police, he would have to run. He'd seen

American police on TV. Some were fast. The slow ones would just shoot him. He saw the professor's assistant and another woman. Not police. The woman with the professor's assistant spoke to him: "Hola. Me llamo Inez. Lo traducire."

"Policia?"

"Yo no estoy con la policia. I am not with the Police. She looked at Owen and repeated this in English.

Owen nodded and said "No police." He turned to Inez. "Ask him if he is Yucutan 2012 who sent me the new star coordinates."

Inez asked him in Spanish.

Humberto said, "Si. Si. .Me llamo Humberto. Soy Yucatan dos mil doce"

Owen: "How? How do you find the new stars?"

Inez translated. Humberto replied with a torrent of words.

Inez translated: "Every night, I look at the sky. I go outside the city, to where it is very dark. I have a Questar. A gift from a friend. Once in a while, I see something new. The Questar is a very good telescope."

Owen paused. Then he said, "Wait here." Inez translated while Owen went into his office. He returned with a large rolled up piece of paper. He unrolled it and asked, "Do you recognize this?"

"Si."

"What's missing from it?"

Inez looked at Owen. Owen said, "Please translate my question."

Inez indicated the chart and asked Humberto Owen's question. She gave Owen a hard look.

Humberto understood he was being tested by a man who claimed to be a professor and couldn't even speak Spanish. He looked at the chart and pointed to a blank spot in the constellation Orion. Then he looked at the professor. He did not understand the look on the professor's face at first. It was blank. Then he saw a smile. Owen spoke to Inez.

She said in Spanish: "Welcome to America and the University of New Mexico."

Humberto noticed the professor's outstretched hand. He shook it. "Gracias."

Inez started to translate. Owen stopped her. "I know. 'Thank you'." To Humberto he said "Denada."

Humberto spoke to Inez. She translated for Owen: "He has a friend waiting downstairs. He'd like to bring her up here if that's okay. He doesn't like the way the boys are looking at her."

"Of course." Owen nodded yes to Humberto. To Inez he said, "Ask him if he'd like you to go with him."

She spoke, and Owen watched Humberto shake his head. Owen had a moment of misgiving: what if Humberto decided to run? He reminded himself that he'd come a long way, and had probably endured a great deal to get here. Still, the boy was skittish. Not that he blamed him. He watched Humberto leave the office.

Inez verbalized his thoughts. "He's probably come here illegally. You know that. Or you should. Her tone suggested that she'd come here legally, or been born here.

Owen said: "Did you see that? Do you know how many people in the world can do that – pick out a missing star from a chart with thousands of them? I can't. No one I know – which is to say most of the astronomers in the world – can do that. There's one guy in Australia who can – maybe. And this kid. For all I know he may be on earth illegally."

"Where are he and his friend going to stay?"

"With me, until I can figure out something else."

"How will you talk to him? Or am I staying with you too?"

Owen considered. "I guess it's time I learned Spanish."

Owen looked out of his window, hoping to catch sight of Humberto. Instead he saw a random cross-section of the UNM student body. Most were talking in small groups or on cell phones. They were, mostly, good kids. Many were eager to please; a few were eager to learn. None would, in their entire lives, accomplish what this poor Mexican kid had already accomplished – find three new stars, or the equivalent in whatever their chosen field of endeavor. None had a gift remotely approaching Humberto's. And yet all were here and safe, by an accident of birth. He would learn a little Spanish. It was the least he could do.

Humberto returned with a pretty, petite young woman who seemed not so much timid as in a state of shock. Humberto introduced her as his friend, Maria.

Owen looked at Inez. "Please tell her she'll be safe here."

Inez spoke, and Owen realized that what she said was a bit different: "Professor Sterling says you'll be safe here."

Chapter 43

Det. Benito Rufino

The smart thing, and the safe thing, would be to alert the Antiquities Police. Tell them Alessandro Sussero had in his possession a Mayan codex. But Rufino knew how that would end – certainly not with the exhibition of the codex in the Museo Nacional de Antropologia in Mexico City. More than likely this antiquities theft would be pinned on Humberto. Some in the antiquities police were honest, but none were competent. Moreover, the codex was germane to his murder investigation. Investigations. For now both McNeery's and El Gato's killers needed to be brought to justice.

Rufino drove. On an isolated stretch he slowed the car, rolled down the window, and threw the police rifles out. Back at his apartment, Rufino searched the web in vain for Alessandro Sussero. There was no webpage. Of course not – a man who routinely handled rare objects and large sums of money would keep a low profile. And yet, this man had to be known to the circle of potential clients: wealthy families looking to buy and sell artifacts. A word-of-mouth business. Rufino was pleased to deduce that the way to get to Alessandro was through someone from a wealthy family, and for him that meant Dr. Isabel Reyes.

He dialed her number. He was surprised when he heard her voice: "This is Dr. Reyes."

"Hello. This is Detective Rufino." He felt that by using his title he had a better chance of keeping Dr. Reyes on the line.

"Yes?"

"I need your help."

"Have you been hurt?"

"No, why?"

"That's usually why people need a doctor's help."

"I need to find an antiquities dealer."

"So you called me, Sherlock Holmes? It's hard to believe crimes go unsolved in this country."

"I called you because your father is wealthy. An antiquities dealer needs to keep a low profile, but he has to be known to potential clients. Can you find out if your father knows Alessandro Sussero, and how to reach him?"

"Is this about McNeery?"

"Yes. And El Gato. And Leon Cortes. And Humberto."

"I'll see what I can find out." She hung up.

Later that day Rufino got a call back from Dr. Reyes. "He lives in Merida. My father doesn't know where, he comes to my father's when they meet. His phone number is - have you got something to write with? 999- 924-7821.

Rufino repeated a number. Then he said "Thank you."

"Don't mention it."

"One more thing. I expect I need a referral. May I say I know your family and that's how I got the name?"

"Are you going to say you're a detective?"

"No. I'll pretend to be a collector, Venezuelan by birth, but living in Mexico. Is there anything special I should do to establish credibility?"

"Have your secretary call, not you. And no, I won't pretend to be your secretary."

"I'll be yours." Rufino waited for a response. When none came, he continued: "I can't pretend to be rich - I don't have the money. But you don't have to pretend. So I'll be your – not secretary – but your agent, your..." Rufino was fumbling for the right word. He wanted to say bodyguard, but knew it was not the word he wanted. He was hoping Dr. Reyes would come to his rescue.

She said, "Business manager."

"Yes, that's good."

"No, it's not. And I'm not rich."

"But you're from a rich family. The point is, people treat you like you're rich and you act rich – you have that air."

"So you're not going to be a wealthy collector from Venezuela?"

"I can't pull it off. We both know that. I don't have the clothes, the car, the hacienda."

"The charm, the arrogance, the sophistication."

"I could probably manage the arrogance." He was hoping to lighten the mood. "I'm surprised this Alessandro hasn't approached your father about the codex. He's a collector, no?"

"Yes, he's a collector. But not when the item comes with a couple of murders as part of the provenance."

"I meant no insult."

"People never do." She sighed. "Say you work for me. Keep my father out of it. He'll offer to come to your - that is - my home, or to meet at a restaurant. Meet at a restaurant. Get some business cards with just your name and phone number and a leather case to put them in. At the restaurant, don't worry about the expense - he'll pick up the tab. Order little or nothing, and one drink only. Stick to business. Say as little as possible – you're my ears, not my mouth. You say you can manage arrogance, but arrogance is mostly judicious silence. If you need to commit me to a meeting, that's fine – I'll break the commitment later.

He's used to that. Actually you'll break it later for me. You're representing me so dress accordingly – that is to say respectfully and businesslike. Please tell me you own at least one good suit that fits properly."

"More than one."

"Don't do that. Don't try to prove anything. It shows insecurity. If he's condescending – and he will be – respond with a hint of impatience. To him, you're a flunky; but to you he's just one line on a list of errands, and you've got other things to do for me. Remember, you can bring the meeting to a close at any time by suggesting he meet directly with me. That's what he wants and when he gets it, he'll stop buying you tequila."

There was a pause

Reyes said, "Are you still there?"

"Yes. That was judicious silence."

"Goodbye Detective."

"Goodbye Doctora. And thank you."

Chapter 44

Det. Benito Rufino

Rufino called Alessandro's number. As expected, he got an answering machine with a polite but short message. He left a name – Señor Cortezar – that he'd chosen because of its similarity to Cortes. He was hoping for confusion, if confusion would get him a message meant for Cortes. When a day passed and he didn't hear back he wanted to call again. He called Reyes. She explained that that was impermissible. He had wanted to mention the codex in this message, but that too was impermissible. This enforced coyness didn't suit his temperament. He told Reyes so.

"Why don't you just say you're a detective pretending to be my businessman? Would that suit your temperament? Your temperament isn't the issue. Play the part."

A day later Rufino received a message on a cell phone he'd bought specifically for this return call. Alessandro apologized sincerely but briefly for the delay in getting back to him. He conveyed his best wishes to Dr. Reyes and her family and suggested a meeting time the next day. Rufino called Reyes. "Do I accept the time offered, or do I have to be coy?"

"You accept. Briefly. Politely, but briefly. You are busy managing things for me, remember? Putting it off means you can't cross it off your list."

"What do I say I'm looking for?"

"Mayan. Something unusual. Not stone. I've got plenty of stone. Explain that the family is contemplating some renovation and were looking for a centerpiece. That will let him know that this isn't some bauble, but a major piece that we're looking for. Then you won't need to say anything about price."

"And then?"

"And then he'll thank you and promise to get back to you when he has some items that might be interesting."

"If he asks questions?"

"He won't. But since you worry, just say you don't know. But he won't. He'll presume that he can better gauge my taste than you can."

"You're serious?"

"Yes. All you need to say is 'renovation' and 'major piece' and you're done. He'll eventually come back at you with a small catalog, maybe the codex or reference to it will be in it. If it isn't, we'll say nothing fits the bill."

******

Rufino met Alessandro at El Templo, a small restaurant on the Calle 59. He was pleased to see that Alessandro was on time. At least he assumed the tall, thin to the point of sharpness man in his mid-40s was Alessandro. "Señor Sussero?"

"Yes. Señor Cortezar?"

Rufino shook the offered hand, found it small but it's grip firm. A waiter seated them at a table under a jacaranda tree and left two menus printed on thick sheets of paper. They ordered drinks: Alessandro had white wine, Rufino/Cortezar had Petrone straight up. Alessandro looked at the menu and suggested the sea bass. Rufino found himself assaying the recommendation for any hint of condescension. He wasn't sure, but decided he would have steak, rare, just to assert himself. In his mind he could hear Dr. Reyes disapproval. The truth was, he preferred steak to fish. He asked Alessandro if he lived nearby.

"Not close enough to walk, even on a nice day, like today." Rufino/Cortezar had tried to make the question sound casual, but he really wanted to know. Perhaps he hadn't been casual enough – he'd gotten an evasion by way of an answer. He decided it didn't matter, the codex was probably not in his home, but stored in a vault somewhere.

"Do you collect yourself, Señor Cortezar?"

"No. My wife buys handicrafts at the market." He decided the safest path was to keep to the truth when answering questions. "Every surface in our home is already covered with knickknacks."

He saw Alessandro nod sympathetically. "Some of the handicrafts are wonderful. Have you been to the market at Oaxaca?"

It was Rufino/Cortezar's turn to nod. He thought to himself, this will be okay. If Alessandro was patronizing him, it was subtle and he could ignore it. The waiter came and took their orders.

"Can you give me an idea of what Dr. Reyes is looking for?"

Rufino/Cortezar shrugged. "I don't think she knows herself." But she's redoing the library and she wants something to act as the focal point. To be honest, I'm hoping that means more to you than it does to me."

Alessandro nodded.

"Oh," Rufino/Cortezar added, "no stones. She said she's got enough of those."

Alessandra smiled. "How big is the library?"

"Fair sized. 10 meters x 8, I would estimate."

"You said no stones, but how about jade?"

Rufino/Cortezar shrugged. "Jade is a stone, technically speaking. But it's not what I think of when I think of stone." Rufino/Cortezar assumed that Alessandro had brought up jade to begin to establish the price range. He took a sip of his tequila. The liquor warmed him and he found himself beginning to enjoy this. "Jade's a possibility," he said meaning, he hoped, that the object being sought could be expensive.

Alessandro said, "To be the focal point, it would need to be a large piece – a bowl or ceremonial headdress."

Rufino/Cortezar watched the hypothetical price range go up, and nodded his agreement. He watched Alessandro sip his wine. Rufino/Cortezar felt the urge to steer the conversation to books – he felt Alessandra had missed the hint, but he remembered himself and waited.

"I'll put together some jade pieces, and a couple of other items. Maybe a surprise or two. Give me a couple days and I'll give you a catalog of ideas to take back to Dr. Reyes."

In the "take back" he heard a faint rustle of condescension, but he let it go. "That would be helpful."

The waiter brought their meals.

Chapter 45

Det. Benito Rufino

Two days later they met again, for coffee, and Alessandra handed Rufino/Cortezar a thin notebook with several glossy pages of artifacts and information. Most were elaborate jade pieces. There was one stele, whose presence Alessandra excused on account of its quality, size, and rarity. There was no codex. Rufino nodded his thanks and left. He called Reyes. "He's not suggesting the codex as we'd hoped."

Reyes said, "I'll tell you what. Come to the clinic and do my job so I can do yours. Maybe he doesn't have it. Where else have you looked?"

Rufino said, "He has it. Maybe he doesn't think you can afford it."

"My father has, I don't know, 10 billion pesos. Alessandro knows that, even if you don't. He knows because it's his job to know. You haven't made it clear how much we're willing to spend. So give him his book back, explain that while nice, there's nothing remarkable here; I barely looked at it. Explain that the library is my father's favorite room. Tell him to try again."

Rufino expected to hear her hang up, but there was silence on the line. Then he heard her say, "Benito, all that attitude I just gave you, let just a little seep through when you talk to Alessandro. Right now you're thinking, 'I'll show that bitch' – I want him to think that too."

****

Rufino/Cortezar called Alessandro and told him Dr. Reyes wanted something else.

Alessandro said simply, "The library. Of course. What Señora wants is a book. A Mayan codex. The only one not in captivity. Rarer than the Gutenberg Bible or the original copy of the Magna Carta."

Rufino/Cortezar said, "Yes. Gracias, Señor Sussero."

****

Rufino was on the phone to Reyes. "He has it."

"You've seen it?"

"I have pictures. He emailed a little catalog to me – for you actually."

"How sweet. How much did he ask for it?"

"Price was not discussed."

"Of course not. First, he wants me to commit with my interest."

"He made a point of how rare it was. Rarer than a Gutenberg Bible, rarer than the original Magna Carta."

"So he did discuss price."

"I don't understand."

"By mentioning those other antiquities he's establishing a floor value. He's saying, in effect, this is worth more than either of those. If you look up the price of those items you will understand what the minimum price is for the codex."

"What difference does it make? We'll agree to some price, and when he shows up with the codex I'll arrest him."

"And how do you imagine this sale will take place? You'll meet him at a highway underpass with a briefcase full of thousand peso notes?"

Rufino was caught off guard. He couldn't visualize the buy, except vaguely and in terms like Reyes had just described. He asked, "How do you usually buy contraband antiques?"

"Generally, people like Alessandro feed their clients a fancy meal. Then they adjourn to a bank safe deposit vault, where the antiquity is inspected. If it's suitable, it's moved from one deposit box to another. Months later the new owner retrieves it from its box and brings it home. Are you still there?"

"Yes." He was trying to imagine how the police would intercept such an exchange. It would require the unlikely cooperation of the bank.

"Problem?"

"Yes. There is a danger to you."

"Not to me. I won't be there. My agent will be there. I wouldn't see this artifact until it's ensconced in my father's library. He won't be there either."

"If I'm the agent, then it's perfect. I'll do the bust."

"You'll be in an underground vault of a major bank, and you'll pull out a gun and your badge and shout 'Policia'? Maybe you'll scare Alessandro. Guards will come when he screams and they will shoot you. Then, like the artifacts, they'll leave you down there for a month and then they'll stick you in the trash. This is your plan?"

Rufino considered the scenario Reyes described. While overly cynical, it had the general ring of truth. He thought he could outshoot a bunch of bank security guards, but that wasn't point. It wasn't much of a plan. It stunk. Reyes had merely pointed the stink out. He said, "So we let the sale go through. The codex goes from Alessandro's safe-deposit box to yours and then we arrest Alessandro."

"And the 100 million pesos that we've paid to Alessandro?"

"We freeze accounts, you get your father's money back."

"Just that easy. I don't think that's what happens. You arrest Alessandro. He's out on bail in an hour. The money is already in Switzerland, or the Cayman Islands – someplace where you can't touch it. Instead of his money back my father gets an apology from the chief of police. Maybe he doesn't even get that."

"So what's your plan?"

"Let him sell it to Cortes. Then confiscate it. Let Cortes worry about getting his money back. Alessandro will rush over with a cashiers check the next day, if he's still alive. But it won't happen, because no one is going to take anything from Señor Cortes."

Rufino was about to object but he heard Reyes hang up.

Chapter 46

Dr. Isabel Reyes

When she hung up, Reyes felt the first familiar pangs: the ache in her joints, the fever. She decided to work through it and treated a woman with second-degree burns that the woman claimed was a cooking accident, and which Reyes suspected was abuse. Next she diagnosed and treated an ear infection in a four-year-old girl. And then, her own aches too strong to ignore, she told her nurse that she was not well, and not to let any more patients in that day. She took ibuprofen for the pain and treated a dehydrated infant, a woman with severe menstrual cramps and yet another dehydrated infant. She asked the next patient "How are you?"

The patient responded, "How are you? You look sick."

"I'm okay. Tell me why you're here? "

"You're not okay. I'm no doctor, but you're sick, and I just have a cough that won't go away. I'll have it tomorrow and I'll come back then. You should go home."

"I'm sorry. You're right. I don't feel well. Come back tomorrow. I'll see you first."

The woman went to pat her hand, thought better of the contact, and left. Reyes collapsed into a chair. She took a mirror from her desk drawer and looked into it, hoping to see what her patient had seen. Then she understood the reason for the amateur diagnosis. Her face and hair were glazed with a sheen of perspiration. Even her blouse was beginning to soak through. Her eyes were sunken in their ocular cavities. Her pallor, while far from white, was a bleached version of its former self. She looked like shit, one didn't need a medical degree to come to that diagnosis. She stumbled into the examining room, crawled onto the table and fell asleep.

When she woke, it was afternoon. Reyes had a moment of terror: the examining table, the examining room all momentarily unfamiliar. Had she undergone surgery? Then a wave of reassurance washed over her as she remembered. Her head and joints ached. She wanted to move, but lacked the strength or the will or some crucial combination of the two. Incapacity frightened her. She felt in her lab coat for her cell phone. Whom would she call? After some fumbling she found her phone. She scrolled past the last numbers dialed – Rufino, her folks, until she came to the Rabbi's number. She selected it and called.

"This is Simon."

"This is Isabel."

"Are you okay? You sound terrible."

"Another bout of Jewishness. Can you come over? I'm at the clinic."

Simon was going to say something smart, but answered the question instead: "I'll be right over."

She hung up. She supposed her receptionist had locked up. She would have to get up to open the door. It seemed like an impossibility. She tried to turn on her side. She wanted to go back to sleep. And what would be the harm in that? She forced herself to her side. She was sweating again. She forced herself to sit up. She was dizzy and had to pause. She slid off the table, leaned against it for support. She was wobbly, but then some old muscle memory clicked in, and she was able to walk. She reached the wall and found the light switch. The sudden brightness hurt – her head, her joints – how was that even possible? – and she leaned against the wall with her eyes closed. She opened them and began to adjust. She walked to the front of the clinic and unlocked the door. And she collapsed into a chair in the half darkness and waited for Simon.

Chapter 47

Alessandro Sussero

On one level, Alessandra did not relish the thought of telling Leon Cortes there was another bidder for the codex. It complicated things, and it meant there would be at least one disappointed client when negotiations were over, probably two. On another level, two bidders meant a higher price; and on still another level, Alessandro wanted to see Cortes' supreme confidence ruffled. Alessandro did not like the man – his showy piety, his presumption, his physical coarseness. Alessandro did not think Leon Cortes would respond well to his news, and that's why Alessandro had summoned the nondescript man that now sat with him in his casita. The man before Alessandro was of medium height and build, of unremarkable appearance; Indian in feature, not Spanish; with dark straight hair. He was dressed in blue jeans and a guyambana, and he wore a Padres baseball cap. He looked like a gardener. He went by CC Almeda. Alessandro thought one of the C's stood for Carlos. He was Alessandro's body guard. Alessandra had summoned him to explain that he needed to heighten his vigilance. He was about to piss off someone powerful and he wanted CC to know.

CC listened with a blank look that Alessandro always found unnerving. CC looked at pictures of Leon, Leon's known bodyguards – Alessandro stressed "known" – and added "of course there are others."

Still, CC betrayed no emotion.

Alessandro went on, repeating himself, made talkative by the intensity of CC silence and his own personal agitation. Finally CC's silence proved contagious and Alessandra stopped talking.

He had hired CC years ago, after a particularly nasty mugging. The muggers were amateurs; they'd taken his wallet, but not his keys and had administered a gratuitous beating. It all happened so suddenly that Alessandro hadn't had time to reach for the gun he carried. If he had, it most certainly would've been used to kill him. When he got out of the hospital he made inquiries and found CC.

There had been another mugging attempt. CC had stepped out of the shadow and crushed one assailant's knee and hit the other's face with such force that it dislodged one of his eyeballs.

After that, the muggings stopped.

Chapter 48

Alessandro Sussero

Alessandro called Leon. He explained that a second party had shown interest. He downplayed that party's interest, but encouraged Leon Cortes to make an offer if he was interested. Then he could tell the other party the codex had been sold, and steer him to a different piece. He explained to Leon that he was not interested in a bidding war – "these things never turn out well" – all he needed was a fair offer from Señor Cortes. Would he like to see the codex again?

There was a moment of silence, and Alessandro wondered if Leon and even been listening. He did not want to repeat himself. Then Alessandro heard Leon on the line: "No, I don't need to see the codex again. Thank you for your candor. You'll have an offer shortly."

Alessandro tried to imagine what Leon meant by "shortly," and decided he would give him a couple of days before he had the same conversation with the Cortezar/ Rufino.

A day later a large envelope arrived from Cortes. At first Alessandro was surprised – he'd been expecting a call or regular envelope. And then he understood: enclosed would be a sales contract drawn up by lawyers, full of stipulations about authenticity and provenance, terms. He smiled as he hefted the envelope, felt its weight. Bullshit, but necessary bullshit from Cortes's point of view. He'd heard this about Cortes, that in his legitimate business dealings he was scrupulous, even fastidious. He couldn't buy a case of toilet paper without drawing up a contract.

He opened the envelope and saw the edge of a glossy photograph. Had Leon taken a picture of the codex? How was that possible? The thought had barely congealed in his mind when he found himself looking at the severed head of Javier, mounted on the hood of his car. The next picture showed a bloody canvas sack on the sidewalk in front of Dr. Reyes' clinic.

Alessandro felt dizzy. He put the pictures and the envelope down. He sat down – collapsed – into a chair. His heart beat frantically as if it were being squeezed by a rough hand and trying to escape. The room itself began to beat, in time with his heart. He closed his eyes and tried to will himself into a state of equilibrium. Finally he opened his eyes and looked at the rest of the envelope. He skipped over the remaining pictures looking for a note. Nothing.

He reached for his cell phone and called CC. There was no answer. He tried again. And again. He looked at his watch and started calling CC at five-minute intervals. He checked the lock on his door. He retrieved his gun, sat facing the door, and resumed his calls to CC.

Finally, an unfamiliar voice answered. Alessandro asked, "Who's this?"

The unfamiliar voice responded, "Who's this?"

"I was trying to reach CC. I must have the wrong number." A wave of relief passed over Alessandro. In his panic he dialed the wrong number and had been hitting redial since.

"Who's this." The voice demanded.

"I'm sorry, I have the wrong number."

"This is the police. Who's this? We have your number, so you might as well identify yourself."

Alessandro paused. So CC had been arrested. He discounted the possibility that CC had just done something wrong – more likely the arrest was for some old crime. He knew some of CC's past – that's why he'd hired him – and CC was no Boy Scout. "Has CC been arrested?"

"No. He's been killed. Since you seem to know him would you come down to the police station and identify the body."

"I'm not well. Can you describe him to me over the phone?"

"Señor, it will only take a minute. I realize this is unpleasant – he was your friend, no? – But it must be done. We're Calle 47 near Calle 16."

"Give me a minute." Alessandro hung up. He poured himself a glass of tequila and drank it down. He took his gun and holster, changed his mind and put the gun in his pants. He took another drink and left.

The sun and the liquor hit him at once when he went outside. He staggered, grabbed the rail and retched. When he was done he went back inside to rinse his mouth and put on his sunglasses. He walked slowly at first, then quickly to the street the officer had given. He saw the flashing lights reflected off the windows of parked cars even before he turned into the street. Halfway down there were five or six police cars and officers in bulletproof vests with "Policia" printed in yellow. Most wore masks that covered their faces – so he knew they thought this was drug-related. He regretted bringing his gun. He would explain; he hoped they would understand. Most of the police held automatic rifles. He forced himself to walk purposefully towards the nearest masked officer.

"I'm Alessandro Sussero, I was asked to identify the victim."

The policeman nodded, grabbed his upper arm and led him to the car. Alessandra recognized CC's Land Rover right away. He could see something splattered on the inside of the windshield and then he realized it was the inside of CC's head. He stumbled, and the officer held him up. "It's his car." Alessandro said. The officer stopped, but kept his hand on Alessandro's arm.

"Okay. But you must still identify the body. I'm sorry."

Alessandra let himself be led forward. He recognized CC from the back, and wanted to say so, but he knew he would have to look at his destroyed face.

"Do you know this man?" A second masked officer asked.

There was a gaping hole where CC's forehead used to be. CC's face wore an expression Alessandro had never seen before and couldn't describe. He nodded. "That's my bodyguard. CC Almeda.

"Thank you."

Alessandro felt as if he'd been turned inside out. An officer accompanied him, silently propelling him through the bright hot streets. Alessandro thanked him when they reached the door to his home, or he thought he did, hoped he did. Later, he couldn't remember. The officer had said "There were no signs of torture. Professional courtesy."

That he remembered. He couldn't get the words to leave. "Professional courtesy."

He knew he should call Leon Cortes. Instead he drank, and retched, and drank some more.

At 10:30 there was a knock on the door. He froze. There was a second knock and he heard the doorbell ring. Then he thought he heard whoever was there leave. He couldn't be sure, so he waited. He moved silently through his house to the upstairs window that looked out on the door. He pulled the blinds open a bit and peeked through. There was no one at the door, just a FedEx envelope. He looked again, not trusting his own sight. Then he went downstairs and retrieved the envelope.

Inside, with the door locked, he pulled the tab to open it. Instead of pictures there was a small envelope. He opened it. There was a check for 5 million pesos and a note: "This is your commission for the article we discussed. Collecting is a small world, as I'm sure you know. It so happens I know the owner and will pay him directly. I know it's the seller who usually pays the commission, but in this case the arrangement I negotiated with the seller stipulates that I pay it. My agent will collect the article this Tuesday, May 25 at 11 at your bank. You will bring a copy of this check as identification. Thank you for your help in arranging this transaction. Sincerely, Leon Cortes."

So that would be the date they put on his headstone: May 25. He would meet Leon's agent at the bank, turnover the codex and sometime later that day end up with his brains splattered on the windshield of his car. Or worse: he did not expect to be shown "professional courtesy" as his profession wasn't murder. He could refuse the meeting. Leon needed him alive. In that case he would be kidnapped and tortured. This was the point where sensible people in sensible countries went to the police. His was not a sensible country.

It occurred to Alessandro to leave it. Go somewhere else – Spain, where he had friends, or Argentina. The United States. But whoever had killed CC was no doubt watching Alessandro's own casitas right now. He resisted the urge to go to the window and peek out. He considered El Gato – a man wise in the ways of this world – and how he had ended up. It occurred to him to have himself arrested. Call the antiquities police. He couldn't very well go there – he would be shot on the steps – but they made house calls, especially in a case like this. He might still be killed in their custody – even by them. He poured himself a shot of tequila but hesitated. He needed his wits about him. He let the glass sit on the coffee table. Tomorrow was Sunday. He had three days.

He paced the room. He looked at the glass of tequila and drank it. At first it dulled his fear. But then it irrigated a new feeling, as the dark bud of his anger began to bloom. He'd liked CC. They weren't good friends, but their frequent proximity had led to an easy camaraderie. And now CC had been murdered, just to make a point. He gave himself over to the full scope of his hatred for Leon Cortes. Cortes was a bully, and evil, and murderous, like his namesake. He – Alessandro – shouldn't be trying to run from him. He should be running at him, guns blazing, to avenge his friend. He poured and drank another shot of tequila. He was a dead man – he knew it. Why not take Cortes with him? Alessandro had gone about his business, an occasionally shady business, without once feeling the need to kill anyone. He had competitors, and he let them live. He had obnoxious clients, and he let them live. He had customers he wanted to kill – who didn't? – and he'd let them live. He managed, like most of his fellow men, to go through life obeying the commandment "thou shalt not kill" and really, it wasn't so difficult. Cortes however, that churchgoing hypocrite, killed as casually as another man would send an email. Alessandro hadn't liked El Gato – had been afraid of him to tell the truth – but El Gato was a prince, an angel, compared to Leon Cortes. He poured another shot but didn't drink it. He needed his wits about him if he was going to kill Leon Cortes.

Alessandro recognized the stages of grief in himself, not grief for CC, but for himself. He was as good as dead. He'd double-crossed Leon Cortes and in Leon's world that was a capital offense. El Gato had multiple bodyguards and was a street tough hombre, and lucky to boot, and look how he'd ended up. Alessandro had one bodyguard, now dead, and had grown up protected in elite boarding schools. Leon Cortes, on the other hand, had been raised by wolves – or so it seemed. It was hard to imagine the upbringing that created such a monster. No matter. Once he accepted the inevitability of his death, Alessandro found he could begin to plan. If you accepted your death, your actions had considerably more latitude. Leon Cortes was no doubt making plans too, but they didn't contemplate this. People flee when hunted; they don't run towards their hunters. Leon Cortes would never see it coming.

Alessandro's first thought was to ask for a meeting with Leon. The problem, Alessandro realized, was that Cortes had no reason to meet with him. Even with the codex as bait, Cortes would send an underling. The actual transfer – deep in the bowels of the Bank of Mexico vault – would be between Alessandro and someone other than Leon. An arranged meeting was out of the question. Unarranged then. A chance encounter. The only part of Leon's routine that Alessandro knew was his Sunday mass at the Church of Santa Maria.

Chapter 49

Alessandro Sussero

Alessandro realized his more immediate problem was escaping his own home. He was being watched; he was certain of it. He didn't think they would kill him until they had the codex, but there was nothing to stop Leon's men from kidnapping him, and torturing him until he gave up the key to the safe deposit box. He'd give it up in a second – and they would torture and kill him anyway.

He wanted that drink now. He had a long day of waiting ahead of him.

He would have to sneak out at night. He could climb from roof to roof – the houses were conjoined. At some point he would have to climb down to the street, but he thought he could manage that. The tequila, he realized, had given him an improved sense of his athletic ability. It had certainly fortified his courage. He looked at the glass on the coffee table, but then he looked away. He'd need to be sober tonight, and he knew the glass on the table would lead to another, and then another. He had to stop drinking now. He grabbed the glass and poured it down the sink. It was an empty gesture - he knew well enough where the bottle was and could easily pour himself a replacement. But that would take an act of will, or at least an act.

He watched a soccer match. He made himself a light dinner. He considered a drink – one drink – but decided against it. He left the TV on in the bedroom as he gathered his wallet, passport, checkbook, cell phone. He put on sneakers and a jogging outfit. He tried to read, and when that didn't work he tried to watch TV, and while he couldn't settle on a program, skipping from channel to channel distracted him. He watched the highlights from the afternoon soccer match. Finally, when he judged it late enough, after midnight, he left the TV on and climbed the stairs to his rooftop patio. It was dark, but not as dark as he would've liked. He crept to the wall and peeked out at the street. He saw a cat dash across the road. He thought of El Gato – he couldn't help it. A chest high wall separated his patio from his neighbor's. The neighbor's patio was empty. He pulled himself over the wall. It was harder than he thought. He walked carefully but quickly across to the next wall. He resisted the urge to check the street. He pulled himself over. The next wall was lower and he cleared it quickly. He was sweating now. His plan was to get to the end of the block. He assumed they would be watching both the front and back of his casita, but that the end of the row of homes would be out of their sight.

He had one more wall to scale before the end of the block. The wall before him was higher than the others, and as he got closer he could see the top was embedded with broken glass. He couldn't believe it. He understood these broken glass parapets on the walls facing the street, but facing a neighbor's patio? It looked like the remains of a bar fight frozen in concrete. He could make out broken bottles and shards of what look like plate glass. The wall was perhaps a foot wide, and there were several rows of this jagged glass. He would have to turn back and go the other way, but he suspected a similar obstacle along that roof top path. The end of the block was in sight. Just this last wall. He was sweating hard now. He heard a noise and strained to hear better. Something small scurried across the patio. He looked around. The roof patio had a permanent grill. There was a round table and wrought iron chairs. The chairs had pads, but they were thin. Still, he considered them. There was a chaise lounge with a pad. This one was thicker. He couldn't tell from where he stood if it was full of air or something more substantial. He grabbed the thin pads from the chairs and piled them on top of the wall. He pressed down tentatively and the broken glass poked through. He took the pad from the lounge. It was canvas and seemed to contain foam, not air. He added it to the pile of seat cushions. He heard the scurrying sound again and stopped. In the silence he heard a door open below and saw light escape from the open door. Then, above his heart beat, he heard the door close. The light disappeared. He carried a chair to the wall and wedged it to it. He stood on it and considered: there was no way to walk over the wall – it was still chest high, even as he stood on the chair. He would have to breast himself over, as he had the others. He looked around for something else, anything else. Nothing. He heard what he thought were footsteps below. He pulled himself onto the wall. He could feel the lumps that the protruding glass made in the pad. He considered standing but the pads were too lumpy and he feared concentrating his weight. He got to his knees – tentatively and turned around so we could slide down on the other side. As he began to back down over the edge, the pad slipped. He managed to break his fall with his feet, but there was nothing he could do about the noise. He tried to listen but all he could hear was his own panic. A dog barked, somewhere up the street and a second dog answered.

There was one more wall, also covered in broken glass, and a two-story drop to the street. The barking dogs made it impossible to hear any other sounds. He grabbed the pads and carried them to the opposite wall. The smaller pads were in shreds and larger pad was gashed deeply. He found a flower pot and bashed the glass teeth of the far wall down. He put the pads down and carried a chair over. He pulled himself up onto the pads and felt a sharp pain rip his chest – the glass. He rolled away from it, cursing. He got to his knees and turned. He planned to climb down using the window ledges, but he was in a full panic now and his feet found no purchase. He thought if he let go he could slow his fall by hugging the building. The barking continued. He let go.

Alessandro hit the ground with a jolt of pain. He was surprised to find he could stand and walk. His ankles throbbed. The jacket was jogging outfit was soaked with blood and he realized he needed to go to a hospital. He looked around. The end of the block was empty. If he could make it to the plaza he thought he could find a taxi, one that would take him to the hospital.

When he approached, the taxi driver rolled up his window and drove away. Alessandro looked at his jacket. Of course - the blood. Nobody wants their taxi covered in blood. He took out his cell phone and called Delia. It was late and he would be waking her. He had not wanted to put her at-risk, but now he felt he had no choice. He looked around. No one else seemed to be out, except a couple of teenagers who paid him no mind. They're involved in mischief of their own, he thought. Finally he heard a groggy voice on his cell.

"I'm sorry to call so late. I need your help. I'm okay, but I had a little accident and I need someone to take me to the hospital. I'm at the plaza, the corner with the newsstand."

Delia's voice was awake now: "I'll be right there."

"Delia, bring something to cover your seat. I'm a little bloody."

Minutes later he saw her car. He looked to see if she'd been followed. When she saw him she pulled over and started to get out. He said, "Stay in the car. I can get in by myself."

He eased himself in the passenger side. "Just go to the hospital." He saw the horror on her face. "I'll be okay. It's just a cut. A nasty one, but just a cut."

Finally she said, "Did someone do this to you?"

"No. I did it myself. It's a long story – for another time. Thank you for coming."

Chapter 50

Ex-Rabbi Simon Press

As he arrived at the clinic and knocked, Simon's cell phone rang. Instinctively he answered it. The voice at the other end said, "It's open, just come in."

It took Simon a moment to realize that it was Isabel on his phone. He opened the door.

"Here." Not the phone this time but Isabel's actual voice. He saw her slumped in a chair. Her hair, except for some stragglers, was caught up in a tight bun. He thought she looked like a seedy ballerina and said so.

"I'd like some soup. Can you heat up soup? And I'd like to be distracted. Can you distract me? And the next time you see me, when I'm feeling better, I will be so fucking gorgeous you'll go blind. The kitchen's that way. I'm sorry, thank you for coming. I should've said that first."

Simon realized it was this imperiousness in Isabel that fascinated him, the way she acted like the queen of some country she'd temporarily misplaced. "You're welcome. I can heat up soup. And by 'seedy ballerina' I meant of course a blindingly beautiful seedy ballerina. A Dégas." He thought he noticed a smile.

"In the fridge."

He saw a plastic container of dubious liquid, that by his own process of elimination had to be soup. He opened several cupboards until he found a bowl and after the contents had been poured and flopped into the bowl he put it in the microwave and nuked it. Then he put the bowl on a plate, found a spoon and carried it to her.

"Should I feed you?"

"No." But she made no move to eat. Then she said, "Yes."

Simon sat next to her and began to feed her soup.

"That's enough." He watched a thin smile form on her face. " I'm going to be sick, get me that bowl." She pointed a large turquoise plastic bowl. He reached it and handed it to her.

She took it and threw up. She wiped her mouth with a tissue and handed him the bowl. "Bathroom's through there."

Simon took the bowl and emptied it in the toilet. He rinsed it and emptied it again. He returned and asked, "You have nurses that work for you – why isn't one of them here? Not that I mind. Just asking."

"There's nothing they can do for me."

"You should drink some water." He looked around for water as he spoke.

"In the fridge."

"Should I get a cup?"

"No. I can drink from the bottle." Isabel took a sip.

Simon offered her a plastic basin. She shook her head, pushed it away.

He said, "Should I take the soup away?"

"Yes, that would help."

When he returned from the kitchen he said, "I'm mainly here to distract you. The waiting on you hand and foot is just a bonus, not really what I came over for. Since you're feeling particularly Jewish at this moment, I thought this would be a good time to start your education. Okay?"

He watched her roll her eyes.

"Good. There's a Jewish tradition that when you learn something we give you a taste of honey – to reinforce the notion that knowledge is sweet. We're probably going to have to forgo that this time. But in the future..." He looked to see if even the mention of honey was going to make Isabel gag.

"Okay. Let's start."

Simon began with the Sabbath, and how to keep it. Then the laws of kashreth, and how to keep them. Isabel asked, "Do you keep them?"

"I'm reformed. So I don't keep them. You should understand what I'm reformed from."

Finally she indicated she'd had enough.

"Shall I go?"

"No. Enough Judaism for one day. Let's talk about something else."

"Maybe you should teach me something."

"Medicine?"

"No something simple."

"Like what? What simple things don't you already know?"

Simon said, "I've always wondered how it is that women make a decision to sleep with someone."

"I would be a traitor to my gender if I told you that. How do men decide?"

"We pretty much want to sleep with everyone. There's no decision involved."

"Surely you're more discriminating than that."

"Barely."

Isabel considered the question. "You're asking as if it is a premeditated decision."

"Isn't it? You're asked on a date. You say yes – to the date – and you're aware they'll be a moment on the date when your date will ask you back to his apartment. You prepare. You bring birth control, or protection. You choose to wear sexy undergarments – or you don't. All because you plan to say 'yes' or 'no.'"

"This is what you imagine?"

"Yes. In the absence of any real information. Am I wrong?"

"What if the man doesn't ask me back to his apartment?"

"I can't imagine that. Maybe he's shy; maybe he's afraid of being refused. But that's beside the point. The decision in most cases is yours. So how do you make it?"

"You think I sleep with men on the first date?"

"If you don't, that's part of your premeditated decision process. That's what I want to understand. But not just you – well you of course – but women in general. How do your friends decide? Do you talk about this?"

Simon watched Isabel appraise him, as if he'd asked a trick question. Or as if he were the clever prosecutor, and she the reluctant witness, with some choice piece of information she was dying to withhold and he was dying to extract.

Simon said, "Start with your friends, if that's easier."

"I feel like I'm betraying my sex."

"Why? Wouldn't dates go better for both parties if men knew this? Wouldn't they act less like jerks?"

"Some of my friends have sex just to get the date over with."

"I don't believe that." He smiled. "But give me their names anyway."

"You ask a serious question, and then you joke about the answer. This is when we get up from the table, go to the lady's room and change into our granny panties."

"Why isn't it okay to joke about serious things? Those are the things we most need a sense of humor about. The silly stuff takes care of itself."

"Because a joke lets you avoid the serious answer. And it's a serious answer you want, isn't it?"

Simon considered. "Yes, it is. So how about you? I promise not to make a joke about your response."

"I can't believe I'm going to answer this."

"But you are?"

"Yes. First, I listen to my heart – do I want to? Then I try to think of any reasons why it will be a bad idea, and the unfortunate consequences."

A pause. Simon felt it, "Consequences like what?"

"Consequences like is he married? I won't sleep with a married man. Is he healthy?"

"Healthy as in disease-free? Or healthy enough for sexual activity, as in you don't want to screw him to death? I'm not making a joke – I'm asking for clarification." He watched Isabel consider him.

Isabel shook her head. "You're impossible."

"No, I'm not. I can understand your not wanting to end the evening by causing a macro cardio infarction – however much that might enhance your reputation. How would you know if the man was disease-free? Isn't that a chance you take; isn't that why you insist on a condom?"

"I don't want to have sex with someone who's dying."

"Oh." Then, "Why not?"

"It would break my heart."

There was a silence between them. Finally Isabel said, "Why don't you ask what you really want to know."

"Which is?"

"Will I ever sleep with you?"

"Okay. Will you? Not now of course – you're not feeling well enough. Not soon – because you think I'm a jerk. But someday?"

"Maybe. Look, I know you mean well, Simon, but you wear me out. I think I can sleep a little."

"I can stay, make you some soup when you wake up."

"I'll sleep better if you go. I'm sorry."

"I can come back."

"That would be nice. I'll call you."

Simon let himself out. He meant to make some clever parting remark, but none came to him. It was late afternoon and businesses were reopening. He bought corn on the cob from a street vendor and settled on a park bench in the plaza to eat it. He wanted a proper meal, but didn't want to eat alone in a restaurant. The sun was bright, and brightness seemed to have its own weight. Not because of the heat – that had its own weight – or the humidity –

likewise – but the very brightness seemed by its intensity to cross from being a visual pressure to a visceral one. The weight of that brightness made him tired. Tourists wore sunglasses to lighten the load, but he did not want to seem to be a tourist. He would bear it, as he bore the heat and humidity. Perhaps because it was so unlike the daily gray of Dublin. And you could duck out of this sun's weight, whereas the Dublin gray followed you inside. He entered a cantina and ordered a Corona. He considered that no one had tried to kill him recently – not since the sack of broken bones and flesh that had been El Gato had been deposited on the sidewalk in front of Reyes's clinic. It seemed reasonable to assume that El Gato had been behind the first attack on him. And that El Gato had killed McNeery. Or someone working for El Gato. So that much justice had been accomplished. As for justice for El Gato's killer, he could only hope that those who lived by violence died by it and that Leon Cortes would get his in the normal scheme of things. Or not: he knew that most senior thugs lived to ripe old ages, too powerful to meet the fate they routinely dealt out to others. He had a chance with Isabel Reyes – a more pleasant line of thought – and he thought about how he might turn her "maybe" into "yes." He ordered a second beer. He looked outside to where the light baked the plaza. He thought of Humberto and Maria and allowed himself to worry a little on their behalf. He assumed that most people who tried to sneak across the border either succeeded or failed but remained alive. And with all these thoughts he discovered his sense of noble purpose leeching away until he was forced to think about his own scholarly work and McNeery's. He wondered why McNeary hadn't simply handed over the codex when threatened. Had he even been given the chance? He decided he would work a little. He paid for his drinks and left. He paused at the door to let his eyes adjust and then he shouldered the weight of that brightness and walked back to his apartment.

Chapter 51

Alessandro Sussero

At the hospital, Alessandro took over 40 stitches. Against the advice of the young resident, he refused to stay.

The resident persisted: "You've lost a lot of blood. There's the risk of infection. If you move about there's a chance you'll reopen the wound. Are you sure you don't want to file a report with the police?"

This last question, Alessandro was sure, was just a ploy to get him to stay. People did not file reports with the police in Mexico. Surely the young woman who had stitched him up knew this. Reluctantly she wrote him a prescription for Levaquin, a broad-spectrum antibiotic. "Any possible redness around the wound and you must come back here for a different antibiotic."

"Of course." By which Alessandro meant no.

Delia frowned. "What would it hurt to stay overnight?"

He took her arm and led her away. "We need to get this filled quickly."

"Are you going to tell me what happened?"

"I locked myself out. I was climbing over one of those glass embedded walls trying to get in the roof door and I cut myself."

"Are you crazy? Why would you do that?"

"I had a mattress to protect me against the glass – never mind. It didn't work out as I planned. So yes, I'm crazy. There is a pharmacia over there. Stop, okay?"

She stopped the car.

"Wait here. I'll only be a minute." Alessandro started to get out of the car, moving gingerly, surprised at how much the slightest movement made his world blaze with pain.

"Sit. I'll get it." She took the prescription from Alessandro and got out of the car before he could protest.

Alessandra heard the car, but didn't see any lights.

He saw Delia stop at the sound. A large man in a black ski mask jumped out and grabbed her. He threw her over his shoulder. She screamed, and then a second man hit her hard in the face. Alessandro saw him turn and stare for just a second before he jumped back into the car. The first man pushed Delia into the back seat and got in after her. Alessandro heard the car slam into gear and it was gone.

He sat there frozen. Then he remembered the gun. He was immobilized a second time by shame. He could've shot the sons of bitches. He still could. He started to get out of the passenger seat and was thrust back by the searing pain. He was breathing hard. Slowly, he tried again. The pain was there, but he was almost ready for it. He slowly got out and moved to the driver side. He lowered himself in against another flood of pain and put the gun on the driver seat. He backed up without looking around – turning his body was an impossibility – and then drove in the direction he'd seen the car go.

The cell rang. He started. *Who?* he thought, but then he knew. He tried to answer but no words escaped his mouth. The voice on the other end said, "I'm a merciful man, but not, it seems, a patient one. Nor am I a fool. Because of a prior business arrangement with the late El Gato, the item you are trying to sell me is already my property. It is in your possession and I would like it turned over to me, its rightful owner, Monday, when the bank opens. Is anything I just said unclear to you?"

Alessandro uttered a hoarse "No."

"Good. Go home. Get some rest. I'll send the car for you on Monday at 10."

No mention of Delia. No need. Alessandro understood. He understood too, that while Leon might let Delia go once he got the codex, no such mercy would be extended to him. He had tried to cheat Leon Cortes. That was El Gato's crime, and it was El Gato's fate that awaited Alessandro. He knew Leon's retribution was always tailored to the victim; he tried to imagine what his own would look like. The mirror of some vice. He had always been kind to animals and women; in fact women were his only vice. This punishment, his slow death would be connected in some way to lust. He shuddered as he considered the prospect of painful castration. In the morning at eight Leon Cortes would go to Mass. Alessandro resolved to meet him there.

The stitches itched. Possibly this was the beginning of an infection. He shrugged inwardly – this was the least of his worries. He was tired. As his adrenaline ebbed he felt prickly and exhausted. He wanted to sleep and knew he couldn't. The itching from his stitches turned into a painful throb. He went into the pharmacy and bought Motrin and bottled water, then took twice the recommended dosage. He drove, not home, but towards the Church of Santa Maria and tomorrow's mass.

Chapter 52

Alessandro Sussero

Alessandro drove through the night – first away from Merida, and then, when he was sure he was no longer followed, back. He planned to sleep a few hours when he got back, in his car if need be. He gobbled a couple more Motrin. He remembered the church, and imagined hiding out in the nave or the pews, waiting for Leon's arrival. He was no crack shot, he would have to get close to Leon in order to shoot him, and he had no idea how to do that. Or rather, he had many ideas, none of them good. While the church was large, and mostly empty in the morning, he did not think he could successfully hide in it, even if he arrived in the middle of the night. If Leon saw him, his bodyguards would be upon him instantly. He wouldn't mind killing a few of them for what they'd done to CC, but then Leon would escape. Perhaps he could sit praying in the first pew, disguised in some fashion. Leon always sat in the first pew. He thought briefly of the Godfather movie. He could arrive at the church early and tape the gun under the pew. Then ask to join Leon at prayer. Make a groveling apology. Then reach for the gun under his seat and shoot Leon between the eyes. He wasn't sure he could retrieve the gun and fire in a single swift motion. Far better to step out of the shadows, aim and squeeze off as many shots as it took to kill the son of a bitch.

He continued to drive, and to think. He could sit with the beggars, gun hidden under a dirty serape, face covered by a wide brimmed hat, an alms basket in his left hand. The regulars would resent him, he expected. Leon would recognize that he was an interloper, even if he didn't recognize him in any other way. So what? By then it would be too late. He would buy the grungy clothes he needed from some beggar. It was easier to think about the costuming than the deed itself. He tried to rehearse that in his mind: he bends over to put a few pesos in my basket and I bring the gun up and shoot him in the face. He knew, viscerally, that the simplicity of his imagining did not match the deed itself. He would practice: he would sit and bring the gun up and pretend to fire it. The image that came to mind was ridiculous. Something a child would do.

The bell tower of Santa Maria caught the new day's light first. Alessandro stood beneath it, shivering a little in the morning chill. He wore a dirty serape and a straw hat that had seen better days. He'd traded his sneakers for sandals made from old tires. He looked down the tower, into the shadows that girded the rest of the church. At the bottom, near the massive wooden doors three old Indian women slept: small, crooked, hair the color of pewter. He was tired himself, but alert, his skin buzzing with adrenaline and fatigue. He looked at his watch. It was not yet seven. He removed the watch from his wrist and stuck it in his pocket. Mass was at nine, and Leon was usually prompt. Although he would be dead in two hours, Alessandro was hungry now. He walked in search of food. He passed several places that were closed and finally found a small bodega. He bought rolls and an orange and a cup of coffee. He thought of buying food for the three crones that slept outside the church, thought again, and finally decided he'd share what he'd bought for himself if they were awake when he returned. He looked back at the bell tower. The sun had slid down a ways, a quarter of the tower was now in light.

He ate quickly, in spite of his intention to savor this, his last meal. He did not return immediately to the church. He explored the side streets. He had begun, he realized, to plan an escape. He would shoot Leon and run down this street, and this one, eventually losing his pursuers. He would hide here, or there. He looked back at the bell tower, where the sun now illuminated a full third. He found himself reconsidering. He would throw himself on Leon's mercy, in church before God and priest and congregation. Give him the key to the codex deposit box. He would see Delia safe. He would seek the sanctuary of this very church. He looked back at the tower, where he could watch the light slide down, a tier of stone at a time. He took his watch from his pocket and checked: almost eight. He put it back on his wrist: he planned to consult it frequently. He could not make up his mind about the gun. He would leave it – or not. He tried to imagine Leon's point of view. Could Leon afford not to kill him? Would that mercy be regarded as weakness? Would Leon ever consider letting him live – was his death so dictated by the circumstances as to be beyond deliberation? The church – the bell tower was now half light half shadow – couldn't save him. Leon's thugs would simply escort him outside to a waiting SUV and then to whereever Leon took people for slow killing. Fear froze him like a stone. His heart pounded in his chest like it meant to break out. A bit of his breakfast came up, burning his throat, and then he was retching violently onto the street.

Alessandro stood, bent over, a vile taste his mouth. The only person he was capable of killing, he realized, was himself. And he didn't have the stomach for that either. Reflexively, he checked the time. First he looked at the bell tower, almost 3/4 light, and then at his watch: 8:35. Then he walked, like a zombie, back towards the church. He bought some oranges for the crones. He handed them out silently; accepted their dull gratitude, and seated himself next to them. They ate and ignored him. He took that as an omen. For all his anticipation, he was surprised when the black SUV pulled up to the steps. He watched as Leon Cortes, the black-suited bulk of him, got lightly out of the back seat. He felt his heart begin to beat insistently inside his chest. Leon mounted the steps purposely, reaching inside his jacket for pesos. He seemed at first to notice Alessandro, and then to dismiss him. He gave a few pesos to each of the crones. Alessandro raised his own empty basket. Leon said, without rancor, "My friend, you should work."

"You should die." Alessandro said it softly, not sure if his words even broke the surface into sound, or whether they stayed in the depth of his throat. Leon Cortes stopped, and looked at him with an expression that seemed to Alessandro quizzical. Alessandro did not feel like the author of what happened next: the gun was in his hand, he pointed it at Leon Cortes and squeezed the trigger. The recoil startled him, as if out of a sleep, and he fell backwards. There were shouts, but no screams. Leon stood there, as if deciding something. Then he saw Leon fall towards him. Alessandro tried to fire another shot. Leon was on top of him, pinning him to the ground. A moment later the gun was ripped from his hand. A blazing pain shot through him as his finger was ripped almost from his hand with it.

Slowly, incredibly, Leon rolled off him. And then he stood up. Alessandro heard Leon mutter his thanks to God, and saw him make the sign of the cross. Two men, or three, he wasn't sure, dragged Alessandro to his feet. His hat was gone now and Alessandro watched the recognition grow on Leon's face.

Leon turned to the crowd that had now formed and said, "Mother of God, I'm okay." He turned to Alessandro, and shook his head. Alessandro saw a dismissive pity in that shake. Then Leon made a gesture to his bodyguards and Alessandro was dragged to the SUV and driven off. He tried to console his damaged finger, but the guards held his arms. The beginning of his torture, he thought, and tried not to imagine worse.

The SUV drove through poor neighborhoods to even poorer ones, neighborhoods of shacks and shanties, and then to buildings that seem to be warehouses and adjacent to them, junkyards. They brought him into a warehouse where tile was stored. Alessandro smelled the diesel fumes from forklifts and the stale odor of stored air. After the air-conditioned SUV the warehouse was hot. There was a bit of light from windows high in the wall. The floor was tamped earth. He barely noticed. His hand was throbbing, his trigger finger dislocated and all but torn off. They did not tie him up. Instead they dictated that he should sit on the floor. One of his guards drew a circle on the floor with toe of his boot. "Don't leave this," he said. Alessandro stood a moment in the circle, and then sat. The guards sat at a table nearby and played dominoes.

Alessandro expected to be tortured. And he was certain he would be, eventually. But now he was just ignored. He considered running, but was certain they would catch him. One of the men left the table to take a piss. When he returned, he stopped in front of Alessandro.

"Let me see your hand." He said it gently, and Alessandro held is mangled trigger finger out. The man touched carefully, but Alessandro still felt a shock of pain and winced.

The man acknowledged his pain, asking "It hurts?"

Alessandro nodded, not trusting his voice.

The man nodded back and grabbed the finger and pulled it off. The black jolt of pain flooded Alessandro and he passed out.

When he came to later, Alessandra saw the men at their dominoes, and his finger on the ground, inches from his face. The man who had ripped it off looked up from his dominoes gave him a brief nod.

A cell phone rang and another man at the table got up and crossed the warehouse to the door. He pulled it open and the white light poured in. Behind the light was another black SUV. The SUV drove to the center of the warehouse, to the dominoes table.

Leon Cortes got out. He gave Alessandro a look Alessandro could not read. He spoke to the man who had torn Alessandro's finger off. "It's like being hit in the chest by a fastball. Hurts like hell. Leaves a big bruise. I'll be okay. Thanks for asking." Then Leon turned to Alessandro. "Give me the key to the safe deposit box."

Alessandro expected the question, but more speech with it. He said "It's in my apartment." The truth, although he didn't know if he would be believed.

"Give me the key to your apartment and tell me exactly where the safe deposit box key is."

With his undamaged hand Alessandro took his keys from his pocket and handed them to Leon. He said, "It's in the top left drawer of my desk. My desk is in the study, the room with all the books." The apartment, the study, the desk, and his books all seemed to belong to someone else now.

Leon took Alessandro's keys and handed them to one of the domino players. The player, tall and heavyset like Leon, got into the SUV and left the warehouse. Leon turned back to Alessandro: "I hope he comes back with that key."

Chapter 53

Det. Benito Rufino

When two days passed without a returned call from Alessandro, Rufino decided to watch Alessandro's apartment. He watched from the roof of the building across and down the street. He saw the SUV pull-up and two men let themselves into Alessandro's apartment: Cortes' thugs. He knew from their thick necks and tight suits. He was off the roof in an instant and in his car, waiting to follow them.

Barely five minutes later, Rufino watched as they left the apartment. One, an older, bullet-headed thug with a Chinese ideograph tattooed on the back of his neck was talking on his cell phone. The other, younger, but with the same weightlifter's thickness got into the driver side of the SUV. Rufino gave them a block lead. He had the license plate if he lost them. He caught sight of them a block later. Rufino followed, several cars back. Soon they crossed into the shanty town and then the industrial district of junkyards and warehouses. There was less traffic, and Rufino registered dismay as the last car between him and the Black SUV turned off onto a side street. Rufino turned at the next intersection. He turned again and ran parallel to the SUV's direction – if it didn't turn. He rode for two blocks and then turned again, hoping to find himself once again behind the SUV, but the road was empty. He drove on, hoping to catch sight of the SUV parked by one of the warehouses. He found himself hoping that Alessandro was being held at a warehouse and not a junkyard. Of course they would hold him inside a building; they would only move him to a junkyard when it was time to drop a ton of scrap metal on his head. He drove on, slow enough to sneak sideways glances at the warehouses and their parking lots. Some held tractor-trailers, some beat up old VW's. Then he caught a flash of a dark car in the mouth of a warehouse for roofing tiles. The door closed on it. Rufino drove by and pulled into the next side street and left his car. The street was empty. He checked his service revolver.

Rufino considered the warehouse. There was a small door near the opening the SUV had disappeared into, secured by a chain and padlock. There would be other doors, other chains and locks. High up, just below the roof, there was a row of small windows – barred glass. The large door opened and Rufino watched the SUV drive out.

Rufino waited for the door to close behind. And waited. Nothing. This glaring lapse in security seemed less a lapse when Rufino considered his approach: he couldn't very well walk across the lot into the open door. He'd be a perfect target, his dark body a silhouette against the bright noon sun. If he snuck up on the opening hugging the wall, he'd be looking into a cavern of darkness. Possibly there was no one inside, he thought, and quickly ran back to where he'd parked his car.

Rufino paused a moment when he reached his car. If they were armed – and of course they were armed – his Corolla would offer very little protection. But he had to get inside, and he preferred to drive. He turned the ignition and drove slowly by the warehouse. The door was still open. He turned into a deserted street and drove back. He accelerated when he turned into the lot and continued to accelerate right into the warehouse. He braked hard. The contrast with the bright outside light made it impossible to see. He took off his sunglasses. The dim interior was empty. He saw a card table and chairs. When his eyes adjusted he got out of the car. He could see the dominoes on the table. On the ground, where he instinctively looked for signs of a struggle, or blood, he saw only a crude circle scratched in the dirt. He cringed: there was a bloody finger in the circle. He placed it in a plastic bag. Forensics would confirm what he suspected – that it belonged to Alessandro.

He took a quick look around. While it was likely that the rest of Alessandro was in the SUV, there was a possibility of finding his body here. He was hoping not to find it piece by piece. He walked, gun drawn, by pallets of orange roofing tile. He looked at the dirt floor for signs of blood. What little light there was filtered down from the high barred windows. He saw what looked like a small windowed office at the back, beyond the pallets of tile. He inched toward it. There was a desk light on, the only artificial light in the warehouse. A pallet of tiles blocked the door. He looked down the aisles of pallets for forklift as he approached the office. There had to be one but it was probably near the entrance. He heard a muffled sound. On the floor, curled up in a fetal position was a woman, hands and feet bound with gray duct tape. She was curled away from him; he couldn't see her face. He grabbed a tile from the pallet and smashed the office window. The woman contracted, but made no effort to look at him. Rufino said quietly "police," and hoisted himself through the broken window. He smelled urine. He could see the same gray duct tape on the side of her face as he turned her. Her eyes were wild with fear. "Police" he said, louder this time. He tore the tape from her mouth and a sound between a sob and a scream came out. He pulled the tape from her hands. "Who are you? Who did this?"

She could not speak. He continued to unwind the tape. When her hands were free she covered her face with them. He removed the tape from her ankles. "How long have you been here?"

The sobs became a whimpering, then a whisper. "Water."

At first Rufino didn't understand. She touched her lips.

Water. He looked around. There was no cooler in the office. He had a bottle in his car.

"In my car. Can you walk?"

She stood slowly. He went to help her but she shied away.

"Be careful of the glass." Reluctantly she let him help her through the broken window. She hung back, waiting for him to lead. He walked toward the light at the end of the warehouse, gun drawn. He looked back occasionally to see that she was still following. He reached the car and handed her a bottle of water. She shook as she held it. She drank slowly at first, then more greedily. "Delia. My name is Delia. Can you take me home? They left me here, on the floor, for a day, tied up. Do you understand what I'm saying? Take me home. I need to clean myself."

"You won't be safe at home."

"Then you stand guard. What have they done to Alessandro?"

"I don't know. Do you know why they took him?"

"They're criminals. He has money. Is it so hard to figure out?"

Rufino open the car door for her. She hesitated. Rufino saw this and said "Don't worry about it."

Rufino drove to the address she gave. When they arrived, he said, "Wait here. Do you have your key?"

She shook her head. "They took my pocketbook. It was in it."

Rufino checked the street and then went into the building and up the stairs to the apartment number she gave. The door was closed, but not locked. They'd been here, as he suspected. He turned the knob and pushed the door open with his foot. He took a quick look and pulled back. The apartment was a mess but appeared to be empty. He entered with his gun drawn, went room to room. He returned to the car and got Delia. "They've ransacked your apartment but no one's there now. What were they looking for? Did Alessandro ever give you any keys or anything to hold?"

"He sends me flowers sometimes. Some jewelry." She looked at her apartment from the door and sobbed. Then she stopped abruptly and went into the bathroom. Rufino heard the shower start. He could use a shower himself. Meanwhile, Alessandro was somewhere being tortured unless he'd given Cortes the codex, in which case he was dead. The shower stopped. A moment later Delia stood in the doorway in a towel. "You have to find Alessandro. Go."

"Did you see him at the warehouse?"

"No."

"Tell me what happened."

"Later. Now you must find him."

"Tell me what happened and I might know where to look."

Delia spoke quickly. Finally Rufino asked "Do you know what bank he used? Do you have a key to his apartment?"

"No."

"Did he have a key to yours? I ask because the door was unlocked, it wasn't forced."

"Yes."

"Have you been to his apartment?"

"Yes."

"All right. Come with me." Delia stared at him. "Put some clothes on. I'll wait outside."

A moment later she was at the door in jeans and a tank top. Rufino led her down the stairs to the car.

Chapter 54

Det. Benito Rufino

"Why would they do this to him? To me?"

Rufino knew, but decided he wanted to hear what she thought. "I don't know. What do you think? Was Alessandro mixed up anything illegal? Drugs?"

"Of course not."

"Why, 'of course not'?"

"He just wasn't, okay. If he was, he would've tried to get me to use. That's what men do. He didn't – so he wasn't."

"I have to ask. He was pretty frightened of these men. Why?"

"I don't know."

"Did he owe them money? He has a nice place. Nice things. How did he earn the money?"

"He sells antiquities."

"That pays a lot of money?" Rufino knew the answer, he wanted to see if Delia did. *How much did she know about Alessandro's work?*

"It can. Commissions are 10%. Some of the items he sells go for millions of pesos. You do the math."

"Where does he get them?"

"From other collectors. From estates. Daddy dies, the kids don't want this old shit, they call Alessandro."

Rufino considered her response. She seemed not to know. He asked, "Who pays the commission?"

"The seller. When you sell a house, who pays the real estate agent: the seller. Do you really not know this? Don't you own a house?"

"I own a house. Different businesses work differently. What do you do?"

"I'm a real estate agent."

"Do you make a lot of money?"

"Not yet. Maybe someday."

Rufino thought about her apartment and decided she was telling the truth, at least about that.

He drove. Finally Delia restarted the conversation: "Where are we going?"

"To see Leon Cortes." He looked at her quickly to see her reaction.

"You just drop in on Leon Cortes? I don't think so."

"I think so. I don't think he'll see me and that's okay. I want to see if you recognize any of his employees." He looked at Delia again and this time he saw her reaction. It was like the look he had seen on her face when he found. "I don't want to go."

"He frightens you? Leon?"

"If you had any sense he would frighten you too. Stop the car. Take me home."

"Somebody has Alessandro. I thought he was your boyfriend. Don't you want to help him?"

Delia looked away. She said to the window, "It's your job to help him. It's your job to find him."

"Yes, and for that I need your help. I think they took Alessandro to the same warehouse I found you at."

"How do you know?"

Rufino remembered the finger. He said "Fingerprints. His prints were there."

"He wasn't with me."

"No, they kept him in the front."

"Can we get something to eat? I haven't eaten in over a day."

She's planning to run away, Rufino thought. He pulled up to a street vendor. "This will have to do for now." He bought a couple of tacos and cokes and handed her one of each. She did not thank him, he noticed. Soon she was eating. "You can have mine too," Rufino said.

Rufino did not expect to see Leon Cortes. Not without a warrant, possibly not even then. He hoped Delia would recognize one of his guards from her abduction. He drove towards Leon's hacienda. When she finished the second taco she put on sunglasses, large ones that covered much of her face. As he approached the hacienda he spoke to Delia: "How about him?" Rufino indicated a bull like man a denim work shirt and jeans.

"No."

"No? Are you sure?"

"No. He wasn't one of them."

"Wait here." Rufino stopped the car. "I'm going to piss him off enough that he'll call for reinforcements. Let me know if any of the others were involved." He got out before she could object. He walked towards the denim man, held his badge in front of him like a shield. The denim man took out his cell and spoke. Rufino stopped a few feet from him and said: "I'm detective Benito Rufino. I'd like to speak with Señor Cortes."

The guard said, "Is he expecting you? Do you have an appointment?"

"I was in the neighborhood. I thought I'd drop by. Sample some of Señor Cortes's famous hospitality."

"Fuck off."

"Perhaps I wasn't clear, asshole. I'm a detective, and I want to see Cortes – now. You are interfering with the investigation. That's a felony." Rufino could see the reinforcements out of the corner of his eye.

The guard said, "Perhaps I wasn't clear – fuck off."

Rufino hoped to guard would touch him – that would allow him to shoot the son of a bitch. There were three other guards – one on either side of the man in denim, and one was gradually moving to a position behind Rufino. The guard on the left, an older man with a silver earring said, "I'll tell Señor Cortes that you dropped by. Do you have a card?"

Rufino realized he was being offered a way out. The silence was broken by a car horn.

The old guard said, "Your girlfriend is impatient. Go to her." He smiled.

Rufino took a card from his pocket and gave it to the older man. He turned. The man behind him stood his ground. Then slowly, with elaborate grace, barely stepped aside. Rufino grazed him as he walked by. He did not see the older man drop this card and grind it into the ground with his boot. When he reached the car he got in and gave Delia a hard look.

She said, "I honked because I recognized him. The older guy was one of those at the warehouse."

"You're sure?"

This time the hard look was Delia's. Rufino considered running them over. A car accident would be easier to explain than shooting them in cold blood. And he thought extracting a confession from the broken victim of a car accident would be easier. But he had Delia in the car; there might be, would be, others out of sight who would come to their aid. Or he could hit-and-run. Except that he had just given the man his card. Backup, if it came at all, would come too late.

Delia said, "Let's go now. I've identified him, okay? Let's go."

Rufino backed the car into a K turn and drove away. When he was off Leon's property, and his house was out of sight, he saw Delia calm down. She was young, Rufino reminded himself. Perhaps she learned this fear of Leon Cortes growing up: "Be a good girl or Leon Cortes will eat you up." Leon Cortes was the new bogeyman, the monster under the bed. He said, "Where should I take you?"

He could tell the question made her uncomfortable. She was just realizing that she could not go back to her own place. She stared ahead. "No friend or relative you can stay with?"

She turned to him: "And put them in danger?"

It was a fair point. His wife was still away, and he thought of offering his place. That would be complicated. Still. "You can stay at my place."

She looked at his ring. "You're married. What will your wife say?"

"She's out of town."

"And that's worse. Do you know anyone?"

Rufino smiled – to himself, he hoped. The rabbi had offered to take Maria in, there was precedent. "I know someone. A friend."

She waited for him to continue.

"It's okay. He's a priest. Not one of ours. A Jew." He saw a look cross her face. "What?"

"Are you crazy?"

"He's a holy man, not some alien from outer space. I'm not crazy. He won't infect you with Jewishness."

She looked at him. "You're serious."

"Yes. You have another idea? Somewhere else to stay?"

"Won't I be putting him in danger?"

"That's not really your concern, is it? The answer is – he doesn't care. He's already mixed up in this. His friend, the murdered priest, was the one who found the codex. So now you've got something in common. Shall I call him?"

"What's his place like?"

"He rents some rooms on Calle 39.

Rufino watched her shake her head. He slowed the car and pulled over. "You can't go back to your apartment. The Jew – the rabbi – will take you in. He speaks Spanish – enough anyway. I don't have any other options. I'm calling him." He looked at Delia, who seemed to finally to understand her predicament. She said nothing. Rufino scrolled through his phone until he found the rabbi's number and dialed it. When the rabbi answered, Rufino said: "I want you to meet someone. Do you still have room at your place?"

Moments later they pulled up to the rabbi's apartment. The rabbi said, "I was on my way out, but I have a minute."

Rufino introduced Delia and told the rabbi her story.

Press said, "You're a nation of priests, and every time you have a woman in trouble you bring her to me. What's your long-term plan?" He addressed this to Rufino.

"We'll arrest Cortes and his gang. Then she'll be safe."

The rabbi said, "That's some plan." He turned to Delia: "You can stay as long as you need to. Now I really must be going."

Chapter 55

Ex-Rabbi Simon Press

Simon went to Isabel's apartment, where he found her feeling a little better. She still let him make the soup, but she fed herself, sitting at the table in her dining room.

Simon said, "I have a new roommate. Rufino brought me a woman in trouble."

"Who?"

"Alessandro's girlfriend. Delia. Very pretty. Very frightened, as she should be."

"Are you telling me this to make me jealous?"

"I'm telling you this. The jealousy is your contribution, but I'm flattered by it."

"Will you sleep with her?"

"If she'll have me, why not? Did I mention how pretty she is?"

Isabel made a face. "She won't sleep with you unless you ask her. Will you make the first move? I'll answer that: no, you won't."

"And why's that?"

"I know you. You won't. You'll decide it wouldn't be fair. She's taken refuge in your house. It would be taking advantage. Besides, if you really were interested in her, you'd be back in your apartment fucking her right this minute, instead of watching me eat soup."

"You're suggesting I would rather watch you eat soup than fuck a lovely young lady."

"I'm not suggesting anything. I'm merely reporting the facts."

"When you get better, you and I are going on a real date."

"Why would I do that?"

"Because I'll ask you," and he was going to add *and eventually you will say "yes"* – but thought better of it.

There was a moment of silence where Simon could swear Isabel was formulating her answer and deciding, once and for all, if she would sleep with him. It was not a moment he expected to witness – the moment of his own sexual fate with Isabel Reyes being decided.

Finally she said, quietly, "When I'm better."

Simon took it as a signal to change the subject "We can no longer bid on the codex. Cortes has it; or will, as soon as he's done torturing Alessandro. The girl was kidnapped by one of Leon's thugs, but she won't bring a complaint."

"And how did she end up going to Rufino?"

"She didn't. He found her bound and gagged in a warehouse where he thought they'd brought Alessandro."

"So we're done with this."

"I still have McNeery's notes. But on the bright side, Cortes will leave Humberto and Maria alone."

Chapter 56

Det. Benito Rufino

Rufino was surprised by how easily he was able to pick the lock at Alessandro's casita. The deadbolt hadn't been set. He entered the casita and locked both. He'd met Alessandro and expected the casita to reflect the man – neat, with an understated elegance – and he was not disappointed. A short foyer led to a living room on one side and the dining room and kitchen on the other. He walked past these. He tried a door on the left and found a bedroom. The door on the right, open, revealed a bathroom. At the end, opposite the door he entered was another door, partly ajar. He pushed it open and found the light switch. He was standing at the entrance to a large study/office. On the left was a floor-to-ceiling bookcase, filled with large quarto size volumes. On the right and ahead were windows. In front of the windows, on the right, was a large glass sheet straddling two stone glyphs. Opposite was a small ornate desk that he would have guessed belonged to a woman. He tried the drawers but they wouldn't yield. He picked the lock of the drawer on his left. When he opened it he saw manila files and quickly recognized them as referring to clients. He picked the lock of the drawer on his right. Files again but with a random series of labels, all in a small neat cursive. He forced himself to read through the labels slowly, methodically. Bank of Mexico. He pulled the file and opened it to find bank statements and a checkbook. It was a large bank, with several branches in Valladolid. The statements gave a federal district address – the Mexico City headquarters. He forced himself to read through the documents carefully, hoping to find some indication of a particular branch. All the statements were from the federal district. He found deposit slips, with sums that made him jealous and resentful, until he remembered Alessandro's severed finger. On the slips were branch numbers, several different ones, indicating deposits made throughout the city but most were from the Calle 36 branch, the one nearest the casita. Rufino shoved them all into his pocket. He tried to open the middle drawer, and to his surprise it was unlocked: pens, pencils, paper clips, business cards – the detritus of middle drawers everywhere. A set of car keys for an Audi. He pulled the drawer all the way out. If there was a safe-deposit box key, this was where Alessandra would have kept it. Perhaps. But there was nothing. And then he saw another key. Rufino assumed it was a spare but he would check on his way out. He put it his pocket, along with the car keys.

There was a printer, but no computer, and a rectangle of dust where one had been. There was no Rolodex because – he assumed – Alessandro kept his contacts on his phone or computer, or because it had been taken. He didn't know if Cortes' thugs had already dragged Alessandro to the bank. He didn't know – for sure – if the nearby branch was where Alessandra kept his safe deposit box with the codex. If he announced himself to the bank he was fairly certain the bank officer would try to contact Alessandro, and warn him. He could sit and watch, waiting for a visit that might have already occurred, while Alessandro was slowly murdered somewhere else.

Finally, he drove to the bank. He asked to speak to a branch manager – he handed a factotum his card and indicated he worked for the Reyes family – yes, that Reyes family. He was brought quickly to an office in the bank, where a short trim man came from behind his desk to shake his hand.

Rufino explained his need for safe-deposit box: did they have any available?

"Yes, of course. Not so many as the main office at Calle 15, none so large. But we have several sizes, adequate for jewelry, documents, foreign currency."

Rufino asked to see the largest and was led by the manager to a vault in the back. There were rows of small boxes set into one wall, larger boxes and the very largest boxes set into an adjacent wall. Rufino decided that the largest box might be adequate to hold the codex.

"What is the procedure? Is there privacy?"

"Of course. You inspect your box in one of these rooms here." He indicated two small adjacent windowless rooms, each with a chair and a small table, and rather too much light for the tiny space. Rufino nodded his approval.

"You present your key and box number to a teller and he will bring your box to the designated room. You sign a ledger; date and time, and again when you return your locked box to the teller.

"May I see the ledger?"

The bank manager stiffened. "We only bring the ledger out when it's actually being used. I'm sure you understand."

"Of course. I'd like one of the larger boxes."

The manager let him back to his office, where Rufino completed the paperwork and was given the key. He asked for an envelope, and a large manila one was quickly provided. He went out to his car, rummaged through the glove compartment and stuffed a couple of maps and an old insurance card in the envelope and returned. The ledger was produced for his signature by a young female teller. Rufino said "I'm sorry. I left the key in the manager's office, would you mind..." He let the sentence drift.

"Of course not." She left and quickly went to the manager's office. Rufino scanned the page, quickly. He looked back a page and found Alessandro's neat signature for May 20th. Before the kidnapping.

The teller returned. She said, "The manager says you took it?" She made the statement a question.

"Perhaps I left it in my car. I'm so sorry." Rufino gathered up his envelope of precious glove compartment trash and returned to his car.

Rufino would wait. He called Max, told him to meet him at the branch. Rufino hung up and thought about Max. Max was the only officer Rufino worked with that he trusted completely. Max insisted that some of his friends were honest police, and as much as Rufino wanted to believe this, he couldn't. He didn't know them, or not nearly as well as he knew Max. Max – others called him Mountie because he had some police training with the Canadian Royal Mounted Police – had been with Rufino for years. He was a chubby, good-looking man. Half Spanish, half Indian. Likable, open, easy-going. He was on his second wife, and second family. More family than a policeman could afford on salary alone. A half a dozen kids altogether. The oldest, Max Junior, was 13. Max himself was just over 30. If they had a drink together, Rufino made sure to pick up the tab. Rufino knew his own honesty came from anger and the sense of superiority it gave him. Max's honesty seemed to come from a more innocent place.

The heat settled on Rufino like a weight. The sun was well up now. Rufino looked at his watch: 11:20. He looked around for some shade. A car drove up. Rufino recognize Max in the driver seat. He dipped his head slightly to acknowledge him. Rufino watched as Max parked his Ford Explorer in the shade of a scrawny pine. Rufino called him: "Stay where you are.."

They waited. At one the bank closed for siesta. Rufino and Max drove to a tacqueria, Rufino for the air conditioning, Max for the food.

"No beer. I can't have you running off to piss in the middle of our stakeout."

"You want this one badly."

Rufino nodded. He told Max about Delia, and about the finger he found.

"Not while I'm eating, boss."

"That usually doesn't slow you down."

Max grunted. Then, when he finished eating, Max made a great show of daintily wiping the corners of his mouth within a napkin. Rufino paid the bill and they left.

The heat had ratcheted up another notch. It hung on them like a sorrow, as demanding as a shrew, as oppressive as a Caribbean dictator. Sunlight exploded off the windshields and chrome bumpers. Rufino watched Max put on sunglasses. His own were in the car.

They drove back to the bank and resumed their watch. No one in his right mind would sit in a car in this heat. They forfeited any chance of being inconspicuous. Rufino could only hope that Cortes, in his arrogance, or indifferent, would pay them no mind if he turned up at the bank.

He corrected himself: when he turned up at the bank. He hoped this afternoon. He hoped soon.

Time on a stakeout moves at different speeds. Minutes crawled, and then inexplicable blocks of time just disappeared as Rufino fell into one reverie or another. The afternoon lurched on.

A black SUV pulled into the lot. Rufino came to full attention. The driver – a man Rufino thought he recognized from Cortes's hacienda – got out and opened the rear door for his passenger. A large man got out quickly - Cortes. On the other side a door opened and a second man got out, slowly, as if having second thoughts - Alessandro. The three men walked into the bank. Rufino would've liked to know if anyone – another guard perhaps - remained in the car. He couldn't tell through the tinted windows. He assumed not. He looked across the parking lot at Max and nodded his head. Max nodded back. Rufino got out and went into the bank.

He saw Cortes and Alessandro speak to a teller. He saw the teller turn the safe deposit box ledger towards them and watched them sign their names. As soon as they finished and were buzzed back behind the counter, Rufino went up to the teller.

He asked to visit his safe deposit box and was asked to wait. He waited a minute and asked again: "I'm really in a bit of a hurry. Can we expedite this?"

The teller in charge said: "I'm sorry. We only have two rooms and some gentlemen came in just a moment ago."

Of course. They come together, but they had different boxes. Both viewing rooms would be occupied. So the teller imagined. Rufino wanted to shake her. Instead he said: "I don't need a viewing room. I just need to get some papers from my box – I can do it in the hall. But I do need to hurry. I have a plane to catch. Can you help me?" He watched as her desire to be helpful wrestled with her need to obey the bank's rules.

"Please."

Chapter 57

Det. Benito Rufino

Rufino said, "I just need to grab some papers." He watched as she glanced around.

"Okay," she said quietly, and buzzed him past the teller counter. Rufino took a quick look around. Cortes's bodyguard was not in the lobby, which meant he was in the back, with Cortes and Alessandro. Max was pretending to fill out a deposit slip. Rufino reminded himself that Leon wore body armor, and he suspected his bodyguard did too. He would, if it came to it, have to shoot both of them in the face. He hoped he wouldn't have to shoot Alessandro, but he had enough experience to know that people behaved strangely, formed unlikely bonds, in crises. He thought of Delia and decided he'd shoot Alessandro in the crotch if necessity required it. He smiled at the teller and followed her back to the safe deposit boxes. The huge vault door was open. He handed her his key and she went inside. To his right he saw the two viewing rooms. Both doors were closed. He remembered from his visit that they locked from the inside. He wondered if the teller would wait: she had broken the rule, would remain hyper-vigilant while he looked through his box? Or would she return to her post in the front?

He was reminded briefly of the story of the lady and the tiger. Which door was Leon Cortes behind? Which door was Alessandro behind? There was a possibility, a likelihood, they were in the same room transferring the codex from one safe deposit box to another.

"Here it is," the teller handed him the large metal box and his key.

"Thank you."

"When you're done —" she didn't finish her sentence.

"When I'm done?"

"Well, that's why we only let people back here when we have a room. You're supposed to lock your box and leave it on the table in your room."

Rufino tried to help her out: "Why don't you come back in 5 minutes and I'll hand it back to you? Okay? Would that be okay?" Rufino thought he heard the sound of people moving chairs in the second room.

The teller stood paralyzed from moment, but then she seemed to reconsider and asked "Five minutes?"

"Five minutes. I promise." Rufino tried not to look at the door that he expected to open at any minute. He needed to draw his badge and his gun, and he wanted to get this woman out of harm's way.

"Five minutes," she repeated. Clearly this would be five minutes of heart pounding anxiety for her. Five minutes in which if her rule breaking were discovered, she would be reprimanded, or lose her job. Five minutes of hell. *You have no idea, Señora*, Rufino thought.

She left quickly, eager to get through her five minutes of purgatory.

The door opened. Rufino pulled his gun and then his badge. Alessandro came through the door first. Rufino watched as a look of surprised recognition crossed Alessandro's face, followed by something darker and frightened. Rufino hoped he would register the badge and then the gun, and that he would register that his hour of deliverance was at hand.

Alessandro stopped.

Rufino motioned him to come forward.

The bodyguard was next through the door. Rufino watched him register the gun and the badge. He said "Police. Keep your hands where I can see them. I know you wear armor, so if I have to shoot, I will shoot you in the face." Rufino stopped and watched as the bodyguard slowly raised his hand. "Good. Leon Cortes – good afternoon. Please, everyone, step back into the room. That's good. Open the box, Señor Cortes." Rufino watched Cortes's face, but he couldn't read the expression. He watched Cortes hesitate. "Open the box. Do it now."

Cortes said, "The key is in this pocket." He patted his pants. "If I reach for it, don't shoot me and claim I was reaching for a gun."

Rufino nodded. He watched Cortes slowly withdraw the safe deposit box key from his pants. Slowly, deliberately, Cortes opened the large safe deposit box.

Rufino said, "Empty it."

Cortes lifted the box carefully and turned it over.

It took Rufino a moment to register what he was seeing. A small jade artifact, some sort of medallion, skidded onto the table, followed by an envelope. Then nothing. Rufino thought for a moment that this was some kind of magic. He looked into the safe deposit box that now lay empty before him.

Rufino said, "Open the envelope."

Cortes opened the envelope and withdrew a sheet of typing paper. "It's the provenance for the jade piece." He shrugged. "Maybe you could put your gun away, before you make another mistake."

Rufino looked at Alessandro, who looked like a walking dead man. He noticed his hand was bandaged. He said to Cortes, "I see Señor Alessandro has had an accident. Let him go before you make another mistake."

Cortes said, "Señor Alessandro is not a prisoner. I am his customer. He came with me; am I permitted to give him a ride home?"

Rufino said, "Señor Alessandro can take a taxi."

The teller opened the door. Rufino did not look at her. He said over his shoulder, "I'm with the police. Come back in ten minutes." He watched Cortes nod, and the teller left.

Cortes said "I think we're done here, Detective Rufino. May we go?"

"Alessandro goes first."

Cortes said, "As you wish." Alessandro seemed unsure of what to do.

"Go," said Rufino. He watched Alessandro look at Cortes.

"Go," said Cortes.

Alessandro left, his shoulders hunched as if he expected to be beaten on the way out.

Cortes asked, "Do you go to church, Detective Rufino?"

"No."

"You should." Cortes left, ahead of his bodyguard.

The frightened teller stood in the lobby with the manager. The manager said, "A word with you, Señor Rufino."

"Not now." Rufino brushed past him. He saw Max hurry after him, but he didn't slow down. Max caught up to him at the car.

"What happened?"

Rufino waved the question away, then stopped. He owed Max at least a partial answer. "The codex wasn't in the safe deposit box. Just some jade trinket. They knew we were watching for this."

"How?"

Rufino said, "How do you think? Someone told them."

Rufino got into his car and drove away. He didn't believe Max would have betrayed him, although he certainly had the opportunity. He hadn't told anyone else. Of course Max was always in need of money. Rufino tried to push the thought from his mind. But it lingered like a filament of spiderweb all the way home.

Rufino called Dr. Reyes several times, but she didn't answer or return his calls. On a hunch he called the rabbi.

"You've reached Simon Press on a recording. Please leave your number and a brief message and I'll call you back."

Rufino left his name and number. Minutes later his phone rang.

"This is Simon. You called me."

Rufino told him about the exchange of the bank, about all that had befallen Alessandro and Delia.

Press said, "He beat you. He has more resources and fewer scruples. It wasn't a fair fight."

Finally, Rufino said what was on his mind: "Why doesn't he just kill me. Or you? Or Dr. Reyes? He has the means. He's not afraid of the law – he owns the law. Why doesn't he kill us?"

"He tried to kill you. If he succeeded then someone more competent would be on the case. You did a good job saving the young woman though."

There was silence, in which Rufino remembered why he hated the rabbi.

Press broke the silence: "Why does Leon want the codex so badly? I understand it's worth a lot of money, but he has a lot of money."

Rufino said, "He feels that belongs to him by right. El Gato found it, and El Gato works – worked – for him."

Press said, "The pirate's code. Any treasure belongs to the captain, to be shared with his crew as he sees fit."

"Yes."

"Why do you want Cortes?"

Rufino said, "He's bad. He tried to kill me."

"Good reasons. What happens now? I mean to you."

"I'll be disciplined, again. Suspended. I'll become one of those guys selling grilled corn in the jardine." He laughed. "I'll end up paying protection money to one of Cortes' underlings."

"Why wouldn't you just shoot him instead?"

Rufino laughed. "Maybe."

"Benito, the night before I came to Mexico I beat up a student. Further proof – should any be necessary – that I was unsuited to the rabbinate. You could've killed Cortes at the bank. You didn't, proof that you're unsuited for police work, as it's commonly practiced. Maybe I should be a policeman, and you should study Talmud.

"Alessandro still has the codex, or he'd be dead. You should have arrested him at the bank. You might've mentioned that Delia's safe – the other thing that Cortes holds over him. Then you wouldn't have to sell corn in the jardine. If it's not too late, you should still arrest Alessandro. He'll be grateful. Just keep him away from the prisoners and the guards."

Rufino said, "So you see why I can't just arrest Alessandro."

"Yes, but what are you going to do? You'll never get the codex now. Why do you want it? Again I ask: why does Leon Cortez want it?"

"It's worth – I don't know – 100 million pesos – $10 million in your money."

"It's worth that if he can sell it. But how can he sell it?"

Rufino said, "A private collector. You don't know this, but the black market for pre-Colombian artifacts is huge."

"I do know that. But this artifact is in a class by itself. Who'll spend $10 million US for something they can't display, for something they can't even acknowledge owning? The other stuff, the other artifacts you can forge a provenance for. People do. But not for this. This is in a class by itself."

Rufino said, "El Gato killed for it – he thought it was valuable."

"El Gato grew up on the streets, he was a hustler, he didn't understand that this was more than an artifact. I think Leon Cortes understands what he has. He knows he can't sell it. Or even display it."

"So, rabbi, why does Cortes want it?"

"Well, for starters, El Gato and everyone like him had to be taught a lesson: don't cheat your boss. I don't think Cortes cares about it one way or another."

"So why does Cortes acquire it after El Gato's been made an example of?"

Press said, "I don't know. It's perplexing."

When Rufino hung up, Delia came into the living room.

She asked, "Did they arrest Leon?"

Press shook his head. "Rufino tried to catch them with the codex but he failed. He saw Alessandro though. He said he looked okay."

"Will they kill him?"

"Alessandro? I don't know. I'm new here. Is that usually what they do? They didn't kill you."

Delia let out a single sob. She whispered, "Yes, they will kill him. For a stinky old book."

Chapter 58

Ex-Rabbi Simon Press

Press picked up a six-pack of beer and a bag of ice and drove out to the site. He found Professor Estavan under the tent, writing in a spiral notebook. He greeted him and offered the beer. Estavan took one and said "Join me."

Press asked, "How's it going?"

The professor took a long drink. "At first I was annoyed to be taken off my own excavations at Coba. But this is an older site. Improbably old. It will change all the timelines. So you understand – this is a big deal."

Press nodded and took a drink. "In a way that's what I came to see you about. I've heard this site is over 1500 years old. Is that even possible?"

Estavan said, "Yes, it is. You know that the Maya are celebrated for two related things: the accuracy of their calendar and their celestial observations. What's remarkable about this site is how old it is, and as it turns out, how old their history of celestial and calendrical accuracy is. They were making accurate celestial observations for over 2000 years, since before the birth of Christ."

Press felt something he couldn't name come over him. He thanked the professor and left the shade of the tent. Sunlight assaulted him and he realized he was never going to get used to that – the brute physical force of sunlight in this land. He put on sunglasses, which took some of the shock away from his eyes, but he still felt the sun beat on every inch of his skin. He got into his car and drove back to Valladolid. He was bothered the entire way back by the shadow of an idea that wouldn't quite reveal its form, but whose presence he felt.

He shouted a greeting to Delia – the previously agreed-upon ritual that would assure her that it was Press, and not one of Leon's thugs, entering the apartment. He would yell "Marco"; she would reply "Polo." He explained that this was a game children in America played in swimming pools.

There was no answer. He shouted "Marco" again. Silence. He stopped, and surveyed his apartment. Things seemed in order. Somewhat reassured, he shouted "Marco" again. Again, no response. The door to Delia's room was slightly ajar. He knocked. No response. He slowly pushed it open and saw Delia lying on the bed. He froze: a sudden panic squeezed his chest. Then she moved her head slightly and he saw the earbuds, and the white wire. He shouted

"Marco" and watch Delia slowly remove the earbud and turn. She said "Hi."

He wanted to explain what a fright she'd just given him, but he thought better of it. "Polo," he corrected her. He closed the door and went back to the living room. But the shadow of the idea was gone. What was left was the shadow of the shadow; a memory. He had been on the verge of something, but now it was gone. He thought he could get it back later by remembering his conversation with Estavan. Besides, a new thought had taken up residence. He found he was thinking of Isabel Reyes.

Press called her and told her the news about Rufino. She did not seem surprised: "Every day I treat women that have been beaten up by their husbands and boyfriends. The same women, over and over. So resignation is – how do you say it? – my default position. So Rufino got beat. Of course he did. Rufino's problem is that he thinks he's smart, smarter than the average policeman – and maybe he is – but he tends to underestimate everyone else's intelligence. Cortes is rich because he inherited money; but he grew richer and more powerful because he's smart. Rufino sees only what Cortes got by inheritance."

Press listened. Finally he said, "So there's nothing to be done? Is that the way it is?"

"There are things to be done. You could ask me to dinner."

"Have dinner with me tonight."

"No, I don't think so. Some other time. You have to ask without being prompted."

Press heard her hang up. He wondered what it was about him that prompted women to talk to him like that. He remembered Mary's taunt – the one that led to all his troubles: "Then spank me." He realized there are many things he wanted to do to Isabel Reyes. He added "spank" to his mental list. Tomorrow he would call again and ask her to dinner.

Delia came in the living room. She was wearing a tight blue dress that seemed to be made of some elastic material. He wondered if it was aimed at him, or someone else, men in general, or women, or no one at all. He said, "You look like you're dressed to go out. I think that's a bad idea."

"I know. I'm not going out." She fixed herself a salad and sat at the dining room table. "They say you are like a priest, that you can't be with a woman."

"I'm like a priest, yes. I'm a Jewish priest, a rabbi. Or I used to be. We have different rules. I can be with a woman. Rabbi's marry, have children." He watched Delia chew it over. "We should find a safe place for you far from here."

"Where would I go? My family, the people I know, are here."

"Just for a while. Until Leon Cortes moves his attention to something else."

"He'll remember." She said it like she was pronouncing a death sentence.

Chapter 59

Ex-Rabbi Simon Press

The next morning Simon called Isabel and asked her to dinner. She seemed genuinely pleased, and accepted. He'd expected her to give him a hard time.

He met her at her apartment. He was surprised to find her ready, but kept it to himself. "Shall we go?"

"I want to show you something first."

He waited while she went into her bedroom and brought out a small silver cylinder, about 3 inches long with flanges at each end. She handed it to him. "I found this in some very old crates in my parent's home. It was wrapped in a silk cloth, but it was hidden with some old silverware. I have a hunch you'll know what it is."

Simon knew what it was even before he took it.

"It opens," Isabel said.

"I know. Inside is a rolled up paper with Hebrew writing."

She nodded.

"It's a mezuzah. Jews place them on their doorways, because the prayer inside commands them to."

"What does it say?"

"'Hear O Israel, I am Lord your God, the Lord is one.' There's more, but that's the main message."

"How old is it?"

"How long has your family been Catholic? It's older than that. Did you find anything else?"

"Like what?"

"Like a prayer shawl – a tallis – a shawl with knotted fringes on it. Or a set of small boxes attached to leather straps – phylacteries – tfillin."

Isabel shook her head. "But we have a lot of chests in the basement."

"It seems like your family was Jewish once."

"My father will be so pleased to find out."

"They usually are. Shall we go someplace kosher for dinner?"

"Does it make me more or less attractive to you – knowing that I'm Jewish?"

"Well, we won't have to argue about whether to raise the kids Jewish or Catholic. I'm sorry: that was flip and the question deserves a better answer. It's a good question, however you think about it. You're asking me how much of what attracts me is your difference, aren't you? I think what attracts people to each other is some kindredness of spirit. But we like it if that spirit is wrapped in an exotic package. Otherwise it's like dating your sister. Does that make sense?"

"Yes. Why do you think were kindred spirits?"

"Because we read the world the same way."

Isabel thought that over. Finally she said, "You might get lucky tonight, Rabbi."

After dinner they strolled through the jardine. The heat had abated. It was warm, but not oppressively so. The jardine was busy: families grouped around the corn on the cob vendors and the vendors of gelato; teenagers in the darker sections, whispering; old men on the benches, talking. A single policeman, wearing a flak vest and holding a carbine, stood near the entrance to the bank, now closed for the night. The front of the church was lit up. A crone with a thin leathery hand outstretched sat on the steps, a statue of begging. She was small – tiny even – almost another species. A child came up to them selling chewing gum. Press paid five pesos for a small package. He offered some to Isabel. He found himself trying to create some significance for the transaction, the crone, the jardine. He mentioned this to Isabel. He asked her if she ever thought like that.

"No. Not here. Perhaps if I were in Dublin. You do this because you are a visitor."

"Maybe. But I used to do it in Dublin too."

"Well then you do it because you are a rabbi. You have the habit of interpretation. The Bible, if that's in front of you; whatever is in front of you. Sometimes I think you try to interpret me."

"All the time. Especially you. Do you mind? Is it flattering to be the object of such hard thought?"

"It seems a little superior of you. But flattering too. I like it that you think about me. But some of your thinking is just lustful fantasy, right?"

"Some, yes. Some isn't." He felt her take hold of his arm. It was an ambiguous gesture – the gesture of a friend? But he felt a surge, as if every artery were suddenly alive and simultaneously reporting in.

She held on until they reached her apartment. She said, "Would you like to come up?"

"Yes." And because a simple "yes" didn't seem sufficient, he added "I'd like that very much."

She let go of his arm to search her bag for her keys. A moment later she found them and unlocked the door.

"Would you like some coffee?" Isabel said.

"I'd like some wine."

"Of course. And you'd like me to have some too."

Simon nodded. And wondered: now? She'd invited him in. Surely that was a sign.

She went to the kitchen and returned with a decanter and two glasses. "Pour."

He poured each of them a glass. He raised his. "L'chiam. It means 'to life.'"

She touched the glass to his. "Say it again."

"L'chiam."

"La chime."

"Close enough."

She sat next to him on the couch. He smiled and drank.

****

Simon rose early, but found that Isabel was already out of bed and fussing in the kitchen. He offered to make her breakfast.

"No. When we have a pajama party in your apartment you can cook breakfast. In my kitchen, I cook. Besides, I know you're grateful. Ruining some eggs isn't necessary."

"I am grateful. And you? Please say you have no regrets."

"I have no regrets."

"But you didn't stay in bed."

"I don't like morning sex. I know men do. I don't."

"Not even when you're on vacation?"

"Not even then." She put two plates of eggs on the table and sat. "Is that a deal cracker?"

"Deal breaker. No."

"Also, I expect you to be faithful to me. So Delia has to go."

"I'm not sleeping with Delia."

"Not now. But maybe she likes sex in the morning. She has to go."

"Okay, but where do we send her? Where can she be safe?"

"So she's my problem now, too?"

"I'm afraid so."

Isabel got up and poured them coffee. "Let me think about it."

Chapter 60

Det. Benito Rufino

On a hunch, Rufino went to Alessandro's. He saw Alessandro leaving, accompanied by the two large men, one who had been with Cortes that the bank. Rufino made a note of the license plate on the black SUV they got into. He called Max.

Max said, "They took my gun and my badge. Also my paycheck. But on the bright side, I'm still alive." Manuel made the bright side sound pretty gloomy. And his "still alive" felt conditional. "We fucked up, my friend."

"We can fix it. Alessandro is on the move with Cortes's thugs. This will be the real exchange."

"No doubt. But we're both suspended. Why not turn it over to the police – wait, I know what you are going to say – they can't be trusted."

"They can't."

"They can't, and that's a shame. But it's not my shame anymore. Nor yours."

"Max, he tried to kill me."

"I'm sorry. You should've shot him in the face when you had the chance. He didn't try to kill me. Not yet." Max laughed a hollow laugh.

"Not yet." Rufino wasn't sure that this would persuade Max. Perhaps, when it was all considered, Max would blame Rufino. Maybe he already did. The phone was quiet. Rufino sensed he'd lost the argument. With nothing to lose he said, "Not yet. They'll come after you, Max. It's my fault, but he'll still come after you, and your family. I'm sorry – you know I'm right." Rufino heard silence.

"Promise me – on your life – that this time you'll shoot him."

"Sure."

"I mean it. Promise."

"On my life, I'll shoot him. What will happen to us?"

"We'll go to America and pick strawberries."

Rufino heard it in his voice: Max wasn't kidding.

Chapter 61

Ex-Rabbi Simon Press

When Simon returned to his apartment, he found the door open. He called out: "Marco?"

No response. He entered his living room. He called again: "Marco." He entered the bedroom where Delia slept. It was empty. He called her cell phone and got her voicemail. He went back to what had been Delia's bedroom. He saw a piece of paper peeking out from under the pillow. He read it quickly:

Dear Rabbi Press,

I have a cousin in Puerto Rico. I'll say with her. Thanks for your hospitality.

Fondly,

Delia

Chapter 62

Det. Benito Rufino

Rufino awoke to the insistent barking of dogs – a barking that did not stop, and seemed to draw more barking to it. He was used to barking, but this had an urgency that made him get out of bed. He looked at his clock radio: 4:42. He grabbed his gun. He would shoot the god damn dogs. Their owners too. The barking was close, it seemed to come from right outside his door. He pulled on pants and a shirt he didn't bother to button. The barking continued as he dressed. A bark and a yelp – a sound he associated with an injured dog. As Rufino moved into his living room there was no question – the barking was outside his own door. He opened his door cautiously and looked out. He could see one dog guarding the corner of the canvas sack on his doorstep. The dog noticed him for a second and then returned its attention to the canvas sack. It was dark, with only a bit of light from the streetlight. He shushed the dog, who ignored him and kept up its barking. He opened the door to get a better look at the sack. It was too dark in spite of the streetlight. He closed the door and went to the closet for his flashlight. The dog continued to bark and windows opened. He thought he heard the sound of a stone hitting pavement. There was a brief interruption in the barking and then it started up again. He found his flashlight and opened the door, letting the light play first on the dog, then on the sack. The sack wasn't canvas in the light of the flashlight beam. It was a heavy plastic, stenciled with the name of an industrial uniform cleaning service. The sack was closed with a drawstring. He took a cloth from his pocket and pulled the string open. He expected to see a face but there was no face looking back at him. Only an open wound where it had it been. There was sticky blood everywhere. The dog sniffed and ran off. Rufino stood up and backed off. He found it difficult to breathe. His first thought was: the rabbi. And then a more terrifying thought came: Dr. Reyes. He forced himself to open the bag and shine the flashlight inside. The body was on its back. It wore what looked like a sweat suit, slick with blood. A man's sweat suit. Not Reyes. Too thin to be the Rabbi. And then he knew: Alessandro. He played the flashlight beam down one arm and then the other. He saw the missing finger.

Where was the head? He grabbed his cell phone and dialed. He got an answering machine. When the message was done he said, "Dr. Reyes, this is Detective Rufino. If you get a package today don't open it. Don't open it. Call me right away."

Rufino's next call was to Max. "Get up my friend and get over here. We have a body. Don't eat breakfast, not even coffee. Just get over here."

He thought Dr. Reyes opened the clinic at eight. So he would have time to get there first, intercept the rest of Alessandro. Several dogs were sniffing the sack. He shooed them away.

The plaza was almost empty when Rufino arrived. The newspaper vendor was putting the steel bars on the piles of *Diario de Yucatan, El Sol de Mexico, Por Esto!* Two small Indian women, the color of nuts, were already huddled by the door to the cathedral. There was no light on yet in the clinic. He nodded to the newspaper vendor and walked quickly to the clinic. The dog was sniffing something by the door, a hat box. Rufino quickened his steps. He kicked the dog away. The box was addressed to Dr. Isabel Reyes. Rufino took a folding knife from his pocket and cut the tape holding the lid on. He looked around. The dog was about 15 feet away growling. He lifted the lid. Staring back at him was Alessandro. He heard barking and looked back at the dog. Beyond he could see a figure in a white coat: Dr. Reyes. He put the cover back on and lifted the box. He heard his name called.

"Detective Rufino."

"Dr. Reyes. Good morning."

"Bringing me a present?"

Rufino let his expression answer for him.

"Are you okay?"

"I'm okay."

Dr. Reyes looked at the box. "That has my name on it."

"That's irrelevant. It's evidence."

"Of what? What is it?"

"A murder. I have to go."

Reyes grabbed his arm. "It has my name on it."

Rufino was surprised at how roughly he shook his arm free of the doctor's grasp. She grabbed his arm again, harder. He stared at her. She stared back but did not let go. Finally he said, "It's Alessandro's head. The body was left at my apartment. You can do an autopsy, but I'm pretty sure about the cause of death."

Reyes let go of Rufino's arm. "Open it."

Rufino stared at her.

"Open it please."

Rufino took the lid off the hatbox. He watched Reyes look, and he watched her face glaze over momentarily.

"Okay." Reyes said quietly, to no one in particular. She said "okay" again, this time to Rufino. He put the lid back on. Rufino started to walk away. "Was he tortured?"

"The body was beaten. I haven't examined it. My man Max is with it. Probably."

Dr. Reyes found that her next thought was of Simon Press. She took her cell phone from her bag and called. When she heard him answer she said, "It's Isabel."

"Is everything okay?" He knew it wasn't.

"They've killed Alessandro. They sent the body to Rufino and the head to me."

Press's first thought - as it was every time a heinous crime crossed his path, even if only the path of his eyes reading the daily tally of carnage in the newspaper – his first thought was how incomprehensible the people who did these things were. He wanted to kill them with an Old Testament vengeance, but he wouldn't and he knew he couldn't. He couldn't kill them any more than Hamlet could kill his fratricidal uncle – and in neither case did religion have anything to do with it. He could punch a student who accosted him – but he could not kill one. Something prevented him, something that didn't prevent the daily parade of his murderous fellow creatures. He forced a question on himself: what if Alessandro had made the call, and the body and head in question belonged to Isabel Reyes? Could he go and shoot Leon Cortes? What would prevent him? He could imagine the towering rage, but not the act. Alessandro had attempted to kill Leon – for good reasons, the Rabbi conceded, that included but were not limited to, self-preservation and revenge. Leon had reason enough to kill Alessandro, at least by Leon's reckoning.

Simon Press had not become a rabbi because of some innate purity. He was incapable of murder. He was incapable of it – plain and simple. He knew, or thought he did, that contemporary psychology regarded murderers as men like us, but with broken impulse control, or weak or nonexistent superegos, or as the victims of such debilitating childhoods that the formation of normal self-restraint never occurred, or else they were biochemically out of balance and unmedicated. But the rabbi held to more primitive (or more advanced – he couldn't be sure in the fullness of time how the matter would play out) notion: they were another species. Some other isotope of humanity. He kept this idea to himself. If only, like Neanderthals, they had heavy brow ridges or some other physical characteristics that gave them away.

He had heard that Leon Cortes was an affable man. People liked his company. He was charming. "Meet it is I set it down: a man may smile and smile and be a villain." Hamlet was onto him and his ilk.

Simon should have been at the mercado buying flowers. A gesture that now seemed warped by the monstrosity of Leon's early-morning offering. Simon found himself walking toward the mercado anyway.

His step was not light as it should've been. An emaciated dog with a canted walk trotted past him. Simon inhaled fresh bread, and rotted fruit in the same breath. Outside the pharmacia two old men sat, not talking. One smoked the nub of a cigarette pinched between his thumb and forefinger. Simon realized he was looking for signs, and possibly for danger. An old pickup truck was unloading crates of cantaloupe. A young, dark man in an Orlando Magic jersey was pulling the crates off the tailgate and onto a hand truck. Simon offered a "Buenos dias" and got one in return.

Inside, the mercado was dark and cool. He walked past the food and vegetable stalls towards the aisle of flowers. He recognized the young gap toothed girl who had sold him his last bunch. She looked at him with recognition, but did not speak. Simon said "Buenos dias."

She replied, "Buenos dias."

Press pointed to the flowers he wanted and she gathered them. When he finished and she held up an armful he asked, "Cuanto?"

The girl quickly figured her way through the bouquet, adding in her head. "86 pesos."

Press shook his head.

"80 pesos."

"60."

They agreed on 70. The girl seemed more pleased than when she'd asked for 86. And then something crossed her face and Press turned.

"Señor Press."

Press saw a young man, thick in the arms and neck, with expensive sunglasses and a gold earring. "Buenos dias." Press said it evenly, without warmth.

"Buenos dias." There was smirking in the phrase. "Would you step outside with me."

Press did not hear the slight rise in inflection that usually accompanies a question. He gave the flowers back to the girl and said, "Please hold these – I'll be back for them in a minute."

Press tried to read the faces of those he passed on his way out of the mercado. But he couldn't read them, they were mostly turned away. Outside he saw a black SUV with tinted windows. He followed the thick necked man to the rear door, which the man opened for him. He hesitated. With a gesture, a young man indicated he should get in. Press stood still, refusing. "If you have something to tell me, do it here."

A voice from inside said, "Rabbi Press, I'm Leon Cortes. A man tried to kill me a few days ago, so I'm wary of public appearances. Join me inside, if you please."

Press found himself getting into the car. The door closed and the thick necked man reappeared and got into the driver's seat.

"I wanted to talk to you. To meet you and talk to you."

"Why not call me?" Press said.

"I like to meet people in person. I like to have them meet me in person. It's better, don't you think, to meet in person?"

"Of course. Still, people generally call first. The meetings are mutually agreed to, and arranged for both parties' convenience."

"You're right of course. You should go if a few minutes conversation now is inconvenient for you." He turned to the driver and asked him to stop. The car stopped. "When would be a better time for you?"

Press smiled, more than he intended. Some of the smile was relief. He wasn't being kidnapped. "Now is fine."

The car moved forward again. "Professor McNeery was a friend of yours. I'm sorry for your loss."

"Thank you." Press decided to play along with this surreal conversation.

"I've read Dr. McNeery's scholarship. Yours too. Are you surprised?"

"I'm surprised when I meet anyone who's read my writing. I'm an obscure academician, generally only other academics read what I write, and then only to find fault with it." He watched Leon smile.

"You're being modest – a pose I've never understood. When you lecture, hundreds come out to hear you. Is that true?"

"True. But many come only in the hopes of getting to take a swing at me. Sometimes I oblige them." Press was annoyed at how easy he found Leon to talk to. Rumors of Leon's charm were not an exaggeration. "Did you want to talk to me about my research?"

"Yes, that among other things. But although I'm reasonably well educated, well read, I really don't know enough to – what was your expression – find fault – with your scholarship. In my ignorance, I would make false assumptions, draw the wrong conclusions. I might have strong opinions about what you've written – I do have strong opinions about what you've written – but they are not more intelligent for being strong. How long have you been in Mexico, Rabbi?"

Press saw the trap, stepped into it boldly: "Only a couple of weeks, and already I have strong opinions about it." He smiled at Leon.

"I have lived in Mexico for 60 years – all my life. My family has been here for 500 years." He flicked a piece of lint from his trousers. "Do you know Borges, Rabbi?"

"Some. Only in translation."

"He writes a story, 'Three Versions of Judas,' in which he puts forth the heresy that the real Savior was Judas, because while Jesus only mortified his body for our sins, Judas was required to mortify his soul. What you think of that?"

Press nodded. "I know the story. He also wrote a story about a heresiarch and his persecutor, in which he suggests that in the eyes of an omniscient God, who sees things differently than we do, they might be the same person."

"'The Theologians.' I know the story. Do you suppose that in heaven, you and I, rabbi and devout Catholic, rabbi and drug lord – for that's how you've come to think of me – might be the same person?"

"Perhaps in heaven, Leon Cortes – devout Catholic and drug lord – might be the same person." Press watched Leon smile.

"I'm sorry I did not get to know you sooner, Rabbi."

He meant it. Press could hear the sincerity in his voice.

"In the bad old days," Leon continued, "Zetas ran the drug business in the Yucatán and several other provinces. They were monsters. They are monsters. People were tortured, people were killed – all the time. For cocaine. We don't use much cocaine here in Mexico. Cocaine is for the United States. So if every Mexican was as drug-free as a choir boy, there would still be a huge illegal business in cocaine here, because of your adopted country. What's the right thing to do, Rabbi?"

"I would decriminalize cocaine."

"Of course you would. Because you're a man of moderation. You could have two beers with dinner, call it quits. So how is your campaign to decriminalize cocaine going? I look at what the Zetas are doing to my city, to my country and I say: not what can I do – but what must I do – while I wait for you to decriminalize cocaine and so prevent the annual murder of thousands of Mexicans.

"What I do is wrong, but not the reason for it. I will go through the purifying fires of purgatory for it. I'm sure of it." Press noticed Leon was no longer looking at him. He was speaking to some unseen presence.

"Why do you want the codex? What does it have to do with any of this?"

"The Bishop of Rome asked me for it."

"The Pope? This Pope?"

"Yes."

"Why does His Eminence want it?"

"It's not my place to ask, only to obey."

"You have it now, don't you? Will the killings stop?"

"When it's safely in Rome. In the meantime, tell Rufino to stop pursuing it."

"Rufino doesn't take orders from me."

"No, nor from his superiors. But you and Dr. Reyes might persuade him."

"Why? How?"

"Ask him how many drug-related murders there've been in the Yucatan since I drove out the Zetas."

"What will he tell me?"

"If he's honest – none." Leon leaned forward to speak to the driver: "The mercado."

In a few minutes they were back at the market. The driver got out and opened the door on Press's side. As he was getting out, Simon felt Leon's hand on his shoulder. "Reread Borges, my friend. We should meet again and talk about him. Read 'The Garden of the Forking Paths'."

Chapter 63

Ex-Rabbi Simon Press

Press returned to the mercado to retrieve his flowers. The girl was surprised to see him. When he asked for the bouquet he'd selected she just stared. Finally, thinking she didn't remember him, he explained: "I was here 15 minutes ago. Don't you remember me?"

She nodded a reluctant yes.

"So, where's my bouquet?"

"I put the flowers back."

"Why? I said I'd be back for them." Press watched her look away. And then he understood. When Leon sent for you, you didn't usually come back. He said gently, "Make me a new one please." He watched her turn and begin to gather flowers. When she was done, she handed him the bouquet.

He might have been imagining it, but Press thought the crowd in the mercado parted for him as he left. Like Moses at the Red Sea, he thought. Before he wandered for 40 years in the desert, he amended.

He walked to the clinic. He expected to find the usual crowd, but the waiting room was empty. Only Reyes's nurse/receptionist was at the desk. She looked terrible. He was going to leave the flowers and call later. The nurse said "Go on back. She's not with a patient."

He walked past the desk down the short corridor to Dr. Reyes's office. He saw her look up from the chart she was reading. He was only halfway down the hall. He had hoped to surprise her – even just a little. "No patients?"

"They don't like to come on days when severed heads get here first. Bad luck. Worse than whatever sickness troubles them."

"I'm sorry." He paused and handed her the flowers.

She took them. "Thank you."

He watched her get up wearily and remove a vase from the cabinet. She filled it half full of water and placed the flowers in it. She spent a moment adjusting the flowers, creating separation, fitting them to the vase. He said, "I took a ride with Leon this morning." He watched her stop and look up at him. "He had his goon get me out of the mercado." He told her the rest. "Have you ever met him? In person?"

"Once. A while back. He asked if I needed anything for the clinic. I told him 'no'."

"You think he was telling me the truth: that he's just following orders from the Vatican? Six men are dead, five on his order if not by his hand." He watched Reyes consider.

She said, "So he didn't do it because the codex is valuable. What does the Vatican want with it? There are plenty of old valuable things. It's not part of the Catholic heritage. Landa burned every codex he could get his hands on. Guilt?"

"I don't think they're capable of guilt. Shame, but I don't see how shame motivates them to steal a Mayan codex after their predecessors went to so much trouble to destroy them."

The phone rang. Reyes picked up and listened. She put the phone down and looked at Simon. "I have a patient."

"In spite of Leon's message?"

"Being 15 and pregnant is scarier than even Leon Cortes."

Press was not sorry to leave. He wanted to talk about Leon's revelation, but he wanted to think about it even more. He believed Leon. He didn't want to, but he did. Did the Vatican want it simply because McNeery, a perpetual pain in their ass, had found it? There were other annoying ex-priests on the loose, doing research and writing about lost gospels, casting doubt on what Jesus had said and what he hadn't, some calling parts of the Catholic enterprise into question. Why was this particular codex so important to them?

The papacy was a religious office. But of necessity it was a political office, an economic office, an intellectual office. It was a military office as well. The rituals could remain unchanged for 1700 years - must remain unchanged – but the management of its secular affairs had to keep up with the times. So there was a website, and complex investments; there were the Swiss guards for show, and a state-of-the-art security mechanism in place because evil might be as old as Cain, but its methods were as up-to-date as the latest cyber attack.

So the Vatican wanted a 1500-year-old Mayan codex. He felt a frisson of pleasure. History still mattered. His own inquiry into the remarkable speed of the adoption of Christianity was not some professional jerk off – as he occasionally feared when he sent yet another heavily footnoted article to the Journal of Near Eastern and Judaic Studies, but an inquiry that might in fact matter to the world and time in which he drew his breath.

He went back to his apartment, locked the door, and took out McNeery's notes. McNeery was a scholar, and his interests were broad, but his main expertise – the expertise that ran him afoul of the church – was in dating the four Gospels. The Gospels presented a number of problems for the church. First, three Gospels roughly agree as to the events described – the so-called synoptic Gospels of Matthew, Mark and Luke; but the fourth Gospel, John, seems to take a different view of the basic facts.

The church just looked the other way, much as the rabbis had ignored the conflicting accounts of creation in Genesis. McNeery, like most Gospels scholars, insisted that the Gospels were not contemporary accounts of Jesus's life written by his disciples, but were actually written some 40 to 80 years after his crucifixion. McNeery was merely the most articulate, forceful, and least deferential of the scholars that sought to bring these facts to the world's attention. The world, of course, was not reading the obscure academic journals in which McNeery painstakingly argued his case for the later dates. But a popularizer had gotten hold of McNeery's articles and had written a bestseller. To his credit the author generously acknowledged McNeery, and the church felt it had no choice but to respond. It responded with the threat of excommunication – a clumsy overreaction that made McNeery briefly even more famous, and kept the controversy alive long past the usual shelf life for these kinds of revelations.

McNeery had gone farther afield than most scholars in trying to date the Gospels. He looked at the usual linguistic markers, parallel histories by the Romans, and (before he fell out of favor) the Vatican's own records and secret files. He looked for anachronisms, clues that the author's contemporary experiences had encroached upon the narrative. So what was he doing in Mexico, in the Yucatán, 5000 miles and a civilization away from his field of study? What was he doing studying a civilization whose first contact with Christianity came 1400 years after the era on which he had spent his entire scholarly life?

Press's first thought was that McNeery was looking for a mythical analog to the Christ story among the Maya. McNeery had argued – in a minor key – that the story of Christ told by the Gospels had been modified to make it conform more closely to the universal myth of the hero who goes to a supernatural realm to bring back a lasting benefit to mankind. The Joseph Campbell argument. Certainly resurrection stories existed in many mythological systems – including those unknown to each other. Was it archetypal in the Jungian sense, part of the race's collective unconscious? Finding a similar narrative among the Maya would bolster that portion of his claim. Still, why this site?

It seemed plausible. And yet – this was a vacant cerebral conjecture. It wouldn't explain why the Vatican wanted the codex. The myth, if it existed would have multiple venues of expression. It would be carved on the walls and on the steles. McNeery's research was always driven by particular facts.

Press went to the refrigerator and took out a beer. It bothered him that he couldn't see the connection between the Maya and McNeery's work on dating the Gospels. He thought of calling up Isabel but she would still be seeing patients. By now they'd be drifting in again, after the morning's superstitious boycott. The itch of not knowing grew so strong that Press considered calling Leon Cortes. Of course Leon wouldn't tell, even if he knew. He drank some beer and paced.

The basic principles behind dating the Gospels were these: 1) The more two Gospels had in common, the closer in date. That was reasonable and obvious. 2) A higher percentage of quotes meant the Gospel was closer to the actual events. 3) The more specific references – place names, names of people – the older and closer to the actual events. McNeery had found stylistic similarities that showed that two of the synoptic gospels - Matthew and Mark - were more closely related. None of this shed the least bit of light on what McNeery was doing in the Yucatán. Press finished his beer, but not his pacing. He considered another beer and decided against it – for now. He knew he was bearing down too hard on the problem. He needed to back off, lighten up, think about something else, and trust the subconscious machinery of his mind to keep working away.

A thought tickled him: a renegade branch of historical inquiry had insisted on a pre-Columbian contact between the old world and the new. The field included some real historians, playing by the rules; some fringe historians who didn't; and an assortment of wack jobs from the UFO community who believed that extraterrestrials were responsible for pyramids in both hemispheres. These arguments had a sort of ditzy charm. Of course there were pyramids in Egypt and the Yucatán – if you wanted to build tall and didn't have steel, or the arch, that's how you did it. Five-year-olds all over the world, without alien assistance, built the same way.

But McNeery had found evidence of Jesus in the Yucatán before Hernando Cortes brought him in 1507. Long before 1507, if the date of the codex could be believed. Press looked at his watch and decided it wasn't too early to call Isabelle and ask her to dinner.

There was no answer so he left a message. A few minutes later his cell phone rang. "Hi. You tried to call me?"

"I did. Have dinner with me." He waited, listening in silence, while she considered.

"Okay. In an hour. Where?"

"La Casita. They have a band tonight. I'll teach you how to samba."

"That will be interesting. I'll meet you there at 7:30."

She did not come directly from work. She was dressed for a night out – heels, a shiny black dress, a shawl of some gossamer dark fabric shot through with silver metallic thread. She kissed him lightly, on the lips. She asked, "Do you even know how to samba?"

"I do. Part of my rabbinical training. You've got to be able to dance at weddings and bar mitzvahs. Want a drink?"

"Tequila."

He ordered tequila and beer. Isabelle said, "So you met Leon Cortes. First you sleep with me, then you go for a ride with Leon Cortes and live to tell about it. You're coming up in the world, Rabbi."

He told her about the reaction at the mercado, about feeling like Moses.

"So what commandments will you be bringing down from Mount Sinai?"

"We talked about Borges. Can you believe it? And the codex is not for him. He's supposed to deliver it to the Vatican."

" Do you believe him?"

"Strangely – yes. What I can't understand is why they would want it."

"To destroy it."

"Okay. To destroy it. But why? After all these years, why? It's not like the Mexican Indians are going back to their Mayan faith."

Isabel said, "A different prophecy of doom? We don't like competitors to our apocalypse."

Press said, "That's come and gone. We're still here."

"What do McNeery's notes say? What's in it?"

"Nothing I haven't already told you about. Star charts. That battle is over too. Galileo won. The church accepts that the sun is the center of the solar system and that the earth revolves around it. Accepts that the solar system is on one arm of our galaxy, one galaxy among many, and not the very center of the universe. Accurate star charts might've been a big deal in the 1500s, but no longer."

The band played a samba. "Dance with me." Isabelle pulled him from his chair. The room was warm and noisy. The samba beat was infectious. They danced. He could see she was surprised by how well he did. It was hard to believe that 12 hours earlier she'd looked at a severed head; and that he had taken a car ride with the man who had done it.

"Let's go," she said when the music stopped.

"Dinner?"

"Later. Let's go right now."

She brought him to her apartment. He was pleased to see his flowers sitting in a vase on her dining room table. She saw him look and whispered a husky, "Thank you."

She was close, holding his hand. He placed his other hand on the back of her head and drew her face towards his. He kissed her; felt her kiss back, felt her hands on his head, felt her lean her body into his. He felt her nibble his ear, her hand pull his shirt from his pants and slide up his stomach to rest on his beating heart. His own hands began to explore her body. Moments later they were out of their clothes and on the bed. He entered her quickly but gently. He felt her legs wrap around him and he fell into the slow rhythm of their coupling. She gave a little shout – her climax - and he felt the warm surge of his own.

He spoke into her hair: "When we have children, we won't teach them to samba until they are least 18."

She squeezed him; said nothing.

"I'm getting up. You can look." She walked to the bathroom. When she came out – still naked - she said "Get dressed. I'm starved. You asked me to dinner."

He watched her put on jeans and her oversized shirt. He dressed quickly. He was ravenous. He said "Back to La Casita?

"Some place quieter."

They walked to El Centro, down a side street from the Plaza. Five tables, only one occupied. It was late now, almost 8:30. They ordered, asked for bread. When it came they wolfed it down and asked for more.

"Would you like something to drink?" He asked.

"No thank you. I feel pretty good."

There was a silence. Press couldn't tell if it was a silence shared, or if it stood between them, an awkward distance that needed to be bridged with words. Usually he didn't have any trouble finding something to say. The mood, while good, seemed fragile.

Isabel asked, "Do you have a girlfriend? Somewhere else."

"No."

"Why not?" It was a challenge. She didn't believe him.

"I have a girlfriend here, I hope."

"There's no one you're sleeping with back in the United States or Ireland?"

"No." He watched her weigh the second "no."

"You're smart, nice, nice looking, you can dance. Why don't you have a girlfriend?"

He thought she was genuinely perplexed, not just baiting him. "Thank you. With a resume like that I should have several girlfriends."

"And, let me add, you know your way around a bed."

"Thank you."

"So how is it you don't have a girlfriend?"

"I haven't found anyone I liked well enough – until now."

"Good answer. I still find it strange. When did you last have a girlfriend? "

"Stop it. How about you? Actually, I don't want to know."

"Why not? I'll tell you."

"Don't. I think men and women must be different that way. I don't want to know. Most men don't."

"Don't you want to know if I have a boyfriend, someone else?"

"You don't. No one you care about. If you did, you wouldn't be here with me."

"So you think you know about women?"

"A little. I was married once, for a long time. 18 years. Remember?"

"At best, that makes you an expert on one woman; if I were to ask her, she'd claim otherwise."

Press felt the conversation lighten. She gotten the answer she'd wanted; or she'd allowed herself to believe the answer she got.

She said "I like you, Rabbi. Don't screw this up." It should have been a punch line, but she said it earnestly.

"I won't. You've been hurt."

"Of course. So has everyone. It's not that. It's that I like you. I want you to go on being the person I like."

"Why wouldn't I?"

"When you fuck men, it changes them."

Press found he had no answer for that.

Press was not surprised when, at the end of dinner, Isabel told him she wanted to be alone. He offered to sleep on the couch.

Isabel asked, "And how long would that last?"

"I would leave you alone."

"Not if I came to you."

Simon walked her to her apartment. He kissed her like it was their first date. Then she pulled away and patted his chest. She unlocked the door and went in. Simon paused before the closed door and then walked home.

He found he was keyed up. He was disappointed not to be with Isabel, but he thought he understood. She'd had had a long and difficult day. She'd looked at a severed head. She admitted to feelings for him – and that made her vulnerable in a way that she found uncomfortable. She didn't trust him – he'd stirred up some old pain. He understood that she needed to sort things out; he could have helped, and he didn't understand why she wouldn't let him. He understood a little – "when you fuck men it changes them."

Chapter 64

Ex-Rabbi Simon Press

Press returned to McNeary's notes. Next to the translation, on the half of the page McNeery reserved for his notes, he found the occasional reference to another Mayan site, sometimes to a specific building or stele within the site.

He felt a surge of restlessness and got up from his chair. The surge was strong - he didn't even try to dissipate it with an orbit of his apartment. He grabbed his hat and walked outside. He headed for the park. It was warm and he felt the sweat gathering in the small of his back. He walked briskly to the park, but once inside his pace slowed to a contemplative stroll. Why pre-Columbian sites? The idea came to him in a rush. All previous attempts to find apocryphal Gospels had centered on the Middle East. But what if those renegade historians who argued that Columbus wasn't the first to make it to the New World were right, and further – this would've been McNeery's interest in this esoteric field of history – what if they had brought with them one of the non-canonical Gospels? It was a wild gamble in its own right, and it was predicated on a renegade version of history that few legitimate scholars even had the patience to refute. But McNeery had been threatened with excommunication, and now he'd been murdered, so someone was taking his inquiry seriously.

The first place to visit was near Merida.

Part of Press's theory predicated the spread of Christianity on its championing of the underdog. 2000 years ago this was a novel idea – although it existed in subtle and not-so-subtle forms in the Old Testament. The second born, rather than the firstborn, are often the favorites in the Old Testament. Abel, the second son, makes the sacrifice that is pleasing to God; Jacob supplants Esau; Joseph was a younger brother – these are the subtle ways the Bible champions the underdog. Not-so-subtle: David's victory over Goliath. And David was the youngest of Jesse's eight sons. It was Press's theory that the Jesus story builds on this. Jesus, a descendent of David, the quintessential underdog, breaks the patrimonial bond - he has no earthly father. He champions the meek, the poor, children, lepers. For the first time in history people could identify themselves as underdogs, and Jesus was their champion. At first the underdogs came from the ranks of Jews; but soon from the ranks of gentiles.

He called Isabel. "I'm going to Merida this weekend. Join me."

"Why?"

"It's the first place on McNeery's list."

"I thought his notes were all translation."

"He made copious notes. Some are places. Other Mayan ruins."

"So McNeery believed that someone else got to the New World before Columbus and the conquistadors?"

"Maybe. His default attitude would be skepticism. The pre-Columbian theories are mostly bunk."

"What is bunk?"

"Nonsense. Henry Ford said 'history is bunk.' Some of it is."

"If he thought it was bunk – why did he make a list?"

"To give it a fair hearing – I think because he was a bit of a renegade he had sympathy for other renegade historians. Anyway, I'm going. Please join me?"

"Yes."

"Can you be ready by cight?"

"9:30."

"Am I suppose to bargain?"

"No. Just pick me up at nine. Don't be early."

Press said goodbye, pleased with himself. He had wanted to return to Merida for some time. Now he had a reason and good company.

He was ready at eight – he'd chosen the original time knowing he would be. He spent the hour before he planned to pick up Isabel studying – again – McNeery's notes.

Press arrived at Isabelle's apartment promptly at nine. When she let him in he was pleased to see a suitcase by the door.

She said, "You're surprised I'm ready."

"A little. But I appreciate it."

She kissed him lightly on the lips. "That suitcase isn't going to put itself in the car. I packed a little lunch."

When they were in the car and on the way she said, "What's in Merida? I mean for you. I'll go shopping. You should come with me and buy a hammock."

"The ruins at Dzibilchaltum. One of the stelae there records a legend of a virgin birth. The stele itself is from 1100 to 1200 CE and the birth it records works out to about 6 BCE by the Mayan long count." Simon searched her face for reaction, but Isabel was wearing sunglasses.

"So somebody did get here before Hernan Cortes." She said it evenly.

"Maybe. Unusual births are not that uncommon in mythology. Aphrodite has no mother – she was born of sea foam – at least that's the politically correct version – or from Zeus's ejaculate, in the original version."

"So the goddess of love is from what you call a jerk off?"

"Pretty much."

"It's a big deal if Cortes wasn't here first. Is it a big deal for historians?"

Press slowed the car. Ahead a farmer was encouraging livestock to cross the road. As he slowed, Simon instinctively looked in the mirror. Behind them was a pale blue VW bug. Behind the bug was a late-model black SUV with tinted windows, like the car Cortes had met with him in. He waited, his eyes on the mirror. He said "It's a long shot. The more likely explanation is it's just a locally grown myth. But it caught McNeery's interest."

The last of the cattle cleared the road. The farmer waved his hat. Simon accelerated quickly.

Isabel said, "You're in a hurry for someone who thinks it's just a local myth."

Press turned to her and smiled. "You don't miss much." He checked the mirror. Both cars were still behind him, but where else could they be? There had been no turnoffs.

Isabel said, "So you believe in what you called 'bunk' yesterday?"

"I'm curious. And like McNeery, I try to keep an open mind." He spoke lightly, but he stole a quick glance in the mirror. Both cars were still behind them. "You know some people think Columbus was a converso. His ships sailed the day before the Jews were expelled from Spain."

"You mean like me. Or so you think."

"What do you think?"

"Medically, maybe. I don't know, do I look Jewish?" She took off her sunglasses and turned to him.

Simon couldn't tell if the question was a joke or in earnest. He shot her a quick glance.

"Could be."

"It takes some getting used to – the idea that I might have Jewish blood."

They passed a cross road and Simon watched the VW slow and turn off. The black SUV was behind him. An 18 wheeler passed him going the other way, and behind it a gray pickup and an old beige Toyota. The road was clear – both sides. As far as he could see the only signs of civilization were billboards for Feliz Pollo – a fast food restaurant. He looked in the mirror. The SUV seemed to be keeping the same distance. He pushed down on the gas, accelerating to 120 KpH.

He said to Isabel, "But you, your parents, your parents' parents – all Catholic going back for generations at this point. Your Jewish blood is pretty diluted."

"Not so diluted that I don't have Familial Mediterranean Fever. My family must've married other conversos, must somehow have been drawn to them. Look at me now – I'm on my way to spend the weekend with a rabbi."

Simon smiled. He glanced in the mirror. The SUV was further back, and hadn't accelerated. He said: "I suppose in the beginning the conversos knew who the others were. It seems natural they would intermarry. Maybe they had no choice – other Catholics would've avoided marrying them."

"Because they were tainted."

"Right. But after a while it would be hard to keep track of who was a converso, who wasn't."

"Not so hard as you think. Family trees are a big deal here. Because intermarrying with the natives did occur, those that didn't were especially proud of that fact. Everybody kept track – of their own family, and of others."

Press accelerated some more. The increased distance dampened his anxiety. The SUV did not keep pace and fell further behind.

"Do you have mestizo blood?"

"No. And I know this is because I have a mustache. A point of pride for Mexican women of Spanish descent. Proves we haven't intermarried with the native population."

"I didn't —"

"No. I wax it. Some women don't."

Press could barely see the SUV in the mirror now. They rode in silence for a while. Up ahead Press saw traffic for the first time, and the reason for it: a road gang was repairing the highway. He slowed and joined the short line of cars and trucks crawling past the work zone. In his rearview mirror he saw the SUV right behind him. The car stopped. The SUV stopped some 10 feet behind him. Simon was looking in the mirror full-time now, so when this traffic started up Isabel had to remind him to go. "What are you looking at in the mirror?"

"The car behind us reminds me of Leon Cortes'. I keep expecting them to open the doors to take me for another ride."

Isabel looked. "Standard drug dealer car in these parts."

Press accelerated to catch up to the traffic. He kept glancing in the mirror; the SUV remained behind them.

Isabel said, "Do you think we're being followed?"

"He's been behind me since outside of Valladolid, but on the other hand, where else would he have to go besides Merida?"

Soon they were on the outskirts of Merida, and Press asked Isabel to read the directions to the Casa Mexico, a small bed and breakfast where they were staying near the Parque Santiago. Press lost sight of the SUV, then found it again in his rearview mirror. When he pulled over at the bed-and-breakfast, the SUV drove past and turned the corner.

Simon grabbed their suitcases. The heat was intense outside, but soon he was in the cool of the lobby. After checking in, a young man in a white guyambana and black pants took the bags and led them to their room on the second floor. He watched Isabel appraise room, then smile. He asked, "Do you like it?"

"This is very nice. Let's eat" - she indicated a shaded patio off their room – "and then let's take a siesta."

As she laid out her picnic on the patio, Simon double locked the door and checked it. Satisfied, he joined her. The patio afforded a view of the street, through lush vegetation. He was pleased to see no black SUVs.

It was warm, in spite of the shade, on the patio. Press decided that if the people in the SUVs were to come for him, they would come at night.

When they finished eating, he felt Isabel grab his hand and pull them back into the room. "Siesta time."

It was after two when he awoke and heard the sound of water running in the shower. The room was warm, and he was tempted to join her in the shower. He decided against it, afraid that she would find it more intrusive than romantic – an invasion of her privacy. He would ask her about it though. He heard the creak of the faucet being turned off. Moments later he heard the bathroom door open and Isabel stepped out, one towel around her waist and one wrapping her hair. He felt an erotic jolt. He watched a wry smile cross her face. She turned away and put on a blouse. He felt, a little sadly that perhaps this was a show she'd put on before, in other rooms, for other men. He said, "Keep this up and you'll need to shower again."

"Later. I want to go shopping and you want to go to the ruins." She dropped the towel and pulled on panties and jeans.

"We could do both together."

"Not yet. I like you quite a bit right now, Rabbi, but you'll ruin that good feeling if I take you shopping. You'll grow impatient and then cranky. Go look for the Virgin. That supposedly is why you came here."

"Will you be back here by six?"

Isabel nodded and grabbed her bag and left.

Press took her damp towel from the floor and wrapped it around his waist. He stepped out on the patio, and watched, moments later, as she came out on the street and headed south. Still no SUV. No one seemed to be following her as she walked down the street.

He showered quickly in cool water, and then dressed. He retrieved his car and drove north to Dzibilchaltum. He checked his mirror and almost immediately saw a black SUV a couple of cars back. There was no mistake: he was being followed. He took some solace in the fact that they were not after Isabel. After several turns, they were still behind him. He decided to stop checking.

He arrived at the ruins. He parked and walked to the visitor center. He asked for the curator, Dr.Lourdes, whom he'd contacted earlier in the week. They shook hands, and the small white-haired man led him to a 12 foot stone stele in the northeast corner. He indicated several glyphs on the stele's east side. "This is what you're looking for."

It was still hot out at five when Simon returned to the bed-and-breakfast. He'd looked for the SUV on the way back, but hadn't seen it. He had a moment of concern that forced him to quicken his step – they had left him to go after Isabel. He found the room intact, and when he entered it he saw Isabel sitting on the patio, reading. She looked up when he opened the door.

"Did you find your Virgin mother?"

"Yes. A couple of glyphs on one stele. I expected it to be a bigger deal."

"I bought you something." She came inside and went to a plastic bag. She pulled out a white guyambana with an off-white trim. "Try it on."

Simon pulled off his polo shirt and put it on.

"Very nice. Now you look like a local and not some obnoxious Norte Americano touristo."

"Did anyone follow you?"

"No. Yes, lots of men, but that's nothing new."

"It's strange. The SUV followed me out to the ruins but then I didn't see it on the way back. It's like they knew I was coming back here." He gave Isabel a quizzical look. Then, "Are you hungry?"

"Yes."

"Did you buy anything for yourself?"

"You'll see. Let's go eat."

Chapter 65

Ex-Rabbi Simon Press

No one followed them home on Sunday. First he dragged Isabel to the Museo Regional de Antropologia, where he took in the essential strangeness of the alien culture, and reflected on the essential strangeness of his own. He told Isabel: "In Dublin there's the Blarney Stone, and kissing it is supposed to give you the gift of gab that the Irish are so stereotypically famous for. So all the tourists kiss it. Knowing this, all the Irish boys sneak out at night and piss on it."

"Did you?"

"Kiss it or piss on it? As a lad I pissed on it as a rite of passage."

"How about the Irish girls?"

"They generally prefer to kiss Irish boys."

"I meant – you know what I meant."

"One or two on a dare. Pissed on it, I mean. No one from Dublin ever kissed it."

They walked to a diorama showing a Mayan infant with his head bound by boards. "They liked oblong heads – thought they were beautiful." Isabel paraphrased the Spanish.

Simon said: "Do you ever wonder that they didn't leave anatomical charts? They weren't squeamish about human sacrifice and their astronomical charts are sophisticated."

"Maybe they did. Maybe they were in the codices that were burned. Who knows what was in them. Look, I don't have much patience for museums. I think they're basically lies. I've never been to one that ever acknowledged that the people portrayed had a sense of humor. I'd like to know what they laughed at. That stele you visited today, the one the anthropologists accord such reverence – wouldn't it be great to know that in reality 13-year-old Mayan boys all pissed on it after dark." She looked at Simon. "You didn't kiss it, did you?"

"Time to go."

A storm came up on the way back. The sky filled with black clouds, lightning forked and soon huge raindrops that seemed like water balloons hit the windshield. It was impossible to see; the windshield wipers were useless. Finally Simon pulled off the road. It was like the inside of a car wash. He felt Isabel take his hand. He turned and kissed her. She kissed back, her tongue active on his lips, and in his mouth. She brought his hand to her breasts, then pushed them down to the waist of her jeans. She unbuttoned them and he slid his hand into her panties. The kisses grew more insistent and his finger found her moist home. The rain seemed to come down harder, her breath quickened and soon she was shuddering through the climax.

The rain began to let up. Visibility returned. Simon heard her say "Take me home; I'll make it worth your while."

Later, much later, Simon found himself back in his own apartment, alone. Isabel had said, "I have to sort some things out – my feelings for you. I can't have you here while I try to do that."

He felt hurt; but he had left when she asked him to. He'd always liked the time after sex, when he felt satiated, his body suffused with a syrupy sweetness, and the pleasant thought of more to come, later.

But now he felt none of these things, only a deflating confusion. He'd asked, "What's to sort out?" But she pushed him gently but firmly towards the door.

He looked at McNeery's margin notes and put a check next to the immaculate conception – Dzibilchaltun. The next trip would be short – a quick jog to Ek Balam. He wondered that he hadn't gone earlier. It was only a dozen miles away, and strange even by Mayan standards. There was no need to visit McNeery's list in order. He'd gone to Dzibilchaltun first because he wanted an excuse to bring Isabel on an overnight, not because it was first on McNeery's list. Now she was thinking things over. He got in his car and drove towards Ek Balam. Instinctively, he checked his mirror. The black SUV was behind him. He was tempted to wave. He found his first feeling was annoyance. He no longer feared the car or its occupants. If they'd meant to harm him they'd had plenty of opportunity on the way to Merida. He thought of calling Isabel, as a precaution, then changed his mind. He thought of calling Rufino, and just as quickly rejected that idea. A dark thought crossed his mind: what if he'd been spared on the way to Merida because Isabel was with him. They – whoever they were, probably Leon's thugs – wouldn't want to involve the daughter of a prominent family in what was sure to be his messy demise. But they weren't that scrupulous. He drove on, the air-conditioning barely keeping up with the Yucatán heat.

His goal was a large chamber in the central pyramid. When he arrived he was disappointed to learn it was closed to the public. Simon asserted his professional credentials, but was still rebuffed. He got the name of the supervising archaeologist, who might or might not be around the following day. He felt his frustration marinate in the hundred degree heat. He was walking towards his car and stopped. He went back, offered to pay for a guided tour of the closed chamber. There was a moment of hesitation, but the answer was still "no." He wondered if offering a specific amount would've made a difference. He resigned himself to the fact that he was new to the ways of mordida. Isabel would've known how much to offer.

In his anger and frustration he failed to check his mirror for the first five minutes. He looked back as he was entering the Valladolid's outskirts. There was no SUV. He called the next day; the archaeologist was not in.

The next day's morning papers didn't carry the news, but there were rumors. It was a day later when *El Universal* described an explosion and collapse at Ek Balam. Simon called the archaeologist in charge at Ek Balam.

The distraught archaeologist answered: "There's an epidemic. Who would do this? Last week, Dzibilchaltun, now this. Why?"

Press was stunned. He'd read nothing in the paper. He said so. The archaeologist said, "It was in the Merida paper. A stele was stolen."

"When? I was just there."

"They found it missing on Sunday morning."

Press felt the slow trickle of ice water inside his chest. The theft of a stele from Dzibilchaltun was one thing; it could still could be recovered. But the destruction of the main pyramid at Ek Balam was something else. He wondered: in addition to being a strange Borgesian Christian/drug lord, was Cortes some Columbus venerating crackpot? Or was it the primacy of his own ancestor – Hernando Cortes – that Leon felt he was protecting? It occurred to Simon that far from being in danger, he was the safest man in Mexico. He enjoyed the protection of a powerful drug lord, at least for the time being, and as long as he led Leon's henchmen to the sites on McNeery's list. He sat down, but in his agitation he found he could not stay seated. He wondered that they didn't simply kidnap him and torture him like they had Alessandro. But in some ways this was easier. And perhaps they didn't know about the list; perhaps they thought he was figuring things out, and for that they needed him alive and cooperative, as he so unwittingly had been.

Press considered his next move. What if he visited the cathedral in Compeche – would they blow that up? Probably not. It was only visits to pre-Columbian sites that interested them.

He jumped when the phone rang. It was Isabel. "I miss you. Come over and I'll cook you dinner."

He resisted the temptation to decline and cite the need to sort things out. "What time?"

"Eight."

He went to the mercado for flowers and wine, haggled halfheartedly for the former. He had some time before eight, which he spent on the Internet, reading about the destruction at Ek Balam.

Miraculously, no one had been killed. The detonation had taken place in the middle of the night. There was speculation that the pyramid could be rebuilt, but the chamber, ground zero for the explosion was a total loss. The glyphs were certainly destroyed.

Press gathered his flowers and wine and left for Isabel's.

Chapter 66

Ex-Rabbi Simon Press

The next morning Press's phone rang. He was disappointed to see it wasn't Reyes. He said, "This is Simon."

"This is Detective Rufino. Cortes and his men visited the bank this morning and retrieved the codex."

"Where are you now?"

"Following them."

"Where?"

"Right now I'm in Mexico City: Jean Pablo Street. Across from the Apostolic Nunciature of the Holy See."

It took Press a moment. "The Vatican Embassy?"

"Yes."

"And they brought it in?"

"Yes. I'm waiting to see if they bring it out."

"I think you'll be waiting a very long time. Thanks for letting me know."

"Simon."

"Yes."

"Leon Cortes is still a very bad man, and dangerous."

Simon heard Rufino hang up.

Press dialed Isabel Reyes. There was no answer. He assumed she was with a patient. He left a brief message: "Hi. It's Simon. Have dinner with me. I have interesting news."

It was an hour later when his phone rang. "Hi. It's Isabel. I'd be delighted to have dinner with you and your interesting news. In fact, I really prefer to have dinner with just your interesting news, but you can come too, to pick up the check."

Press couldn't tell if she was teasing, or if she was truly angry. "If I tell you the news now, will you still have dinner with me?"

"Would it be so hard for you to just say 'I miss you terribly – I must see you – have dinner with me tonight'? 'Have dinner with me – I have news' – does that shit work in Ireland? Or America? I might as well have dinner with the paperboy. He has more news than you do."

He refused to be baited. "Let's start again. Please have dinner with me. I want to see you. And by the way, Leon Cortes took the codex to the Vatican embassy in the DF."

"I have your news now. What do I need you for? But I'll see you at 7:30." She hung up.

Press considered his romantic options. He decided to buy flowers. He thought he might manage that without incident this time, since Cortes was in Mexico City.

The Pope didn't want the codex destroyed. He wanted to see it. Press assumed the Vatican had scholars who could translate it. But when he thought about it some more, he wasn't sure. The Mayan code, as it had been called, had been difficult to break. It was a Russian, Yuri Knorisov, who proved that the Mayan hieroglyphics were phonetic as well as logographic. McNeery had taught himself to read the glyphs – but McNeery was brilliant, and had a facility for language. Still, the Vatican commanded vast intellectual resources, directly and indirectly. They'd get it translated. The problem, he realized, was keeping that translation secret. He assumed the Vatican would send it out in parts, to different translators. The trick was to know how fine to chop it. To do that they had to have some idea of what they were looking for.

He had arrived at the mercado. He was amused to find that he still moved within a bubble of deference when he walked among the stalls. He was the tough hombre who had gone for a ride with Leon Cortes and had lived to buy flowers again. He tried a different flower vendor. An older man – brown, leathery – collected the flowers Press indicated. "Cuanto?"

"100 pesos."

Press offered half that.

"70." Press gave him 70 pesos and acknowledged his perfunctory "Gracias" with his own quiet "Denada."

He met Isabel at the restaurant. She took the flowers and gave him a kiss and a warm hug. He let his surprise show.

Isabel saw it. "What? You brought me flowers. Positive reinforcement." She hugged him again and kept hold of his hand. She said, "Cheer up, Rabbi. Tell me your news."

"I already told you. Leon took the codex to the Vatican Embassy in the DF."

"So now the Vatican is part of the plot. Sounds serious." She was teasing him.

"Remember how you felt when you were called to do McNeery's autopsy and you realized he hadn't been killed by a jaguar? Go ahead, make fun of me."

Isabel patted his hand. "I solved the medical mystery. Have you solved the intellectual mystery? Why does the Vatican want the codex? Not because it's worth millions. You've been thinking about it. Don't deny it. You should have spent some thought on us, but never mind. Why does the Vatican want it?"

"Independent proof of the Star of Bethlehem." He looked at Reyes for her reaction.

"So why steal it? Just let the Mayan Experts in Mexico translate it, then brag about the results. It's better for the Vatican if the confirmation comes from an independent source."

"As you point out, stealing it makes no sense. It bothers me."

The waiter came over and they ordered drinks. Isabel said, "After dinner, let's go dancing. I know you want to think about the codex, but trust me, dancing will help."

"Dancing will help me think about the codex?"

"Dancing will help you get me in bed. Now – right this second – are you thinking about the codex?"

"Not really."

"You're stuck, and yet subconsciously, you're still working on it. You'll see: dancing will help with the codex too."

They finished dinner and went to La Casita. They heard the pounding salsa beat before they came to the entrance. Couples with drinks and cigarettes loitered around. The man at the door greeted Isabel and they hugged.

Isabel said, "That's Marcel. A friend. But I thought I saw the shadow of jealousy cross your face. Good." Inside, the room was too loud for the rabbi to hear. Another man – young, dark skinned, well-dressed came over to Reyes and kissed her on both cheeks. She introduced him to Simon, but his name was lost in the music. The young man asked her to dance. She hesitated. Simon said, "Save the sambas for me." He watched her salsa onto the dance floor.

An hour and several sambas later he felt Isabel pulled him toward the door. "Time to go home," she whispered in his ear and then kissed it.

"My apartment's closer," Simon offered.

"My apartment's nicer."

He didn't argue. He walked fast and was surprised that she kept up with him.

******

When Simon awoke, Isabel was already dressed and smelled pleasantly of soap. He said, "What time is it?"

"6:45. Have you figured out why the Vatican wants the codex? Your subconscious had plenty of room to work, your conscious mind was pretty much shut down."

"Is there any coffee?"

"I left some in the pot. I've really got to run."

"I'll call you later."

"You'd better."

Isabel left. Simon padded off to the bathroom. When he returned he dressed, drank some coffee and left. He wanted to think about the codex but he found his thoughts returning to Isabel Reyes instead.

He walked to his apartment and opened McNeery's notes. Then he changed his mind – he couldn't say why – and looked up Diego de Landa on the Internet. Landa had changed – from a brave monk who single-handedly stopped a human sacrifice to someone who ordered and oversaw torture that even the Spanish governor at the time found abhorrent. What changed? At the moment Landa was burning the codices, monks throughout Europe were carefully copying out the pagan mythology of the Greeks and Romans. What had set him off?

The Vatican knew Cortes; they knew his methods. They knew McNeery had been killed. The codex had blood on it – and still they wanted it. Spiriting it out of Mexico – stealing it from the Mexican antiquities authorities - was a violation of established protocol regarding indigenous artifacts. They flouted this. And why did they insist on stealing the original, when surely the Mexican authorities would have graciously provided them with a high-quality copy?

Press understood – better than most – how dangerous an idea could be. He'd spent his entire academic life studying how the idea embodied by Christianity had simultaneously undermined both paganism and Judaism. In the 300 years from 100 CE to 400 CE the whole western world – Europe and the Middle East, had changed its mind about its most important beliefs.

McNeery had been looking at dates for a celestial event, a footnote to an old controversy. He'd stumbled onto something else. He'd been killed for that misstep.

Chapter 67

Ex-Rabbi Simon Press

Press considered his next move. Coba was further down the list, but it appealed to him now for several reasons. The ruins were huge – 25 square miles – and largely unexcavated. He could visit several locations within the ruins and let Cortes's henchmen guess which was key. (It occurred to him that they were remorseless and would simply destroy them all.) He would stay away from El Castillo – the second-highest pyramid in the Yucatán – in the Nuhoch Mul group. According to his guidebook, the stelae were worn to the point that the carvings were unreadable. Carved stone had returned to just stone. Another advantage was their proximity – they were about 80 km from Valladolid. He could see them in a day.

He phoned Isabel to let her know his plan. She did not offer to join him as he hoped she would. She remarked – Simon thought more callously than was necessary – that she had "real work" to do. She told him to bring insect repellent.

He set off for Coba. The black SUV appeared with the consistency of shadow in his rearview mirror. There was no need, he realized, to keep checking. But the habit was hard to break. An hour later he was at Coba. He put on the insect repellent before he got out of the car, and hoped Cortes's men – not knowing the destination – had failed to bring any. He rented a bike – an unlooked for benefit – and he soon lost his followers in the maze of dirt paths that spiderwebbed the site.

He found the stele McNeery's notes had indicated. The glyphs were worn but still recognizable. Press couldn't interpret them, but he took careful pictures. Later, with help, he would decipher them. He quickly remounted his bike and rode off towards the lake, if the sign could be trusted. Whenever Leon's thugs caught sight of him, he planned to stop and make a show of examining whatever stele or ruin was present. Then he would bike back to his car and leave.

He saw the turquoise expanse of the lake through the jungle foliage. He pedaled a bit faster, wanting to put more distance between the true site and this new place where he hoped to be discovered by Cortes's men. Something darted from the vegetation on the side of the path and he swerved. It disappeared into the thick underbrush on the other side. He pedaled again, more slowly now.

He heard the crunch of wheels on gravel and looked back to where the path emerged from the jungle. The ever present buzz of the jungle seemed to increase a notch. He expected to find others at the lake, but he was alone. Two bike riders emerged from the jungle trail. Press expected them to feign indifference to his presence, even as they kept a sharp eye on him. But instead they began to pedal towards him. This broke with the protocol of their previous tailings. The birds, agitated by the new visitors, increased their cawing. Press felt trapped. He mounted his bike. They kept pedaling towards him, now 50 yards away. He saw a second opening in the jungle to his right. He started to pedal towards them, to build some speed. They were 25 yards apart. Cortes's men slowed down. Press turned suddenly towards the jungle opening and pedaled hard. He took a quick look over his shoulder as he entered the path. They had turned and were following him. They were no longer seated on their bikes, but standing and pedaling hard. The dirt path was narrow and rough. Branches of jungle vegetation intruded, whipping Simon as he rode through them. He crouched low on his bike, pedaling hard. He came to a fork. On the left the path seemed a little wider, a little better traveled, and he hoped it would lead him back towards civilization. It was dangerous to look behind him, and pointless. They would follow him. They weren't far enough behind for him to lose them at the fork. It was a simple race: get back to the parking lot and witnesses, before they got to him. Ireland was a country of bicycles and he'd done his share of cycling as a young man. He rode hard, but he knew that they were younger and more fit and that Mexico was also a country of bicycles. Another fork loomed ahead. Again, he chose the wider fork, this time the right. He crashed through another branch, felt it sting his forehead. Ahead he saw a sign indicating the parking lot. He took the fork that indicated 2 km. He was beginning to tire. He thought he could sprint the last 2 km. He forced his aching legs to keep pedaling. His thighs burned from the exertion. The path was wider and free of branches. He snuck a look back and saw them, about 100 yards behind. If he could keep up this pace he would make it to the visitors' area and safety. If.

He put his head down and pedaled harder. He reached the lot and jumped off his bike. He ran to his car. He opened the door. His hands were shaking, but he managed to get his key in the ignition. The car started. He looked back at his pursuers. They were straddling their bikes and laughing at him.

Chapter 68

Det. Benito Rufino

The dogs were barking again. Rufino pulled on a pair of pants and grabbed his gun. He looked out his window onto the street. He saw the tail light of the dark car pulling away. The dog was sniffing at a hat box and barking. His first thought was: the rabbi. The second thought – he tried to force it back down – was Isabel. The thought that followed was more bitter than he could stand: he'd had a chance to kill Cortes at the bank, and outside the papal embassy and he hadn't. Everyone had asked him the same question: why don't you just shoot him in the face? Rufino opened his door slowly and looked both ways down the street. The dog ran to him, then ran back to the box. He walked to the box and kicked the dog away. The hatbox was tied. He took a folding knife from his pocket and cut the ties. The cardboard was damp at the side. With the tip of the knife he lifted the lid. The face that stared back was beaten and swollen, but there was no mistaking whose face it was: Max.

The dog came back to sniff and Rufino kicked it viciously. He heard its ribs crack and it let out a horrible yelp. It limped off, making the horrible sound of uncomprehending animal pain. Rufino brought the hatbox into his house – not bothering to put on latex gloves. There was no mystery to be solved. He would drive to Cortes' house – he would drive into Cortes' house, he would... He grabbed his keys and a shirt and got into his car. He drove fast, not stopping for lights or signs. He thought of ways of torturing Leon. Most were impractical – he didn't own a junkyard or wrecking ball. He could break every bone in Leon's body – one by one – with the aluminum baseball bat he kept in the trunk of his car. But he would have to kidnap Leon to do that, an unlikely scenario given Leon's bodyguards. He could shoot them first. It bothered him that he didn't know how many guards Leon had and that he had no way of finding out. He realized, reluctantly, that Leon would be expecting him and would be prepared. What they'd done to Max was both a warning and a provocation. He felt himself involuntarily draw his foot back from the accelerator. For the first time it occurred to Rufino to see if he'd been followed. There were headlights behind him, but he couldn't tell what make of vehicle they belonged to. He made a series of terns off the main road to see if they followed. And then he realized – what's the use? Of course he was being followed. Leon couldn't afford to be surprised.

Rufino knew he should see Max's wife. He knew it was his responsibility to bring her the news. He remembered his visit to Luis's girlfriend. He remembered her question: "Why don't you shoot the son of a bitch?" He didn't want to be asked that again. He would see Max's wife when Cortes was dead. He owed her that much.

The headlights were still behind him. He pulled onto the highway. They pulled on after him. A desperate plan formed in his mind. The highway was empty at this hour except for his car and the car headlights behind him. He slowed; they slowed. He accelerated suddenly. They followed, but at a distance. He increased the separation. The headlights seemed content to lie back, biding their time. Rufino continued to accelerate and then suddenly slammed on the brakes and turned the wheel sharply. He felt his car spin around and he was facing the way he'd come. He accelerated again. He was going the wrong way now and heading towards the headlights. They were less than a kilometer away and closing at 200 km/h. He took dead aim at them. He thought he could see them slow down, even as they grew closer. He pushed the accelerator all the way to the floor. He saw them veer to the other lane. He veered so that he was still aimed directly at them, closing the distance. They honked. There was half a kilometer left between them. He flipped on his high beams. Their horn was constant now. 200 meters. 100 meters. The headlights swerved off the road and he blasted by them.

Rufino looked at the speedometer: he was going almost 150 kph. He slowed and pulled onto the shoulder. He looked in his mirror, where the car that had been following had swerved off the road. The lights he'd seen materialized into a semi – the driver honked and gave him the finger as he passed. Rufino drove on the shoulder to the entrance ramp, and still going the wrong way, left the highway. There would be no following him. Cortes' men were ready to kill for Leon, but not to die for him. Still, a direct assault on Leon's hacienda would not succeed. They would be ready for him and he would die in a hail of bullets. And Leon would not leave his hacienda, not after word of this wrong way charge reached him.

Except to go to mass. Rufino took the back roads to Merida, where he expected a heavily guarded Leon Cortes would attend mass in the morning. After Alessandro, the beggars would be cleared from the front steps. The church would be searched before Leon entered it – or perhaps not. Violence in a church was unthinkable to Leon Cortes.

Rufino suddenly felt exhausted. As the adrenaline washed out of him he felt an overpowering need for a short nap. He pulled down an alley and turned the car off. He was asleep instantly.

A moment later he woke with a start. He had no idea how long he'd slept, but when he looked at his watch he saw only about 20 minutes had passed. He drove on towards Merida and the Church of Santa Maria.

Chapter 69

Ex-Rabbi Simon Press

Press often thought about the workings of the mind in general and his own mind in particular. But the one mental phenomenon he found inexplicable was the one he was feeling now: that there was an idea on the tip of his mind, the way that a desired word could hover, just out of reach, on the tip of one's tongue. He knew, for instance, that the idea had to do with the Gospel of Matthew in McNeery's translation of the codex, the way he would know the word on the tip of his tongue began with an "r" and eventually, if he thought about something else, the word would appear. "Recant." That was the last word to tease him in this way.

He paced his apartment, and when that didn't work he left and walked to the plaza. He was aware that he was putting himself in danger, but he was convinced it was a very limited danger: another beating, another ride with Leon Cortes. He looked around, a habit he'd acquired in Mexico. He assessed the capacity of random men to inflict harm upon him. He thought about McNeery's translation in view of the fact that the codex was old – 1500 years old if Rufino sources were correct. And again he felt the teasing pressure of an idea just beyond his grasp.

He really couldn't make it appear. His best hope was to think about something else. He thought about Isabel and he imagined her in Dublin. He thought she would hate the weather, and the gloomy gravitas of the thousand-year-old churches and castles. Maybe she'd read *Ulysses*, and he could take her to the places that Bloom visited. He would be a Dubliner recapitulating the itinerary of Dublin's most famous – albeit fictional – Jew. One way to see Dublin. Would she be amused by this conceit, or not? He could imagine her preferring to piss on the Blarney Stone and then returning the next morning to watch the American tourists kiss it. Or would she demure and suggest a setting with better food and better weather. Would she, like a movie run backwards, go to Spain and embrace the fate of her most distant ancestors – return to her Jewish roots, a re-Converso.

He decided to try to imagine that fateful first meeting between those six century Christians – newly triumphant - with the bloody paganism of the new world. How quickly would they have gotten around to mentioning Jesus? The desire to spread Christianity wasn't what fueled the Portuguese maritime venture. It was the lust for money: spice money, slave money. Mammon, not Jesus, was the God of exploration. He thought it was an awkward problem for the Judeo-Christian heritage that the omniscient God of the universe hadn't even dropped a clue that there was an entire other world – the so-called New World – on this, His favorite planet. There were clues to the coming of the Messiah – Isaiah was full of them - but no clues for this, a whole new world. Press looked around. He was standing in the Plaza, near the newspaper vendors, with no recollection of the walk that had delivered him here. He had reached his physical destination before his thoughts had reached theirs. He paused to pick out a new destination. He thought about walking back to his apartment. He had a sudden burning desire to know what sort of oceangoing boat was available to the sixth century evangelists, the bringers of the Gospel of Matthew to the to the Yucatan. He called up images of the famous Roman triremes - images from movies. He'd seen pictures of Columbus's famous ships. There must be some intermediate link, but the warehouse of his images produced nothing except the Viking Longboat. A pagan boat, however seaworthy. What sort of boats were Christians sailing in 500 A.D.? He was walking briskly now.

When he arrived back at his apartment a quick Internet search revealed nothing suitable for crossing the Atlantic Ocean in 500 A.D. And yet the codex insisted that some Christian had made it across. How else explain inclusion of the Matthew Gospel? He no longer felt the presence of the thought that had been on the tip of his awareness. It was lost for now. He consoled himself with the notion that these elusive thoughts had a way of returning to him when he gave up his search for them. He remembered his strange conversation with Leon. Leon said he wanted the codex because the Vatican had asked him for it. Why did they want it? Why do they want it now, long after the Spanish and Portuguese division of the New World had ceased to matter?

He stopped pacing. It took Simon a moment to realize that he was standing still as statue in the center of his living room. In 4 B.C.E., who's to say which world would discover the other? The primitive Maya were better astronomers then the Hebrews or the Romans. And astronomy was the key to ocean navigation. If he were God, Simon thought, he'd hedge his bets. Give the New World its own Christ. History always wears the mantle of inevitability, and yet professional historians know how little separates one possible history from another.

And then he saw how things stood with the Pope. Columbus wasn't the issue. A parallel Christianity, one in every respect like the one born at Bethlehem, had sprung forth in the Yucatan, among the Maya. No pre-Columbian contact, no alien intervention was required to explain what McNeery had found and the codex had documented at least as faithfully as one of the Gospels: God had sent the world two Sons. Make that worlds. He had sent each of two worlds - unknown to each other but of course known to God – His Son.

The Gospel of Matthew hadn't arrived on the impossible boat. It was indigenous. God planted his Messiahs in two worlds: in the one He flourished, after a rocky start. In the other, the one the rabbi paced in now, He never quite caught on, in spite of the indigenous predisposition for human sacrifice. But this codex – and undoubtedly other codices – told His story until Landa burned them. In 1562 Catholicism was already reeling from Martin Luther's Protestant Reformation. The last thing it needed was a strangely familiar gospel coming from the New World. The Catholic enterprise could, and did, withstand many challenges, but not a second Christ.

Chapter 70

Det. Benito Rufino

It was morning. The sun was up, but just barely, and most of the streets were still in shadows. Rufino was alone on the street. A stray dog saw him, barked once, and trotted away. Rufino walked towards the church. He stopped suddenly and turned. There was no one behind him, the street was still deserted. He saw the church from across the plaza, but he circled around and approached it from the side. He found an open door there and entered. The church was lit by a few sconces and a bank of hundreds of votive candles. Even with the candles the light was no match for the vast dark space of the cathedral.

Rufino checked his watch. Not quite seven. He entered the confessional and knelt. He heard the door slide open. "Good morning, my son." Rufino watched the priest make the sign of the cross.

"Forgive me father, for I have sinned. It has been many years since my last confession. For these sins..." Rufino decided to confess one more sin. "I have killed a man."

The priest absolved him and assigned him his penance.

He was done. He got off his knees. He thought: this is what Leon Cortes does. He kills my friend. He says these words and he's forgiven. He suppressed the urge to stab the priest in the throat. He melted back into the vastness of the cathedral. The cathedral seemed lighter now, his eyes having adapted to the half-light. He gave up an elaborate plan that would have put him in the confessional, dressed as a priest, hearing Leon's confession, and absolving him with a bullet between the eyes. The bodyguards didn't matter. By the time they reached him, his soft nosed bullet would be leaving the back of Leon's head, taking most of his skull with it. He hoped he would have time to kill the guards too, but it didn't matter. As long as he got Leon.

Rufino walked halfway back to the pews and then knelt. He said the penance the priest had given him. He crossed himself, rose, and walked to the vestibule. It was 7:20 – the beginning of his last hour. He thought of Isabel Reyes and, unbidden, she was joined in his thoughts by Simon Press. He'd never been able to reconcile his feelings toward the rabbi. He was a rival, and an arrogant son of a bitch, and to make matters worse, he would be alive at the end of the day. And yet there was something likable about the man. He thought about Max's wife. He hadn't been able to bring himself to tell her, as he should have until he'd avenged her husband, his friend, and then it would be too late. She'll get the message. He doubted she'd forgive him. But who would take care of her, her family? He thought – the answer came hard on the heels of the question – who else? – Simon Press. That seem to be the rabbi's role – to take care of the widows of Leon's victims. He thought he should call the rabbi and tell him. And then he thought there's no need. The rabbi would figure it out; and if not, Isabel would tell him. He wondered what the codex said, that had caused so much death, and realized he didn't care. Leave that to the rabbi too. An old woman entered the church and limped slowly toward a pew in the back. A few minutes later a young woman entered with a child and found a pew closer to the front. Rufino checked his watch: almost 9. Each time the church door opened the vestibule was flooded with the morning light. An old man entered, walking within an erect carriage that belied his age. Through the open door Rufino saw the black SUV at the curb.

He squeezed back into the shadows of the vestibule. He had a moment of misgiving, which he conquered by remembering Max's face. He removed his gun from its shoulder holster and released the safety. He waited: while the driver opened the door for Leon; while Leon got out; while Leon ascended the church steps; while Leon gave pesos to the poor crones by the cathedral door – still his habit even after the assault by Alessandro; while his guard entered through the church door.

"Max Guiterrez sends his regards."

Rufino watched Cortes and his bodyguard turn towards his voice. He squeezed the trigger and watched the head of the guard closest to him jerk back. He fired a second shot into the confused expression that Leon Cortez wore on his face. He fired a third shot into Leon Cortez's face, and watched as blood and gray brain splattered onto the farthest guard who was already reaching for his gun. He fired a fourth shot at the face of the bodyguard. He saw – incredibly – the guard point his gun at him and -

******

Some news travels fast. It was 9:15 when Simon Press answered his phone and learned from Isabel Reyes that Leon Cortes and Benito Rufino were dead. Although he did not speak the words of the Kaddish – it wasn't his place – the words came to his mind: Yisgadal vyiskaddash... He told Isabel he was coming over and she didn't object. He asked "Are you in danger? Of the retaliation?"

Isabel said, "I don't think so. I don't know. His lieutenants will fight over the throne. There will be more killings before the day is over. Things will get crazy, like in the bad old days. I told him to do it, you know."

"Told whom to do what?"

"I said to Rufino: 'Why didn't you shoot him in the face when you had the chance?'"

"You weren't the only one. And he didn't do it because you told him. He did it to avenge his friend."

"When does it stop?"

"When we run out of hate. When we run out of friends."

Chapter 71

Cardinal Santini

The Pope's studio in the Apostolic Palace, the Vatican

Cardinal Santini sits in one of six identical white upholstered chairs, before the Pope's writing table. The table and chairs sit on an island of Persian rug, which in turn sits on the white and gray parquet marble of the floor. Opposite him, on the white-on-white wallpapered wall is a large 16th century picture of the Virgin Mary holding the Baby Jesus. In the painting, Mary is seated on an ornate wooden throne on a small dais. As is the custom in religious depictions of Mary and Jesus, both are haloed. Mary's head tilts toward her infant son. The writing table is made of dark wood, old but unmarred. On it, open, is the codex.

Four of the chairs are occupied by Santini's fellow cardinals. The translator, a short, dark skinned man, stands. Opposite Cardinal Santini, in the only chair without upholstered arms, sits Giuseppe Giovanni, Bishop of Rome, Pope Pius XIII.

The translator speaks quietly and haltingly: "After Chacec was born in Becan, during the time of the Serpent King, sorcerers from the east came to Calakmul and asked, "Where is the one who has been born king of the Maya? We saw his star when it rose and have come to worship him." The translator paused.

Santini: "Continue."

"When the Serpent King heard this he was angry, and he had called together all the chief priests, he asked them where the – I'm sorry, this is an untranslatable word – was to be born. 'In Becan' they replied. Then the Serpent King called the sorcerers secretly and found out from them the exact time the star had appeared. He sent them to Becan and said, 'Go and search carefully for the child. As soon as you find him, report to me, so that I too may go and honor him.' After the sorcerers had heard the Serpent King, they went on their way, and the star they had seen when it rose went ahead of them until it stopped over the place where the child was."

The translator pauses and looks at Cardinal Sabatini.

"Go on."

The translator returns to the codex: "When they saw the star, they were overjoyed. On coming to the house, they saw the child with his mother, and they bowed down and worshiped him. Then they opened their treasures and presented him with gifts of gold, jade and feathers."

The Pope raises his hand slightly, the subtlest of gestures, and the translator stops. "How old is this Codex?" The question is aimed at Santini.

Santini answers it: "Fifteen hundred years old, give or take a hundred years. But the event described is older of course."

The Pope cannot disguise his growing impatience: "Of course. How much older?"

Santini: "The codex was dated by carbon decay, hence the range. But the dates in the codex, the Mayan dates, can be calculated by working back from the end of their calendar. Their calendar ends in our year 2012. Working backwards, the date of the birth of Chacec – their Jesus – is 22 BC.

The Pope rises from his seat. The cardinals rise from theirs. The Pope closes the codex and looks at Santini: "Burn it."

Epilogue

"It turns out that the mind of God is less like our own than even Borges could imagine. It's not just that God chooses not to distinguish between inquisitor and heresiarch, as Borges suggests, but that simultaneous events occurring in different places are the same event, or that (this is an anthropomorphic approximation) every event has its shadow elsewhere: such is the power of the light of God."

— Ex- Rabbi Simon Press

ABOUT THE AUTHOR

Howard Allan is the pen name of Howard Luxenberg. Short fiction of his has appeared in *Tin House, The Iowa Review, The Sun, The Gettysburg Review, Alaska Quarterly Review,* and *Other Voices* and has been included in the anthology *Best of Tin House.*

.

91109684R00276